D1121484

Tom Bradby is Political Editor of ITV News. He began his reporting career with the company as Ireland Correspondent almost fifteen years ago, during which time he covered the unfolding peace process and wrote his first novel, *Shadow Dancer*. As Asia Correspondent, based in Hong Kong, he was shot and seriously wounded whilst covering a riot in Jakarta. After a spell as Royal Correspondent, he went on to become UK Editor before taking up his current post in the summer of 2005.

Tom Bradby is the acclaimed author of five novels. *The Master of Rain* was shortlisted for the Crime Writers' Association Steel Dagger for Best Thriller of the Year 2002. *The White Russian* was shortlisted for the Crime Writers' Association Ellis Peters Award for the Best Historical Crime Novel of 2003. *The God of Chaos* was shortlisted for the Crime Writers' Association Ellis Peter Award for the Best Historical Crime Novel of 2005.

Acclaim for:

The White Russian

'Sad, atmospheric and richly entertaining, *The White Russian* is the kind of historical fiction that may send you back to the real history books to learn more'
Washington Post

'Unfailingly evocative . . . reminiscent of *Gorky Park*'
The Times

'A tumbling pace, emotionally torn and credible characters . . . and twists and dubious allegiances enough to leave readers wondering until the closing pages . . . A chilling crime yarn and a cautionary tale about the sometimes painful exigencies of love, *The White Russian* is a literary cocktail with a decided kick'
amazon.com

The Master of Rain

'Tom Bradby's expert evocation of the hothouse atmosphere of Twenties Shanghai makes an exotic backdrop to a cracking murder mystery . . . An immensely atmospheric, gripping detective story with just the right mixture of exoticism, violence and romance. Bradby has used his years as a foreign correspondent to imagine splendidly the opulence, corruption, debauchery, violence and mutual racism of a city that fused some of the worst of Asian and European values'
The Times

'Beneath the surface of this clever book, a thrilling yarn of murder and mayhem, we find a wise, richly layered and utterly convincing portrait of what was the most evil and fatally fascinating of all the modern world's cities. No one has managed to bring Shanghai so alive, in all its ghastly splendour'
Simon Winchester

'A brilliant evocation of one of the world's most fascinating cities, which uses the classic thriller genre to draw the reader into this hypnotising milieu. Bradby creates colourful three dimensional scenes which are real and meaningful . . . *The Master of Rain* also works as a wonderful travelogue. It will make you yearn to go in search of the old Shanghai'
South China Morning Post

The Sleep of the Dead

'The second novel by ITN's talented young Asia correspondent lives up to the promise of its remarkable predecessor, *Shadow Dancer* . . . Bradby has the talent of a reporter but the heart of a storyteller. And his new novel proves it triumphantly. Once again he draws on his experiences as a reporter in Northern Ireland, but this time adds the ingredients of an Agatha Christie thriller with a distinctly contemporary twist: *Cracker* meets *Miss Marple* by way of *Silent Witness* . . . Elegant, spooky, and a compulsive page-turner, *The Sleep of the Dead* confirms Bradby's considerable promise as a thriller writer'
Geoffrey Wansell, *Daily Mail*

'A real race-against-the-clock thriller and complex psychological drama'
Irish Independent

'This second thriller from Bradby confirms him as very much in the know when it comes to matters military . . . Intriguing and emotive, this is a slow-builder that proves to be worth the wait'
The A List in the *Mirror*

Shadow Dancer

'Remarkable first novel . . . Bradby handles the tension with skill to produce a gripping tale that is at the same time a compelling argument against allowing the culture of killing to take over any cause, however just'
Peter Millar, *Times Metro*

'An exceptional first novel. On the surface yet another thriller about the murky world of the intelligence war in Northern Ireland, it is also a compelling, incestuous story of love and torn loyalty in a community and family ravaged by hate and betrayal. There are no cardboard cut-outs here. Tom Bradby succeeds in creating real characters. Far too many novels on this subject take refuge in cliché and caricature — Bradby refuses to. Detail is piled on detail until you find yourself immersed in the Republican ghetto of West Belfast . . . The book's accuracy makes it stand out from almost any other that I have read on the subject. The language, the tension, the funerals, the fear — all are portrayed vividly and correctly'
Sean O'Callaghan, *Daily Telegraph*

'This is the best book on the northern conflict since *Harry's Game* . . . *Shadow Dancer* is an excellent read on any level. It scores heavily both as a thriller and an accurate, unblinking look at what is happening right now just a few miles up the road'
Irish Independent

Also by Tom Bradby

SHADOW DANCER
THE SLEEP OF THE DEAD
THE MASTER OF RAIN
THE WHITE RUSSIAN

and published by Corgi Books

THE GOD OF CHAOS

Tom Bradby

CORGI BOOKS

THE GOD OF CHAOS
A CORGI BOOK: 0552151459
9780552151450

Originally published in Great Britain by Bantam Press,
a division of Transworld Publishers

PRINTING HISTORY
Bantam Press edition published 2005
Corgi edition published 2006

1 3 5 7 9 10 8 6 4 2

Set in 10/12pt Palatino by Palimpsest Book Production Limited,
Polmont, Stirlingshire.

Corgi Books are published by Transworld Publishers,
61–63 Uxbridge Road, London W5 5SA, a division of
The Random House Group Ltd, in Australia by Random House
Australia (Pty) Ltd, 20 Alfred Street, Milsons Point, Sydney,
NSW 2061, Australia, in New Zealand by Random House
New Zealand Ltd, 18 Poland Road, Glenfield, Auckland 10,
New Zealand and in South Africa by Random House (Pty) Ltd,
Isle of Houghton, Corner of Boundary Road & Carse O'Gowrie,
Houghton 2198, South Africa.

Printed and bound in Great Britain by
Cox & Wyman Ltd, Reading, Berkshire.

Papers used by Transworld Publishers are natural, recyclable
products made from wood grown in sustainable forests. The
manufacturing processes conform to the environmental
regulations of the country of origin.

To Claudia, Jack, Louisa and Sam.
And Mum and Dad.

Acknowledgements

Thanks to my inspirational and exceptional Claudia, who has always been my partner in the production of these novels; my mother Sally who has provided invaluable research and great ideas at every stage; my agent, Mark Lucas, who is simply terrific; and, last but not least, my editor Bill Scott-Kerr, the nicest man you could ever hope to meet and a brilliant publisher to boot.

Acknowledgements

Thanks to: my inspirational and exceptional wife, Claudia, who has always been my partner in the production of these novels; my mother, Sally, who has provided invaluable research and great ideas at every stage; my agent, Mark Lucas, who is simply a genius; and, last but not least, my editor here at Transworld, Bill Scott-Kerr, the nicest man you could ever hope to meet and a brilliant publisher to boot.

CHAPTER ONE

CHAPTER ONE

Cairo, June 1942

The *khamseen* had blown all night, rattling doors, slipping through keyholes and whistling down corridors, before burying its cargo deep in the skin. The Egyptians said the suffocatingly hot desert wind commemorated the period of fifty days during which Cain had carried the body of his brother Abel. It certainly felt like a punishment.

Quinn rubbed tired eyes, tugged at his shirt collar and tried to shift the grit from round his neck. He had not slept but, then, he had not expected to. This day had approached with grim inevitability.

'Sir?' Madden said.

'Yeah.'

'Are you awake?'

'Very funny.'

'Then what do you think?'

Quinn closed his eyes. Sure, they knew what he was really thinking. It was a day upon which any distraction was welcome, but none would hold his attention for more than a few moments.

What did he make of the issue at hand? What other conclusion was there? The document in front of him was stamped, 'MOST SECRET. Cairo, Evacuation Plans', and was an admission of failure that Allied chiefs dared not make but could not avoid much longer.

He glanced at the maps on the wall. The first depicted in pink the British Empire in Africa and the Middle East as it had been at the start of the war, stretching from Libya to Palestine. The second showed how fast it was shrinking. The waves of defensive line upon defensive line, drawn and redrawn in grease pencil, were moving closer to Cairo. The Desert Fox was no more than a day's drive away.

'Where's Rommel this morning?' Quinn asked. He no longer attended briefings. The British top brass had made it clear he wasn't welcome.

'It's still confused, but we appear to be massing here . . .' Madden placed his finger between the sea and the Qattara Depression. 'Just by the railway halt at El Alamein. They reckon it won't give him much room for manoeuvre.'

Quinn thought of the battle-weary troops he'd seen pouring in from the north at dawn. 'So this is the last stand? If Rommel breaks through to Alexandria, the way to Cairo is open?'

'I suppose so. You know what they're saying – that the Nazis can read our every move.'

As a rule, Quinn ignored gossip: if it was to be believed, the city was awash with Rommel's spies.

He listened to the sound of a train rattling into the station below and glanced out of the window. One of the city's scavenging kites hovered high in the hard blue sky. He wondered if Mae was up yet, imagined her dressing in front of the chipped gold mirror in the corner of their bedroom. She'd want to look her best today.

'That's what the unit commanders are saying in the field,' Madden said soberly.

'Hmm.' Quinn took out a packet of Cape to Cairo cigarettes, lit one and threw the thin carton across the table. Madden helped himself and passed it on to Kate Mowbray. They smoked in silence. Quinn tapped the edge of a report Madden had typed on their previous case. He needed to sign it off this morning. 'What happened last night?' he asked. He'd driven them through the previous investigation until they were all hollow-eyed with tiredness.

'Seven arrests. Nothing to interest us.'

Quinn had left Madden on duty, but he ought to have been there himself. The city was edgy, fractious, tormented by the weather and the relentless nature of Rommel's advance.

'I walked across to the railway station,' Madden went on, 'just after midnight.'

'And?'

'Very crowded.'

'Panic?'

'Getting close to it. I saw the last train to Jerusalem pull out.'

'People fighting to get on?'

'Not fighting, but . . .' he shrugged '. . . it was crowded.' He stretched his long back. He was a tall man, the impression heightened by a gaunt frame and a thick mop of curly ginger hair. The desert sun had burnt his pale, freckled skin.

Quinn heard laughter in the next room. He stood up and saw, through the window in the partition door, that a woman was talking to one of his assistants,

Sergeant Cohen. As she leant back in the chair, her long, dark brown hair cascaded over her shoulders. Cohen was laughing, too.

Quinn caught sight of Effatt, chief detective of the Cairo Police, who appeared to be sharing the joke. At least it was good to see *him* smiling. 'What'd you suppose Effatt's doing here at this time in the morning?' he asked. In theory, his friend dealt only with crimes among the local populace, Quinn exclusively with those involving the hundreds of thousands of soldiers circulating through the city. In practice, they often worked together.

Neither of his companions answered, so Quinn put his half-finished cigarette in the wooden ashtray on the desk and opened the door. The clock between the windows on the far wall showed just before eight. In the richer, more textured light of evening, you could make out the tips of the Pyramids from here, but for the rest of the day they were indistinguishable through the haze. 'Good mornin',' Quinn said.

Cohen stood alongside Effatt, but the woman remained seated. 'This is Mrs Amy White.'

'Sure, we've met.' Quinn offered his hand. She took it, her grip firm and palm dry. Cool green eyes scrutinized his. She wore a white silk scarf to shield her face from the dust outside, a brown jacket and cream trousers.

'You know one another?' Effatt asked.

'Mrs White is a volunteer at the same hospital as my wife.'

Effatt coughed. 'She came to my office a few minutes ago. She said she had heard a commotion in the apartment above her own but received no answer when she went up to check upon its cause.' Effatt spoke

14

English with a faint American accent, the legacy of a year spent at the University of Michigan shortly before the war.

'Not really a matter for us,' Quinn said.

'Mrs White went up a second time. She found the apartment had been ... disturbed. She believes the gentleman who occupies it works at GHQ.'

'What's his name?'

'Captain Rupert Durant,' Amy said.

Quinn nodded at the sergeant. 'Cohen, go get me—'

'Q Branch, sir. I've already checked. He works at Movement Control.'

Quinn frowned. Movement Control was a sensitive department, its staff processing detailed information on the deployment and fighting strength of every unit in the field. He waited for Amy White to continue, but she made no sign of intending to do so. 'Tell me, ma'am, what did you find inside?' he asked. He kept his tone formal. He'd met her a couple of times while he was waiting for Mae in the hallway, away from the stench of the wards.

'The apartment looked like a bomb had hit it,' she said. 'I didn't figure Durant as the untidy kind.'

'You knew him?'

'To exchange greetings.'

'How'd you know he worked at GHQ?'

'It was something I heard.'

'You aware of what he did there?'

'No.'

'You didn't know which branch he worked in?'

'No, Major, I did not.'

'When did you last see him?'

'Yesterday. Maybe the day before.'

'What about his *sufragi*? You—'

'He doesn't employ one.'

'He ain't got no servants?'

Ed Madden and Kate Mowbray were also frowning. For a British officer in Egypt, it was unusual.

'Not that I know of. You'd have to ask him.'

There was the sudden wail of an air-raid siren from the roof. Commonplace at night, it was rare in the day, but increasing in frequency. Quinn walked to the balcony and pushed open the doors. The siren howled against an empty, peerlessly blue sky. Quinn squinted, trying to make out the black dot of an aircraft, or the rumble of its engines, but he could hear only the bustle of traffic around Bab el Hadid. He watched the kites circling the tall spires of the Turkish mosque in Saladin's citadel, then looked across to the railway station. A large crowd had gathered: people were sitting on suitcases or searching for pools of shade. Two uniformed military policemen strolled among them, with their distinctive red caps and webbing. A waiter dressed in a white *djellaba* and bright red fez skipped at their heels, offering a silver tray laden with small glasses of tea.

He turned back in, closed the doors against the heat and the wind. He sat down, leant against the Imperial typewriter on Cohen's desk and rested his feet on a grey filing cabinet. The phone trilled beside him and he lifted the mouthpiece, then let it fall. Amy White hadn't moved. 'So, you heard a commotion in Durant's apartment?' They were in the centre of the atrium between the two corridors, so his voice was partially lost to the circling fans high in the domed roof above.

'Something like that. A thump, chairs pushed around.'

'How'd you figure—'

'I wanted to check if he was all right.'

Quinn examined Amy White's face. It seemed to him that there was a note of self-justification in her voice, which the circumstances did not appear to warrant. He turned. 'Kate, go—'

'I saw him.'

He swung back. Amy White's expression was sombre now. 'You saw whom?'

'Ten minutes or so after I first heard the commotion, the door opened upstairs and there were rapid footsteps. I pulled open my own door.'

Quinn waited. 'And what did you see?'

Amy leant forward, her arms wrapped round her shoulders, as if she was trying to ward off a chill. 'A man. Tall. He hesitated a moment, looked at me, then walked on past. He didn't say anything.'

'You get a good look?'

'He wore a hat, a fedora, pulled low over his eyes. He was about your height and dressed in a white linen suit, with immaculate shoes. His eyes were bright, like a wolf's.'

'A white guy?'

'Yes. He had a cleft chin. Like you.' She pointed to Quinn. 'A smaller nose, a distinctive mole in the centre of his right cheek.'

It was a lot to take in from a single glance. 'And after he'd gone you went upstairs?'

'No. I went back into my apartment. But I got to thinking. What was the noise I'd heard? Why hadn't anyone answered my knock? Was Captain Durant all right? So I went back up.'

The office was filling up, the typists, language officers and specialists of the central pool arriving at their

17

desks. On the far side of the atrium Major Alastair Macleod, head of Field Security, stood outside his office, arms crossed, deep in conversation with his Egyptian adviser, Reza.

'Hang on there.' Quinn ducked into his own office to retrieve a revolver from his desk drawer. As he did so, he saw Kate Mowbray looking at him through small pebble glasses, her straight auburn hair damp with sweat against her forehead. Instinctively, he knew she did not approve of Amy White.

Technically Kate was only his driver, but she was smart and efficient, and since he was chronically short of staff he'd integrated her into their unit, the detective division of the Royal Military Police. She was from Cape Town and had come here with the South African Women's Auxiliary Arms Service.

Quinn pulled on a desert jacket, concealed his revolver, then checked he had his pink Special Investigation Branch warrant card. 'Ed, better go round to Movement Control, see if you can find Captain Durant. If you do, bring him over to his apartment. Don't tell him nothin'. We'll see you there.'

'You're going out?'

'Yeah.'

'Colonel Lewis is holding an evacuation briefing over at GHQ at lunchtime. You haven't forgotten?'

'We'll be back in an hour.'

'Colonel Lewis said our presence was mandatory, sir.'

'We'll be there.'

'He asked me to give you this.'

Ed Madden was holding an envelope. Quinn took it. He glanced at his name on the front, then pulled out the note inside. *Dear Joe*, it read, *I shall be thinking of you today. I can only imagine how difficult it will be to get through, but thank you for all your hard work and dedication over the past year in such trying circumstances. Best regards as ever, yours, Charles.*

Quinn slipped the note into his pocket, looked up. They were all watching him. 'How'd he know it was today?'

'It would be hard for any of us to forget,' Ed said.

'Sure.' Quinn felt embarrassed. 'Thank you.'

He led the way out of his office and across the atrium. As he reached the stairs, he noticed Reza standing on the half-landing, gazing out of the window as a couple of his assistants unloaded a group of Egyptian men from the back of an Austin utility vehicle in the courtyard below. The prisoners' arms were bound behind their backs with white rope, which suggested they were probably students from one of the universities – 'subversives', as Macleod and Reza called them.

Reza liked to conduct interrogations himself, and sometimes, as you passed over the ventilation grilles by the main entrance, you could hear cries from the cells below.

The Egyptian turned, a waft of his perfume catching in Quinn's nostrils, his dark eyes fixed on the party coming down the stairs towards him. He was short, almost like a dwarf, his black hair pomaded to disguise its thinness, his skin dry and marked like that of a dead snake. He wore a ring on each of his fingers and carried a short silver and ivory stick.

Quinn didn't offer a greeting or break his stride. He'd learnt to avoid being drawn into conversation with this man. It didn't help matters.

19

CHAPTER TWO

The morning sun shimmered behind a hazy sky filled with dust whipped up by the *khamseen*. A couple of mechanics sheltered beneath a lone palm. They did not stir as Quinn strode across the courtyard. At this time of the year Cairo was a city that lived from dusk till dawn. As the sun climbed towards its zenith, even the foraging dogs and beggars surrendered to its blistering heat.

A battered jeep pulled in and disgorged a handful of redcaps and a European in handcuffs. Officers from the uniformed section were constantly sweeping the souks and bazaars, looking for the deserters who had become the bane of this war. Men were abandoning their units in droves in favour of the relative anonymity and safety of Cairo's back-streets. Many got themselves into rackets. The previous investigation had been into the murder of two Australians found in an alley in Clot Bey with their genitals severed. They had been selling very young girls to off-duty soldiers until they had fallen out with their Greek partner.

Auchinleck, the new commander-in-chief, had

20

cabled London for permission to shoot any deserters they caught.

Quinn got into the back of the car, alongside Amy White, and wound up the window to keep out the dust. As the Austin Seven pulled through the gate, a group of children charged forward. Four or five dark faces appeared just inches from his own and fists thumped on the window. One or two were holding up flywhisks for sale. Kate accelerated into the dusty street and the children dropped away in search of other targets. Quinn followed Effatt's glance to the wall of the mosque. It was covered with posters depicting the British king, George VI, with a large red cross through his face. They were everywhere now, exhorting Egypt's citizens to turn against their rulers.

There was even more traffic than usual around Bab el Hadid, the crowd outside the railway station still growing. Quinn turned to Amy. 'You still working at the hospital?'

'Sometimes. I'm not there as often as your wife.'

'She could be running the place.'

'You don't sound like you approve.'

'She gets something out of it. That's the main thing.'

'She gives something to it. Isn't that what it's about?'

'You notice if the man was armed?' Quinn asked her.

'Which man?'

'The one on the stairs.'

'Not so far as I could tell.'

'You see if he was sweating?'

She seemed bemused by the question and pulled the white scarf across her face as a primitive mask.

'How long you been in Cairo, Mrs White?'

'Not long.'

21

'You're from New York?'

She turned. Her startling green eyes pierced his. 'That's right.'

'Manhattan?'

'Yes.'

'How 'bout you tell me what brought you to Egypt?'

'Maybe the thing that brought you, Major Quinn.'

He doubted it. 'Your husband posted here?' he asked.

'Sure.'

'He's a military man?'

'No.'

'In business, then?'

'You could put it that way.' Amy's eyes had not left his, but there was something cold and distant in them until she smiled. Quinn could recall seeing her in the darkened interior of the Kit Kat club a couple of nights before, cigarette in hand, framed by the moonlight reflecting off the river.

He'd never have got Mae to the Kit Kat.

Kate drew up the car outside a house on the far side of Garden City. The tarmac street was almost deserted and – for Cairo, at least – quiet. A temporary guard post had been erected beneath the shade of the banyan trees thirty yards away. Quinn couldn't see anyone inside it. 'Who's that for?'

'Brigadier Wilson,' Kate said. 'At least, I think so. Do you want me to check?'

'Don't bother.' Ever since the British had sent tanks to the Abdin Palace and forced a change of government on King Farouk, some of the top brass had insisted on a guard detail. They were not far from the British embassy here, and only a few minutes from GHQ.

He got out, slapping the dust from his elbows.

The building was a three-storey villa built in what magazine features called the 'modern style' of Paris and Marseille. It was painted white with battered wooden shutters. It was typical of this part of town, Cairo's answer to the Upper East Side or London's Mayfair. It had a long wooden and glass veranda along its right-hand side.

Effatt led the way. The Egyptian detective was tall and rotund, dressed in a neatly cut dark suit. His hair was receding and his forehead shone with a film of sweat. A banyan tree in the small courtyard garden was coated with dust, an untended pot plant wilting in the heat. Quinn coughed and Amy White held the silk scarf across her mouth. Kate polished her glasses.

There was a brass plate on the door of the second-floor apartment announcing its occupants as Mr and Mrs Avril White, but nothing indicated the identity of the inhabitant of the one directly above. Quinn knocked once, but there was no response. He and Effatt drew their revolvers.

CHAPTER THREE

Quinn knocked again. 'Captain Durant?'

There was still no answer.

'Captain Durant?' he said. 'Major Quinn, Royal Military Police. Come to the door, please.'

They waited a few moments, then Quinn gently depressed the handle and pushed open the door. They moved along a corridor into the living room. Its shutters had been closed against the morning sun, but the place looked, as Amy had said, as if a bomb had hit it. The drawers of the desk had been opened and upended, their contents scattered. The sofa had been tipped onto its back and ripped open with a knife.

Quinn walked through to the principal bedroom. Captain Durant's bed had been turned over, the mattress torn open. All of his uniforms had been taken from the cupboard and thrown across the floor. Quinn picked up a photograph frame that lay face down, its glass broken – a studio portrait of an attractive woman with medium-length curly hair and two pretty daughters, no more than five years old. They appeared close in age, leaning together, their faces split by huge grins. Waiting for Daddy to come home.

Quinn held it a moment longer than necessary.

The medicine cabinet in the bathroom had been emptied. Even in the second bedroom, which was sparse and apparently unoccupied, the bed had been torn apart.

Quinn opened the shutters. 'Effatt, you'd better get some of your boys down here. Fingerprints and a couple of officers to search the area.' His own division was notoriously short-staffed and he relied on Effatt for the back-up he'd once have taken for granted.

'Should we call Field Security?' Kate asked.

'Not yet.' He turned back to Amy. 'You telling me it was like this when you came up?'

'Yes.'

'Just the same?'

'Pretty much.' Her face was drawn.

Quinn glanced into the kitchen. It looked clean – unnaturally so, compared with the rest of the apartment. He opened the refrigerator, which contained only a small selection of fruit. It looked fresh. 'Tell me what happened,' he said. 'Exactly.'

She breathed in. 'I had just got up.' She glanced at Effatt. 'I was in the shower. I heard a thump on the ceiling. I didn't think much of it. I got out of the shower and went to the bedroom.'

'Your husband with you?'

'No.'

'Gone to work?'

She nodded, but her expression told him she thought it none of his business where her husband was. 'I walked through to the bedroom. I heard another bang right above my head, then scraping sounds, then another thump. At first, I'd thought Captain Durant might have been moving the furniture around, but now it was more like a struggle. I got dressed and walked up the stairs to see if anything was wrong. It was quieter. I couldn't hear anything. I knocked, but there was no answer.'

Quinn waited for her to continue.

'I went back down, and about ten minutes later I heard the footsteps on the stairs, as I told you.'

'And after he had gone, you came back up?'

'Yes.'

'And this time you came in even though there was no answer?'

'Correct.'

'You sure Captain Durant doesn't have a servant?'

'None that I'm aware of.'

Effatt had picked up the telephone and was barking instructions into it. Quinn tried to think of an excuse to get his friend on his own. He wondered what decision he'd come to over his son. How much time did the boy have left?

There was a knock and Ed Madden stepped through the doorway, stooping to avoid banging his head. 'A bit of a mess,' he said. He turned to face Quinn. 'Movement Control don't know where Captain Durant is, sir.'

'That's careless of them.'

Madden didn't smile.

'When did they last see him?'

'Yesterday.'

'What time?'

'He left the office about seven.'

'They got an idea where he might be?'

'No. But his superior, Colonel Wheeler, is anxious.'

Quinn thought about this. A man toiling away in the engine room of the war, working long hours, his

26

head crammed with sensitive information. Not the kind you wanted to go missing. 'Durant ever failed to turn up to work before?'

'No. He's popular in the office, by all accounts. No-one could think of any reason why he would fail to appear. They were visibly concerned.'

'Anybody talk to him last night after he left?'

Madden shook his head.

'They have any idea where he might have gone?'

'Unless he was going to a concert or the cinema, he always went straight home. That was their impression anyway.'

'You know him, Ed?'

'I've met him once or twice at briefings. He seemed an unusually charming fellow. Quiet, but with a dry sense of humour.'

Quinn turned and looked down into the street. An old woman swathed in black was resting in the shade.

'One thing did strike me,' Madden said quietly. 'I spoke to his secretary. She chose to inform me that he'd taken to leaving work earlier. Until about a month ago, it was not uncommon for them both to be at their desks at ten o'clock at night.'

'So why the change?'

'She doesn't know. He was getting tired, she said, but I got the idea there was more to it than that. I didn't push too hard. She was becoming distressed.'

'A love affair?'

'She didn't say.'

'A good-lookin' broad?'

'No.'

Quinn watched the woman outside gather herself and move into the sunlight. He wondered if he should leave this to Madden or hand it to Macleod at Field

27

Security. He ran a detective division, not a missing persons bureau. 'Go back to GHQ, Ed, and tell them that a Captain Durant from Movement Control is missing. But don't tell 'em what's happened to the apartment.'

Madden looked as if he wanted to ask why not, but thought better of it. 'Who should I talk to?'

'Nobody except Colonel Lewis. And go straighten out Durant's secretary, tell her she's not going anywhere. I want to speak to her this morning.'

Madden ducked back through the doorway.

'Poor Ed,' Kate said, when he'd gone. 'He still doesn't look like he's enjoying himself much.'

Quinn looked at her, but passed no comment. The Honourable Edward Madden, blue-blooded son of the Empire and heir to a sizeable fortune and estate back home (or so it was said), made it plain that he thought several centuries of family history dictated his proper place was at the front. But Quinn didn't want to let him go. The kid was unusually good at his job, and if he agreed to a transfer the chances of getting a decent replacement were slim. He fought every application and Madden knew it. 'Don't go touching anything, Kate.'

Amy White walked away. Quinn listened to her footsteps on the stairs, then wandered through to the bedroom. He ignored his own instruction and scooped up another photograph frame. This one contained a picture of Durant and his wife. They made a handsome couple. Durant had bushy eyebrows and a thin face with full lips. Quinn removed it, folded it carefully and slipped it into his pocket, along with the one of his wife and their daughters.

He bent down and looked under the bed. Beyond

28

it, he spotted a leather briefcase, which appeared to have been kicked beneath the chest of drawers.

It contained a small leather pocket diary, a packet of Lucky Strike cigarettes, a few pens, a pencil-sharpener, a collection of rubber bands and a leather photograph album. There was also a sheaf of uncontroversial memos from the office – one about a change in the date monthly pay cheques were issued, another about new security arrangements at the gate, a third about procedures for taking leave. The album contained pictures of Durant with his wife and daughters. He handed it to Kate and opened the diary.

He flicked through it carefully. On the page for 5 January, Durant had written 'Clare's birthday' in a small, neat hand. Three weeks later, he'd made a note of 'Lucy's birthday'. All other entries appeared to apply to social events. Every Sunday, Durant had written 'CSO' followed by a time, usually '5 p.m.' Each Monday, it was 'Continental, 5 p.m.'

'CSO?' Kate asked. She was at his shoulder.

'Cairo Symphony Orchestra.' Quinn knew about Squadron Leader Rignold's Sunday concerts because Mae sometimes tried to persuade him to go. 'And I figure there's always a concert on the roof garden at the Continental on Monday afternoons.'

There were many entries at the start of the year saying 'rehearsal' and plenty more for visits to the cinema. One week it was *Gone with the Wind*, alongside which Durant had written 'Ruth', another *The Great Dictator*, by which he had written 'Shirley'. A month later he had been to see *Elizabeth and Essex* with 'Emily'. These names appeared alongside films throughout the year. 'A man with many lady-friends,' Kate remarked.

'Most likely girls in the office. Taken on rotation by the looks of it. Maybe that was why he was so popular.'

'What were the rehearsals for?' Kate asked.

'Could be he was an actor.'

'A singer, more like. Isn't the amateur theatrical group here always doing musicals?'

Quinn went on turning the pages. On 19 June, Durant had written, 'W.e.B. 33, top floor'. This had been crossed out, but there was a similar entry for 25 June, which was that evening. There was a time: '9.30 p.m.'

'"W.e.B."?' Kate said. 'Is that Wagh el Birket?' It was the central street in the Berka, the city's red-light district, a squalid and dangerous warren of filthy alleys that was firmly out of bounds to all ranks.

'You got it.' Quinn searched through the pockets of Durant's uniforms. He put the dressing-table back in its place and gathered up a pair of silver hairbrushes, an old Rolex wristwatch, the glass smashed, and a battered leather cuff-link box, most of whose contents had been spilled across the floor.

Quinn tapped the diary. 'Get a call in to Movement Control. I want to know who Ruth, Shirley and Emily are.'

'He's officially missing, then?' Kate asked.

'Until we round him up, yes.'

'And where will we find you, sir?'

'I'm just going to see if Mrs White has anything to add.'

CHAPTER FOUR

The door to the apartment was ajar. 'Come in,' she called.

She was nowhere to be seen. The room was almost as sparsely furnished as the one upstairs. There were no pictures on the wall and only a photograph on the mantelpiece broke its whitewashed monotony, with a couple of simple wooden artefacts. There was a sofa, a table, a couple of rugs on the floor. It felt temporary.

'I'm in here,' she said.

Quinn did not know whether it had been a summons or an instruction to remain where he was. Halfway down the corridor a door opened, spilling out dull red light. 'Sorry,' she said. 'I'm in the middle of something. Come on in.'

The darkroom was about eight feet by five. It had been crudely adapted, with makeshift shelves. 'Sorry about this,' she said. 'I'll be done in a minute.'

Amy was bent over a Bakelite tray, her face creased in concentration, watching a photographic image take shape. There was another pegged to a line above her head, of a Desert Rat standing in front of a tank, arms raised in exultation. She had scribbled a caption beneath it: 'A British soldier celebrates a moment of triumph in the battle for Egypt.'

Quinn watched her rinse the new print, then hang it up to dry. It was a moment or two before he realized it was the same shot. Or, rather, it was the original picture, from which the captioned version had been cut.

He bent sideways to get a better look. In the original, a body was visible in the foreground. It was evident that the soldier, far from celebrating, had in fact raised his hands in grief and despair at the death of a comrade.

Amy started developing another print. The silk scarf she had used as a primitive filter against the dust was still wrapped loosely round her shoulders, concealing her neck. Her crisp white shirt was open far enough to reveal a V of bare skin.

'Who do you work for?' he asked.

'The Chicago Sun.'

Quinn looked again at the two photographs. The strange thing was that in the cropped version the soldier still seemed ecstatic with relief and joy, even if you knew that was not so. 'And this is what the readers of Chicago want?'

'I was trying to get something past your censors. They're sensitive about the messages we send – maybe you've noticed.'

'You don't approve?'

'I don't get on a high horse about it. We all need to know which side we're on.'

Quinn's eye was drawn to a series of photographs she had pinned to the wall. They had been taken in battle, perhaps during the same skirmish, and showed two infantrymen dug into primitive trenches, a pair of vehicles burning in front of them. There were close-ups of the men's faces, grainy portraits of fear, heat and exhaustion. They were gritty and real. 'Where did you take these?' he asked.

'South of Tobruk.'

'How long ago?'

'About four weeks.'

'What happened?'

She looked up at the pictures. 'We were trying to run through to the Free French at Bir Hacheim. We were ambushed, pinned down, had to come back.'

'How did you get there?'

'I arranged an escort.'

Most reporters, even American ones, now checked into the transit camp at El Daba and picked up a 'duty officer' for a tour of the battlefield. Amy had taken quite a few pictures of a raffish British captain in front of a tank. 'The escort?' he asked.

'No.' She pointed at another set of pictures, of a man in a hospital bed, swathed in bandages. It was just possible to make out the vestiges of the same lopsided grin. 'He lost both legs in the ambush.'

Quinn surveyed the sequence of images. 'It's a dangerous occupation,' he said.

'This is a war.'

'It's not a life most would choose.'

'You mean it's no life for a woman?'

'I mean there ain't a whole lot of people who'd put themselves in the line of fire when they didn't have to.'

'Danger is a matter of perspective, isn't it? It depends how much you have to lose.'

They were silent. The air in the room was warm,

heavy with the scent of the chemicals and a hint of perfume. He thought he could smell something sweet on her breath.

The last line of photographs on the wall had been taken in the slums and back-streets of Cairo. They were all of children, filthy and hungry. 'I'm sorry,' she said, catching the direction of his gaze. 'About what happened. I mean, it's none of my business, but your wife—'

'She likes to talk about it.'

'And you don't.'

'No.' Quinn turned away from her. 'When you—'

'I could do with a drink,' she said.

She walked down the corridor and took a seat at the table next to the open window. She folded away one of the battered wooden shutters, then offered him a glass of iced water. He declined, so she poured one for herself. 'So, you've lost your Captain Durant,' she said. 'Maybe he's deserted, gone to Palestine.' She tapped her glass with an elegant finger. 'You're sure you don't want one?'

'No.' He took the seat opposite, glanced around the room. 'You've no reminders of home,' he said.

'Where's home for you, Major?'

'Here.'

'Your wife says you grew up in Manhattan, on the Lower East Side.'

He didn't answer.

'I had a cousin who lived on Seventh Street, name of Weinberg.'

Quinn considered this, but couldn't place a Weinberg. It was odd because Seventh was one of those neighbourhoods where all the kids stuck together. Even in the depths of winter they would turn

34

out to light packing-box fires in the gutters and play stick and stoopball until called in to bed. 'Hold on, sure I know him,' he said, recalling a tall thin kid with thick glasses. 'Aaron Weinberg. Lived next to the Orthodox church, opposite Brewskey's. Father was German.'

'They're good people.'

'That's your maiden name – Weinberg?'

'Yes.'

Quinn looked out of the window at the swaying branches on the far side of the street. He caught a glimpse of someone in the shadows. The figure was unmistakable. Reza shifted to the right, as if for a better view of the doorway. Quinn leant forward. 'Are you all right?' Amy asked.

Quinn turned back to her.

'Joseph to your friends, or Joe?' she asked.

'Quinn.'

'That sounds . . . unyielding. You weren't in the military back home, though.'

'No.'

'You were a cop there, too?'

'Ma'am, I'd love to talk but we've got a job to do here. Are you telling me you only ever met Captain Durant on the stairs?'

'Yes, that's right.'

'He talk to you?'

'Of course.'

'What'd he say?'

'Desultory conversation. Good morning. Fine weather . . . It's going to be hot today.'

'He got any idea you work for an American newspaper?'

'No.'

35

'So how'd you know he worked at GHQ?'

'Like I said, Major, it was what I heard.'

'From whom?'

A flicker of annoyance crossed her face. 'It's a reasonable assumption. I never saw a car. He walked off down the street in that direction with his briefcase, so I made an educated guess.'

'Did he—'

'You think he's lost?'

'Right now, ma'am, he is. Way I look at it, Captain Durant's life here is likely more interesting than it appears.'

'He's an English officer, Major. Aren't they all like that?'

Quinn didn't smile. 'Would you recognize the man in the fedora if you saw him again?' He thought of the photographs on the wall in her darkroom. With that kind of eye, it seemed likely.

'I guess so.'

'You never seen him before?'

'No.'

'You sure?'

'Positive. It was not a face I'd forget.'

'What nationality would you say he was?'

'I've no idea.'

'He was a white man?'

'Yes.'

'I'll get one of my guys to come around, draw a picture.'

She was hesitant. 'Yes . . . of course.'

'You ever see anyone else go up to Durant's place? I mean, before today.'

'No.'

'You sure? No other officers, servants?'

'Yes.'

Quinn looked at her. 'You got no servants here?'

'The boy's father is ill so I sent him home. The cook comes in the evening. I don't like having them under my feet.'

'You don't like having servants?' If it was true, she was the first expatriate wife Quinn had heard express this view.

'I don't need them all day, every day.'

'You lived here long, Mrs White?'

'A couple of months.'

'When did you come to Cairo?'

'A couple of months ago.'

'Where from?'

'Casablanca.'

There was a soft knock at the door. It was Effatt, his face sombre. 'Quinn, I think you'd better come.'

CHAPTER FIVE

Quinn heard Amy White's sharp intake of breath as they emerged into the small garden at the rear of the apartment building. Captain Durant's body hung from the branch of a eucalyptus, suspended by a rope wrapped round his shoulder. The corpse had stiffened with rigor mortis. A length of piano wire was still embedded in its neck, which had been almost severed. The face was red and covered with a thick pelt of flies.

'Cut him down,' Quinn said. Kate Mowbray stood with her back to the river, her face white with shock. Quinn took a pace towards Amy. 'Maybe you better go inside,' he said.

'Yes.' She was staring at the body. One of the constables was cutting the rope as another took the weight of the corpse.

'Is that Durant?'

She hesitated a moment. 'It is Captain Durant. Yes, that's him.'

'This ain't something for the correspondents' club.'

The constables lowered Durant's corpse. It landed with a dull thump. Quinn bent down and waved away the flies. He picked up one end of the piano wire,

38

which had a crudely fashioned handle. It had been worked all the way through the neck and into the bone.

For a moment, he stared at the gaping wound. It had been ferociously done and with great strength. He studied the arm, where they had fastened the rope, then the rope itself.

He tugged back Durant's khaki shirt, which had been ripped open, then put his foot beneath the corpse and tried to roll it onto its back. In doing so, he got a clearer view of Durant's chest. 'Eh, Effatt, you seen this?'

An icon had been cut crudely into the skin, a fork-tailed canine with a narrow, drooping snout, a figure from Egyptian mythology. Beneath it was a single word in Arabic. 'What does it say?' Quinn asked.

Effatt didn't answer.

'Effatt?'

'The figure represents Seth, God of Chaos. The word translates as "Liberation".'

'What does it mean?'

'It was the slogan for a group calling itself the Arab Brotherhood. They had a few supporters in the army, some students. They weren't as big as the other anti-British groups or as well organized, so their activities petered out. But they were vicious – assassins.' He pointed to the word. 'I haven't seen the word used like this since before the war.'

'Who is the God of Chaos?'

'The Voice of Thunder, Lord of the Northern Sky, God of Chaos. Seth has many names. In the under-world, he is said to seize the souls of the unwary. He is often associated with foreigners.'

Quinn bent close to Durant. Now that Rommel was at the gates of the city, there were plenty of Egyptians who saw the Axis powers as the best chance of

39

liberation from British rule – Macleod and Reza were bringing in alleged 'subversives' by the truckload every day – but he found it hard to imagine even the most radical choosing to single out a lone British officer in this part of the city.

'Effatt, you see any sign of blood upstairs?'

'No.'

Quinn rocked back onto his heels. 'A lone British officer, in his own apartment, in a part of town crawling with soldiers ... it doesn't feel like a political hit to me.'

Effatt shook his head.

'There's a guard post outside, just down the street,' Quinn said.

'I've already sent the boys to check.'

Quinn waved away the flies once more and searched the body. He found a crushed packet of cigarettes in the breast pocket of Durant's shirt, a silk handkerchief, a roll of Egyptian pounds and a small knife in the trousers. He turned over the cigarette packet, emptied out its contents. He spread the handkerchief in the dust, sifted through the banknotes, then opened the knife. He looked again at the marks on Durant's chest.

He stood up, lit a cigarette and offered the packet around, looking out over the slow-flowing waters of the Nile, from which they were separated by a low picket fence. The garden, if it could be called that, consisted of a yellow patch of grass leading back to the veranda of the ground-floor apartment, fringed by dust-encrusted palms and the eucalyptus, its white bark shimmering in the sun. The apartment's shutters were closed, the veranda strewn with broken furniture. It looked unoccupied.

The building was set back from the others, closer to

the edge of the Nile, so that at a different time of year, with a little more care and attention, it might have been a pleasant place to while away a winter evening.

Quinn watched a felucca float past, its big white sail billowing in the flaccid air. Beyond it, he could see the startlingly green polo fields of the Gezira Sporting Club. He thought of two little girls far away who were not yet aware that their father would never come home. He looked down at Captain Durant's contorted features, then removed the photograph from his pocket. There was a clear resemblance, although the body was bulkier than the photograph suggested. 'Far as I can make out,' he said, 'our captain's been dead ten hours or more, going by the rigor mortis. And yet Mrs White heard signs of a struggle only a short time ago.'

'We only have her word for that, sir,' Kate said. Quinn could see she was trying not to look at Durant's corpse, attempting to hide her reaction to it.

'You think she's lying?'

'Well . . . No . . . It's just that—'

'I figure you could be right.'

'Maybe the killer came back,' Effatt said.

'Why would you return to the scene of a crime?' Quinn countered. 'How many killers you known do that?'

Effatt tugged at his moustache.

The Egyptian detectives had trodden through the dust, so it was pointless to check for footprints. Instead Quinn moved slowly along the path, looking for any sign that the body had been dragged. He found none. 'He's a big man. Difficult to carry on your own, without leaving some trace.'

He walked into the building and knocked on the

41

door of the ground-floor apartment. When there was no answer, he climbed the stairs to Durant's flat. Inside, he went straight to the bedroom and retrieved the briefcase. He looked through it once more, took out the memos and folded them into the diary. Effatt checked the living room.

'By the way, you were right,' Kate said. 'Ruth, Shirley and Emily are all secretaries in Movement Control.'

'They worked for him?'

'Not directly. His secretary is a rather formidable-sounding woman called Mrs Markham. The other girls were in a central pool. Captain Durant used to take them to the cinema. In rotation, as you guessed.'

Quinn handed Kate the diary and papers, then crouched to check the mattress and the floor. He could find no blood anywhere.

'Can I help?' Kate asked.

'I figure Durant must have been killed in here.'

Quinn went to the spare room and ran his eye across it. He returned to the living room, watched Effatt for a moment, then went into the kitchen. He opened the refrigerator. A cockroach scuttled out between his feet, so he banged the side hard to scare away any companions, then bent down and ran his fingers along the floor beneath the appliance. The first few inches had been cleaned, but the rest had not been touched. 'Effatt.' He lifted the fridge as the Egyptian and Kate reached the narrow doorway. 'Dried blood.' He put it down. 'Durant was killed in here.'

Effatt looked at him with doleful eyes.

'He was murdered in here,' Quinn said. 'The killer carved the symbol on his chest, took the body below, strung it up, then came back to clean up.'

One of Effatt's assistants entered the room. 'The guards say they didn't see anyone come or go last night,' he said, in more or less fluent English.

'They drunk, not paying attention or lying?' Quinn asked.

'I don't think they were paying attention.'

Quinn went to the window and stared down at the dusty street. The men were leaning against the trunk of a palm. He could see no sign of Reza now. 'Half asleep or not,' he murmured, 'that's why they hung the guy out back.'

'I'm sorry, sir?' Kate said.

'That's why they took Durant out back. I figure they'd have wanted to dump him miles from Cairo. That way, he's just a mystery. Maybe he's deserted, panicked at the German advance, taken an early ticket to Jerusalem. But because of the guard post they couldn't risk it, so they hung him out back. Now they've got a murder inquiry.'

'What do you want to do?' Kate asked.

'I figure we need a little more pressure on Mrs White. Then we'll take a look at number thirty-three Wagh el Birket. It sure seems like a strange place for Durant to have been going. After that, we'll see what we can lift at his office. You want to come with us, Effatt, or stay here?'

'Of course come. The men will speak to neighbours. They will report later. Shall I call Nawab, or you want to try one of the military doctors?'

'Call Nawab,' he said. He would at least offer the benefit of speed.

Quinn led the way out of the apartment. He knocked on Amy White's door, but received no answer. 'Gimme a couple of minutes,' he told Kate.

CHAPTER SIX

Quinn turned the handle and pushed gently. It was not locked. 'Mrs White?'

The window was open and a shutter flapped against the frame. There was a pungent smell, a mixture of vomit and cleaning fluid, and he could see the smear of moisture on the floor. It hadn't been there earlier. 'Mrs White?' he asked again.

The shutter flapped harder.

Quinn walked forward, his leather soles noisy on the hard floor. He could still smell vomit. Perhaps the scent had lodged in his nostrils. He paused by the darkroom, but its door was open and there was no light on. 'Ma'am?'

He kept walking.

She lay with her back to him. 'Mrs White?' The bed was wide, with a plain white cover. There was a jug of water beside it, but only one glass. On the far side, there was a single photograph of a couple in a leather frame.

'Ma'am?'

She didn't respond.

'You all right?'

44

She was staring at the wall, her right hand clutching her left shoulder. Her face was pale.

'Mrs White?'

She still didn't answer.

Quinn sat down on the end of the bed. 'You OK?'

'I'm fine.'

Two long bare legs were stretched out towards him. Quinn could just make out the sound of voices below. 'I understand,' he said. 'It ain't a pretty sight.'

'What did they do to him?'

Quinn didn't answer. He doubted she wanted to know.

Amy rolled onto her back and sat upright. As she did so, the silk scarf slipped from her neck, revealing what it had been placed there to conceal. She had livid bruises on either side of her windpipe, as if someone had tried to strangle her.

She realized her mistake, blushed, pulled the scarf back up. 'I'm sorry,' she said.

'For what?' He waited for her to explain, but when she did not, he asked, 'Want to tell me how you got those?'

A truck passed by outside. 'No. It's not your concern.'

'I got a murder inquiry on my hands, ma'am. Everything is my concern.'

She did not answer, so Quinn stood up. A tall glass door led to an iron balcony. He unlocked it and stepped out. Kate was talking to two soldiers by the guard post, taking notes in a leather book. 'You notice the guards much?' he asked.

'No.'

'Got any idea how long they've been there?'

'A few months. Ever since we moved in.'

'They down in that box day and night?'

'Does it matter?'

'Maybe.'

'At first it was just at night. But lately they seem to have been there more often.'

'You ever spoken to any of them?'

'No.'

Quinn stepped back inside and turned the key. 'You seen corpses before, though, right?' he said.

'Of course.'

'I guess, in your line of work, you see them all the time.'

'Not all the time, no.'

'You knew Durant well enough to feel something for him?'

'I knew him. That's all.'

Quinn glanced at the single glass by the bed. 'Your husband not around much?'

'No.'

'What kind of business he in?'

'Oil.'

'And—'

'He spends a lot of time in Suez, but he's coming back to Cairo today.'

Quinn sat down again. 'You never know people's stories, do you, ma'am? That's the truth of it.'

'I suppose not.'

'You ever know a girl named Mary Gibson?' he asked. 'Lived on Seventh in a couple of rooms close to your cousins, right next to McSorley's. She was a pretty girl, about your age.'

'No.'

'Her husband was usually dragged out of McSorley's by his boots, but when he sobered up he liked to go home and knock the life out of her, day after day, week after week, year after year.'

She was watching him.

'People saw her face all bruised, didn't like to get involved. But there was a guy who lived opposite, worked down the docks. One day he hears the screams and the sobbing, goes across the hall, knocks on the door and pulls the husband out. Now the bad guy is getting his punishment. Ends up, he falls down the stairs and breaks his neck.'

'That the kind of justice you believe in, Detective?' she asked.

'I believe in the right kind.'

'Unusual for a cop, wouldn't you say? I'm guessing there's a moral to the story.'

'Ma'am, that case never saw the inside of a court of law, but if you want help, you gotta ask for it and you gotta tell the truth.'

'I don't need any help.'

'You sure about that?'

'Yes. And I am telling the truth.'

'Seems to me you knew Durant better than you're letting on.'

She shook her head.

Quinn waited a moment, took a notebook from his pocket, tore out a piece of paper and wrote down his office telephone number. He handed it to her. 'You think about it, ma'am.'

'I don't need to think about it.'

'Maybe, but see, it works like this. My job now is to spread the net, see what we reel in. I don't want to see someone like you getting into trouble.'

Her face flushed. 'I've told you everything I saw. I've nothing more to say.'

'We'll see. Where will you be?'

'I'll go to the Gezira for a few hours, if that's permitted.'

'I'll catch up with you there.' He returned to the door. 'Oh, and I'd appreciate it if you didn't leave Cairo.'

'I've a job to do.'

'Ma'am, so do I.' He turned to go.

'Good luck today,' she said. Quinn stopped. 'Please give my best wishes to your wife.'

Quinn walked briskly through the apartment. He wondered if anyone in Cairo did not know that this was the first anniversary of his son's death.

He stepped into the corridor. He could hear voices in the lobby. He took another few paces, then halted again. She hadn't really answered any of his questions.

Quinn retraced his steps, nudged the door open and re-entered the apartment. He listened to the muffled sound of her crying and looked about him. Something about these rooms was not quite right. Even in wartime Cairo, wives, in his experience, could not resist a degree of impromptu homemaking. They bought an imitation Flemish tapestry from one of the reproduction antique stores in Zamalek, or got a Greek artisan to make up a fake Hepplewhite sofa. It was almost as if the Whites had arrived yesterday. The furniture was rudimentary. There were no rugs, or glass jugs, no copper ashtrays or antique wooden boxes from the bazaar. It felt unusually temporary.

The sound of sobbing had faded to a whisper.

Upstairs, Effatt was alone in the apartment. It was a moment or two before he noticed his friend's presence.

'The broad's lying,' Quinn said. 'We're going to have to turn her over. You get your boys to trace her servants, speak to the neighbours. I'll put the others onto her husband.'

Effatt nodded.

'You made a decision?' Quinn asked quietly.

Effatt looked at him, eyes dulled by fatigue. They both knew the other was not sleeping. The partnership of the wakeful, Effatt called them. 'No,' the Egyptian said. 'If I don't let him go, he will die. If I do, who knows? Perhaps it will be the last I see of him.'

'Mae says it should only be for a few weeks.'

'I know.'

'She figures that—'

'I admire her faith, but it may soon be out of our hands. Rommel inches closer every day. If they make the journey, who is to say they will be able to come back?'

Quinn did not argue. Effatt's eight-year-old son, Rifat, had tuberculosis. They had taken the boy to the hospital where Mae worked as a volunteer, then to the richer practitioners at the Vittorio Emmanuele Hospital. But the only chance of recovery appeared to lie with a sanatorium in Jerusalem, run by a doctor who specialized in pioneering surgery. Mae had sought it out, and was willing to take the boy, but it presented Effatt with an agonizing choice. His wife had died giving birth and he had three other children to raise. He couldn't go himself, but if the boy went alone it might be the last he saw of him. 'I will have to let him go,' Effatt whispered. 'In my heart I know it. And yet I cannot. What if Cairo falls? We could be divided by a front line. You tell me. What is really happening out in the desert? Our office is alive with rumours.'

'Like what?'

'That the British high command has already taken a secret decision to abandon Cairo.'

'And you believe it?'

'Do you?' Effatt asked.

'No.'

'Why not?'

'They lose Cairo, they'll lose the war.' Effatt didn't look convinced. 'The story from London is that Stalin is demanding a second front in Europe. Churchill can't deliver, so he's sold the idea we'll beat them back out here. If Cairo falls, the Russians will try for a separate peace. That's what Churchill keeps telling his generals.'

'But the Germans are pressing on.'

'The US equipment is arriving. New aircraft, new guns . . .'

'Come on, Joe. If they break through to the delta, you will be gone in an afternoon. I'll be here one side of the front line while you and Rifat are the other.'

'Maybe, as a non-combatant, you'd get through.'

'I want to know what is happening. According to your newspapers, the Germans are being beaten back. But their Arabic service says Rommel has booked a room at Shepheard's for the end of the week. I don't know who to believe.'

'I'll see what I can dig up,' Quinn said.

Neither man moved. 'If he goes,' Effatt said, 'I cannot ask Mae to take him.'

'She wants to.'

'Even so, I—'

'It means a lot to her. You know that.'

50

Effatt's eyes searched Quinn's. 'How is she today?' he asked.

'Swell. She wants it to be a celebration.'

'She is a remarkable woman.'

'Yeah.' Nothing made Quinn feel lonelier than being reminded that he was the only person alive who wished his wife was less remarkable.

Effatt took his arm. 'Time heals all wounds.'

'Maybe it depends how much time you've got.'

CHAPTER SEVEN

Quinn sat in the back of the car. He wanted to open a window, but knew it would only make matters worse. There was no escape from the heat. He took out a handkerchief that had been clean and dry this morning and mopped his brow. It was already damp. As they swung onto Kasr el Aini, Kate was forced to an abrupt halt by a horse-drawn gharry. She honked her horn, long and loud – the Egyptian way – lurched past, then clipped the corner of a donkey cart loaded with vegetables. She swung the wheel violently. She was sweating even more than Quinn.

Quinn opened the window to let in a sliver of air as they accelerated, but they were almost immediately caught behind an ancient Thorneycroft bus, belching fumes, so he shut it again. 'Kate, when we're through in the Berka, you and Ed go turn over the broad's life. Effatt's boys are working the neighbours and servants, so try the husband. I figure he had good reason to nail Durant. By tonight, I want the scoop on these folks: when did they arrive, where are they from, what's his business? Go talk to some of the other press guys and the fellas at the Anglo-American Association.

Does the press guy at the legation know her? Send a cable to the *Chicago Sun*. How long has she been on the staff? And they came from Casablanca. Anyone know what they were doing there?'

'You think she did it?' Kate asked.

'I figure she's lying. So there's got to be a reason. Get Cohen down to draw a picture of the guy she claims she saw. See if she can stick to the same story. And she was talking about a couple of cousins lived in my neighbourhood back home. Way I remember it, they were German Jews, came over in about 'thirty-five. Her family name is Weinberg, so cable the United States Immigration Service and have them check if they've got any record of an Amy Weinberg. Residential address would have been Seventh Street on the Lower East Side.'

Quinn watched the tide of humanity flow past the window, local men in dazzling white robes and coloured turbans weaving through knots of pink-faced soldiers in faded khaki uniforms. There were far fewer soldiers on the streets now. Almost all leave had been cancelled and men sent north to their units in the desert west of Alexandria. They passed a convoy of trucks, which, like their occupants, were covered with dust.

The car ground to a halt. 'You get a look at Reza back there?' Quinn asked. Kate and Effatt both turned, frowning.

'Where?' Effatt said.

'He was standing the far side of the street while I was talking to Mrs White. Before we found the body.'

'You're sure?'

'Yes.'

The others thought about this in silence. They all

detested – perhaps even feared – Reza. But, more importantly, it was the one subject on which Quinn knew they mistrusted his motives. 'Maybe he heard what was happening and decided to follow us,' Effatt said.

Quinn wiped his brow again and brushed away a fly that had landed on his nose. It was like being baked alive. He glanced over his shoulder. They were trapped. He pushed open the door. A traffic policeman had his hand up, halting the flow in both directions to allow a detachment of the Mounted Troop to cross. The soldiers were all on white Syrian Arab stallions, with red sashes across dazzling white uniforms. They appeared to be bound for the palace. Quinn got back in. 'Go round, Kate,' he said.

She ignored his impatience.

A few minutes later, they passed the signs that marked the entry into the Berka. The streets were narrower and darker, dotted with tawdry red booths. Effatt was craning forward, looking at the buildings, none of which was marked with a number.

The Egyptian detective tapped Kate's arm and indicated she should pull over by a pavement café. He got out, shouted at one of the waiters serving coffee, then climbed back in. 'Further,' he said, a note of tension entering his voice, as it always did when they ventured here.

Quinn took out his revolver and checked the chamber. They stopped again, and Effatt ducked into a tiny tobacconist's. Quinn watched a butcher talking to a boy beside a pyramid of melons. The old man's head rested against a carcass hanging from the shop front. Quinn caught sight of another, younger, boy

54

standing in the doorway. The child gazed at him with wide eyes.

'How is Effatt's boy?' Kate asked.

Quinn tore his eyes from the child. 'What?'

'I just wondered if he was all right.'

'Who told you about that?'

'Ed.'

Quinn breathed out. 'He's alive.'

'He'll be all right?'

'It depends.'

'On what?'

Effatt emerged and pointed with greater confidence to a red booth twenty yards up the street on the right. Beyond it was parked a British military jeep.

'Stay with the car, Kate,' Quinn ordered. He and Effatt crossed the street and slipped into a narrow alley festooned with laundry. Two women reclined on a low wooden balcony. It was darker down here, but shafts of sunlight lit the end of the street like a stage set, behind a thin curtain of dust. Quinn mopped his forehead and examined the crudely painted hoarding at the entrance to a peep-show. It depicted a donkey having sex with an Egyptian woman twice its size. The smell from the open sewers caught at the back of his throat.

Effatt checked the darkened doorways ahead. A group of children rounded the corner, kicking up dust and waving a selection of pornographic magazines. 'Hey, Mister, hey, Mister!' One of the boys jumped up and slapped one against Quinn's chest. 'Hey, Mister, you want my sister? Very clean, all pink inside like Queen Victoria!'

Effatt barked at them in Arabic and they retreated reluctantly. Quinn was still watching the alley. A long line of peep-shows and cabarets stretched down it, their attractions advertised as bluntly as those of the fat woman and the donkey. Beyond them, on another main thoroughfare, he glimpsed a river of turbans and tarbooshes bobbing along in the sunlight.

Effatt pushed aside the children and led Quinn past the donkey. A woman as large as the one in the picture leant forward, her hands dripping with elaborate jewellery. She knew they were not customers. Quinn glimpsed a row of red booths, each with a shabby curtain, circling a tawdry stage in the room next door. He listened to his partner's curt questions, none of which the woman answered. Finally Effatt pushed past her. Quinn followed, ignoring her bleated complaint.

They pounded up the stairs to a large room, decorated in red and gold, with tall, ornately framed mirrors and a satin *chaise-longue* upon which two women sat, open-mouthed. '*Rokhsa*,' Effatt said, demanding the Ministry of the Interior employment cards that were obligatory for anyone over the age of fourteen, then handed them the photograph of Durant.

Quinn watched them shake their heads, but he had no doubt that they knew the man in the photograph. Both glanced warily at a closed door in the corner. Quinn heard a low whimper. He moved a little closer to it and listened. Now he was certain. A girl was crying. He pushed open the door.

She lay on a big brass bed, nursing a bruised, tear-stained face. Blood trickled from her nose and lip. There were leather straps on the bedposts, from which she had just been released. A soldier stood next to her, naked and whippet thin. The room was heavy with the scent of massage oils and hashish.

56

There was another faint cry, followed by a barely audible tapping. The girl could not resist glancing anxiously at a cupboard door. For a moment, they were silent.

But the tapping continued. Effatt moved towards it. 'What the hell do you think you're doing?' the soldier asked, in a thick South African accent.

Effatt opened the cupboard.

A little boy knelt inside, sobbing. He wore a new cotton shirt and trousers and clutched a toy car. He was no more than four years old. Effatt picked him up, but he gestured to his mother, calling for her. Effatt carried him across to her.

The girl clutched the sheet round her, pushed her hair behind her ears and took the child. She bent her head.

'What the hell do you think you're doing? I paid good money for—'

In two strides Quinn had the man by the throat, pinning him to the wall. For a split second, caught off guard, the soldier didn't resist. He kicked up ineffectually with a knee, then landed a better punch. He went for Quinn's eyes – one quick stab with a single finger – and broke free. But Quinn was angry. He grabbed the man again, kicked the legs from beneath him and pinned him to the ground. He took hold of his hair and banged the back of his skull against the stone floor. The man screeched, but he was strong. He punched back.

Quinn held him by the throat. The man went for his eyes. 'I paid the bitch—'

'Joe!'

Quinn saw a flash of metal as the man brought a knife towards his neck. He caught the soldier's arm

57

and smashed it against the stone floor. The knife spun towards the bed.

The man screamed again. Quinn reached for his revolver.

'Joe—'

'You piece of shit,' Quinn muttered, as he forced the muzzle into the soldier's mouth and down to the back of his throat. He saw the realization grow in the soldier's eyes, fear turning to panic. 'People like you,' Quinn muttered. He began to depress the trigger.

CHAPTER EIGHT

Quinn felt a blow to the back of his head and his knees buckled. The soldier scrabbled to his feet, genitals flailing. 'Jesus,' he said. 'You're a fucking maniac.'

Effatt's face appeared above him. The Egyptian offered a hand, helped him to his feet. Quinn lunged at the South African again, but Effatt shoved him back against the wall. 'Get a grip, Joe.'

'Take him away, for Christ's sake,' the soldier shouted.

'What's it going to change?' Effatt whispered. 'Nothing for you, nothing for me. This isn't the way to deal with it ... Are you all right?'

'Sure,' Quinn said. The world had stopped turning, but his head throbbed. The girl knelt on the bed, lit by the oil lamp on the dresser. Her son had wrapped his thin brown arms round her neck. On a low table there was a silver plate of Turkish delight and sweet pastries, along with two empty coffee cups and the water-pipe they had used to smoke the hashish.

'Get dressed and come outside with us,' Effatt told the soldier calmly.

'What do you mean, come outside? Who the hell do you think—'

'Shut your fuckin' mouth,' Quinn said.

The man picked up a shirt and covered his genitals. Quinn took another pace towards him. 'Get him out of here!' the soldier screamed.

Effatt moved to the door and waited. As Quinn shuffled past, he shut it behind them. He took hold of Quinn's arm, steadied him again. 'I'm sorry, Joe,' he whispered again, 'but what's it going to change?'

'It'd be a start.'

'It would be a mess. Playing God won't help either of us.' He reached up and scratched the end of his nose, revealing the sign of the cross on the underside of his wrist. Effatt was a Copt, a member of Egypt's Christian minority. As such, and as the servant of an Imperial power, his was a complicated existence. He gripped Quinn's hand. 'This is a job we have to do, that's all. Let's not try to make it something else.'

Effatt returned to the women on the far side of the room. Now they were frightened, and angry enough to fight back, raising their voices in response to his questions. Quinn massaged his skull. A cane armchair stood beside him, but he resisted the temptation to sit.

The door opened and the soldier reappeared, fully dressed, a cigarette pressed to the corner of his lips. 'Who the fuck are you?' he asked.

His face was tanned and weatherbeaten, his hair almost white. He had hollow cheekbones and the luminous eyes of a jackal. Quinn wondered if this was the man Amy White had seen on the stairs. It was hard to imagine him in a white linen suit. There was no mole on his cheek. 'Chief investigator, Special

Investigation Branch, Royal Military Police. This is the chief detective of the Cairo Police.'

The man looked at him. Maybe it was Quinn's imagination, but the soldier's demeanour had changed: his manner was less aggressive. He seemed wary, uncertain.

The girl emerged with the child on her hip. She was tall and beautiful, despite the bruises, much too pretty for a shit-hole like this. But, then, weren't they all? 'What's your name, son?' Quinn asked.

The soldier didn't answer.

'I hope you paid her well,' Quinn said.

'That's none of your business.' His voice was quieter.

'It's none of your business, *sir*.' The soldier glowered at him.

'I thought all leave had been cancelled.'

'I came in from Jerusalem a few hours ago, I drive back tonight.' The soldier looked across at Effatt, then back at Quinn. 'What do you want?'

'What do we *want*? Listen, son, you better watch your step, you hear? Next time I won't be so gentle. Tell us exactly what time you arrived in Cairo.'

'I wasn't looking at my watch.'

'Who was with you?'

'No-one.'

'You completed the journey alone?'

'Yes.'

'What were you carrying?'

'Uniforms.'

'For whom?'

He shrugged.

'What did you do with them?'

'I dropped them at the citadel.'

'Let me get this straight. You dropped a bunch of uniforms, had the man sign for them, then left your transport and came here?'

'Yes.'

'Let me see your papers.'

The soldier reached slowly into his pocket and pulled out a dog-eared pay-book, the means of identification for lower ranks. 'Corporal Jooste,' Quinn read aloud. 'From South Africa?'

'Yes.'

'Afrikaner or English?' Quinn had learnt in this job that a few South Africans of Dutch descent had joined up to fight. As a result of the scars of British imperialism, their loyalty was considered potentially open to question.

'My mother was English.'

Quinn held the papers up to the light. He examined the area around the photograph and the overlapping stamp. He'd seen enough fakes to be reasonably certain this set was either real or a very good forgery. He handed the pay-book to Effatt and wondered what the hell an officer like Durant had been doing in a seedy place like this. He turned to the girl who'd been beaten, examined her face. She avoided his eye. Her son's head was resting on her shoulder.

Effatt handed the papers back and indicated that he, too, thought them genuine. He appeared to understand Quinn's curiosity: one of the few hard facts they had about the accident that had killed Quinn's son was that the man driving the car had been a deserter travelling on false papers.

'You know Captain Durant?' Quinn asked.

'Who?'

62

'Captain Rupert Durant. English officer, about your height, dark hair. Worked at GHQ.'

The soldier shook his head. 'What's happened to him?'

Quinn narrowed his eyes, watched the man's face. 'He a friend of yours?'

'No.'

'But you know who he is, right?'

'I've never heard of him.'

'You been in here before, Corporal?'

'No.'

'You certain about that? The girls seem to know you.'

'Yes.'

'How'd you know about this place?'

Jooste raised an eyebrow.

'It doesn't advertise itself,' Quinn said.

'The area's full of whores. Maybe you didn't notice?'

'It was the picture of the fat lady and the donkey, was it?'

The man didn't smile. 'What do you want?'

'You sure you don't know Durant?'

'I've said so.'

'He was a regular here. Or so it's said.'

Jooste didn't answer.

'You seen any other officers here?'

'No.'

'But, then, you've not been here before, so how could you have done?'

'Exactly.'

Quinn took a step back. 'Where you stationed, Corporal?'

'In the citadel.'

'That's where I'm gonna find you?'

63

'Yes.'

'You're making the run between Jerusalem and here?'

'Yes.'

Quinn made the man wait. 'All right, Corporal Jooste. You can go, for now.'

The man took back his papers, then strode away across the wooden floor. 'Oh, Jooste . . .'. He stopped, turned around reluctantly. 'Why'd you ask what had happened to him?'

The soldier's bewilderment was plain.

'When I asked if you knew Durant, you shook your head. Then you asked what had happened to him.' Quinn smiled. 'Not a question that would have crossed your mind 'less you'd known who he was.'

For a moment, Jooste dropped his guard. 'You're a cop so—'

'Far as I recall, I didn't say anything had happened to him.' Quinn glanced at the woman, who was still standing in the doorway, a white cotton sheet round her shoulders. 'Want to change your mind?' he asked the soldier.

'About what?'

'Whether you knew Captain Durant, or have been here before.'

'No.'

'You know, I could run you in for lying to an officer and obstructing an investigation.'

'I'm not lying.'

Jooste disappeared down the stairs, hobnailed boots thumping out his anger. Once he'd gone, Effatt quietly resumed his conversation with the women. Quinn offered a silk handkerchief to the whore Jooste had been abusing. She took it and dabbed her nose and chin. The boy's arms were still round her neck. After a few moments, Quinn took back the handkerchief and cleaned her cuts himself.

Her dark eyes searched his. They betrayed neither anger nor relief. When he'd finished, he pushed the handkerchief into her hand and gently removed the wooden car from the boy. He examined it with exaggerated care, then bent down and ran it round the wooden floorboards. It was crudely made, the wheels barely turning. Quinn straightened, offered the car back. 'Good,' he whispered in Arabic, as the boy took it from him. 'Fast.'

Effatt was watching him. 'These two claim the owner's not here,' he said softly, as if reluctant to interrupt. 'They say they've not seen Jooste before, and have never heard of Captain Durant.'

Quinn watched as the woman clutched the sheet to her chest and returned with her son to the bedroom. She closed the door. 'What are we going to do?' Quinn asked Effatt.

'About what?'

'About this.' He pointed at the bedroom door.

'Come on, Joe.'

'The creep going to come back?'

'I doubt it.'

Quinn heard a commotion in the street and went to the narrow window. A group of Australians rounded the corner, singing;

> 'King Farouk, King Farouk, you're a dirty old crook
> As you walk down the street in your fifty-shilling suit
> Queen Farida's very gay, 'cos she's in the family way . . .'

As they passed, Quinn noticed Corporal Jooste standing in a doorway, scanning the street nervously, as if he was waiting for someone. 'Take a look at this.' Effatt joined him. 'Think he's a deserter?' Quinn asked.

'Easy, Joe. His papers are good.'

'Or good fakes.'

'Maybe, but one problem at a time, eh?'

'You see the way he looked at us when we told him who we were?'

Effatt was still watching the street. 'I've seen him before, I'm sure of it,' he said.

'Where?'

'I'm not certain. I'll get out the arrest records.'

'What's he doing, though? Who's he waiting for?'

As the soldiers passed, the South African stepped out and moved off.

Without discussing it further, Quinn and Effatt made for the door. By the time they were in the alley, Jooste had disappeared. They ran in the direction he had gone.

Quinn ducked beneath washing-lines and ignored the insistent begging of groups of children and the occasional shouted invitation from whores on low-lying balconies. There was more light ahead. They were getting close to the north side of Ezbekiya Gardens.

As they emerged onto the square, the wail of a muezzin calling the faithful to prayer started up from a nearby mosque. They were close to the corner where the new searchlight battery had been installed, behind the open-air cinema screen. A tram stopped and disgorged its passengers. In the old days, before the war had taken hold, bands of British troops played in the gardens after dinner and there was still a shop on the corner that sold and repaired nothing but bagpipes.

They watched Jooste get into a taxi. 'Keep going?' Effatt asked.

'You bet.' Quinn hailed another taxi and they clambered in. Effatt spoke urgently to the driver.

The car, a battered Citroën, smelt of dust, petrol and leather, and wheezed like an asthmatic as it rattled down into the warren of lanes that made up old Cairo. Eventually, it ground to a halt behind a donkey cart. Quinn rubbed the dirt from the window and looked out at a vine-hung terrace and the intricate latticework that lay behind it. Effatt got out and led them on foot, Jooste bobbing like a cork as he navigated the human tide flowing towards the Khan Khalili, the oldest section of the city's bazaar.

Quinn and Effatt entered a narrow alley filled with the aroma of spices, of cumin – like lemon grass – mingled with cinnamon and cardamom, their footfall quiet on the dusty floor as they moved through pools of dappled light and shade. Dead hawks and other birds of prey hung above shop entrances to ward off evil spirits. Here and there men sat reading aloud from the Qur'an.

Jooste turned up another alley lined with stores selling cotton. Long djellabas, smocks, sheets and European-style shirts hung from every available space, almost blocking out the sunlight. He turned left, then right again, still apparently in no hurry. Row upon row of jewellery and mounds of finely polished copper glittered all around.

Quinn recognized this part of the warren. They were close by Fishawy's, the coffee shop at the heart of the bazaar. Jooste headed towards it.

Quinn and Effatt dawdled outside a shop selling copperware and leather. The owner enthusiastically extolled his wares until Effatt silenced him. Quinn picked up a large copper pot and tried to look like an off-duty soldier.

Fishawy's was small and spilled out into the alley so the life of the bazaar flowed freely through it. Jooste was seated on the bench closest to them, but Quinn could only see his legs and the top of his head. He turned the copper pot in his hands, eyes scanning the café.

On the next bench, two men shared a water-pipe, the aroma of Me'assell tobacco sweet in the still air, one resting a thin arm easily upon the other's knee. A young girl sipped coffee at a table nearby. She had gold rings on her fingers and ran a length of coloured cord between them while her escort sat unnaturally still.

Quinn listened to the clink of coffee glasses, watched the waiters strut through their domain. His eyes returned every few seconds to the South African. He saw the man's foot tap on the stone floor. A waiter glanced in his direction. Quinn turned to Effatt, pretended to mutter something, then swung back.

The guy had gone. Quinn pitched himself forward, down a narrow lane to their right. He reached a crossroads and stopped, then ran on again, into the dazzling light of the square alongside the Al-Hussein mosque.

The place was bustling with life and, as Quinn scoured it, he knew they'd lost him.

CHAPTER NINE

Standing by the car back in the Berka, Kate Mowbray faced a large, curious crowd. An elderly gentleman in a deep red turban was shouting at her, waving his stick. Effatt spoke first to the old man, then the crowd.

'Having trouble?' Quinn asked her.

'I don't think they see too many white women down here.'

'A new career for you, then.'

'Ha, ha.' They climbed into the car. 'Where have you been? I was about to give up on you.'

'We took a trip to the bazaar.'

'Thanks for telling me.'

'No time to talk.'

'What did you find?'

'One of your countrymen who likes to knock women about.'

The crowd was dispersing. 'They knew who Durant was,' Effatt said quietly. 'The women, I mean.'

'Something's not right,' Quinn said. 'We'll come back tonight.'

'I can hardly wait.' Kate turned the key and the Austin rumbled into life. 'We'd better go straight to the briefing or Colonel Lewis will have our guts for garters.'

They turned onto Clot Bey and crawled south. A convoy of five or six black and white taxis headed in the other direction, towards the station, packed to the gunwales with Europeans and their luggage.

The traffic was even slower as they approached the opera house, then stopped altogether. They heard the rhythmic chant of a street protest in the distance. Quinn and Effatt got out and watched a large group of students march down the far side of the road, a succession of defiant, agitated faces, fists punching the air, aiming towards the presidential palace. Such things had been commonplace a few months ago, after the British had deposed the government, but they had petered out. Perhaps the students had been emboldened once more by Rommel's proximity, and the German radio broadcasts in Arabic in which the Grand Mufti of Jerusalem promised imminent liberation and the annihilation of the Jews.

Quinn climbed onto a low wall. There were several thousand demonstrators. He scoured the crowd for some sign of Reza or his assistants, watching and taking photographs. On the far side of the procession, a despatch rider had dismounted from his motorbike. Behind him was what looked like an ambulance convoy on its way in from the desert. The students began to chant, '*Bissama Allah, fi alard Hitler*'; In heaven Allah, and on earth Hitler. A billboard above them advertised a production of Verdi's *La Traviata*.

Two mounted policemen were jostled and called for assistance with high-pitched whistles. For a moment the crowd looked as if it would get out of hand. But the protest was too big and purposeful to be deflected, and it moved on. Behind it, a tram waited to continue on its way towards Gezira.

When the last of the students had passed, they slipped back to the car. Kate edged them through the watching crowd and crossed the square to Boulevard Muhammad Ali. As she did so, they pulled up behind a troop-carrier fresh from the front. On it, soldiers slept, stacked unevenly like sacks of wheat, oblivious to the heat, the dust or the anger of the citizens they were fighting to protect. Only one appeared to be awake and he raised his fingers in an ironic V for victory.

There was a queue of cars in the dusty street outside British Army Headquarters, waiting to be cleared through the security barrier. Quinn sat back. Most of the soldiers and officers flooding in on foot were British, but he spotted one or two Australians and a tall Free French officer in a kepi waiting for their credentials to be checked.

GHQ had originally been sited in the gloomy surroundings of the Semiramis Hotel on the banks of the Nile, but as the war for North Africa had gathered pace, the top brass had been forced to switch to this block of flats, known as the Grey Pillars, at the southern end of Garden City.

Quinn and Kate climbed to the top floor of the central tower.

As he walked towards the Map Room, Quinn felt the coolness of the air-conditioned offices to his right and left. This was practically the only place in Cairo that enjoyed such luxury. Several offices were empty: General Auchinleck and his deputy had taken themselves up to Eighth Army Field Headquarters in the desert.

The briefing had already begun. Colonel Charles Lewis, a tall, imposing man with slicked-back hair and movie-star looks, stood in front of a huge chart of Egypt and Libya, billiard cue in hand. Beside him was a polished mahogany table, upon which sat a battered tray of tea and biscuits. Lewis was head of Military Intelligence and Security in Cairo, and therefore Quinn's nominal superior.

Lewis moved to the window and closed the blind to shield himself from the sun. He tapped the leather soles of his bespoke shoes on the polished parquet floor. Cairo had been circled in black on the wall map, as had Alexandria, about five hours' drive to the north. To the west, the coast ran down to Libya, and it was along this axis that Rommel and his troops were advancing. 'In order to get through to Alexandria,' Lewis said, 'we see no alternative but for Rommel to cut through the narrow gap here between the sea and the Qattara Depression. The depression itself is impenetrable to any modern army. Its northern walls are too steep and its salty floor too soft for tanks. And it is huge – as though a giant hand has scooped out several thousand square miles of desert.

'I'm afraid, however, that we must now accept that this bottleneck close to the railway halt at El Alamein is our *last* hope of preventing a rapid advance across the delta. If Rommel does break through it, he will be in Alexandria in half a day, and here a day at most after that.'

Quinn glanced at a map of the Middle East on the wall in the corner. A large black arrow from a previous briefing was a reminder that most here did not even wish to consider. The Nazis were also driving south through the Caucasus towards Iran and Palestine. The

British in Egypt were being caught in a vast pincer movement.

Maybe there would be no escape route, after all.

Lewis slid the end of the cue along the coast to Mersa Matruh, several hundred miles to the west of El Alamein. 'The bad news is that Rommel appears to be behaving as if he knows our every move. By rights, we believe he ought to have paused here at Matruh, gathered his strength. Instead, he appears to be punching on towards El Alamein and Alexandria. He has an extremely long supply line, which we are harrying from the air, day and night, but this is not deterring him.' Lewis surveyed the room gravely. He lowered his cue. 'The unfortunate truth, gentlemen, is that we may have to give the order to evacuate Alexandria today, perhaps tomorrow. Naturally it is not something that should be discussed beyond the confines of GHQ or we'll have a flap on our hands.'

You've already got one, Quinn thought, recalling the crowd outside the station and the weight of extra traffic on the roads.

'I wish there to be no misunderstanding, however. Cairo is, and from now on will be, an entirely different matter. The Defence Committee received this communication overnight from the PM. I think it outlines the situation with customary clarity. It orders, "mobilization for battle of all the rearguard services. Everybody in uniform must fight exactly as they would if Kent or Sussex were invaded. Tank-hunting parties with sticky bomb and bombards, defence to the death of every fortified area or strong building, making every post a winning-post and every ditch a last ditch . . . No general evacuation, no playing for safety. Egypt must be held at all costs."'

Lewis surveyed the room as his staff officers contemplated the threat of hand-to-hand street-fighting in appalled silence. 'The evacuation plans you have been issued with are now redundant. Let me reread that sentence. "No general evacuation, no playing for safety, Egypt must be held *at all costs*." It is possible, of course, even likely, that our opponents in the city here will attempt to assist Rommel's advance, or hamper our retreat, or both. We think the Germans are trying to facilitate this. Today's ally, or at least assistant, may be tomorrow's enemy. So we will require you to display greater than ever vigilance. We will fight for every last inch of this city. The Defence Committee is drawing up a set of emergency plans.'

Quinn contemplated his superior. Undeniably charismatic, he possessed every attribute of the great public speaker except sincerity. Whoever ended up fighting in the streets of Cairo, he was pretty sure it wasn't going to be Charles Lewis.

'There is one further matter. It should be perfectly obvious to you that the policy I have just outlined guarantees there will be no orderly evacuation. So my message to you today is to destroy anything that you no longer need. Prepare to burn the rest at the shortest possible notice. The last thing any of us would wish to do is give the Nazis intelligence that may assist them in the future, or to let down in any way all those locals who have helped us.'

There were around thirty men in the room – Kate was the only woman – and when they sensed that Lewis had finished, they turned away soberly. Quinn was about to do the same when he found Madden at his shoulder. 'Colonel Lewis wishes to see us, sir.'

'Now?'

74

'He insists.'

'All of us?'

'You and me.'

Quinn glanced at Kate. 'You'd better come along.'

'Sir . . .' Madden interjected, but he saw the look on Quinn's face and dropped it.

Madden led them through to Lewis's office. The colonel sat behind his desk, legs crossed, smoking a cigarette. For all his aristocratic languor, Quinn found his superior a hard man to dislike. Macleod and Reza sat alongside him. It was said both Lewis and Macleod came from Shanghai, but despite their shared history – or maybe because of it – they appeared to have little fondness for one another. Quinn glanced at Reza. The Egyptian's dark eyes were fixed upon him, beads of sweat glistening on his scalp between thin strands of carefully stretched hair. He reminded Quinn of a vulture, constantly searching for its prey. 'That will be all, Miss Mowbray,' Lewis said. 'Thank you.'

'She may as well stay.'

Lewis frowned. 'With the greatest respect to you, Joe, she has been with us little more than a month and she *is* still only an auxiliary.'

'She don't bite.'

'She's a driver, not a detective,' Macleod said.

'Loosen up. She's part of the team. Maybe she's only been with us a month, but she's been here eighteen so she knows her way around.'

'Joe—'

'If you gave me more men, Colonel, maybe I wouldn't need to employ auxiliaries, but she's here and she's smart, so I say she stays.' Quinn watched Lewis and saw the hesitation in his eyes. Another day, he'd have forced the issue, but not today. Kate

75

Mowbray had flushed bright red, but she smiled at him with gratitude. Lewis waved his hand in exasperation. 'All right, take a seat. Time is short, so let's cut to the chase.'

CHAPTER TEN

Lewis leant forward. 'You'll not have had a moment to file a report on the murder of Captain Durant yet but—'

'I've done a preliminary summary,' Madden said. He stepped forward, unclipped the flap of his briefcase, took out a folder and placed the report in front of Lewis.

The colonel bent over it. There was a knock. A tall blonde woman in a tight-fitting skirt stood in the doorway, Lewis's third secretary in as many months. Quinn caught Kate's eye. Lewis's reputation was legendary. 'Brigadier Collins for you,' the woman said.

'Tell him I'll call back,' Lewis replied, without looking up. He turned over the first page of the report. When he'd finished reading, he handed it to Macleod. 'The thing is, I hope you'll not take offence, Joe, but in the current climate I'd prefer Alastair to handle this case.'

Reza gave a thin smile.

'Why?' Quinn asked.

'Because I think it belongs in his domain and the investigation may provide leads that he will need to follow up. It was my inclination when Madden reported earlier, but this confirms it.'

'I don't get it.'

Lewis leant forward. 'Durant wasn't some Johnny from the ranks. We need to think about what lies behind this.'

'He bled the same.'

Lewis took the papers back from Macleod. 'It's here in your own report. The Gyppo symbol, the word "Liberation" . . .'

'Murder is murder.'

'Joe,' Lewis said, with a barely audible sigh of exasperation, 'why you fight for every case defeats me, but it seems plain that what we've got here is local extremists *assassinating* a senior officer. Why else would they scrawl this symbol? But, if so, who is behind it? How big are they and how well organized? These are the questions to which we need immediate answers. Alastair will be able to use his informers in the army and the underground groups to get at what is really going on.' Lewis glanced at Reza. 'He is the head of security, after all, so now if—'

'Extremists?'

'It's in your report – the Gyppo symbol, the word "Liberation", the way poor Durant was hanging from a tree. The question we have is, will this be the first of many such attacks? Are others being planned even as we sit here? Does this represent a new terrorist threat that we have yet to fully—'

'That isn't credible.'

'It sounds pretty credible to me,' Macleod said.

'So we all want another case on hold, do we?'

They all knew what he meant. 'Given the circumstances today,' Lewis said, 'I'm going to let that pass without comment.'

'This ain't a political murder,' Quinn said. 'No way.'

'What makes you so sure?' Reza asked.

'Captain Durant wasn't killed in the back garden where we discovered his body. He was murdered upstairs, in his own kitchen, by someone he knew. The killer came up behind him, put piano wire around his neck. There were no bruises on his face and hands and no sign he had time to struggle.'

'Then why the word "Liberation" carved on his chest?' Macleod asked. 'And that curious symbol, the God of Chaos . . .'

'A red herring. Hoping for a dumb cop who was going to buy a scenario.'

'You'll not concede there's anything in it at all?' Macleod asked.

'No.'

Lewis glanced at Macleod. Like everyone else in Cairo these days, he seemed inclined to defer to him. Quinn thought they were frightened that without the Scot – and his army of thugs and informers – they'd be unable to keep the city in check. 'So why was Captain Durant murdered?' Lewis asked.

'If I had an answer,' Quinn said, 'we'd have made an arrest.'

'Well, you're going to have to give us something.'

Quinn resented the way superiors, even good ones, wanted the conclusion to a homicide investigation five minutes after it had got started. 'It's been made to look like a political murder, sure. What could be a more natural play? A time of war, a city on edge . . . they figure they'll get some local cop who doesn't want to make a case or it'll get bumped to something like Field Security and then the trail leads nowhere.'

They were watching him.

'I figure Durant was taken by surprise, in his own place. I'd say it was something to do with a girl. Maybe the husband found out, lay in wait. Maybe he hired someone else to do the hit.'

'A love affair?' Reza asked.

'On what basis?' Macleod added.

'That the married woman who reported the attack is lying.'

'About what?' Lewis asked.

'How well she knew Durant.'

'How do you know that?'

'It's an instinct.'

'And she's your suspect?'

'I didn't say that.'

'Who is she?'

'An American photographer.'

Lewis glanced at the clock on the wall. 'You know, we're going to have to tell the Auk this afternoon. You can imagine how he's going to respond.' The Auk was General Auchinleck. 'I'd like to tell him it's all some squabble over a wretched girl, believe me, but whatever you say, the ritual nature of the murder and its symbolism is going to leap out of any report we send up. They'll be breathing down our necks from dawn till dusk. And that's without even thinking about London's response.'

He paused. 'All right, gentlemen.' They all stood up. 'Not you, Joe.'

When they were alone, Lewis closed the door. He offered Quinn a cigarette, lit it for him, then perched on the edge of his desk, swinging one long leg. The

formality of a few moments before had melted away.
'Did you get my note?' he asked.

'Yeah.'

'I'm sorry, perhaps I shouldn't have written.'

'I appreciated it.'

'Thank you . . . I know it's difficult, but try not to let your judgement be affected by what's happened. I understand that—'

'Nobody understands.'

'Of course. And you might say, with reason, that it's none of my business, but as a friend I cannot believe your relentless nihilism is going to help anyone, least of all you. God may move in mysterious ways but—'

'I leave God to my wife.'

Lewis sighed. 'Very well, Joe. I haven't forgotten that I promised we'd have a result by now.'

'It's been a year.'

'I know, but we're close. We really are.'

'To what?'

'We have a suspect, an accurate description of the man driving the car and the name he used on his last set of false papers. We've been scouring the city for him and it can't be much longer.'

'What's the name?'

'I can't tell you that, Joe. You know I can't. But I understand your frustration.'

'Macleod and Reza have found nothing. A year, and they've got nowhere. Too busy beating the hell out of a bunch of harmless students down in the basement.'

'That's not true. They've interviewed over three hundred and fifty deserters in detail. They have a pile of statements that would reach the ceiling. And, if I may say so, I think a little gratitude to all of us wouldn't go amiss. It was an accident. We know the driver was in all likelihood a deserter who sped off because he didn't want to be caught. On any objective analysis, this would barely be any sort of priority. But because we know how much it means to you we've poured thousands of man-hours into trying to locate him.'

'You've got to want a result.'

'What's that supposed to mean?' Lewis asked.

'Come on. How dumb do you think I am? The only important witness, Corbett, was reassigned to England a week after the accident. The only description we have of the guy comes from him.'

'That was a routine matter planned long before.'

'Is that what Macleod tells you?'

'Joe, I'm not sure I like your tone. I'm familiar with your views and I've tolerated them because of the circumstances, but I assure you that Lieutenant Corbett's transfer came through more than a month before your son's death. And, whatever you may think, Alastair is not in the business of protecting his informers from charges of—'

'Corbett worked for Macleod. Mysteriously he's the only witness to the theft of the car outside Shepheard's. You've spoken to three hundred and fifty deserters, but not one has recognized the description he gave of the thief. When the guy hit my son, he was turning in *towards* the barracks. So what was he doing? Coming in to give himself up? That car was never stolen in the first place. Corbett ran informers for Macleod. I say one of them had his car and was driving into the barracks for a meeting. Whoever the guy is, Macleod wanted him protected. He persuaded you he should handle the investigation and Corbett was ordered to

82

tell a few lies until he could be reassigned so I couldn't get at him.'

'That's enough, Joe.'

'I want all the papers on it handed over to me.'

'That's out of the question.'

'He was my son.'

'Don't be a bloody fool,' Lewis snapped. 'You think I'd let you within a million miles of something like this? Do you remember what happened back home, or should I remind you?'

Quinn stared at the ground.

'You're lucky to have a job, Joe. It's only because of me that the small matter of your departure from the New York Police Department was overlooked. And you didn't mention it in your papers, as I recall, so I'd have had double the reason to throw you out. Without Effatt and Ed to keep an eye on you, I'll be honest, I don't think I could have you out there.'

'Let's leave it.'

'I'd like to, Joe, believe me. I would if I could believe you'd really changed, that there was no chance you'd ever snap again.'

'You never done anything you regret, Colonel?'

'Oh, plenty. But you *don't* regret it, that's the problem. I've asked you twice to leave this investigation to Alastair, but you've been questioning people at Shepheard's, trying to get hold of the deserters' statements – don't deny it, Joe, I know you have. Alastair says you've been trying to bribe one of the secretaries in his—'

'Asking.'

'It's the same difference.'

'Maybe to him.'

'Well, I—'

'He was my son.'

'And everyone understands that. But I can't allow an investigation to become personal. Surely you must see that.'

'Macleod isn't a cop.'

'He ran the detective division in Shanghai for a decade. And, for your information, it was a much more violent city than any you'd have known back home. I asked him to look into your son's death because I thought he'd do a good job and I had to keep it away from you for obvious reasons. I'm afraid I don't understand why you seem to have a grudge against him.' Lewis looked at him. 'You're a good bloke, Joe, but you let it get personal back in New York and it didn't work out well, so do yourself a favour and leave this to us. You went off the rails after your father's death and I'm not having the same thing happen here. We'll crack it in the end. Have patience.'

Quinn was pretty damned tired of these lectures. It would be a whole lot easier to have patience if he didn't hear that Austin gunning its engine every night in his dreams.

'The work of the department must go on. As an outfit, we need to pull together, now more than ever. Look at what's going on around you. The city's coming to the boil again and the Defence Committee is bloody petrified. The last thing we need is a revolution on our doorstep. If Alastair and Reza said, "Jump," right now the Committee would ask, "How high?" I recognize that you don't like either of them, but this is the time to put that to one side and—'

'They do a job. Normally there's no problem.'

'Their sources could be useful to you. They've got ears in every corner of the city.'

84

'Wouldn't know about that. I ain't never seen any of their reports.'

'Macleod says you never ask.'

'I'm a cop. It's not my business.'

'So is he. A chief of police in his time, no less.'

'Maybe a different kind.' Whatever he might have done in the past, Macleod's job now was to hunt spies and keep the local populace in its place. It was a task to which both he and his assistant appeared well suited. Quinn debated telling his superior that he'd seen Reza outside Durant's apartment *before* they'd discovered the body today but, under the circumstances, thought better of it.

Lewis returned to his seat. 'And here's another thing. The way I explain you to critical superiors, Joe, is to play upon their anxieties. A city packed with colonial soldiers needs an uncompromising policeman, I tell them. Such eccentricities as you may display, including, may I say, an at times spectacular lack of tact, have to be put down to "cultural differences".'

'We're allies now.'

'Perhaps, but don't think for a moment that's going to improve matters. You can imagine how well my colleagues are responding to being told by Americans that their conduct of the war is inefficient, not to say incompetent.'

'Look, I'm just doing a job.'

'So you say. But not playing the game.' Lewis tapped the paper in front of him. 'You could at least have got Madden to write me a report that omits to mention the symbol and the hanging corpse. Then I could have passed it on with a clear conscience and left the Durant case quietly in your hands.' Quinn didn't react. He doubted Lewis was kept awake nights by his conscience. 'You know what this is about for us, don't you?' Lewis went on. 'You understood what I was saying back there?'

'Yeah, I heard you.'

'The last thing we want to have to tell the Auk is that he's got a terrorist problem in the rear.' He pointed to Madden's report. 'What if this *is* something new? A new bunch of local lunatics? A new rebellion? You've seen the demonstrators out there again. Who's organizing them? Is this all co-ordinated in some way?'

'Durant's death has nothing to do with that.'

'Are you absolutely certain of it? Or is this just a New York detective's hunch?'

'Call it what you want. Give me a couple of days, I'll have the answer.'

Lewis shook his head. 'All right, I'm going to rewrite this to send on up the chain, playing down the references to the God of Chaos or we'll be bombarded with questions. I'll say we think it's an old-fashioned love triangle and tell Alastair he can't have the case. He has enough on his plate so I can probably mollify him, but you'd better be right.'

Quinn stood up, but he didn't move towards the door. 'What's really going on up in the desert?' he asked.

'What do you mean?'

'How long have we got and what are our chances of winning?'

Lewis waited a moment. 'Given the bottleneck, our chances ought to be fair. Rommel's soldiers are tired and his supply line stretched, but he possesses a supreme confidence. If you're worried about Mae, I'd get her out now. If you're asking me officially, of course we'll win. Off the record, I'd dust off your rifle. You may need it.'

Quinn went to the door.

'Joe,' Lewis said. 'Ed Madden and Kate look like they're dead on their feet.'

'They're working hard.'

'Not everyone has the same agenda.'

'What does that mean?'

'If I knew what your agenda was, perhaps I could say.'

'We're just doing a job, like I said.'

'Morning, noon and night? That's not healthy for any man, is it?' Lewis picked up an envelope. 'I got another letter from Madden's father.'

'What'd it say?'

'Similar sentiments.' Madden's father, himself a former colonel in the Grenadier Guards, didn't think an attachment to the Special Investigation Branch in Cairo was an appropriate step in his son's military career, especially not in time of war. 'I'm going to have to send him up to the front line,' Lewis said. 'I can't delay it any longer.'

'Do I have a say?' Quinn asked.

'No. Sir Jeremy has too many connections.' Lewis looked at him again. 'You can have your case, Joe. But you'd bloody well better be right. We'll have morning conference here every day at nine. I want a typed summary delivered overnight.'

'You got it.'

'And a copy to Alastair,' he said, as Quinn pulled the door shut.

CHAPTER ELEVEN

Captain Durant's office was two floors below, encompassing a series of rooms off a long, gloomy corridor. His boss, Colonel Anthony Wheeler, was a bookish man with narrow features and thick spectacles. He sat at a desk too tall for him, surrounded by piles of paper. Quinn introduced himself, but the colonel barely looked up. Clearly no-one had informed him of his deputy's demise. 'You've found Captain Durant?' he asked.

'Yeah. We got him.'

'Good. We were concerned. It's most unlike him to be so late.'

'He's going to be more than late, I'm afraid.'

Wheeler's eyes flickered behind his spectacles. He knew something was wrong, Quinn thought, had been expecting it, even. Quinn let him wait it out. 'I'm sorry to have to tell you this, Colonel,' he said quietly, 'but we found Captain Durant's body just a short time ago.'

There was a long silence. 'How? I mean . . .'

'He was in the garden of his apartment.' Quinn took a seat. Ed Madden and Kate remained standing behind him. 'I'm sorry.'

Wheeler shut the file on which he had been working, angled his face towards the wall. 'My God,' he whispered.

'He was a friend?'

'Yes ... I mean not a friend precisely, but ... a decent chap. A conscientious subordinate.' Wheeler's reaction was curious. Unless Quinn was mistaken, shock was mixed with fear. 'It will be a matter for Field Security?' Wheeler asked. 'Captain Durant's murder, I mean.'

Quinn took a notepad and pencil from his top pocket. 'In time, maybe.'

Wheeler looked relieved.

'You know Macleod?'

'No.' Wheeler shook his head, evidently sensed he'd given the wrong impression. 'No.'

'Why did you say murder?' Quinn asked.

Wheeler frowned.

'I told you his body had been found.'

'I don't understand.'

'What about an accident? Or suicide?'

'I—'

'Murder ain't what people expect, even in a war, is it, Colonel?' Quinn watched Wheeler's Adam's apple bob. 'You couldn't imagine Durant doing himself in?'

'No. Exactly.' Wheeler was grateful for the assistance.

'Maybe you could tell us what Durant did here.'

'In the office, you mean?'

'Yeah.'

'Well, all of our junior staff reported to him.'

'About what?'

'The activity in their sector.'

'What activity?'

'The location and movement of all our units in the field. Their fighting strength and so on.'

Quinn saw that Wheeler was aware of how sensitive this had made Durant's position. 'And Durant passed all this stuff to you?'

'Not routinely, no. If he was going to a meeting upstairs, perhaps he might let me have a copy of his summary as a courtesy. But my job here is to manage the personnel rather than the flow of information.'

Quinn removed some grit from his mouth. He realized that Wheeler had been anxious to make sure he understood this point. Durant had been a fulcrum for information being passed between junior field staff and the top brass, which made his position unique. 'Any of the juniors able to put together the same kind of picture?' he asked, to be sure he had understood correctly.

'In theory, but not . . .'

'Not without drawing attention to themselves?'

Wheeler nodded.

'How long had Durant been with you?'

'A few months.'

'How few?'

'Six or seven. I'd have to check his records to be sure.'

'I'd like to see them.'

Wheeler stood up, went to a nearby cabinet and searched through it. Quinn's eyes moved to a calendar on the wall with photographs of British landscapes. It seemed out of place. Next to it a framed poster advertised a production of *The Pirates of Penzance* by the Cairo Amateur Theatrical Society at the Royal Opera House.

Wheeler sat down again, opening a red folder. 'September last year.'

'From England?'

'Yes.'

Quinn held out his hand and Wheeler stood again to hand over the file. He noticed how easily the colonel forgot the natural deference due his rank. The record was sparse. Durant had been an accountant in somewhere called Harrogate before the war. He was married, with two children. He'd joined up in September 1940 and was sent to Cairo a year later. 'Where did you meet Major Macleod?' Quinn asked.

'What do you mean?'

'You said you knew him.'

'No . . . I, er . . .' Wheeler's face creased with confusion. 'I didn't say that.'

'Is that so? My mistake.' Quinn made a show of returning to the file, then looked up. 'What was Durant like, Colonel?'

'He was a decent chap. Very decent.'

'"A decent chap"?' Quinn mimicked Wheeler's accent.

'Yes.'

'What was he really like?'

'I don't understand.'

'"A decent chap" doesn't tell me nothin'.' Quinn leant forward. 'Someone almost cut his head off. That ain't an everyday occurrence, even in Cairo.' He took a photograph from his jacket pocket and dropped it onto the desk. Durant's daughters smiled up at them. Wheeler didn't look at it. 'The way I see it,' Quinn said, 'Captain Durant was a man who inspired strong emotions.'

There was a long silence.

'You got the advantage, Colonel. You knew Durant, and I didn't. Why would someone want to kill him?'

'You might speak to his secretary, but I—'

'You didn't like him?'

'We were colleagues.'

'No more?'

'No.'

'Then how did you find him as a colleague?'

'Very pleasant. A thoroughly decent chap, as I've said. Reliable, conscientious. A good eye for detail. That's important in this job.'

'Come on, Colonel,' Quinn said. He had lowered his voice. 'You want me to take you down, show you the body – or what's left of it?'

Suddenly Wheeler seemed about to weep. Quinn didn't think it was for the loss of Durant. 'He was popular,' Wheeler conceded, 'but—'

'He liked to take the girls to the pictures?'

'So I believe.'

'He was hitting on them?'

'Of course not.'

'They liked the guy?'

'Yes.'

'But you didn't?'

'I didn't say that.'

'You ever see him outside work?'

'No.'

'Never?'

'Well, I wouldn't say never, exactly, but—'

'Where?'

Wheeler frowned. 'I'm not sure. It might have been at the Gezira.'

'You go there often?'

'Quite regularly, yes.'

'A swim at lunch. A few moments to relax on the Lido?'

92

Wheeler stiffened. 'When my workload permits.'

'You see him with someone else, a girlfriend?'

'No.'

'You know a broad called Amy White?'

'No.'

Quinn contemplated the colonel's anxious face. 'It's gonna fall to you to inform Captain Durant's wife.'

'Yes.' Wheeler was happy to be led to safer ground. 'Of course. What should I tell her?'

'That he died during a visit to the front. I don't think she needs to know all the dirty details of her husband's life in Cairo, does she?'

'No.' Wheeler made no attempt to contradict him.

'It's a common enough story. A husband far from home, the pressure of war, a strange and exotic city.'

'I'm sure.' Wheeler was staring intently at his fingers.

'Durant got a girlfriend?' Quinn asked again.

'No. I mean, I don't know.'

'You made the assumption, then. A married man a long way from home . . .'

'Of course I didn't.'

'You never saw him in the Berka?'

'It is not an area of town I frequent, Major.'

Now Quinn was sure Wheeler knew more than he was saying. 'There was no gossip in the office?'

'If there was, I wasn't aware of it.'

Quinn interlocked his fingers, his eyes never leaving Wheeler's. 'You notice anything different about the last few months?'

Wheeler shook his head.

'Nothing at all?'

'Well . . .' Wheeler had sensed he was being lured into something. 'No, I don't think so. I mean, Captain

Durant was quite a good-humoured fellow in the office. I don't believe I noticed a change in his demeanour. No, I didn't.'

'He gettin' moody?'

'If he was, I wasn't aware of it.'

'There anything about Captain Durant's behaviour that aroused your suspicion?'

'I don't know what you mean.'

'He was leaving the office earlier?'

'What makes you think that?'

'Durant's secretary informed Lieutenant Madden here that a month ago your guy started to leave the office right on seven. Before that they'd be here late, maybe till midnight. As the commander of such a sensitive unit, it's a detail I figure you'd have noticed.'

Wheeler stared into the middle distance.

'You mind if we look at Captain Durant's office?' Quinn asked. 'And I'd like to talk to his secretary and the girls from the typing pool.'

Wheeler got to his feet, flustered. 'Yes, I mean, no, but . . . I must tell Mrs Markham and the others first.' He took two paces, stopped. 'About Captain Durant. Please give me a few moments.'

CHAPTER TWELVE

Wheeler was gone ten minutes, perhaps more. The three sat in silence, reluctant to share impressions when there was a chance of being overheard. Quinn was happy to be alone with his thoughts.

The colonel returned, and indicated they should follow him. Mrs Markham sat at her desk, clutching a white handkerchief in one hand and a pair of reading-glasses in the other. Her eyes were red and swollen. Wheeler withdrew, without bothering to introduce them. Quinn detected his air of relief.

Durant's office was small, airless, and a testament to Mrs Markham's passion for dogs. Her section was covered with pictures of different breeds, and a large calendar with a new photograph for each month of the year. 'I'm sorry, Mrs Markham,' Ed Madden said softly. 'We spoke earlier. This is my superior, Major Quinn.'

Mrs Markham was the kind of woman who prided herself on not succumbing to emotion, Quinn guessed, except where animals were concerned. She was struggling, therefore, to pull herself together. It proved no easy task. 'I'm sorry,' Quinn said.

She didn't answer.

'I know it's tough but—'

'You have a job to do. I quite understand.'

Quinn waited for her to compose herself. He thought he would learn more in a few seconds here than he'd have discovered in hours with the prickly Wheeler. 'When did you last see Captain Durant?' he asked.

'Last night. Just as . . .' She could not bring herself to complete the sentence. Just as usual, she meant. But this linguistic illustration of the disturbance of the natural order set her on a downward spiral again. Tears crept into the corners of her eyes. 'It's this wretched war, isn't it?' she said. 'Do you know, he wrote to his daughters almost every day? Clare and Lucy. I don't suppose I shall ever meet them now.'

Quinn waited for her to elaborate.

'Damn this war,' she said.

He tried to decipher what she meant. 'Captain Durant was married . . .'

'What do we expect?' Mrs Markham asked. 'These men, so far from home. Of course they get lonely.'

And now Quinn understood. Mrs Markham did not approve of adultery, but she had been uncommonly fond of Captain Durant. 'He had a girlfriend,' Quinn said.

'We shouldn't be surprised,' Mrs Markham said, 'should we?'

She wanted his agreement. 'Maybe not,' he said. 'What was her name?'

Mrs Markham sighed. 'I don't know.' More tears rolled down her cheeks. 'Those poor little girls. What do they know of such things?' She dabbed at her face.

then stood up and snatched her bag. 'I'm sorry, Major. Would you excuse me?'

Quinn also got to his feet. 'I just need a name—'

'I don't know,' she said. 'I really don't know. Please, if you don't mind, I'd like to go home now.'

'Mrs Markham—' She began to leave. 'Mrs Markham!' he barked. She stopped. 'I apologize, ma'am,' he said, 'but this is a homicide. I'm not done.'

'I can see what you wish to know, Major, but if Captain Durant did . . . well, if there was someone, then I am not aware of who it was. I know you will have other questions, but if you could spare me a few hours to compose myself, I shall do my level best to be helpful to you.'

Without waiting for an answer, she left. Quinn did not call her back.

For a moment, they stood in silence. Quinn stepped forward to examine the calendar, but it was purely decorative with nothing marked on it. He turned round and sat at Durant's desk, switched on the fan, then a lamp.

The desk was neat, all paperwork stored in two wire trays. Quinn pulled over the one marked 'Out', removed the documents and sifted through them. Even the most cursory examination confirmed what a wealth of information had crossed Durant's desk. The first sheet, dated the previous day, read: '112 Squadron pull back to Landing Ground 102. Eighty per cent serviceability. New Kittyhawks arrived, 69 sorties flown today.' Beneath this, someone had scrawled: 'Total in service in theatre: 235 fighters and dive-bombers, 62 light bombers, 67 medium bombers.'

Quinn turned the page. He wondered if there was anyone in Cairo, apart from the most senior commanders, who had known as much about where Allied forces were deployed and in what strength. 'Remnants of S. Notts Hussars at Alamaza Camp reformed as battery of medium artillery. Armed with new 5.5 inch guns. Put into 7 medium regiments.' Next to this, Durant had written: '8th Army Tactical HQ moving to Ruweisat Ridge.'

And so it went on, a flood of detail. There was a report from the Medical Research Section, entitled 'Fatigue in Tanks', suggesting the long summer days were taking a severe toll on the men's ability to fight in the desert, and another detailing the serviceability of tanks in the field and the movement of supplies. Durant had scrawled on the bottom: 'Lack of armour-piercing equipment still major factor.' Quinn handed it to Kate.

'Sir?' Madden said. He had been looking through the gigantic filing cabinets and stood back to show how a section of one folded down to reveal a safe. Quinn went to examine it. It had a Chubb lock. 'We didn't find a key on him, did we?' Madden asked.

Quinn returned to the desk to look for one. He opened all three drawers and sifted through the odds and ends inside. He couldn't find a key. 'Do you want a hand?' Kate asked. Without waiting for an answer, she selected a paperclip from a china bowl on Durant's desk, then bent and snapped off a length of wire from a tray. Quinn watched as she walked over to the safe and examined the lock. A few seconds later, he heard a loud clunk and Kate swung back the door.

'How the hell did you learn to do that?' Quinn asked.

'It's a long story.'

He was amazed. 'Doesn't seem right for the

daughter of a chaplain at a private school in a Cape Town suburb.'

'My father used to be a prison chaplain. We had some strange people staying at the house.'

Quinn peered into the safe. Inside, he found a couple of documents and a leather box. It contained a necklace. Quinn took it out and held it up, a delicate butterfly hanging from a gold chain. Diamonds on the butterfly's wings glittered even in the dull light.

'Good Lord,' said Kate. Quinn trailed the chain through his hand and held the butterfly in his palm. 'Expensive,' she added.

'Sure.'

'You're wondering where he got the money?' she asked.

'I was thinking more it showed the guy had taste.' He placed the butterfly in Kate's hand and let the chain fall slowly into her palm. 'It's something you would buy for someone you love, Mowbray, don't you think?'

She blushed. 'I spoke to the press attaché at the American Legation while you were with Colonel Lewis and Ed tried the Anglo-American Association. Seems like Amy White's husband is in oil exploration, some small company that's a subsidiary of a big firm in the States. They're digging out the address of the office here for us.'

'What about her?'

'She's definitely a photographer. That much checks out. She arrived with her husband two months ago, filled out all the forms for accreditation. When she's not up in the field, she works as a volunteer at a military hospital, but you know that.'

'She got any friends?'

'The guy I spoke to had seen her around, but nobody else sprang to mind.' Ed Madden indicated that he'd picked up nothing more. 'They didn't know anything about Casablanca,' Kate went on, 'but we'll cable the embassy in Lisbon. Ed thought that if they'd come from New York to Casablanca, maybe they docked there first.'

'Good idea. Get a cable off to the New York Police Department as well,' Quinn said. 'I'll give you a name. See if they've got any kind of record. And I want a list of known associates here. If she is the girlfriend, I need something concrete, someone who's seen them together.'

Quinn turned his attention to the documents. The first was an apparently unremarkable list detailing the arrival of supplies in Cairo and their movement up to the front line.

The second sheet read, 'MOST SECRET. Sabotage Units to mount simultaneous sticker bomb attacks against aircraft on nine Axis aerodromes, 26th June. Will reach objectives by parachute and long-range desert patrol.' In the margin, the deputy chief of staff had written: 'Rupert, if they require any special supplies, please ensure they are moved up as a matter *of the highest urgency*.'

The last document was a carbon copy. It was headed 'Allied Forces in Theatre', dated 24 June, and contained a long, detailed list of every unit that would be involved in the defence of Cairo and Alexandria. Each fighting section was broken down, with an estimated strength, location at brigade, sometimes even company level, and an approximate summary of the serviceable tanks, vehicles and other heavy equipment at its disposal.

It was a summary of everything Durant would have known. Quinn handed it to Kate. 'Where's the original?' he asked.

He checked that there was nothing else in the safe and swung the door shut. 'Kate, tell the girls in the typing pool we want to speak to them one by one. Then set Colonel Wheeler to send someone after Mrs Markham. We got to talk to her again today. This evening at the latest.'

After Kate had gone, Quinn and Madden stood in silence. Kate had returned the necklace to Quinn and he played with it, dangling the butterfly in his palm. 'You're very quiet today, Ed.'

'It's hardly a day to encourage eloquence, is it?'

'What do you think our captain was up to?'

'Love, I'd say. As you guessed.' Madden sat down heavily. He looked so dejected that Quinn took pity on him. 'Colonel Lewis got another letter from your father today.'

'I've asked him not to write any more.'

'I told Lewis I wouldn't stand in the way of any transfer requests you make.'

'Thank you,' Madden said. 'That's very decent of you.'

'That's what you want, right? Straight up to the front line?'

'Very much so. Do you have any idea . . . I mean, when?'

'Nah, but I'm sure it'll be soon. Not sure what I'm going to do without you.'

Ed Madden tried to smile. 'I know you hate writing up reports. I've enjoyed the work – found it rewarding.'

'You done good by me.'

Madden shook his head modestly. 'I have no gut instinct the way you do. I can't feel my way through a problem.'

'Maybe that's a strength. But I don't see your future as an inspector at the Yard.' Madden tried to smile again. He seemed unusually lugubrious today. 'At any rate, you gotta take me on a full tour of the baronial hall if I ever make it to England.'

Madden nodded.

'In the meantime, let me tell you what you gotta do today.'

Madden took a notebook and pencil from his jacket pocket. 'Go on, then.'

'When we're done with the typing girls, I'm gonna see how Nawab is doing. But I want to get this net around the Whites. You nail the husband. Find out the registered address of the company today, go down and take a look. What kind of set-up is it? I need a good list of their associates. Who do they see, where do they go? I'm real interested in the Casablanca connection. Why does an American suddenly leave home and head for Morocco? Effatt's working on the servants. If you've time, talk to one or two of the British correspondents, like Buster Morrison from the *Express*. I'd be interested to see what they make of the broad.'

Madden was still writing. 'Then take a run down to the citadel. We met a Corporal Jooste in the Berka. His P64 said he was from the Service Corps and he claimed to have just come in on a run from Jerusalem. The papers looked genuine, but I figure I should have pulled him in, so check out whether they have any record of anyone under that name.'

Madden finished scribbling. 'What did Colonel Lewis want?'

'He says your reports are too detailed.'

'Really? But—'

'It's a joke, Ed, same old story. He's hoping I'll give up, get off his case about my son.' Quinn faced his deputy. 'Tell me something. You've worked here long enough. Do you figure Macleod and the colonel as friends?'

'They don't seem to like each other very much.'

'Sure, but how come they ended up here together? Macleod's the chief of police in Shanghai and Lewis runs the biggest company there. They've got to have known each other. Why would the colonel get this guy a job here if he didn't like him?'

'I'm sorry. I know it must be very frustrating for you.'

'We'll find the guy.'

Madden looked worried. 'But do you think ... I mean, will you get a charge to stick after all this time? There's no military offence, is there, and you know how difficult the mixed courts are about—'

'We'll get him, Ed. That's all that matters.'

Kate returned. 'Wheeler doesn't know where Mrs Markham has gone, sir, and he's let all the girls from the typing pool go home for the rest of the day. He says he'll contact us as soon as he can get hold of them.'

'Christ,' Quinn said. 'There's another task. Go get the girls from the typing pool and straighten out Mrs Markham. See when we can have a real talk. Oh, and try to nail Wheeler. I got a feeling you might get more out of him.'

'Is that all, sir?' Madden asked drily.

'That's all, son. It'll be much easier when you get to the front.'

CHAPTER THIRTEEN

The pathologist was like a gigantic pudding: small and so disproportionately fat it was a wonder he could get his arms into his blood-spattered white coat. He was almost entirely bald, save for a crown of dark hair that looked as if it had been cultivated within an inch of its life.

'This is Major Quinn's assistant, Miss Mowbray,' Effatt said, but Nawab did not offer his hand or meet Kate's eye. It was a familiar story here. Quinn frowned with displeasure but the doctor pretended not to notice.

Captain Durant lay on a marble slab, covered with a bloodstained sheet. There was an overpowering stench of formaldehyde, sewage and decay. Kate put a handkerchief to her mouth and looked away.

'Dr Nawab believes the killer was a man,' Effatt said. He took out and lit a cigarette to hide the smell, then offered his case to the group. They all accepted.

'What makes you so sure?' Quinn asked.

'Because the incision is deep,' Nawab said, 'and the angle at which it cuts into the throat suggests that the killer was of about the same height as the victim,

104

perhaps even a little taller. A woman, however strong . . .' Nawab stopped. 'No, I am sure. Had it been a woman, the trajectory would have been different. It was a man, about six feet tall and strong.'

'We think Captain Durant knew his killer,' Quinn said. 'There ain't any cuts or bruises, nothin' on his hands or face, no sign of a struggle.'

'That is correct.'

'Which would only make sense if he was relaxed and caught unawares.'

'True,' Nawab said.

'Time of death?'

'Midnight.'

'Hmm. When would rigor mortis have set in? Seven, eight in the morning?'

'Something like that.' Nawab looked down at Durant, placed his index finger above the gaping wound in the man's throat. 'It's an unusual case.' He looked at them, to see if they divined his meaning. 'It is not like wire through cheese,' he said, clutching his own neck. 'Piano wire would act like a ligature.'

Quinn knew what he meant, but Kate evidently didn't.

'One can exert considerable pressure,' Nawab said, 'before even the skin is broken. Normally we would expect only a shallow cut. The killer would have closed the trachea, strangled his victim, before the wire had become deeply embedded.' Nawab took a step closer to the body, unable to contain his enthusiasm. 'Look, the wire cut through the skin, then the fat beneath it, then the connected tissue layers, then the strap muscles of the neck, then the trachea and finally the cartilage of the voice box, before it became embedded in the vertebra at the back of the neck.'

Kate shook her head.

'That's why I say a man, and a strong one. The wire has been worked to and fro. Like this.' Nawab mimicked the action. 'Most of the damage was inflicted well after the point of death.'

No-one spoke. Nawab picked up the clipboard and glanced at his notes. 'There is one other matter. I should say that Captain Durant had engaged in sexual activity immediately prior to his death. There are signs of semen on the inside of his underpants, his penis and upon his stomach.'

'His stomach?'

'Yes.' Nawab glanced at Kate for the first time. 'He has a great deal of hair there and upon his chest and . . . Well, you understand.'

'Sexual intercourse or masturbation?'

Nawab reddened.

'Is there any sign of lipstick, long hairs or perfume?'

'None.'

Quinn took a final long drag on his cigarette and ground it out beneath his foot. 'What about the image carved on his chest?'

'What about it?' Nawab was suddenly defensive.

'It was cut with a knife?' Quinn said.

'Yes, a sharp one.'

'At the time of death?'

'No – later. There was no bleeding.'

'It was done after rigor mortis had set in?'

'I should say so, yes.'

'You seen anything like it before?'

'The word "Liberation", yes . . .' Nawab eyed Effatt '. . . but not for some years.'

'What about the drawing of Seth?'

Nawab didn't answer.

'Why the God of Chaos?'

'I'm a pathologist.'

'Haven't you seen something like it?'

'No. And I told the dwarf the same, whatever he claims.'

'Reza?'

'Yes.'

'When did you speak to him?'

'He was here earlier.'

'Why?'

'Security business, he said.'

'What did he want to know?'

'He asked the same questions as you, and I gave the same answers. How am I to know why a madman scrawled the icon of a god? That's his job.'

Quinn watched him a moment more, then turned his attention back to the body. He thought of the immaculately clean kitchen and the blood beneath the refrigerator. 'He could have been kneeling down when he was caught.'

Nawab frowned.

'He was killed in the kitchen. He opens the door of the refrigerator, kneels down to take something, then . . .' Quinn ran a finger across his throat.

Nawab looked less certain. 'But still a man,' he said.

'If you say so, Doc.'

They were silent again.

'Do you want a copy of the autopsy when it's ready?' Nawab asked. He didn't like his conclusions to be challenged, Quinn knew.

'Sure.'

They filed out and climbed the stairs to Effatt's office. It was an open-plan room on the first floor, almost the size of a tennis court, humming with life.

Effatt's desk was at the far end, to one side of a pair of tall glass doors that opened onto an elegant wooden balcony. It afforded one of the best views of the city. Effatt ushered them onto the terrace, then got one of his assistants to fetch them coffee from a street stall.

Quinn leant over the balcony. The late-afternoon sun quivered in the haze, casting long shadows across uneven rooftops covered with laundry. It was a little cooler now, but the scent of diesel fumes and horse dung was still oppressive. He glanced at his watch. He'd have to leave in a minute.

Effatt joined them with three cups of thick coffee on a silver tray, and they sat in a group of wicker chairs. Quinn stirred his coffee, and watched Effatt listening to the wail of the muezzin. 'I sent a constable to retrieve the sheet from Durant's bed,' Effatt said.

'And?'

'It is hard to be certain, but it would seem there are some . . . stains.'

'You find anything else? Discarded underwear, lipstick . . .'

'No.'

'What about your fingerprint boys?'

'They've found at least one set of prints beside Durant's. They almost certainly belong to a woman. You want to try for a match with Mrs White, right?'

Quinn nodded.

'Then we'll need something from her apartment to run a check against.'

'I'll lift something,' Quinn said.

Effatt took a notebook from his pocket and consulted it. 'There are a couple of other things. My men found a glass, or at least fragments of one. It must have fallen from the desk when it was knocked over. There's a faint whiff of whisky or something similar. One or two of the fragments are large enough to have prints on them and they've already established these don't belong to Durant. They asked whether they should test them against our criminal files, but I didn't think that would achieve anything.'

They all knew it wasn't that kind of case. 'A man's prints?' Quinn asked.

'Yes.'

'Tell them go back, look again, see if they can find matching prints anywhere else in the apartment, especially the kitchen.'

'All right.' Effatt looked down at his notes again. 'We haven't located Mrs White's *sufragi* yet and none of the servants in nearby houses had anything to add. We got the same story from the guards outside Brigadier Wilson's home. But my boys had some luck with the caretaker of the block next door. He's an elderly Albanian, a former soldier. He used to stand guard on the doors at Cicurel until he was retired.'

Quinn didn't interrupt. Cicurel was the city's leading department store.

'He was certain he saw a car pull up outside the building yesterday afternoon, a grey Ford V8.'

'He see anyone get out of it?'

'A woman.'

'He get a good look at her?' Quinn had bought Mae a grey Ford V8. There were several in the city.

'No.'

They were interrupted by the screech of a car horn below. Quinn took a sip of the coffee, which was sweet and laced with cardamom. 'There's something else I think you should know,' he told Effatt. 'When I got down to GHQ this morning, Macleod was trying to take control of the investigation. I said it was a homicide and refused, but if you'd rather leave it to me, I understand. I don't want to drag you in any further.'

Effatt looked out at the minarets and domes of the old city. 'Joe.'

'I'm just—'

'It's too late for all of that.'

Back at Bab el Hadid, Madden was at his desk, typing. 'Before you ask,' he said, 'I haven't done everything you requested, but I thought I'd better get started on the morning report for Colonel Lewis. He'll expect detail. Or, at least, Major Macleod will. I sent Cohen down to do this drawing you wanted, and I've got an address for Mr White's oil company. And I spoke to Buster Morrison from the *Express* about Mrs White.'

'What'd he say?'

'He'd seen her around, said she was hard to miss, but he didn't find her that talkative or friendly. A frosty American bitch, he called her.'

'He know who she hangs out with?'

'Not really. He thinks she's well connected, reckons he's seen her with King Farouk's crowd once or twice in the Kit Kat. He's never met the husband. He said she rarely turns up at GHQ press conferences and he's only ever seen her once up at El Daba. Her correspondent seems like a reasonable fellow, so I've put in a call to him. What about you? How was Nawab?'

'Fat.' Quinn took his jacket off and hung it on the back of the chair. 'He thinks Durant had sex before they slit his throat and claims the killer was a man.'

'The husband?'

'Maybe. It looks that way. She says he was down in Suez, so we need to check his movements.'

'I can do that,' Kate said. 'If you've got the address, I'll chase it up.'

Quinn and Madden nodded. 'I haven't put anything about fingerprints in the report,' Madden said. 'Shall I call Effatt or—'

'They've found one other major set, apart from Durant's. They belong to a woman, probably the broad, but I'll need to lift something with her prints to get a match. There's also a fragment of glass with a third set, which appears to belong to a man, maybe the husband. Effatt's guys are going back over the apartment to see if they can find anything else.'

Madden reached for his notebook. 'A few other points. I spoke to Wheeler again. He wasn't any more help.'

Quinn lit a cigarette, offered one to Kate and sat on his own desk. 'What's he got to hide?'

'I don't know. But one of the girls in the typing pool had come back and, once she'd stopped crying, she was more talkative.' Madden was flicking through his notes. 'I spoke to the other two on the telephone. They liked Durant a lot.'

'How old are they?'

'Ruth, the girl I saw, was in her mid-twenties.'

'English?'

'Yes. From Dorset, father's a farmer. They're all ATS girls.' The ATS was the Auxiliary Territorial Service, set up in England to fill administrative jobs so that more men could be freed up for front-line service. It was similar to the section Kate had joined.

'Attractive?'

'I'd say so. Durant was in the habit of taking one or other of them to whatever new picture was showing. Afterwards, he'd buy them tea at Groppi's or, if it was

111

an evening show, dinner or a drink on the terrace at Shepheard's. I'd guess there was some good-tempered competition for his attentions. Ruth said he had a dry sense of humour and was fond of teasing them. Then, three weeks ago, it ceased abruptly. No more visits to the cinema, no more teasing. Durant was a great deal more serious.'

'They figure out why?'

'They guessed the same as Mrs Markham, but had no idea who the woman might be. They were surprised. All three said he'd talked a lot about his wife and children.'

'Does that mean anything?' Kate asked.

'Maybe not. The broad's good-lookin'. Enough to turn a man's head.'

Madden flicked over a page. 'There was one other thing. On these outings, Durant was generous and insisted on paying for the tickets and dinner, but they all separately formed the impression that he watched his wages carefully and money was tight.' Madden looked up. 'I was just thinking of the necklace in the safe. It seems all the more extravagant a gesture.'

'All right.' Quinn removed his jacket from the back of the chair. 'I'll get one of the other drivers to take me down to the citadel to check out the South African, Jooste.' He turned to Kate. 'Make sure you double-check where Mr White was. Talk to his company. Did he really go to Suez? Can he prove it? How did he get there? Where has he been staying and when did he come back?'

'You're going to the citadel, sir?' Madden asked.

'Sure am. We should have pulled in the South African this morning, put him under some pressure. It was my mistake.'

'You think he's a deserter?'

They were both watching him. 'Maybe.'

'I guess you won't be back for a while,' Kate said. She bent down and emerged with a bunch of red canna lilies from behind the desk. 'I hope you don't think it a liberty but we both thought that ... well, you know ...'

There was an awkward silence, until Quinn realized he must step across and take the flowers. 'Thank you,' he said. 'Sure, I'm going in a few minutes, so I'll ... Thank you. I appreciate it.'

Half an hour later, as Quinn was driven through the gate of Saladin's great stone fortress and up the hill, he watched a swarm of kites circling around the narrow minarets of the Ottoman mosque, black shadows against a dusty red sky.

The driver swung into an inner courtyard and stopped the car between a tennis court and the back of a white stable block. Quinn got out and told him to wait. He passed the façade of a tall ochre building with battered wooden shutters and walked down through neatly tended flowerbeds to the offices of the administration section.

It took him a few minutes to find the right official. When he did so, he got the answer he had half expected. No-one there had ever heard of a Corporal Jooste. Nor did they recognize his description.

After a few fruitless minutes, Quinn retreated to the courtyard and sat on the edge of the fountain, scooping up handfuls of cool aquamarine water and tipping them over his skull. He dried his hands, then took out the artist's impression of the driver of the car that had killed his son. Cohen had drawn the guy

113

from Corbett's description, but Quinn thought he had put too much faith in this for too long. He now accepted that, almost certainly, Corbett had lied.

The image bore little resemblance to the South African. He folded it up and put it away.

The light was fading rapidly, but the air was still close. Quinn watched a gardener dig in a flowerbed on the far side of the courtyard. Two young stable-boys led a pair of Arab horses, hoofs clip-clopping noisily over the cobblestones.

He took the butterfly necklace out of his pocket and held it up to the dying light. What was a man of Durant's class and popularity doing consorting with a South African deserter in the sleaziest hovel in the Berka? It didn't make sense. Were all the girls in the office wrong about him?

Quinn thought about the meeting that had been planned for this evening. Was it Durant's choice to go at night, or that of the person he had arranged to meet? The dangers would have been all the greater. If the Berka was an unlikely destination for any officer by day, only a fool would venture there alone at night.

He wondered what had driven the man to such an end.

With a supreme effort, Quinn forced himself upright and walked back to the car. Inside, he rested his head against the back of the leather seat, one hand on the lilies.

He glanced at his watch again. Now it was time. Mae would be waiting.

CHAPTER FOURTEEN

Quinn arrived a few minutes early and Mae was not there, so he sat upon the dusty stone wall by the entrance to the cemetery and waited. He lit a cigarette and kicked at bits of stone. He watched a group of boys playing football on a patch of scrub-land. On the section closest to him, a father was laying out the string of a kite for his son. After a few minutes, when they had got it straight, the man walked towards the kite and held it up. The boy ran back a few yards and the simple cloth and wood structure caught the breeze and soared into the air. The child gave a little whoop of joy.

Quinn saw a grey Ford V8 pull up at the top of the pathway and watched his wife get out. Marjorie Stubbs was with her, wearing a white cardigan stretched tight over her ample figure despite the heat. She raised a hand at Quinn who acknowledged the gesture with a wave.

Marjorie Stubbs organized the volunteers at the hospital. Mae said she had a heart of gold, but she sure did like to talk. Quinn had spent Christmas cocktail parties avoiding her ever since they'd arrived in Cairo.

Maybe she'd come to check that Mae was 'all right'. That would be typical.

Mae walked towards him, wearing a long, smooth white skirt, a pink band in her hair and red sandals on bare feet. She carried a bag under one arm, Ryan's bear under the other and a bunch of flowers in her hand.

She looked pretty, real pretty, every inch the girl who'd made his heart skip a beat so many nights on Seventh. Her nose was a fraction too large, but her face was wide and warm. She was smiling, her cheeks dimpled; her long blond hair was glossy and newly washed. 'Are you ready, Joe?'

'Sure.'

Mae opened the bag, took out the Yankees cap Quinn had given his son before they left home. 'I thought maybe you'd want this.'

He took it and she offered him her hand. They stepped through the gate and faced the setting sun.

They walked up the central path, kicking up tiny puffs of dust. Mae's gaze was steady, resolute.

They turned left and caught sight of the tiny grave in the shadow of the wall, the last of the sun catching a corner of the headstone. Mae gripped his hand harder and Quinn pushed on, focusing on the stone. They stopped in front of it.

Ryan Quinn.
1.3.1937–25.6.1941
Adored only son of Joe and Mae.
May God have mercy upon his soul.
Rest in Peace.

Mae handed Quinn Ryan's bear and, as he looked at its worn face, tears ran in rivulets down his cheeks. Mae rested her head on his shoulder.

116

They waited, eyes closed, the sun still warm upon their faces. It was the perfect evening for going to the Gezira and Quinn could see his son's laughing face above him as he was thrown into the air above the aquamarine waters of its pool.

He placed the cap on his head, thought of the days in the garden when he had tried to teach the kid to pitch.

The breeze tugged at Mae's hair.

The graveyard rang to the sound of children at play, the sunset painting great streaks of red and orange across a powder-blue sky.

Quinn wiped his cheeks. He took off the cap and placed the lilies Kate had given him at the bottom of the grave.

Mae released his hand and knelt down. She placed her own flowers, rearranged his, then wiped the dust and sand off the headstone. It was immaculate.

It had always been immaculate.

Mae brushed the stones and dust from her knees, then stepped back. She took his hand and turned. They walked away. As they reached the corner, Quinn could not resist a last glance. Mae did not falter, but her grip loosened until their hands fell apart.

They reached the gate and stepped onto the path. Quinn watched the father and son playing with their kite. He tried to light a cigarette, but his hand was shaking. Mae took the match and lit it for him. She relieved him of the bear and the Yankees cap and slipped them into her bag.

The silence lengthened. He tried to think of something to say. 'How was your day?' he asked. 'You were at the hospital?'

'Yes, just as I said.'

'How was it?'

'It's worse in the heat.' She adjusted her hair, took out her lipstick and reapplied it. They were silent again. Quinn glanced up towards the car, where Marjorie Stubbs was leaning against the rear door. 'What's she doing here?'

Mae ignored the question and his tone. 'Are you coming home, Joe?'

'No.' He leant back against the wall. 'I spoke to Lewis today. He claims they've got a suspect now, says they know the guy's name.'

Mae didn't appear to be listening. 'I hope he knows we're here,' she said.

'I still figure I'm going to have to take over the case. They're still lying about—'

'Does it matter, Joe? What are they going to do if they find him?'

'I'll see him hang.'

'For what? For driving too fast? You drive too fast, Joe. You always have.'

'He was drunk.'

'You don't know that.'

'Then how come he didn't stop?'

'Even if it were true, would it solve anything to hang him? Would it change anything?'

Quinn stared at her uncomprehendingly.

Mae sighed. 'Please let's not talk about this today.'

'We never talk about it.'

'Maybe, but that's because you've always wanted the clocks to stop and time to stand still. But life goes on, Joe. Perhaps it's not the life we'd have chosen, but we're still alive. He's still with us. He's up there. He's watching. He's being cared for, that's all that matters.'

'He's dead.'

'Not to me. I think he'd want to see us celebrate his life today, so that's what I'm going to do. If you finish your work, I'll be at home. Hassan will have prepared some food. I'd like to see you if you can make it.'

Mae walked steadily away. Quinn watched her to the car but, again, she didn't look back.

Sergeant Cohen – the pool's most fluent Arabic speaker – and two colleagues were staking out the peep-show beneath the brothel. Egyptian detectives were further down the street and in the tobacconist's near the entrance. Effatt stood on the corner, masquerading as a pimp, bathed in moonlight.

Kate and Quinn waited in the car, which was parked in an alleyway. Effatt had insisted they stay out of sight until the last minute, lest anyone recognize them. Quinn was in the front passenger seat, a revolver on his lap. He opened the window an inch and winced at the smell of drains.

'Are you all right?' Kate asked. They'd barely spoken since she'd picked him up at the office.

'I'm fine.'

'You look tired.'

A siren flared briefly, then melted into the honk and clatter of the Cairo night. Kate tapped the large black steering-wheel.

'Impatient, Mowbray?'

'Not yet. By the way, I found Mr White's company on Fuad. It's called Casablanca Oil, so I guess that gives us a clue why he went there from New York.'

'Yeah, but why Casablanca of all places?'

'His secretary wasn't very helpful. She kept on saying I could speak to him when he got back.'

'When's that?'

'Tonight. She said he'd been in Suez and she was expecting him any minute.'

'There any proof he made the journey?'

'She showed me his diary, but there was no hard evidence he actually *went*. I'll check with the hotel. I've got the name of the company he was supposed to be going to see so I'll cable them, make sure he turned up to the meeting.'

'What was the office like?'

'Small, just two desks in a room. There were maps all over the wall, but that was it.'

'It's run on a shoestring?'

'There was no evidence of conspicuous wealth.'

There was a new sound, the low rumble of an aircraft's engines. Quinn peered up into the night sky.

'Is it a raid?' Kate asked.

'Mmm . . . Maybe.'

The roar grew louder and Quinn saw a flash of the bomber's dark underbelly. A few seconds later, papers rained down like confetti. Quinn stepped out to retrieve one. He held it up, then returned to the car and lit a match. It was a crudely reproduced enlargement of an Egyptian pound, with a few sentences in Arabic scrawled on the back. Effatt headed towards them, clutching another. Quinn wound down the window. 'What's the good news?'

Effatt was smiling. 'It says it is no longer worth the effort to pick these up – in a matter of days they will be worthless.' He dropped the note on the street and returned to his position.

'It's been nice to see a real relationship,' Kate said.

'Which one?'

'You and Effatt.' They both watched the figure on the corner. 'I suppose it's difficult for him,' she said.

'Why?'

'All the uncertainty over our future.'

The door to a café in the street ahead was flung open, spilling slivers of light and a brief burst of drunken laughter into the alley before it was slammed shut again. 'In your heart of hearts, do you think Rommel can be stopped?' Kate asked.

'Miracles happen.'

'You don't believe in God.'

'I don't, no.'

'Sometimes I wonder if it would make any difference to most of the locals if Rommel did get here.'

Quinn turned to her. 'Sure it would. Look around you. This is one of the most tolerant places on earth. We've got Muslims, Copts and Jews. We've got Armenian tram conductors, Bosnian salesgirls, Bulgarian telephonists. When I arrived here before the war, the smartest tailors were British, the best photographers German, the finest confectioners Swiss or Italian . . .'

He lapsed into silence. He recalled the excitement of flying over the city for the first time, the hope of a new beginning, his baby son on his lap, the surge of optimism of the kind he'd felt as the boat from Belfast steamed towards Ellis Island all those years ago.

Kate was tapping her finger on the steering-wheel again. 'What will we do,' she asked, 'if the Germans break through?'

'You'll be sent to Jerusalem. After that, who knows? Maybe I'll have to slug it out street by street as Mr Churchill demands.'

'I don't want special treatment.'

'But I hope you'll follow orders.'

Her eyes were fixed on his and he returned her gaze. If she was not quite beautiful, she had a stillness that could be mesmerizing. She brushed her hair off her forehead. 'What will your wife do?' she asked. 'Are you planning to send her ahead to Jerusalem?'

'I haven't decided.' It wasn't true, but he didn't want to have to explain about Effatt's boy.

'I would have—'

'It's not so simple.' He tried to soften his tone. 'It's not so simple, Kate.'

She waited. 'How was today? I mean—'

'We lived through it.'

'Then that's something. Sometimes, looking back, I feel we only existed for most of the time. The mistake we made was we forgot how to live.'

Quinn gazed out of the window. Two weeks ago, Kate had told him she'd lost her twin brother as a child. 'So, who taught you how to break locks, Miss Mowbray?'

'When he was chaplain at the prison, my father helped people back onto the straight and narrow. One thought it would be fun to teach me some of the tricks of his trade. It was a terrific rebellion.'

'And that's what brings you from there to one of the seediest red-light districts in the world?'

'Rebellion?'

'Yes.'

'Perhaps, but it was more boredom.'

'That's it?'

'Mostly. I came because I didn't want to marry a former pupil of my father's who was going to set up a mission in Northern Rhodesia. When you're seeking an escape, you take what's available.'

'You come to war?' he asked.

'Why not?'

'You telling me this was the only choice?'

'No, but . . .' She was quiet for a moment. 'My father is very strict and my mother doesn't like to argue with him. They're loyal servants of the Crown and take our British heritage seriously, so this was something they couldn't really object to. My grandfather fought in the Boer War and decided to stay on in South Africa. My father always wanted a son who would take up the military tradition, so it was hard for him to express his anger at my decision, even if he felt it.'

'Going to go back?'

'It depends what happens, but I doubt it.'

'Where will you go?'

'I like Europe, so maybe—'

'You've been to Europe?'

'No. I mean I like the idea of it.' She smiled at him. Her cheeks were a little flushed. 'Maybe I should try Ireland. What about you?'

What about him? It was a good question, Quinn thought, and one to which he had no easy answer.

'Why did you come here?' she asked.

'It's a long story.'

'We might have all night.'

'It ain't that interesting.'

'Why don't you let me be the judge of that?'

'My wife was a curator. This was her big interest. Her father lived here some time around the last war. He was an expert, a lecturer, so she'd always wanted to come.'

'To visit or to live?'

'To visit.'

'That doesn't sound convincing.' She looked at him. They say you killed a man, were lucky to escape a

123

long stretch in jail. They say you were thrown out of the New York Police Department and told to leave the city.'

'Who's they?' Quinn asked.

'It's the gossip in the office.'

'Don't believe everything you hear.'

'Is it true?'

'The verdict was suicide.'

'But was it correct?'

Quinn watched Effatt move from light to shadow and back again. 'Maybe, maybe not.'

'What happened?'

'I put the barrel of my revolver into a man's mouth.'

'And then what?'

'The look in his eyes told me he knew I'd never dare pull the trigger.'

'But you did?'

'The report says he pulled it himself.'

'Who was he?'

'It doesn't matter.'

'I guess it did to him.'

'His name was Styles. And he was going to get away with murder.'

'What did he do?'

'He carved up some broads in the Bowery. It's a poor neighbourhood. My father had been a patrolman and I knew one or two of the girls. We pulled him in, had him cold.'

'But he got off so you killed him?'

'We went around to his apartment, told him we'd be watching. It didn't work out the way we intended.'

Quinn could see the red-brick wall, the distant lights casting shadows across Styles's face. He could hear the hoot of a cargo ship coming through the Narrows.

He knew he ought to feel regret. Bang. No more Styles. No more tortured, mutilated women.

'Playing God,' she said. 'Isn't that what all detectives end up doing? You throw away the rulebook and start to play God. That way you can try to make the world seem a just place after all.'

'Is that one of your theories, Miss Mowbray?'

'It's an observation.'

'Maybe you read too many detective novels, or spent too much time with convicts.' He leant back in his seat, tipped his chin onto his chest. 'Mmm. A stakeout. Just like old times. Wake me when something happens.' He shut his eyes.

Almost immediately they heard an approaching vehicle. Effatt turned away from the thoroughfare and pulled his fedora over his eyes. A few moments later a jeep flashed by, travelling fast in the darkness. They heard doors being opened and shut.

Effatt glanced up the main street, then joined Quinn and Kate. 'That was Macleod.'

CHAPTER FIFTEEN

'What?' Quinn got out of the car. 'Are you sure?'

'Reza was with him. Another man arrived a few minutes ago from the other direction. It was hard to tell in the shadows but I think it was the South African, Jooste.' Quinn followed Effatt to the corner. He could tell the Egyptian was uneasy. 'Are your men inside armed?'

'Only with knives.'

'Is this a set-up?'

Effatt grimaced. 'How could it be?'

'We were here earlier.'

'But why should we come back? How could anyone know we have the diary and are aware of the meeting?'

Quinn wondered if they'd stumbled into the middle of some covert Field Security operation but, if so, why hadn't Macleod said something at the meeting earlier?

A man emerged from the alley and walked fast towards them. Effatt breathed in sharply. 'It's him,' he hissed, but Quinn had already made the assumption. He took hold of Kate, pushed her against the wall and pressed his mouth to hers. Her skin was damp, but her lips were sweet. She was a good seven or eight inches shorter than him so he had to bend his head. Effatt spoke quickly in Arabic, as if he was insulting or exhorting them.

The South African, Jooste, did not break his stride. He walked straight past them towards the Austin. Quinn saw him glance briefly at the car before he was swallowed by the darkness.

Kate gasped as Quinn removed his mouth. He turned away from her and followed the man into the darkness. Effatt came with him. They reached a cross-roads and kept going, splitting up and taking to the shadows on either side of the alley.

The South African stopped. He waited, as if watching them. Quinn could hear his own breathing.

The man broke into a run. Quinn shouted, pounded after him. Jooste swung right, into a tiny alley criss-crossed by low-hanging washing-lines. He was fast, ducking and weaving in the moonlight, taking down several lines as he passed. Quinn shouted again, then tripped and careered into a wall. He picked himself up.

'Joe!' Effatt yelled.

'Here.'

'He's in this building.'

Effatt was waiting in a doorway. As Quinn stepped inside, he heard someone mounting the stairs. Then silence.

They waited, panting. Quinn wiped the dust from his revolver as Effatt edged forwards. A police whistle blasted, then a shot rang out and ricocheted off a metal banister. They heard glass shatter and wood splintering. Quinn charged past his colleague. There was a thud as the man landed on a tin-roofed shack. Quinn reached the window, was about to jump when he felt a hand on his arm. 'Is it worth it, old friend?'

127

Quinn hesitated.

'He might be waiting.'

'He'll be running.' Quinn pushed himself through the opening and the metal shack collapsed beneath his weight, catapulting him into the dust. By the time he was upright, Effatt was by his side.

They ran up to a crossroads, but in each direction the road led off into darkness. There was no sign of Jooste.

Quinn brushed himself down. 'I'm getting slow,' he said.

'You were always slow. That must be why you're still alive. But I know what you're thinking.'

'I'm not thinking anything.'

'A deserter, with a connection to Macleod . . .'

'It sure is interesting, wouldn't you say?'

'His description doesn't match the drawing you have.'

'The drawing is baloney. Corbett's evidence was a pack of lies. We know the driver was a deserter and we know Macleod has been trying to protect him.'

'We don't *know* it, Joe. It's all guesswork. Let's not jump to any conclusions.'

CHAPTER SIXTEEN

Kate drove them through the darkened city in silence. Madden had stayed behind with Effatt to question the girls in the Berka again. As they reached the edge of Bulaq and headed over the bridge to Gezira, Quinn said, 'Where did you learn to kiss like that, Mowbray?'

'Oh, very funny.'

Quinn smiled, then lapsed back into silence as the Austin trundled over the island. They passed a tram, then reached Zamalek Bridge. To their right, the white spire of the Kit Kat mosque gleamed in the moonlight, and wooden houseboats along the far shore spilled slivers of light onto the smooth waters of the Nile. Kate glided slowly to a halt beneath a pair of eucalyptus trees. They were behind two taxis waiting for a fare. As they got out, a group of boys emerged from the hedgerow, demanding, 'Baksheesh, baksheesh,' until they were chased away by guards in white uniforms, who sprang from the iron gate.

The boys scattered up the road in the direction of the bridge. When calm was restored, the guards ushered Quinn and Kate through the gate. Quinn came to the Kit Kat often. As Cairo's most notorious nightclub, it was where the business of the city's underworld was conducted.

Steps led down to a long terrace. Beyond it the club was in a long wooden houseboat, as if it did not belong to the city and could be cast adrift at a moment's notice. Intricately carved wooden panels and huge pot plants gave way to a dark, smoky interior and the promise of sophisticated pleasures. The heat was tempered by a breeze from the river. Here, Quinn had seen too many long winter nights melt into dawn.

The boat was lit from end to end by the subdued glow of flickering candles, smoke curling languorously up towards rhythmically beating ceiling fans. They handed their revolvers to the attendant and Quinn waited while Kate went to apply some makeup. He slipped his hands into his pockets and tried out his rudimentary Arabic on the doormen.

Kate returned. 'A vision,' Quinn said, but she avoided his eye.

Before they could move, they heard an engine being revved outside, followed rapidly by screeching tyres. Doors were slammed, voices raised.

The King of Egypt came in, a corpulent figure bursting out of a dark suit, brandishing a large cigar. Flanked by two women, one Levantine, one European, and four bodyguards, he looked like a Mafia don. Half a step behind skipped his loyal assistant, Mario Fabrizzi. They swept into the nightclub, heading towards the corner table that was always kept vacant.

Fabrizzi pushed a pair of dark glasses up his angular nose. His skin was pockmarked and rough. He had once been a driver to Farouk's father, King Fuad, but was now one of the young king's most influential officials. Quinn could never understand how he had avoided the British internment camps.

The stragglers of the party were behind Fabrizzi: an ageing White Russian roué, Grand Duke Boris Vladimirovich, and his wife Irina. The grand duke was variously said to be a spy for the Russians or the Nazis, and it was claimed Farouk had personally secured a visa to allow him to move here from Florence.

Quinn stepped into the club. Farouk's bodyguards already ringed his table, as discreet as a herd of elephants. Known to Allied soldiers as 'Fatty' and the British ambassador in Cairo simply as 'Boy', Farouk cut an alternately absurd and threatening figure.

Quinn was about to turn towards the bar when he saw Amy White. She was seated in the opposite corner to the king and his party, in a long cream dress that set off her dark hair to startling effect. Diamonds glittered at her throat. A tall, elegant man in a dark suit stood beside her. Quinn recognized him as her husband from the single photograph in their bedroom. Even in the opulent surroundings of the Kit Kat, she provided a splash of movie-star glamour. He wondered how she'd concealed the marks round her neck.

'I had a feeling she'd be here,' Kate said.

Quinn pulled a silver cigarette case from his pocket, offered it to her, took one for himself and lit both. He guided her to the bar.

The Egyptian barman slid towards them. 'Evening, Mr Quinn.'

'Mac, you know Miss Mowbray?'

'No.' He extended a slender hand across the bar.

He was a handsome fellow, Quinn thought. He watched Kate's eyes linger on the boy's face.

131

'What will it be tonight, sir?'

'Scotch, on the rocks.'

'I'll have the same,' Kate said.

They watched as Mac swept a couple of sparkling glasses from a high shelf in front of the mirror, then turned to face the Hungarian girl whose willowy frame was floodlit by the only electric lamp in the club. She sang well, seeming to linger on every word, as if she was making love to every pair of hungry eyes. She wore little, her ample chest barely contained by a sequined robe that had been cut to reveal an expanse of bare, bejewelled stomach. King Farouk had stopped talking to the Russian and was unable to keep his eyes off her.

The woman was certainly alluring, beautiful even, but she couldn't hold a candle to Amy White. Quinn found himself glancing across the room to where the American sat. She was engaged in earnest conversation with an army officer in her party. Her husband listened, leaning against one of the doors to a balcony overlooking the river.

Quinn turned back as Mac placed a glass in front of each of them. Although there were forty or fifty people in the room, he and Kate were the only pair at the bar.

'How's business, Mr Quinn?'

'Swell, Mac. And you?'

The boy smiled.

'Say, what brings our royal friend here tonight?' Quinn asked.

'The same as always.'

Quinn checked they were not being watched with undue interest, then removed the photograph of Durant from his pocket and slid it onto the counter. 'Ever see him?'

132

'Yes.'

'Recently?'

'Sure.' Mac straightened as another waiter approached, pushing the photograph back towards Quinn. He dealt with the order, then returned.

'He was a regular?' Quinn asked.

'He came in perhaps half a dozen times.'

'On his own?'

'He always arrived alone.'

'He was meeting someone?'

'The last few occasions it was the couple there – don't look now. The striking woman in the cream dress, dark hair.' He was talking about Amy White.

'Yeah, and her husband too?' Avril White was standing on the candlelit balcony now, leaning over the rail. Quinn watched Fabrizzi slip out to join him.

'Your man seemed surprised to find them here,' Mac said.

'You ever see him meet the broad alone?'

'The last time. He was waiting for her, drumming his fingers on the table. He seemed nervous.'

'They leave together?'

'No. He left first. She stayed a while, smoking and staring at the girl on the stage.' Mac pointed to the table where they'd been sitting, next to a blackout blind that was rarely used.

'How long ago was this?'

'The night before last.'

'The night before his death,' Quinn said.

Mac raised his eyebrows. He picked up a cloth and began to buff the glasses laid out in front of him, holding each up to the candlelight in turn.

'You ever talk to him?' Quinn asked, pointing at the photograph.

133

'No.'

'You see him talk to anyone else in here?'

Mac gestured towards a large table next to the window, occupied by the nightclub's owner, a Greek who was even larger than Farouk.

Kostandis was in his fifties and always wore an immaculately pressed white linen suit. His handshake was clammy, his forehead damp with perspiration. He had thinning grey hair and a nose that would not have disgraced a Roman emperor. He was the most notorious homosexual in the city, with a consuming passion for young soldiers, one of whom – a handsome young blond – was at his elbow tonight. As Quinn watched, Kostandis touched the man's arm, then let out a burst of exaggerated laughter. He usually found them here or in the Berka, then paid them for sex in the National Hotel, where he kept a suite.

It was another strange connection for an officer like Durant to have made.

Mac returned to the other end of the bar.

Kate stared into her whisky, swirling it around the glass. 'I never said thank you for including me in that meeting with Colonel Lewis this morning. I know you shouldn't have. I'm grateful for the opportunity. If there's anything I can do, you only have to ask. You know that, don't you?'

'You're not obliged to kiss me every night.'

'No, but I mean—'

'It was a joke, Mowbray.'

'I know. I understand. What do you think Macleod and Reza were doing there tonight? I suppose they can always claim it was some hush-hush Field Security op.'

'They can.'

Kate looked momentarily uncertain. 'I suppose it's possible it might have been just that.'

'It's possible.' Quinn finished his cigarette and lit another. He was having a great deal of trouble keeping his eyes off the liquid in Kate Mowbray's glass. He'd promised Mae a couple of months ago he'd quit the booze. Some nights she'd told him she thought it would kill him – she was probably right. 'Mac,' Quinn shouted, 'a whisky.'

Mac turned slowly in his direction. Amy White was on her feet. Quinn caught sight of her in the mirror. She looked as if she was leaving, but didn't move from the table. She was still talking.

'I thought you didn't drink,' Kate said.

Quinn pointed at his glass.

'Even I can tell that's not whisky,' she said. 'I'm guessing you have some arrangement with Mac here.'

Without meeting his eye, Mac placed a glass of whisky in front of him, took the tea away and poured it discreetly into a bin beneath the bar. 'For you, madam?' he asked.

'I'm fine.'

The Hungarian was performing an Ella Fitzgerald medley, as if trying to soothe away the cares of war for every man and woman in the room. The mood appeared to be affecting Kate. She removed her glasses and placed them on the bar. She looked quite different without them. In this light, her blue eyes shone and her skin glowed. Perhaps it wasn't just in this light. She had an oval face, with pink lips and freckles on each cheek. She had curves. Maybe a couple too many.

Amy White left the table and walked across the room. Quinn assumed she would stop, acknowledge them, maybe indulge in small-talk, but she did none

135

of these things. He drained his glass, waved at Mac for another.

'Were you always a murder detective?' she asked. 'Back home, I mean.'

'No. I walked the beat—'

'Like your father?'

'Like my father, yes. Yeah, I'd forgotten I told you my dad was a cop.' Out of the corner of his eye he was watching Amy White glide through the reception area. 'I got a transfer to the detective division, spent a long spell in Homicide.'

'Were you always a good cop?'

'Define good.'

'One who gets results.'

'A cop who gets results isn't necessarily a good cop.'

'Did your father want you to become a policeman?'

'He sure did.'

'Is he still alive?'

Quinn recalled a vivid image of the old man leaving the door early in the morning, his blue uniform newly pressed. 'No.'

'Did he—'

'He died a long time ago.'

At that moment, Charles Lewis strode in. In contrast to Quinn, he looked as if he had just walked out of a uniform press, his blond hair neatly combed. He looked across at the king's entourage, took out and lit a cigarette, then strolled towards the bar. 'Good evening, Major, Mowbray.'

Quinn noticed Kate's eyes shone when she glanced at Lewis. Did he have this effect on all women? He tried to think of something neutral to say, but Lewis was already walking to the Whites' table, where he greeted Amy's husband warmly. Wherever there was power and influence, Quinn thought, or glamour, there you would find Charles Lewis.

Quinn raised his hand and pushed his glass down the bar towards Mac.

An air-raid siren wailed in the distance. Then, as it faded to an echo, there was a single shrill scream.

CHAPTER SEVENTEEN

The band stuttered, then stopped. A few chairs scraped back, but Quinn moved first. The scream rang in his ears, and the hazy air became electric. He saw the startled expressions on the faces of staff in the lobby. The door was open, one of the men half out of it. Quinn pushed past him, ran up the steps and through the iron gate. The road was empty. The guards appeared too frightened to move. Neither Farouk's chauffeur nor the taxi drivers had climbed out of their cars.

He saw a flash of white and a figure crumpled in the dust. She was in the shadow of a palm down a narrow street that ran away from the river. As he came closer, she moved and tried to sit up.

There was blood on her face, her wrist and her neck. He searched for the source. He brought her wrist to the light. The incision was just above her palm and didn't look deep. Quinn took a handkerchief from his pocket and bound it tight, then looked again at her neck. The cut here was equally shallow – little more than a scratch – but he could see swelling around it.

One of Farouk's bodyguards stood in the centre of the road ten yards away, pushing a revolver back into its holster as he satisfied himself that there was no threat. Others were spilling from the nightclub. The guards still hadn't moved from the gateway.

Kate Mowbray appeared at his shoulder and offered him another handkerchief, with which he removed the blood from Amy's throat.

Moments later, her husband was beside them. 'My God,' he said. 'Are you all right?' He took hold of his wife's uninjured wrist, and Quinn handed him Kate's handkerchief.

White was a handsome man, with a chiselled, clean-shaven jaw and short dark hair. His dark suit was immaculate, even now. His actions were meticulous but uncertain, like those of a father unused to dealing with his child. After a few seconds, he stopped dabbing at his wife's neck and held her hand, but Quinn noticed she did not return his grip. 'I must thank you,' White said. 'Who knows what might have happened?'

His accent was precise, cultured and soft and, like his wife, there was a touch of the movie star about him.

Quinn turned and saw Lewis watching them. Others still spilled from the shadows at the club's entrance. 'Get a taxi,' Quinn ordered Kate. 'What happened?'

Amy looked at him, but didn't answer.

'You see the guy?'

'No,' she mumbled. 'I'm sorry, but—'

White leant forward. 'My wife has had a terrific shock. Do you mind if we talk about this in the morning?'

'Sure I do.'

White straightened, fixed him with a steady, hostile stare.

'We found your neighbour strung up from a tree in the garden. Now your wife is almost nailed with the same MO so I'd like to know what she saw.'

White kept cool. 'I'm sorry – it was all so fast,' Amy said quietly.

'One man or two?'

'One.'

'What was he wearing?'

'I just felt this sudden movement, then . . .' She touched her neck.

'You didn't get a look at him?'

'No.'

'A white man or a local?'

'A white man, I think.'

'What were you doing out here, ma'am?'

'Are you sure we can't deal with this in the morning?' White asked. 'She's had a terrific shock.'

'I'd like to know right now why she's wandering down a darkened lane at—'

'Under the circumstances, this almost amounts to harassment. I shall complain to your superiors.'

Quinn saw Lewis watching him. 'Go right ahead.'

'Please, Major,' Amy said softly, 'I'll do my best to assist you in the morning.'

Quinn gazed at her. He stood up. 'If you wish, ma'am, but don't go far.'

A black and white taxi swung round in front of the club and turned down the alley. Quinn beckoned it alongside them. The air-raid siren wailed again. White helped his wife to her feet, and they both escorted her to the vehicle. She did not look at her husband, or acknowledge his presence. Inside the car, her head lolled back against the seat.

Quinn watched as the old Fiat rattled away into the night.

The siren faded and those closest to the entrance of the club filtered back in. Lewis was beside them. 'Was she all right?' he asked.

'Yeah.'

'What happened?'

'The broad got assaulted.'

'Someone was trying to kill her?'

'Looks like it.'

Lewis turned back to the club. 'Damned strange place to do it. Was he waiting for her?'

'Must have been.'

Quinn wanted Lewis to go, but the colonel showed no sign of doing so. 'She's a remarkable-looking woman.' Lewis examined him frankly. 'Is that your love triangle, Joe?'

He didn't answer.

'I hope you know what you're doing.' With that, Lewis slipped away, leaving Quinn alone with Kate.

He swiped the dust from his jacket and slacks, then coughed. Once he'd started, he couldn't stop. Kate slapped his back tentatively until he straightened. 'What happened?' she asked.

Quinn looked down the alley, which trailed off into darkness. 'She must have sensed someone behind her, raised an arm. But it sure seems odd.'

'What was she doing out here?'

Quinn had asked himself the same question. 'Go back inside,' he said. 'Straighten out Kostandis. Leave Mac. I'll talk to him in a minute.' Quinn pointed to his left. 'The balcony behind where the Whites were

141

sitting has its own causeway to the shore. There's a narrow path up to the staff entrance, which comes out around the corner there. Farouk sometimes arrives that way as a practical joke. I'll check whether the gate is locked, but I'd like to know if any of the staff saw someone on the balcony, or heading towards the path.'

Kate disappeared. Quinn assumed she would encounter a wall of silence, but he wanted a few moments to himself. He walked away from the Kit Kat, down the alley. At either side of him tall fences shielded spacious gardens shrouded in darkness. If the occupants of nearby houses were at home, none had seen fit to investigate the source of the scream.

He looked back at the nightclub, listened to the music. He imagined Amy White standing there, smoking a cigarette. He moved closer to the light, squatted down, tried to make out a pattern in the dust. There had been too many footprints. He straightened again and walked slowly back in the direction of the Kit Kat. He glanced up the road towards the bridge, then at Farouk's white Rolls-Royce.

He reached the staff entrance, hidden from view round the corner. The gate was ajar. An electric bulb attached to a tree above created a wide pool of light. He pushed the gate back. From here, the path curved round a hedge. At the bottom, he could just make out the causeway that led to the rear balcony of the nightclub.

He shut the gate and descended the steps. At the bottom, he saw Farouk's courtier, Fabrizzi, leaning over the balcony, smoking a cigarette and gazing into the dark water below. He had not heard Quinn's approach.

'Evening,' Quinn said, as he crossed the causeway.

Fabrizzi started. 'A girl is injured,' he said. He spoke with a thick Italian accent.

'She'll live.'

'Good,' Fabrizzi said. 'Good.'

'You see anything?'

'No.'

'You see anybody leave the club this way?'

'No . . . no.'

Quinn stepped into the Kit Kat and walked to the bar, conscious of the eyes on his back. Lewis was in the far corner, talking to a group of brother officers. Kostandis was nowhere to be seen. The king had not moved, the girls leaning a little closer to him. Perhaps it was his imagination, but the Hungarian seemed to be singing louder. He sat down and gestured at Mac to get him another drink.

When it came, he took a large slug. 'Is she all right?' Mac asked.

'Yeah.'

'What happened? Everyone is speculating.'

'The girl got attacked – seems like someone was waiting for her. He used piano wire, the same MO as the murder of our friend Durant.' Quinn glanced about him. Mac had always been his eyes and ears in here. 'You recall who was still in place after the scream?'

'What do you mean?'

'Last time I looked, the broad's husband was standing by the door to the balcony. I heard the scream and I moved. I wasn't looking to see who might have slipped out. Was the husband still around?'

'He was here. Just after the scream, he came to the bar and ordered a drink. Then he realized something was wrong and went out.'

'He ordered from the bar?'

143

'Yes.'

'Right after the scream?'

'More or less. He didn't seem interested in what was going on.'

'What'd he order?'

'A whisky.'

'Then what happened? Precisely.'

Mac shrugged. 'I went to pour the drink and he drifted off. Quite a few people had left by now, so he followed them.'

Kate returned. She looked exhausted. Quinn examined his glass, drained its contents. 'Come on, Mowbray, let's get you home.' He slung some money onto the bar, said goodnight to Mac and led the way out of the club.

Neither spoke until they reached the car. Quinn watched the street urchins creeping down the road towards them, trying to get close enough to call for *baksheesh* without arousing the ire of the guards. 'I'm afraid I got nothing out of them,' Kate said, as she slipped the key into the ignition and pressed the starter. 'Your Greek friend doesn't seem to like you much. He says having detectives in the place is bad for business.' The engine rumbled into life. 'What did Mac tell you?'

'Some interesting details.'

She swung the car round and drove back towards Zamalek Bridge. 'You have a theory, then,' she said.

'Maybe.'

'Do you want to share it?'

'I'm trying to figure it out. What was the broad up to out in that dark alley? Feeding the birds?'

'Taking the air, perhaps.'

'At this time of night? And someone just happened

144

to be waiting for her?' He shook his head. 'It has to have been a rendezvous.' They leapt involuntarily in their seats as the car flew off a bump on the far side of Zamalek Bridge. Quinn wiped the sheen from his forehead. 'But Mac says that as soon as she screams the husband's right up to the bar to order a drink.'

'What's odd about that? He didn't know it was his wife.'

'Everyone's attention was on what was happening outside. The music'd stopped. So who'd think of walking to the bar and ordering a drink? And why not order at the table, like he'd been doing all night?'

'I'm not sure I understand that.'

'He's establishing his presence, right? And he's doing it with the one guy in the joint who can be guaranteed to remember and tell me. It was like he knew the broad was going to get nailed and wanted to make sure he was ruled out.'

'He employed someone else to try to murder his wife?'

'That's what I'm trying to figure out.'

145

CHAPTER EIGHTEEN

Outside Quinn's apartment block in Zamalek, the caretaker, Fraser, was fast asleep in a rocking-chair on the wooden veranda, his blotched, sunburnt face tilted up towards the light. He was snoring, the ends of his bristly white moustache twitching.

Fraser was an elderly British expatriate who had inhabited the building for far longer than its other residents. He was an irascible figure whose principal task appeared to be to shout at the servants, particularly Ahmed, the shy garden boy. It was said Fraser was a veteran of the Boer War who had washed up in Cairo on his way home, but it was hard to be certain. He didn't venture more than a sentence at a time.

He awoke as Quinn approached and leapt to his feet to mutter, 'Good evening.' Since he had discovered Quinn was a policeman, Fraser had offered him an exaggerated respect that he went out of his way to deny other residents, particularly the harmless elderly Italian couple on the floor above. He was not to know that Quinn had prevented them being interned.

The building was a former palace in the Italianate-Ottoman style, laden with stucco and painted a dirty lime green. It had been converted to apartments two or three decades before and had received little attention since from its Greek owners, the paint peeling in large chunks from its ornate ceilings. Mae had chosen it because of its spacious gardens. In winter, when the nights were cooler, they would sit on one or other terrace, dining beneath the shade of the banyan trees.

Quinn stepped into the lobby, still listening to Kate's Austin accelerating away up the street. But as he turned the key in his lock, he heard a hacking cough and hushed voices. In the apartment the air was dense. The fans had been switched off. For some reason, Mae never felt the heat. He wiped the dust off his shoes. Beside him on a cane sideboard was an old sepia photograph of Mae's father in front of the Pyramids, the study of which had been his life's work.

He could see candles flickering in Ryan's bedroom and he glanced in through the door. Mae had put out the photographs, a candle before each one.

There was another cough, more wrenching this time. It seemed to go on and on. As he glided down the corridor, Quinn caught sight of the servants standing in a huddle by the entrance to the living room. Hassan, the Nubian *sufragi*, was in front, the young cook and the boy tucked in behind him. They jumped to attention and chorused, 'Good evening, sir.' He muttered a reply and hurried on past.

Effatt's son was in the grip of a coughing fit and he lay doubled up with pain on the sofa, Mae on one side of him, an Egyptian woman on the other. There were more candles and photographs of Ryan on the mantelpiece, along with his bear, the Yankees cap and various other items that had been precious to him.

Effatt stood with his back to the window. They all

147

waited for the boy to catch his breath. 'Rifat,' Effatt said, 'you remember Major Quinn.'

The boy tried to stand. 'Please,' Quinn said. 'Of course, I remember you.' He tried to conceal his shock at the child's appearance. He had shrunk since their last encounter, his frame sickly and gaunt, and fatigue was etched into shallow cheeks. Mae's hand was on his bare arm. 'They decided we should go,' she said quietly.

'Good,' he said.

'It's a burden,' Effatt said. 'I understand that, but we—'

'It's no burden,' Quinn countered.

Effatt turned towards the Egyptian woman, his manner stilted and formal in front of Mae. 'This is my sister, Deena. If it is ... if it is acceptable, she will travel with the boy.'

'Of course,' Mae said. 'Of course she must.'

Rifat sat up straight and, for a moment, he appeared to have recovered strength. But the coughing began again. This time, it brought tiny bubbles of air and blood to his lips. 'Maybe he should lie down and get some sleep,' Mae said.

She and Deena helped Rifat to his feet and escorted him down the corridor to the guest bedroom. Effatt stood ramrod straight, staring at the bare wall. They listened to the boy coughing and the women's soothing voices. 'The day after tomorrow is best,' Effatt said. 'I want him to have time to adjust.'

'Yes.'

'It is an imposition, but I'm—'

'It's no imposition.' Quinn's voice was soft. 'You know that.' He switched on the fan beside him.

'I have not yet booked the tickets,' Effatt said. 'Tomorrow I—'

'I'll do it.'

'I cannot allow it.'

'It will be easier for me. The trains are full. If there's no hospital train going through, we'll need a compartment set aside.'

The boy was coughing again. This time it was mercifully brief. They listened, ears straining for the first telltale wheeze, but the night was still. After a few minutes, Mae returned. She sat with her legs close together and her elbows resting on her knees. 'Joe, Effatt wants to know more about where I'm going to take Rifat and what the surgery will involve.'

'Sure.' Quinn sat down and the Egyptian perched uncomfortably on the edge of a chair.

'It is not an easy procedure,' Mae said, her voice hushed almost to a whisper so that Rifat could not hear, 'which is why relatively few surgeons practise it. But those who do have achieved a good measure of success. The problem with the disease is that it begins slowly, then spreads inexorably.' She held up two hands. 'What some surgeons have found is that by first collapsing the lung and then – possibly – removing part of the infected area, they can arrest and eliminate it.'

Quinn watched his wife. Her eyes shone with a brightness that stirred a distant memory. She had spoken to the doctors and spent hours in the library reading about this disease.

'There are other factors as well.' Mae spoke more quickly now, as if sensing Effatt's discomfort. 'The sanatorium is above Jerusalem, so the rest, diet and relatively clean air . . . well, it should all help. There is a good chance. There really is.'

'It is the only way,' Effatt said forcefully, as if he

were trying to convince himself. He stood. 'I am grateful. If I could say goodbye to the boy . . .'

They watched him go, listened to him ease the door shut. Mae smiled at Quinn. 'Have you eaten?' she asked.

'No.'

'Hassan has left some food out for you.'

He got up and went down the corridor, the servants fleeing at his approach to their quarters out at the back. He lifted the plate that covered the food and flapped at the flies. It did not look very appealing. Or maybe he'd just lost his appetite again.

He took down an almost empty bottle of Scotch and drained the contents into a glass. He sat at the table. Ahead of him was a two-foot-tall model of the Great Pyramid of Cheops at Giza, made from matchsticks. He removed the top to reveal a series of tunnels and inner chambers and ran his finger along the wood. He'd used too much glue, which was irritating because he'd have to find a way to file it down. A cockroach scuttled along the floor and he caught it with his boot.

From here, he could just see the light from his son's bedroom on the corridor wall.

It was half an hour, maybe more, before Effatt emerged and when he did so, his expression was hollow. It was clear that he did not wish to linger, so Quinn accompanied him into the hallway. 'I will see you in the morning,' Effatt said.

'Yeah.'

'I talked to the women in the Berka after Macleod left. They said—'

'It can wait.'

'I'm sorry not to have brought any . . .' Evidently

Effatt did not wish to use the word 'money'. 'Once I decided, I wanted to get him here and begin . . . I will give it to you in the office tomorrow.'

'You know I ain't gonna take it.'

'Then I cannot allow him to go.'

'Please, Effatt.'

'I could not permit it. You must understand. Amid such kindness, how could I?'

'What did you tell me earlier, when I wanted to put a slug in that South African in the whorehouse? What difference would it make? Here's something that will. You have three children left to support. We've got none.'

'But still—'

'You've seen the look in Mae's eyes. She needs this. Don't make me beg, old friend.'

'I do not deserve you. But God is kind.'

He moved away, but Quinn grasped him. 'It's going to be all right.'

The Egyptian held his gaze, his eyes filled with sorrow, fear and regret. How could either of them know it would be all right? It was one thing for Mae to take refuge in informed optimism, but they'd seen too much turn out for ill to believe everything would resolve itself to the good. 'You thought about going with him?' Quinn asked. 'All of you?' Quinn stepped closer. 'Look, you got to keep this to yourself, but the Defence Committee has a cable from London. They'll evacuate Alexandria to preserve the navy, but we're to fight for every inch of the delta and Cairo. Canal by canal, street by street, building by building. They ain't going to let us give up this town without a fight.'

'They will destroy the city rather than lose it?'

'They're going to slow him down.'

He could see Effatt's shock, even in the half-darkness. 'And you will let them?'

'The orders are from London. They won't give up Cairo. But we could arrange a job for you in Palestine.'

'As what?'

'Every city needs a cop.'

'A colonial policeman, Joe? For the rest of my days?'

'A temporary solution.'

'Who can say what will prove temporary in this war?' Effatt dipped his head. There was a long silence. 'What am I going to do, Joe?' His voice was barely a whisper. 'I see you. I know about the long dark nights. I understand I'm headed for the abyss, but I am helpless.'

'He'll be all right.'

Effatt looked up. 'This is me you're talking to, Joe.'

'We'll survive.'

'But do we want to? I can see the price you have paid – I see it every day.'

'You've got to believe it can turn out well.'

'Why?' Effatt's eyes strayed up the corridor.

'There's no other way.'

'I need to have faith, you mean. Like you do?'

'That's different.'

'Why is it different? Every day I come in and pray I'll see that smile on your face again. I look for a sign that you've crawled from the abyss, but I don't see it, Joe. I only see you lost in the darkness.'

'You saying I should get over it?'

'I'm saying you can't offer me hope when you have none for yourself.'

Effatt slipped away. Quinn followed him out and watched his figure vanish into the night.

CHAPTER NINETEEN

Mae lay on her side on the bed, fully dressed, a ghostly white face caught in a sliver of moonlight. Her thin cotton gown had slipped to reveal the smooth skin of her thigh, but she was shielded behind a veil: the mosquito net was all around her, suspended from the ceiling by a metal hoop and tucked under each corner of the mattress. The room was filled with the metallic smell of Cairo's most popular mosquito repellent. On a table, next to the bed, Quinn could just see the outline of the Flit gun, with its chunky barrel and pump handle, which his wife kept close at hand.

There was another photograph of Ryan on the dresser with a candle in front of it. It was the one taken at the Gezira on the day Quinn had been teaching him how to pitch. 'What's going on?' he asked.

Mae did not turn round.

Quinn moved to the dresser, blew out the candle and placed the photograph face down. 'What are you trying to do?'

She propped herself up on an elbow. 'I'm not trying to do anything.'

'Suddenly the house is covered with pictures.'

'Is there something wrong with that?'

'This was the day he was killed. You want to ram it down our throats with every step we take through the house?'

'He was a gift, Joe. Today I wanted to celebrate what he *gave* us.'

Quinn exhaled. 'I don't know how you do it.'

'Do what?'

'You're acting like it happened in a different life. You always have. You go to the hospital and pour your soul into all these guys you've never met, hold their hands, write their wives and watch them die. Every day someone says to me, "Joe, your wife is real remarkable. Isn't it swell? We don't know how she does it." Then we come to the day he died and we're *celebrating*. We got to be happy. We gotta say how *great* life is. Well, I apologize, but it *ain't* for me.'

'I've got over it, Joe? Is that what you think? Is that what's bugging you? You think it doesn't mean anything to me any more?'

'I didn't say that. We've all got to do it our own way.'

'So you're angry because I won't spend the rest of my life in the pit with you?'

'I ain't out of the pit! I admit it! Most days, I don't figure I'm ever going to be out.'

'So that's it. Life is finished? We give up?' Mae asked. 'I know what you think, Joe. I got the picture a long time ago. I see it in your face when you ask me about the hospital.'

Quinn rubbed tired, bloodshot eyes.

'What upsets me so much,' she said quietly, 'is that you are still, after all these months, lost to me. One

154

case follows another, each a matter of life and death, or so it seems. And all you can talk of is the day you'll find the man who drove that car.'

'I'm gonna get him.'

'And then what? You going to put a gun in his mouth like you did back home? Where did that get us, Joe?'

'It'll get us justice.'

'Will it? Can you honestly say that's what it's about? Maybe it was just an accident, after all.' They heard the sound of Rifat coughing again. It faded quickly. 'Why don't you go and talk to him? He's excited at staying in the house of the New York cop who works with his father.'

'I ain't got nothing to say.'

'He's Effatt's *son*.'

'I'll talk to him in the morning.'

'You'll be gone in the morning.'

Quinn slipped off his uniform jacket and leather holster. He undressed, raised a corner of the net and slipped in. Mae turned away from him. 'You know, it's not an insult to Ryan's memory to care for another child.'

'I never said it was.'

He covered himself with the thin cotton sheet. It was hotter under it. Perhaps that was why he never slept.

Quinn was on his feet, tangled in the mosquito net, sweat clinging to his face. He was staring at the darkened bed below. 'It's not true,' he shouted. 'There's nothing I could have done. Nothing!'

'Joe?'

'There was nothing I could do.'

155

'Joe!' Mae's sharp voice penetrated the darkness.

'Why did he do it? Why did he run? I couldn't have yelled sooner, I was just . . .'

'Joe, stop it.' She stood beside him. 'It's me.'

He stared into her troubled eyes and gradually his mind retrieved focus. Now he knew where he was. His nose and mouth were full of the bitter taste of Flit. She took his face between her hands. 'Please, Joe. Enough.'

'I can't go on like this,' he said.

'It's all right,' Mae whispered. 'We're all right.' She took his arm, her grip fierce. 'You'll wake Rifat. Let's go back to sleep.'

With her guiding him, he returned to the bed and lay down on the sweat-soaked sheet. The images of his son stayed with him: of Ryan letting go his mother's hand and running towards his own outstretched arms, of Ryan dropping the ball and changing direction to retrieve it.

Quinn watched the shifting patterns on the ceiling. He knew from experience that the dawn sunlight, when it came, would seep through the blinds and spread slowly towards him. But that was a long way off. He could hear a clock ticking on the dressing-table. It marked out the interminable passage of these nights.

Half an hour later Quinn slipped out of the apartment. He tried not to disturb the snoring Fraser, whose arms were plastered with white mosquito-repellent tubes, which shone like glow-worms in the darkness. Sometimes Fraser would awake to witness these nocturnal perambulations, but he never offered more than a polite 'Good night' upon Quinn's departure or

'Good morning' on his arrival. Perhaps he thought it was police business, or something more interesting.

Quinn strode down the street outside, a faint breeze bringing partial relief from the leaden heat of the apartment. The road was lined with oleander and jacaranda trees, alternate splashes of blue and white just visible in the dim light of the streetlamps. Here there was the sound of a piano, there the hum of a distant tram. On the corner, a light shone from a first-floor balcony. Underneath it, an Italian woman sat in a faded red dress, fanning herself with a newspaper. Her husband owned the garage where Quinn had taken their Ford V8 to be mended before the war, but now he languished in an internment camp up in Fayed, the machinery idle and his workshop empty. Quinn raised his hand at the woman as he passed. She never seemed to sleep. He didn't like to think how she kept herself alive.

Quinn passed the padlocked gates of the Italian school. The Italians had once been thick on the ground in this neighbourhood and Quinn could recall standing on his terrace listening to the Blackshirts yelling, '*Duce, Duce,*' in unison with the children in the playground.

He took a handkerchief from his pocket, mopped sweat from his brow. He passed the little Armenian store where he bought two-month-old copies of the *New York Times*, and the Levantine café where, in quieter times, he had sat to read them.

Quinn sank slowly into the mire of his thoughts. Before he knew it, he had reached the banks of the river and was looking across at the twinkle of the houseboat lights on the opposite bank. He could still hear music drifting across from the Kit Kat, the white minaret of the mosque behind bright in the moonlight. He glanced at his watch. It was almost five.

He heard laughter below and looked down towards the river. A group of children was hanging off the branch of a mimosa tree that stretched over the water. They let themselves drop one by one, throwing up great plumes of dark water, before bobbing to the surface further down. Quinn could see their makeshift shelter beneath the bridge, fashioned from wooden packing-cases. He thought they were the same kids who demanded *baksheesh* outside the Kit Kat. They were making enough noise to wake the residents of the houseboats opposite.

He sat on the grass bank, lit a cigarette. He could just make out the first dawn light above the horizon.

He remembered Kate's question to him earlier. What were he and Mae going to do when the war was over? Originally they'd come here to visit, but he thought now that the tiny gravestone meant they'd never leave.

Quinn watched the kids for twenty minutes, maybe more, then got to his feet and began the journey home.

The phone rang, sucking Quinn from sleep. He slid off the edge of the sofa and stood up. Dawn crept through the shutters and the temperature was rising.

He walked to the other side of the room and picked up the receiver. 'I'm sorry, sir. It's me, Madden.'

'Yeah?' Quinn's mouth was so dry he could barely speak.

'I think you'd better get in here, sir. Uniform branch is sweeping the Berka. Apparently they got a call from Field Security overnight. The signals chaps down at GHQ picked up some kind of transmission.'

'What kind?'

'It's a station identification. No message, but direct to Berlin. It looks like there really is a spy in Cairo.'

Madden's tone was apologetic, as if he, like Quinn, did not share the city's obsession with the threat of espionage. 'Not our area, I know, but I thought you might be interested, what with Durant having access to all that information . . .'

'OK, Ed. I'm on my way.' He replaced the receiver, tried to rub the sleep from his eyes. He must have dozed off finally.

'What's going on, Joe?'

Quinn swung round. Mae was awake, her blond hair tousled. 'Sorry,' Quinn said. 'Gotta go.'

'What is it this time?'

Quinn faced the window. 'We had a case yesterday. Another homicide.'

'Who's been killed?'

'Some officer. We found him hanging from a tree with his throat cut.'

'Who killed him?'

'He's got a broad living downstairs, knew him better than she's saying. You know her from the hospital. The American girl.'

'Amy White?'

'Yeah.'

'She's your suspect?'

'Maybe.'

'She's really nice, doesn't seem the type.'

'They never do.'

'Perhaps you should be less cynical. It mightn't hurt once in a while. When will you be home?'

'Late.'

It was the answer she'd expected. She pointed to the room where Rifat and his aunt were sleeping. All was quiet and Quinn had only heard a few bursts of coughing in the night. 'Will you go and speak to him?'

159

'Later.'

Mae was frowning. 'You'll book the tickets this morning?'

'Yeah.'

'You won't forget?'

'No.'

'They say the trains are packed.'

'We'll make room.' Quinn strapped on his holster and picked up his jacket.

'There was a rumour yesterday,' Mae said, 'that Rommel had already taken Alexandria and was on his way here.'

'He's getting closer.' Quinn slipped his revolver into the holster. 'I'll try to get home in good time,' he said.

But it was a pledge neither believed.

160

CHAPTER TWENTY

Cairo's minarets were still bathed in moonlight as the first rays of the morning sun washed the horizon a delicate pink. They crossed into the suburb of Bulaq, and Quinn looked out at the city coming to life: shopkeepers carrying baskets full of produce, horse-drawn gharries bowling along the streets, bodies stirring in the doorways. A man sat outside a shop selling milk and eggs, legs stretched, smoking a hookah as he watched the world pass by. A woman swathed in black carried a huge pile of empty golden cages on her head.

The traffic slowed almost to a halt as they approached a tram that had turned over in the road. Kate swung off Fuad el Awal Avenue into the narrower streets at the southern end of Bulaq.

She drove slowly. It was a different world down here, far from the vibrant place that strode ever more confidently towards parity with Europe or America. Quinn saw whole families asleep beside piles of rubbish, fathers shielding children with long, scrawny arms. Mae was always telling him that half of Cairo's infants were dead before they reached the age of five, but you had to tour these darkened streets in the dawn hours to appreciate the agonies of its poor properly.

Kate was leaning forward, eyes close to the windscreen as she navigated them back out onto a deserted section of Fuad. They emerged opposite a series of billboards advertising Bata shoes, Dr Boustani's cigarettes and Shelltox – *The Insect Executioner!* The Military Police Barracks on Bab el Hadid had been built to resemble a crusader fortress, and was as ugly as it was forbidding. It was three storeys high, the ground floor entirely occupied by a row of cells and the duty desk, the first the preserve of the administration sections of the uniform branch, the whole of the second given over to SIB, Quinn's department, and Field Security. Quinn's offices were in one wing, Macleod's in the other. The field agents, analysts and language experts they were supposed to share sat in the central atrium. Beside them, along one wall, was a gigantic bookshelf with endless rows of box files.

As they drove past the sentry into the courtyard, there were already signs of activity: a couple of jeeps fresh in from the desert were unloaded in front of the cell doors. Kate parked alongside them and, even in this light, Quinn could see the exhaustion etched into the grimy faces of the men who climbed out.

An Austin utility pulled in, followed by a pair of Bedford trucks. In British military parlance, there was a flap on.

Quinn sidestepped the throng in the lobby and climbed the stairs to his office. He saw Sergeant Cohen leaning against the banisters, talking to David Dexter. Quinn liked both men. Cohen was a Palestinian Jew, a slight man, with a narrow, dark face. Dexter had been born and brought up in India and Ceylon and spoke fluent Hindi. His skills had proved useful in a corruption case involving an Indian mechanized regiment the previous year. 'You've heard, sir?' Cohen asked.

'Yeah.'

'What do you think?'

Quinn assumed, as Madden had, that an intercepted radio transmission meant a Berlin-trained and -equipped agent. Cohen picked up a sheet of paper from the desk behind and handed it to Quinn. It was an artist's impression of a handsome man with a pronounced cleft chin and a distinctive mole on his right cheek. He was wearing a fedora. It was the man Amy White claimed to have seen going up to Durant's apartment. 'She say it's a good likeness?' Quinn asked.

'Yes.'

'You think she really saw the guy?'

'Well . . . no,' he said.

'How come?'

Cohen glanced about him. 'It was just a bit like Corbett's description of the man who stole the car and killed your son. She was too eager to accept whatever strokes of the charcoal I made. Usually it's so laborious and I have to go over it again and again until they accept it's a likeness.'

Quinn held it up. 'Thank you.'

He walked towards his own office. Madden was standing just inside the door. 'I'm sorry to call you so early, sir,' he said, handing Quinn a note. 'This is what Field Security sent down to the uniform branch. I retrieved it.'

Quinn took the paper.

Signals Monitoring Section. 26 June 1942, 12.01 a.m.

Intercept of short burst transmission. Station identification.

Recipient: Berlin.

Transmitter and location not identified. Cairo area.

'Apparently Field Security have known about this for months,' Madden said. 'They intercepted half a dozen brief station identification messages to Berlin, but this is the first time they've been able to get a fix. They traced it to the Berka, so they've done a major sweep.' Quinn handed the piece of paper to Kate, then moved to the other side of his desk and sat down. There was a buff-coloured envelope before him, with his name typed on the front.

No-one spoke.

'What do you make of it, sir?' Madden asked.

'It's not our problem.'

'You don't think it's relevant?'

'We've got the broad on a double count of lying. That's what we've got to focus on.'

Madden looked at his notebook. 'We received two cables back overnight from New York. The police department say she's got no criminal record, but you were right about her family. The immigration service confirmed she arrived from Berlin in 1932. She is German.'

'A German Jew, Ed. Not the same thing.'

'Of course. I've also found Mrs Markham. She's waiting for us over at GHQ. I said you would wish to talk to her as soon as you were in. And Colonel Lewis has postponed the morning meeting because of the search in the Berka.'

Quinn slit open the envelope and slipped his hand inside to remove the letter. He felt scraps of paper and

164

upended them upon the table. Inside were the remains of a photograph, which had been cut into small pieces. He scooped them up, put them back into the envelope. He looked at the name. *Major Joseph Quinn.*

The photograph was one of Ryan and Mae he kept in his desk. To be certain he checked the top drawer. It had gone. 'Are you all right, sir?' Kate asked.

They were both looking at him. 'I'm fine.'

'What is it?'

'Nothing.' He strode out of the room, through the atrium and down the corridor to the toilet. He locked a cubicle door and leant against the cool stone wall. Then he tipped the contents of the envelope onto the shelf behind the lavatory and tried to reassemble the photograph. His hand shook. It was a hopeless task: it had been cut into too many pieces. He put them back into the envelope.

'Are you all right, sir?'

It was Madden. Quinn composed himself and wiped his eyes. He glanced at the envelope and slipped it into his pocket. 'Sure.' He flushed the toilet, opened the door. Madden stood with his hands in his pockets. He was clearly embarrassed. 'Kate said I ought to check if you were all right.'

'Yeah, of course,' Quinn stepped forward to the basin to wash his hands.

Madden didn't budge. 'Exhausted, I suppose, after yesterday.'

Quinn reached for the towel. 'It was a photograph of my wife and son, since you're wondering. I used to keep it in my desk here. Someone cut it up and stuffed it in an envelope.'

The colour drained from Madden's face. 'My God, why?'

'I have no idea.'

'But, sir, that's—'

'It's all right, Ed. Maybe we're upsetting someone. This happens. Don't worry about it.' Quinn walked past him to the door.

CHAPTER TWENTY-ONE

Quinn agreed to a brief detour so they swung into the Berka and drew up where they'd waited last night. Military jeeps and uniformed policemen thronged the narrow streets, and small groups had gathered to watch the search. Quinn pushed the door open, but was prevented from getting out by a small flock of sheep. Each animal had a red cross marked on its back.

A boy darted past, carrying a tray of freshly baked flat breads upon his head. Beside the car, a café owner swept a pile of debris out into the gutter, pausing occasionally to see what was happening. A pair of scantily clad whores craned their necks from a nearby balcony.

There were two jeeps outside number thirty-three. Macleod leant against one, Reza beside him, dwarfed by the sign of the fat woman and her donkey. They reminded Quinn this morning of mobsters like Lucky Luciano back home, who'd grown fat on Prohibition. They held themselves with the same swagger and confident belief that they were above the law. A group of uniformed military police poured from one house and hammered upon the door of the next. 'Police!' they bellowed in English. 'Open up!'

Quinn glanced at his colleagues.

'Police!' the men yelled again. The sergeant in command lost patience, put his shoulder to the door and charged through. Quinn heard a howl of protest, then the sound of a scuffle.

Moments later, the sergeant pulled a man in a blue robe out of the house and hustled him towards the back of a jeep. He'd been handcuffed, and looked as if he'd been pulled from his bed. In the doorway, the man's wife and a little boy witnessed his departure, both bleary-eyed and nervous.

Quinn watched the progress of the search. Ever since the start of the war, they had been faced with the threat of espionage. All of the Germans and most of the Italians in Cairo had been interned, but that still left the Vichy French and any number of Greeks, Albanians, Bulgarians, Romanians and White Russians . . .

'How to win friends,' Kate muttered. 'What's going on? They're looking for the radio?'

'I guess, but let's get going. Like I said, it ain't our problem.'

There was no answer at the Whites' apartment, so they went instead to the office on Fuad. As Kate had suggested, it was situated on the third floor of a run-down building. Gunmetal grey paint was peeling in large chunks off the walls and the ceiling and the only sign of any investment was a plaque outside, which had been newly inscribed with the words 'Casablanca Oil'.

The door was locked. Quinn knocked once, but there was no answer. 'This open last night?' he asked.

'Yes,' Kate said. 'There's a small reception area where the secretary sits, and his office is beyond it.'

Quinn tried again, but there was still no response. He put his shoulder against the door and pushed gently. It felt as if it would give easily. 'I don't think we should do this, sir,' Madden said.

Since the Whites were not military personnel, they technically had no jurisdiction over them. They would need Effatt here to justify breaking in and, even then, he wouldn't want to do it without a search warrant. Quinn put his shoulder to the doors and pushed hard until they gave.

'Christ,' Madden muttered.

The anteroom was bare. It consisted of a single desk with a telephone on it, an old Imperial typewriter and a wooden pot filled with pens and pencils. White's office inside was only a little less sparsely furnished. There was a wooden bench covered with coloured shawls, a few armchairs and a brass coffee table. A couple of small Persian rugs lay over palm-leaf matting. The desk was clear, but the walls were covered with maps: of Cairo, the area around Suez, Egypt as a whole and the Western Desert.

Quinn sat in the cane chair behind the desk. He tried the central drawer, but it was locked. He looked for something to force it and alighted upon a silver letter-opener.

It gave easily and he took out the papers inside. Madden was standing by the door. 'We really ought to go, sir. White's an American citizen. If he catches us here, there'll be hell to pay.'

Quinn looked through the papers, which consisted mostly of letters from government ministers and departments, and carbon copies of the replies. Almost all seemed to relate to a concession to dig for oil in an area around Suez. 'Hmm,' Quinn mused. 'I figure he ain't getting far.'

Towards the bottom of the pile, he found letters heavily embossed with the royal family's crest. They were all signed 'Mario Fabrizzi', the Italian who remained the king's most influential official. They were equally noncommittal. The last one read,

> We note your continued interest, but should advise you that, in the first instance, you should continue to deal with the Minister of Trade and his officials. We are sorry that you have not received as careful attention there on the matters you have raised as you desire and we shall attempt to use our influence to move matters on more quickly.

'Looks like he's getting the brush-off,' Quinn muttered.

'Sir,' Madden said.

'All right.' Quinn put the papers back in the drawer and used the letter-opener to lever it shut. He and Madden moved back to the hallway and closed the doors as best they could. 'We'll straighten out Mrs Markham. I want you to find out where the Whites are,' Quinn said.

'Any idea where I should start?' Madden asked, as Quinn descended the stairs.

'Get Cohen and Dexter to help.'

Mrs Markham stood in the middle of her office. Today, she appeared determined to retain her composure. 'Please have a seat, ma'am,' Quinn said.

She placed her handbag to one side of the desk,

then readjusted the pots of pens and paper-clips in front of her. Quinn glanced at his watch. 'You're in early,' he said.

She sighed.

'You OK?' he asked.

'It's just . . . one minute we're careering along, and the next . . .' She glanced at Kate. She evidently didn't approve of putting young girls in uniform. Mrs Markham, he guessed, had been locally enlisted. The wife of a senior officer, a university lecturer or district official. Her eyes wandered to the papers in Quinn's hand, then to the cabinet that contained the safe. 'I haven't yet spoken to Colonel Wheeler about Captain Durant's possessions.'

'We've taken what we need. You'll get 'em back.'

Suddenly she was looking at them with suspicion, as if they were from the Gestapo.

'A lot of information passes through this office,' Quinn said. 'It's a real treasure trove.' He pulled Durant's chair over and sat opposite her. 'How long you work with the captain, Mrs Markham?'

'A few months.'

'Since he came out from England?'

'Yes.'

'You work in this office before that?'

'With Captain Metcalfe, yes.'

'What happened to Metcalfe?'

'He requested a transfer back to his unit.'

'Why?'

'Why does anyone? He wanted to be at the sharp end, didn't feel he'd be making a contribution unless he was.'

'So you got Durant.'

'Yes.'

171

'You liked the guy?'

'Yes, very much. He was a ... kind man. Considerate.'

'In what way?'

'He made a point of asking after one's well-being. That is attractive in any man,' she said, with feeling.

'He was a friend?'

'I wouldn't have made that presumption.' It took Quinn a moment to work out what she meant.

'He ever talk about his wife or children, ma'am?'

'Not about his wife, no.'

'But his daughters ...'

'Yes. He adored them.'

'He took out the girls from the typing pool?'

'Yes, but—'

'He ever hit on them?'

'Of course not.'

'You know who his friends were?'

'No, Major. I liked the captain, but ours was a purely professional relationship.'

'You see him around town? Some cocktail party?'

'Not that I can recall.'

'But you knew he had a lover?'

If, in a moment of vulnerability yesterday, Mrs Markham might have been willing to concede her superior's infidelity, today, in a stronger frame of mind, she was prepared to make no such admission. She glared at him with all the considerable disdain a British matron of a certain age could muster. She seemed about to rebuke him, but remained silent.

'Any idea who the broad was?'

'I spoke hastily. I cannot be certain that—'

'This was in his safe,' Quinn said. 'You seen it before?' He took out the necklace and dangled it from

172

his hand. She shook her head. 'You know who he bought it for?'

'Perhaps his wife.'

'But he didn't tell you that?'

'No. I wasn't aware of its existence.'

Quinn slipped it into his pocket. 'We'll keep it for now.'

'I shall inform Colonel Wheeler you have taken it.'

'You go right ahead.' Suddenly Quinn felt terribly tired. 'Mrs Markham,' he said quietly, 'we ain't trying to blacken Durant's name, you understand that, don't you?'

She did not look up, but he saw her jaw slacken as the tension receded.

'A woman loses her husband, two little girls a father.' Her face softened. 'If I don't find out why, they're going to be fed a convenient line. Maybe it won't be true.'

She let out a little sigh. 'You have a job to do, Major, I understand.' She looked him in the eye once more. 'Captain Durant was a wonderful man, warm, intelligent, funny and loyal to his friends. He gave the impression he hadn't a care in the world, but I saw beyond that. He was lonely and, like many officers working here, felt he should have been up in the blue – the desert.'

'So, in the end, he fell for a girl.'

She didn't answer that.

'He request a transfer?'

'Not that I know of.'

'So he wasn't that keen to take a bullet?'

'Well—'

'Was that part of the problem?'

'I know he was anxious to see his daughters again,

173

but he wasn't a coward, Major, if that is what you seek to imply.'

'There's no disgrace in wanting to live, ma'am. Did he and Colonel Wheeler get along?'

'As far as I know. They always seemed to.'

'Take a look at his diary.' Quinn stretched a hand towards Kate, who removed it from her bag. He held it up. 'You recognize this?'

'Yes.'

'He ever ask you to put entries in?'

'No, it was his personal diary.'

'He had another for the office?'

'He didn't need one. I keep . . . I kept a record of any appointments.' She pointed to a green book on her desk. It had not been there yesterday.

'May I?' Quinn asked. He took it from her and flicked through. It was packed with details of meetings and deadlines for reports required and pending. It had all been entered in Mrs Markham's ultra-neat hand. 'Mind if I take this for the day?' he asked.

She seemed poised to object, then perhaps had second thoughts. After all, what would she need it for now? As this thought dawned, it visibly weighed her down. Quinn tried to offer some reassurance, but she did not smile back. He glanced through Durant's personal diary and handed it to her, open at the page for the previous night. 'Take a look at that. "W.e.B. nine thirty".'

'I don't know what it means.'

'Wagh el Birket. A meeting at nine thirty.'

Mrs Markham shook her head to indicate she'd not the faintest idea what he was talking about.

'We know there was a broad, Mrs Markham. But we got to find out if there was anything else. We kept

174

a watch on this meeting and some interesting guys turned up.' Quinn waited. 'He know Macleod from Field Security?'

'I don't believe so. I mean, I suppose he would have been vetted when he came on stream for this job. We all are.'

'But they weren't friends or associates?'

'No.'

'Macleod ever call here?'

'I don't believe so.'

'What about the other guy, Reza? Small Egyptian with a marked face and skin like a dead snake. You ever see him down here?'

Mrs Markham shook her head vigorously.

'What about a Greek called Kostandis?' Quinn could tell he was losing her again. Whatever had brought Durant to the Berka, she knew nothing of it. 'Just one or two more questions, ma'am,' he said softly. He handed her the sheet of paper listing the order of battle in the desert. 'We found this in the safe. Did you type it?'

'Yes.'

'It's a carbon copy. You know where the original is?'

'No, I can't say that I do.'

'You gave both to Durant?'

'Yes.'

Quinn took it back. 'What was this for, ma'am?'

She shook her head to indicate that, once again, she did not divine his meaning.

'There's a bundle of real detailed information.' He held up the paper. 'What was this sheet for exactly?'

'I'm afraid I don't know, Major. Captain Durant asked me to type many things. He usually wrote them out by hand. I never asked what they were for.'

'Was it unusual to type something up in this detail? It's got all the units out in the field, exact locations, planned movements, fighting strengths . . .'

'Not unusual, no.'

'You type up this kind of document before?'

'About once a month, I would say.'

'Why is it in the safe?'

'Captain Durant was a meticulous man. He was careful not to leave things lying around.'

She was holding back, her face flushed. There was something here. 'He ever take anything like this out of the office?' Quinn asked.

'No . . . I mean, yes.' She stared at the desktop. It was a heavy admission. 'Not to begin with . . . but more recently, he did, yes.'

'Go on,' he said.

'About a month ago, he started to leave work earlier. I told your colleague.' She glanced at Madden. 'He would put papers in his briefcase and take them home for the night.'

'The last orders we seen say no paperwork from any building, ever.'

Mrs Markham appeared profoundly embarrassed. She knew this as well as anyone.

'You ever discuss it with him?' Quinn asked.

'No,' she said regretfully. 'I didn't. Perhaps I should have done. Maybe things would have turned out differently if I had.'

'What do you mean?'

'Just that you might not be here. That's what you think, isn't it? That's why he was killed. You think he was being blackmailed.'

'Why do you say that?'

'A man in his position . . .'

'I mean, how'd you figure he was blackmailed? About what?' Her cheeks flushed again. 'Did you know who the broad was, Mrs Markham?'

'No.'

'You sure about that?'

She nodded.

'But you knew he had a girl.'

She hesitated, breathed in deeply. 'Yes ... well, I thought ... yes.'

'A woman's intuition?'

'If you want to put it that way.'

'You see any change in him? Any sign he's under greater stress?'

'No. In fact, the reverse. He was quieter, it's true, but he appeared happier, more relaxed.' She looked at the documents in Quinn's hand. 'I know that I should have said something about the papers, but it ...' She bit her lip. 'We had been working very hard. Like everyone, of course. The tension had begun to get to him. I assumed he was taking the papers home to his apartment and working through them there so that he had the chance to relax for a few hours. I know I should have—'

'Don't worry, Mrs Markham,' Quinn said, in as soothing a voice as he could manage. 'No-one's suggesting you're to blame.'

'But he shouldn't have been taking them, I knew that.'

Quinn glanced at the map on the wall. Like those in every other office in the building, the redrawn pencil marks provided a graphic reminder of the gravity of their circumstances. 'Durant make any secret of what he was doing?'

'I don't understand.'

'He wasn't trying to hide it from you?'

'I don't think so.'

'See, if he'd been the victim of blackmail,' Quinn said, 'and it was the papers they wanted, he'd have been trying to hide the fact he was taking them home.'

Mrs Markham seemed impressed with this line of argument.

'He ever get telephone calls here from women?'

She avoided his eye. 'Sometimes, possibly. I don't recall.'

'You're a shrewd observer, ma'am. Any broad come through where you thought, Oh, yeah?'

'No.'

'An American call?'

'I don't remember one.'

'You sure about that, ma'am? It's important.'

'I don't recall one.'

Quinn stood. 'Thank you for your time. We appreciate it. You can be sure we'll call again.'

She looked relieved that the ordeal was over and then, just as quickly, unutterably sad.

When Quinn and Kate reached the corridor outside, Madden was waiting for them. 'I've found her, sir, but we're still looking for him. She says he should be in his office.'

CHAPTER TWENTY-TWO

Quinn had never had an affair, never even thought of it. But as he watched Amy White pull her long, slender body from the gleaming pool at the Gezira, he could see how, so far from home, she might have lured even the most virtuous into temptation. Amy stooped to pick up a towel and buried her face in it. She had long legs, slender hips and the finely sculpted physique of a woman who exercised every day. She dried herself slowly.

Quinn sat in a wicker chair on the terrace in front of the green and white clubhouse. The place had been designed to resemble an ocean liner's lido deck, from which it derived its name. It looked out over the swimming-pool and the croquet lawns, tennis courts, cricket pitch, polo field and racecourse that covered most of Gezira Island. When Ryan was alive, he and Mae had come here every day, but it had been months since he'd last paid a social visit.

Amy pulled on a robe, then strolled in his direction. She took the seat opposite him, still towelling her hair. Quinn had sent Kate to check out her husband's trip to Suez, while Madden tried to find out where he was now. 'Good morning,' she said.

Quinn could see a livid gash along her neck and a bandage round her wrist. 'You all right?' he asked.

'I'm sorry if I didn't display much gratitude last night, but I did appreciate your concern.'

She leant forward and rested her elbow on the table. She raised her good hand at a waiter, who scurried over. 'Coffee, please.'

'Make that two,' Quinn said.

Amy got up and walked to a nearby chair to retrieve her bag. She delved into it and produced a leather folder, from which she pulled a batch of photographs. She watched him as he examined them. They were all of Mae and Rifat at St George's, the military hospital.

Carefully Quinn piled them together, then pushed them across the table.

'Keep them,' she said. 'I hoped I might see you today so I put them in my bag. I promised your wife I'd drop them by.' She glanced at one of the pictures of Rifat. 'Your wife said she hoped to take him—'

'Ma'am, I ain't here to talk about my wife.'

She looked at him briefly, then reached into her bag again. 'I'll find something to put them in, or they'll get damaged.' She picked out a paper bag and slipped the photographs inside it.

Quinn took the packet. He pointed at the wound on her neck. 'You going to tell me what happened?'

'To business, then?'

'I'm sorry. There's a lot to do.'

'You could call me Amy.'

'Whatever you like. If you'd just answer the question.'

'I went out to catch some air.'

'Why?'

'Does it matter?'

'Yeah.'

180

'I just did.'

'There's not a woman in Cairo who'd walk down that alley in the dead of night to "catch some air". So, what was it? You wanted a few minutes away from him?'

'From whom?'

'Don't play me for a fool, ma'am. How did you come by the bruises on your neck?'

She didn't answer.

A waiter arrived with their coffee. Quinn poured milk into his and stirred it slowly. 'Look, maybe we can help each other out here. I got a few problems, a few pictures that don't fit. I got you telling me you only met Durant once or twice on the stairs, for example. But it ain't so.'

'I didn't know him well.'

'You go out with him?'

'One night at the Kit Kat he recognized us, came over. We spoke for a few minutes.'

'You see him again?'

'Yes.'

'Where?'

'In the same place.'

'Your husband there?'

'Not always, as your spies must have told you.'

'You ever see him outside the Kit Kat?'

'No.'

'You ever go to his place?'

'No.'

'You see him the night he died?'

She took a deep breath, then exhaled. 'Yes.'

'You arranged to meet?'

'In a manner of speaking. He pushed a note under my door, asking me to join him.'

181

'Alone?'

'That was the implication.'

Quinn sipped his coffee. 'So you went?'

'Yes.'

'Why?'

'He was a pleasant man, handsome, in his way. In fact, he was more than pleasant. I felt a little sorry for him.'

'Any particular reason?'

'He was lonely. Like a lot of men here. He didn't have a wife in Cairo.'

'You take invitations from every lonely man in the city?'

Her mouth tightened. 'He was a neighbour. I knew he was a senior officer. I thought he might be useful. Your high command doesn't go out of its way to make it easy for us photographers—'

'Your husband know about the meeting?'

'That's none of your business.'

'He was in Suez, ma'am?'

'I've told you that.'

'So, Durant was interested in having an affair?'

'It seemed likely.'

'How about you? You got a similar inclination?'

'I don't believe that's any of your business.'

'He make a pass at you?'

'No.'

'You didn't go to his place?'

'No.'

Quinn took out the photograph of Durant's wife and daughters and spun it across the table. 'You know he was married?'

She stared at the picture.

'He ever talk about his daughters?'

'Yes. I mean . . . no.'

'You know he was a father?'

Her eyes were still fixed on the photograph. 'No.'

'It would have made a difference?'

'What do you mean?'

'You'd still have gone to meet him?'

'Your insinuation is offensive, if I may say so.'

Quinn left the photograph where it was. 'What was his mood like? He seem relaxed to you?'

'Not really.'

'Why not?'

'He didn't indicate.'

'What did you guys talk about?'

'The war, Rommel. His progress, our dilemma.'

'What'd he say?'

'The same as everyone else.'

'Which is?'

'Your generals are incompetent. Rommel will win.'

'He say any more than that?'

'Not much. He wasn't spilling secrets, if that's what you're asking.'

Quinn leant forward. 'You thought any more about what I said, ma'am?'

'About what?'

'The girl on Seventh.'

'I understood your story, if that's what you mean.'

'You got nothing you want to tell me?'

'No.'

Quinn took out Cohen's artist impression. He unfolded it and placed it in front of her. 'One of your colleagues drew it,' she said.

'Yeah, but you never saw the guy. And if you did, it wasn't him.'

Her cheeks flushed. 'Are you saying I'm a liar?'

'I think maybe we're missing an opportunity to help each other, that's all.'

'In what way?'

Quinn stared at the blue waters of the pool. 'You work with images, right? I've seen what you do in the darkroom. You cut an image one way, it looks like this, cut it different and it means something else. So, I'm looking at you. I see a girl, German family, comes over from Berlin to Manhattan in 'thirty-two. A Jew, but one who still chooses to go to Casablanca and live under the Nazis—'

'The Vichy French.'

'Same difference. See, you got to look at it from my side. You give me a hint right away you're German. Is that deliberate? I ask myself. And if so, why? I figure you're lying about how well you knew Durant, lying about the man you claim you saw on the stairs, maybe even lying about the guy you say attacked you outside the Kit Kat. So it looks bad, but I also figure you're hurting somewhere. So, I'm thinking, maybe we can cut a deal.'

'You're not so smart, do you know that, Major Quinn?'

'Ma'am, I don't claim to—'

'You can see the images all right, but not the picture that's staring you in the face. When you came down to pick up your wife from the hospital, I watched you and I could see that you just didn't get it.'

'I'm not here to talk about my wife.'

'But hold up. You got a story to illustrate a point, then so have I. You figure she's getting over your tragedy by pouring herself into the lives of all those broken men, and now I've met you, I understand her despair. You think she's running away, but all she's doing is trying to get back to where she was before. She's waiting for you to come in from the cold, and until then, she's just filling in the time. It doesn't make her feel any better and it doesn't make her feel any worse. It isn't hard to work out, Major. Anyone who knows her would tell you the same. It was practically the first thing that woman Marjorie Stubbs told me when I went to the hospital. But you look at the picture and you see something else.'

'That don't change the fact you've been lying.'

'We did come to New York in 'thirty-two. Congratulations. But, sadly for us, we had to go back home. By the time we wanted to leave again, it was too late. I was stuck in Berlin with an ailing father and only one way to get us both out, so I took it.'

'You speak English like an American.'

'We lived there four years. I wasn't deliberately drawing your attention to anything. My father was an engineer with Farben. In better times, they sent him to work in New York. I went to high school in Brooklyn. Then we were told we had to go back to Germany. I was desperate to stay and so was Mother, but Father insisted Berlin was our home.' Amy White stared at her hands. 'By the time she was taken away, it was too late. My father was given a temporary reprieve because he was an "essential worker". I wrote to the only person I thought would be able to help us, and he did.'

She did not need to articulate what had been the *quid pro quo*. 'Where is your father now?' Quinn asked.

'He's still in Lisbon. Old, poor and in ill health. It was where we travelled to when Avril got us out.'

'How was your husband in a position to help?'

'His family is rich. His uncle is a senator. They had many interests in Germany.'

185

'How did you know him?'

'Through my father's business in New York.'

'What is he doing out here?'

'Repairing the family fortune. Or trying to. They lost money at the outbreak of war in Europe. Avril was sent to Casablanca, then here to investigate what opportunities might present themselves in the oil business once hostilities have ceased. It's his chance to prove himself to his father. Other conclusions you can draw for yourself, but I did see a man on the stairs and I'm sorry you find fault with my description. I was not having an affair with Durant and I was assaulted last night outside the Kit Kat. I'm sorry that I did not get a look at the man, but I didn't. It happened very fast.'

'What was he wearing?'

'Something like . . .' She pointed at Quinn's desert jacket.

'He wasn't in uniform?'

'No.' A breeze tugged at the awning above them. 'I need something to eat.' Amy got up and went to the buffet. While she did so, Quinn slipped her water glass into his pocket, careful not to rub away any fingerprints. She came back with a bowl of fruit and, as he looked at it, he felt the first stirrings of hunger. Had he eaten last night? He could not recall. 'Where to next?' he asked, lightening his tone. 'You going back up to the front?'

'They say Alexandria is going to be evacuated tomorrow.'

'First I've heard of it.'

'I thought I'd go take a look.'

'I'm going to leave you to your breakfast.' Quinn stood up. 'I'll need to speak to your husband today.

186

If you see him, you mention it. You can be sure we'll talk again.'

'I can hardly wait.'

Quinn was surprised to find Kate already waiting for him as he came down the steps from the Lido. 'You get anywhere?' he asked.

'I telephoned the hotel in Suez from the clubhouse. He definitely stayed there. He came back yesterday afternoon.'

'They're sure about that?'

'Yes. They checked it while I was waiting. What did she say?'

'That she and Durant weren't screwing.'

'And do you believe her?'

'No.'

Quinn gazed out through the windscreen. He could just see the tops of the Pyramids. He reached into his jacket pocket and removed the glass, wrapped in his handkerchief. He held it up.

Kate could see she was expected to respond. 'It's a glass,' she said. 'I was hoping for a rabbit.'

'A glass with her prints on it.'

Kate raised an eyebrow. 'What are you going to do with it?'

'Take it to Effatt and see if her prints match those his boys found all over Durant's apartment. If we can prove she's lying about how well she knew him, we'll be getting somewhere.'

CHAPTER TWENTY-THREE

Effatt sat at a large mahogany desk, running a finger along his moustache, his face drawn. The room was already buzzing, his men gathered in small groups around trays of coffee and tea. He handed the file he was reading straight to Quinn. 'Don't jump to any conclusions. Take a seat on the balcony,' he said. 'I'll get some coffee.'

The file contained an arrest record. The South African, Jooste, stared out from the attached photograph. They'd pulled him in eighteen months ago on suspicion of receiving stolen pay-books, but there was no record of a charge.

Quinn took the file out to the balcony and sat in one of the wicker chairs.

Effatt arrived with a tray of coffee. 'I thought I'd seen him before. A couple of my plain-clothes officers picked him up. They saw a group of boys pickpocket a soldier in the Khan Khalili and hand over his wallet and identity papers to a man sitting in a nearby café. The officers arrested him, brought him back here for questioning. I looked in for a few minutes, but it didn't seem serious.'

'The file says he was passed into Macleod's custody.'

'They let him make one telephone call. Macleod and Reza arrived to pick him up.'

'Why?'

'They didn't say.'

'What did you do?'

'Nothing. A soldier with some connection to Field Security . . . it was none of our concern.'

'He's been here a while, eighteen months. It's a long time to be dodging uniform branch patrols in the back-streets unless you've got protection.' Quinn dropped the folder onto the table, then pushed it towards Kate. 'A fellow countryman,' he said.

A young boy in a white djellaba brought out two birdcages and hung them at either end of the balcony. Their occupants fluttered and chirped above the distant hum of traffic. Quinn handed the glass to Effatt, still wrapped in his handkerchief. 'That has Amy White's prints on it. Ask your guys to see if they match those in Durant's apartment, especially in the bedroom. You found the *sufragi* yet?'

Effatt took the glass. 'Not yet. We're hunting Durant's as well.'

'I thought he didn't have one.'

'According to the neighbours, he did. Until about a month ago. The man was originally from Alexandria and went home after the captain dispensed with his services. I've alerted the station up there, but we only have a name. How about the husband?'

'Ed's looking for him. You say Durant got rid of his servant a month ago?'

'More or less.'

'Around the time Mrs Markham thinks the broad

came onto the scene.' Quinn contemplated this. 'Kate, you got the office diary?'

She stood up to retrieve it from her bag and handed it to him. Quinn began to read it, sipping his coffee as he turned the pages. It was detailed, but not illuminating. Mostly it listed the meetings Durant had been required to attend. There were many of them: monthly summary meeting, weekly summary meeting, Northern Sector meeting, daily briefing ... and so on. Only Monday afternoons were kept free. Quinn recalled that that was when Durant had gone to concerts on the roof garden of the Continental Hotel. Maybe with Amy White.

Kate was still looking at the South African's file. 'You ever see him about?' he asked her.

'No. Do you think he's significant? To this case, I mean. Obviously, I know about ...' She tailed off awkwardly, didn't want to mention that this might have been the guy driving the car that had killed his son.

'He's a Dutchman,' Quinn said.

'Well, Afrikaner, yes. I guess he must have an English mother or something.'

They were silent. Nobody knew what to say about the prospect of a deserter with links to Macleod. Quinn got to his feet. 'Hell, he's small fry,' he said. 'We ain't got time for a wild-goose chase. Is Ed back at the office?'

'Not yet. I tried just now. He's still out searching for White.'

'Where is the son-of-a-bitch? Look, maybe we can work on why our friend Durant had so many strange connections. We'll go talk to the Greek.'

*　　　*　　　*

Kate went to get the Austin and bring it to the front entrance while Quinn waited for Effatt. Effatt appeared and shoved a brown envelope into his hand. 'What the hell . . .'

Effatt took a few rapid paces, but Quinn caught up and pulled him aside. 'You're out of your mind.' He thrust the envelope hard into the Egyptian's jacket pocket.

'I cannot let you take him, clothe him, feed him . . .'

'We've been through this.'

'The boy is sick, Joe. Think about it. How can I know what will happen? The Germans are coming here.'

'They're hundreds of miles away.'

'But they *will* come, and then what? How long can you fight street by street and house by house? What will be left? You can run. You should run, but I can't leave. What happens if I cannot cross the lines? What if you need to take him away from Jerusalem to somewhere safer? I must contribute what I can. Please accept it.'

'You seen how Mae feels,' Quinn murmured. 'Do it for her.'

'It's not enough. I feel ashamed.'

'Then do it for me.' Quinn took a step closer, shoved the envelope further into Effatt's pocket. 'I need you to stay. Without you, I'm blind.'

'That's not true.'

'It is. How else will I catch this guy?'

Effatt appeared to understand instinctively that Quinn was not referring to Durant's killer. He dipped his head a fraction. 'Is it still so important, Joe?'

'I have to find him, look in his eyes.'

'Why?'

'See if he was drunk. Maybe he—'

'And then what?'

Quinn met his friend's steady gaze. 'I'll figure it out.'

Effatt did not offer a response. He did not need to.

'You'll be there tomorrow?' Quinn asked. 'You coming to say goodbye?'

'No.'

'You sure?'

'It will not help him. I have said goodbye already. He is excited to be with you now, wants to be able to talk to the cop who came all the way from New York.' He sighed. 'Where now? You want to find Kostandis, right?'

'Until we get the husband, yeah.'

The dining room of the National Hotel was a dark, gloomy place, with wooden panels, ornate brass light fittings and a plethora of potted plants. It was redeemed only by the smell of freshly baked croissants. Quinn ordered coffee and Effatt sent a boy from the desk in search of Kostandis.

Their table was behind a pillar. Quinn sat with his back to it, watching the door via a mirror beneath a huge oil painting of Saladin's citadel.

Kostandis entered the room deep in conversation with a companion. 'It's Wheeler,' Kate whispered. The colonel was clearly overwrought, but was too far away for them to be able to make out what he was saying. Kostandis raised his hands helplessly and Wheeler stormed out. Without asking if it was wise, Effatt followed.

Quinn slipped into a seat opposite Kostandis before the Greek had registered his presence. 'Morning, Constantine.'

The Greek sighed. 'It's not if I'm going to have to dine with you.'

Quinn took a croissant from the basket in the centre of the table and began to eat. He and the Greek had history, of the kind cops develop with the flotsam of the criminal class the world over. Deserters were Kostandis' weakness. Perhaps they were more pliable, or more desperate. They heard his name and sought him out, for money, false papers or both. Quinn turned a blind eye to this in return for occasional assistance. Over the past year it had become more than occasional. From the Greek's point of view, it was not a happy compromise. 'You continue to be the most obliging host,' Quinn said.

'What do you want?'

'I'd like to talk about Colonel Wheeler.'

'Who's Wheeler?'

Quinn put down the croissant, pushed aside the plate and leant towards him. 'Don't jerk me off, Constantine.'

Kostandis thrust the linen napkin into the collar of his shirt, spreading its corners across the lapels of his white suit.

'You sleeping with him?' Quinn asked.

'Don't be ridiculous.'

'Then what's he doing here?'

'He came to find me.'

'Why?'

'It was nothing of importance.'

'He sure was expending a lot of nervous energy for a man with nothing of importance to talk about.'

Kostandis sipped his coffee. 'He wanted a discount for a group of people at the Kit Kat.'

'Wheeler doesn't go to the Kit Kat.'

'Well, he wants to now.'

'You got to do better than that, Constantine.'

'I can't tell you, Joe.' Kostandis' expression was earnest, and he'd never used Quinn's Christian name before. 'You can threaten whatever you like, but I can't.'

Quinn frowned at his informant's uncharacteristic reticence. 'You're going to have to give me something.'

'I can't.'

Quinn glanced at the optimistic headline on the *Egyptian Mail* beside him. The censors ensured the city was fed a permanent diet of self-denial. Kostandis toyed with a piece of croissant as he attempted to recover his equilibrium. 'I don't like you much, Quinn, but I have no wish to see you come to an abrupt end.'

'That sure sounds dramatic.'

'Make light of it if you will. But if I were you I would get up and leave now.'

'Why is that?'

'Because if this conversation continues, it might lead to a situation you will regret.'

'That a threat?'

'It's an instinct.' Kostandis wiped a crumb from the corner of his mouth. 'People will always get rich in a war. Good people have their attention on more important matters, which gives the less scrupulous a chance to attend to their future. Look at what is happening out there in the desert and you will see this is truer than ever. Rommel is close. Loyalties are dwindling, dying even. And although you and your British friends still think you rule Cairo, believe me, you barely scratch the surface.'

'You going to give me something more specific?'

'The kind of people who will get rich in this war

are the kind who would not hesitate now to eliminate a troublesome detective who wears his heart on his sleeve and cannot keep his nose out of other people's business. Who would ask the awkward questions after you've gone, Major Quinn? Perhaps you should consider that. The war will be over soon. Why trouble yourself?'

'You going to tell me what Wheeler's doing here?'

'You may see for yourself. I think you'll find him upstairs. But I wouldn't go crashing in. You might get an unpleasant shock.'

'Before I go, tell me about Durant.'

'Now, there's a name to conjure with.'

'We found his body hanging from a tree. They almost cut his head off. I'm told he was a pal of yours.'

Kostandis continued to eat.

'Wheeler was his boss.'

'Was he indeed?' Kostandis chewed slowly. 'I didn't know that. But you are misinformed. Captain Durant and I were acquaintances only, and barely that. I was introduced to him in the club, once, twice at most.'

'Who by?'

'An American couple.'

'The Whites?'

'I believe that is their name.'

'Why'd they introduce you?'

Kostandis shrugged. 'Does there have to be a reason?'

Quinn looked towards the mirror at the far end of the room. He watched the fans spinning languidly overhead. Kostandis was right about one thing. Even if the Germans got here, nothing much would change in places like this: one lot of colonial masters out, another in. Kostandis and his like would cut a new set of deals, learn to speak bedroom German instead of English. Quinn tried to imagine a bunch of Gestapo officers sitting in this restaurant, but it was difficult. It didn't seem right. 'You get the impression Durant and the American girl were lovers?'

'Hmm.' Kostandis pulled over a plate of freshly cut pineapple. 'That's an interesting question.'

Quinn waited.

'Yes. But anxious not to give that impression.'

Kate reappeared and caught Quinn's eye. 'Yes?' he said.

She beckoned to him to step away from the table. 'Wheeler has taken a room upstairs, sir. The soldier arrived a few moments ago. Effatt said it's the deserter, Jooste. He went straight up there.'

CHAPTER TWENTY-FOUR

They waited in silence, listening to the steady scrape of a straw brush in the corridor below them. It stopped, and Quinn pushed himself upright. There was no mistaking the signal. They heard quick, urgent footsteps, then hobnailed boots pounding down the stairs.

As they parted company, Effatt pushed the master key into Quinn's hand. 'Don't lose him,' Quinn said.

The servant started sweeping again, watching them. Quinn hesitated outside Wheeler's room. He nodded at Kate, then turned the key in the lock and pushed the door back. The colonel lay on the bed, frozen with shock, his naked body half covered with a sheet, but it was the mirror that caught Quinn's attention. It ran from floor to ceiling, the length of one wall.

Quinn went to take a closer look, then returned to the corridor, without having acknowledged Wheeler's presence. Kate followed him. The servant was still sweeping, a little too energetically, and the door to the adjoining room was ajar.

The room appeared unoccupied. It was sparsely furnished, with an undisturbed bed and wall-to-ceiling cupboards that stretched the same distance as the mirror next door. Quinn examined them, then pulled open the central section. Inside, he saw two chairs and a camera with a view of Wheeler's bed.

'Hold on to the guy with the brush until Effatt comes back,' he said to Kate, 'and when he does, get a description of who was in here.'

'They were—'

'You bet they were. They must have run for it the second they saw us go into Wheeler's room.' Quinn flicked open the camera. The film compartment was empty. Through the mirror, he could see Wheeler lying on the bed. He had curled up into a ball, his ribs visible through the taut skin on his scrawny back. He was crying softly.

Quinn watched as Wheeler began to rock. As he went back into the man's room, Wheeler covered his face with the sheet. 'Colonel?'

Wheeler did not answer, but the stifled sobs ceased. He removed the sheet from his face, but his eyes remained fixed on the wall by the window. Quinn picked up a chair and sat close. 'You all right, Colonel?'

'I have committed no crime.'

'You know who he was?'

'My private business is none of your—'

In one swift movement, Quinn grabbed the chair and hurled it through the centre of the mirror. Wheeler sat upright and his face registered shock, surprise, disbelief and, finally, horror. He went deathly pale. He tried to stand, tripped, fell to his knees and vomited onto the threadbare carpet by the door.

Quinn scooped up the sheet, dropped it over Wheeler's shoulders. The colonel crouched on the floor, groaning. 'It's all right,' Quinn said, 'we'll work it out.' He wrapped the sheet round Wheeler, helped him up and returned him to the bed. He took a spare pillow and threw it onto the pile of vomit.

Then he retrieved the chair, went to the bathroom and poured a glass of water. He offered it. The colonel was shaking. 'Drink some,' Quinn ordered.

Wheeler pushed himself upright, took a few sips, then sank down again. 'Thank you,' he said. 'Thank you very much.'

Quinn closed the door. He pulled the chair over to the window and together they listened to the traffic far below. 'You been here before?' Quinn asked.

Wheeler shook his head. 'No.'

'You know who he was?'

'He asked me to call him Alan.'

'You pay him?'

'No.'

'Where'd you meet?'

'Groppi's.'

'How long ago?'

'Last week.'

Quinn took out and lit a cigarette, then offered the pack to Wheeler. The colonel accepted gratefully. 'Kostandis introduce you?'

'Yes.'

'You and he ever—'

'No.'

'So what were you guys arguing about downstairs?'

'He wanted to charge an exorbitant rate.'

'For what?'

'This is his suite. Alan suggested we meet here. I telephoned Kostandis and he agreed. This morning he hadn't vacated the room and, when he did, I found a note telling me what he expected me to pay for the privilege. It was outrageous.'

199

'Why did "Alan" want to come here? What'd he tell you?'

'He said he knew it would be ... exciting.' Wheeler's voice was almost inaudible. He pressed his hand to his forehead, cigarette smoke curling through his hair.

'You tell yourself this was the last time?' Quinn asked quietly.

'Yes.'

'You tell yourself that every time?'

'Yes.'

'You knew he was a deserter?'

Wheeler hung his head. 'Yes,' he said heavily.

'You got any idea of his real name?'

'No.'

'You talk about his life in Cairo, what he does, where he goes?'

'Very little.'

Quinn studied him for a moment. Wheeler avoided his glare. 'We picked him up yesterday. On the P64 he showed us, he calls himself Jooste. You ever hear him use that name?'

'No.'

Quinn leant forward. 'OK, Colonel, this is where it gets real interesting and now you've got to help me out. Durant is supposed to pitch up to a meeting in the Berka the night after he dies. When we stake it out, your friend "Alan" turns up. You going to tell me what that's about?'

'I haven't any idea.'

'You telling me it's a coincidence?'

Wheeler's eyes were watery with fear and self-loathing. 'We only talked about his life at home. He said he grew up on a farm in the eastern Transvaal, but his family moved to Johannesburg when he was a teenager.'

'I ain't got no interest in his family history, Colonel. We got a deserter running about the city who don't seem too worried about getting caught so maybe he's got some high-up protection. And he just happens to know both you and Durant.'

'I really can't explain that.'

'I'm trying to help you, Colonel.'

'I know that and I'm grateful,' Wheeler said. 'You can see I am.'

'You aware "Alan" knew Durant?'

'No. I swear it.'

'Durant ever talk about the guy?'

'No, but Captain Durant and I were not close.'

'You met this guy last week, you say?'

'Yes.'

'You done this with him before?'

'You mean . . .?'

'Yes.'

Wheeler shook his head. His shame and misery were almost palpable. 'I'm sorry. What will you do with me?'

Quinn stood up. 'I'm going to find this guy, but I want you to sit here and figure out a way to tell me what's been going on. Maybe then we can keep this to ourselves. Don't go nowhere except the office, then home. Where's your apartment?'

'I live on a houseboat, close to the Kit Kat. Number three . . . just after you turn right off the bridge.'

'Make sure you're there tonight.'

There was a knock on the door. 'Detective Effatt is back, sir,' Kate announced. 'He's speaking to the servant now.'

'Where'd our friend go?'

'To Fishawy's. Effatt's boys are watching him. I've called Ed and asked him to get a few of our men down to help.'

CHAPTER TWENTY-FIVE

Effatt didn't speak until they were in a car driven by one of his constables. 'The South African is in Fishawy's again,' he said, 'as cool as you like, smoking, sipping coffee.'

The driver slammed on his brakes, blasted the horn and hurled a stream of abuse at a battered taxi that had just swerved in front of them. 'What did Wheeler have to say?' Effatt asked.

'Somebody's frightened the life out of him, but I've got a feeling he'll talk.'

The brakes were jammed on again and the driver let loose more invective.

'Effatt, could you ask him to stop that?' Quinn turned to the window. Two Egyptian soldiers in summer uniforms stood guard outside the wrought-iron gates of the Abdin Palace. Their tunics were dazzlingly white, but their tarbooshes were askew and they looked half asleep.

The driver braked, then lurched forward again. Quinn closed his eyes, tried to shut out the heat and aggravation.

*   *   *

A few minutes later, they got out of the car and plunged again into the heart of the Khan Khalili. Men sat in pools of shade, scanning copies of *El Messa* and *El Ahram*, barely raising their eyes to watch the interlopers pass. Effatt ushered them into a store behind Fishawy's, selling water-pipes, tin chandeliers, oil lamps and jewellery. It was so tiny that Quinn and Kate had to sit on benches set into the wooden latticework while Effatt and the owner held an earnest, animated conversation. Evidently they knew one another.

In an alcove opposite, a wizened craftsman was bent over a burnished copper plate. Two men played backgammon, the rattle of their dice just audible above the cacophony of the bazaar.

A boy appeared in the doorway and began talking to Effatt and his friend. They both shook their heads and the lad disappeared again. Effatt hoisted up his trousers. 'He's still there,' he told Quinn. 'Sitting on his own.'

'Let's take a look.'

'Give it a minute.'

Quinn glanced at Kate. Beads of sweat were gathering on her forehead. 'Hot, Mowbray?'

'Kind of you to draw my attention to it, sir.'

The scout returned and whispered in Effatt's ear. Quinn pushed himself to his feet. They followed Effatt and the boy through the kitchen at the rear of Fishawy's. 'He's out front with his back to us,' Effatt said. 'But be careful.'

The air was heavy with the smell of incense, exotic herbs, mint tea and Me'assell tobacco. Shelves were stacked with water-pipes and a stuffed alligator hung on the wall. Fans circled ineffectually overhead. The waiters were noisily rearranging the tables and chairs.

Two women examined a pair of earrings being shown off by a friend.

An old man in a white turban sauntered in and sat down. Without discussion, a waiter produced a pipe and pushed tobacco into the top of it. He returned a few moments later with a tray of hot charcoal.

Quinn edged forwards.

The call to prayer erupted overhead, booming out over the crumbling rooftops, from the Al-Hussein mosque on one side and the Al-Azhar on the other. Jooste stood up and moved off. Quinn felt Effatt's hand on his arm. 'Hold on.'

A few minutes later, the scout materialized from the crowd. Effatt listened to his hushed, urgent report. 'He's gone to the Al-Azhar mosque, met another white man.'

'Get the glass he was drinking from,' Quinn instructed Kate.

Effatt led them out to Al-Hussein Square. As they drew near to the Gate of the Barbers, a flock of birds took flight, momentarily blackening the sky. They joined the flow of men following the muezzin's call. 'You'd better wait here,' Quinn told Kate, as she caught up with them. He had to lean close to her to be heard above the din.

Inside, it was cooler. Effatt consulted with the boy, then slipped off his shoes and led them towards one of the keel arches in the mosque's vast white marble courtyard. 'The men are in the prayer hall,' Effatt whispered. 'He thinks we should not risk to go further.'

They found a place to sit. A crowd of young students glided past silently, then a steady stream of the faithful. Effatt and Quinn attracted a few curious glances. They retreated to a corner.

The scout wandered into the prayer hall and returned a few minutes later. 'They're just whispering, inside the door,' Effatt said. 'Are we going to arrest them as they leave?'

'Let's see where they go, who else they take us to.'

They watched in silence. The courtyard was a peaceful oasis, Cairo a distant presence beyond its intricately carved white walls. Quinn listened to the subdued clamour of the city, stared into the pools of shade creeping across the marble floor. The faithful came in dribs and drabs, wandering from light to shade and back again until they disappeared into the prayer hall on the far side.

Effatt consulted his watch. 'Did you know that Napoleon once mounted a cavalry charge through this courtyard?'

Quinn smiled.

'I don't believe it was considered amusing at the time.' Effatt turned back to face the prayer hall. 'They're coming,' he said, beckoning Quinn towards the shelter of the arch.

The South African was on the left. Beside him was a man in a white linen suit and a straw fedora.

CHAPTER TWENTY-SIX

'You know him?' Effatt asked.

'Avril White, the American woman's husband.'

Quinn started to move, but Effatt held his arm. 'Give them a few seconds to put their shoes on.'

Effatt led again. They were slowed by having to recover their shoes, but they watched the two men climb the steps and walk away, heading for the bazaar.

A tram approached and, at the last minute, the pair ducked in front. 'Effatt,' Quinn whispered. He ran up the steps from the mosque. The tram rattled slowly past. The square beyond was crowded and it took him a minute to locate them. They were still together, walking now in the direction of the Al-Hussein mosque, as if intending to bypass the bazaar on their way to the heart of the old city.

'How many men have you got out here?' Quinn asked.

'Enough.'

'Who have they been told to follow?'

At that moment, the pair split. Avril White kept on walking straight, towards the old city and Bab al-Nasr, and the South African, Jooste, swung sharp left and vanished into one of the alleys that led to the bazaar.

'I'll take the South African,' Quinn said. 'You follow White.'

Quinn began to run. As he turned into the alley, Effatt blew his whistle, long and loud. Without looking over his shoulder, Jooste broke into a run, attracting startled glances.

An Egyptian between Quinn and his quarry took to his heels in pursuit. Clearly one of Effatt's boys, he, too, blew a whistle, but he was not quick enough. In an instant, Quinn was at his shoulder, then past him.

They swung through Fishawy's. Jooste sent a brass coffee-table flying, Quinn caught a water-pipe.

The South African was fast. It was like chasing a rabbit. He swerved from left to right, ducking beneath low-hanging cotton smocks and shirts; at one minute he was visible, the next hidden. Chairs flew, a mound of copper pots tumbled. Unintentionally Quinn ripped a copy of a newspaper from a man's hands, then almost flattened an off-duty soldier trying to buy an inlaid backgammon box.

He reached an arch. Jooste jumped the steps down from it, landing on two women carrying heavy bags. The women struggled to their feet in the scattered debris. Quinn swerved round them. He shouted for someone to stop the man, but the packed alley swallowed his call.

There was a downward incline and he tried to gather speed. The guy was sure on his feet, a natural athlete. They had reached the jewellery section of the bazaar and Quinn sidestepped one intricate stand, only to knock over the next. There were more angry shouts.

He reached a crossroads. 'Which way?' he yelled. No-one answered. The nearest store-owner shrugged. 'Police! Which way?' The man pointed, but Quinn didn't believe him.

Effatt's plain-clothes constable arrived and asked the same urgent question in Arabic. The shop-keeper seemed no more enthused, but this time he pointed to the left.

They followed this course, but after a hundred yards, Quinn realized they'd lost him again. He stopped, eyes scouring the alley for some sign of the man. Sweat was pouring down his face.

He cursed violently.

CHAPTER TWENTY-SEVEN

Avril White sat in the centre of Effatt's office with his back to the door, fanning himself with the straw fedora. The doors to the balcony were shut, the blackout blinds already drawn across the length of the far wall. It was warm, the heavy air beaten by ceiling fans, and quiet, but for the periodic thump of a typewriter's keys. Effatt was talking to the uniformed officer at the duty desk, but he hurried over. He pushed Quinn and Kate back into the corridor, out of sight. 'We pulled White's car over as he turned out of the gate at Bab al-Nasr. I explained we'd been keeping the South African under surveillance and asked if he knew he was a deserter.'

'What'd he say?'

'He denied meeting anyone, claimed he'd gone to the mosque to look around. A man approached, offered to explain its history and act as a guide. He refused, but the conversation continued as he left the mosque.'

'He came without a fight?' Quinn asked.

'I said you'd be grateful for his assistance . . . a grave matter for the conduct of the war and so on. He didn't complain.' Effatt looked at Quinn. 'Don't worry about the other man. We'll find him.'

'We should have arrested him while we had the chance.'

'We'll get him.'

'What if we don't? What if he makes a run for it?'

'I think he will stay around for a while. Why run if you're confident you can get out of any trouble?'

Quinn digested this thought. He watched White, his head still pounding from heat and exertion. 'You spoken to your fingerprint boys?' he asked Effatt.

'Not yet. I'll go down now.'

'Take this glass with you.' Quinn held out his hand to Kate for the coffee glass she'd retrieved from Fishawy's. 'Check this against the fragment you found in Durant's place. Maybe White hired the South African to do his dirty work.'

Quinn went down the corridor to get a glass of water. He drank three, stared out of the window at the traffic passing below, then put the glass back on the shelf and returned. 'Mr White?' He offered his hand. 'We met last night. Joe Quinn.' White stood, shook his hand, then sat down again. 'Thanks for coming in.'

Now that he had the luxury of a little time, Quinn studied White closely. The guy had a square jaw, deep-set, intense blue eyes and jet-black hair combed high on a wide forehead. He was a strong man, muscular and broad. The kind you might expect to object to being brought in and made to wait. His suit and shirt were of the finest cut, but his shoes worn and battered.

'Has your wife recovered?' Quinn asked.

'My wife?'

'From last night.'

'Oh, yes. Thank you.'

211

'Nasty business.'

'Have you found the man?'

'Not yet.' Quinn leant against a desk. 'But we will. You're from Manhattan also? You sound—'

'DC.'

'OK. My father went to Washington once. He liked it. He was only a beat cop from the Bowery, nothing special, but they took him to the White House, made him feel like a hero. He got a whole three sentences out of Calvin Coolidge!'

White looked at him without interest.

Quinn let the silence run. 'Tell me,' he said, 'I'm curious . . . You know the guy in the mosque?'

'No, as I've already explained to your colleague.'

'You never seen him before?'

'No.'

'So you were just looking around?'

'Yes.'

'And he comes up, offers to tell you about it?'

'That's correct. He wouldn't take no for an answer.'

'So what'd he say?'

'About what?'

'The mosque. Did he tell you how old it was? You hear the story about Napoleon?'

White glared at him. 'It hardly matters.'

Quinn took a few paces, then sat on the corner of a desk opposite. 'What took you there on this particular afternoon?'

'I had met someone in the bazaar.'

'At Fishawy's?'

'That's right. The gentleman I was meeting expressed some surprise I had not already visited one of the city's great landmarks. He suggested I do so at once.' White leant forward. 'Now, I wish to be helpful,

212

Major, and if I can give you a closer description of this man or—'

'You were meeting a contact in the bazaar?'

'Yes.'

'Who?'

White stood up and put on his hat. 'I don't see that it's relevant, but it was Signor Fabrizzi. Perhaps you know him.'

'Of course. What were you seeing him about?'

'A private business matter.'

'Sit down, Mr White. I ain't finished yet.'

'I have work to do.'

'So do I. You knew Durant?'

White didn't move. 'I've heard of his unfortunate demise.'

'He was a friend of your wife's, right?'

'An acquaintance.'

'No more than that?'

'No.'

'You never worried they seemed too friendly?'

'Of course not.'

'You think she could have had anything to do with his death?'

'That's a ridiculous suggestion!'

'You know how she got those bruises on her windpipe?'

White didn't flinch. 'I have no idea.'

Quinn stood up again, took a few paces. 'See, Mr White, there's a few things about this I don't get so maybe you can help me out. Last night, when we heard your wife's scream outside the nightclub, you walked up to the barman and ordered a drink, right?'

'I hardly see how that has any relevance.'

'Why not order at the table?'

213

'The waiters seemed distracted.'

'But you weren't?'

'Apparently not.'

'Your wife screams and you—'

'I didn't know it was my wife.'

'Sure, but everyone else in that club is wondering what's going on. Some have already gone out, others are talking about it, looking at the door. But you're ordering yourself a whisky, which you never drank, by the way.'

'Major, this is all fascinating, but I'm afraid I have work to do.'

'You and your wife ain't answering the questions, Mr White.'

'On the contrary, I have tried to be helpful and I'm sure my wife—'

'I catch you out, you'll hang.'

'I shall report that threat to your superiors.'

'It ain't a threat, it's a fact.'

Effatt was at Quinn's shoulder. 'Excuse me,' he said to Avril White. 'Joe, I think you'd better come.'

Quinn hesitated. He stared at White. 'That'll be all,' he said. 'For now.'

In the basement, they marched down a long, unlit corridor. Quinn could just make out a sign on the door saying 'Fingerprint Division' in English. Effatt knocked once, then entered.

A young man sat on a stool, bent over a table, examining a set of fingerprints beneath a single electric lamp. The blackout curtains were drawn across the windows behind him; the atmosphere, like that in the bigger room, was stuffy and close. 'Good evening, Anwar,' Effatt said. 'You recall Major Quinn?'

The boy looked startled. He had a thin face, with a wispy beard and great pools for eyes. 'Yes, of course, sir. Good evening.'

'Tell Major Quinn what you have found,' Effatt said.

The boy blinked.

'Quickly,' Effatt said.

'The prints of the woman, Mrs White, are all over the apartment, sir. Everywhere except the bedroom. That's been thoroughly cleaned. But on the bathroom, by the window, on the chair . . . It's almost as if they were man and wife.'

'Go on,' Effatt instructed.

The boy examined his notes again. 'That's it, apart from your own and Detective Effatt's prints from the search. Obviously I checked those against the green book.'

'Tell him about the fragment of glass,' Effatt said.

The boy breathed in deeply, looked at Quinn. 'That has your print on it, sir.'

'Mine?'

'Yes, sir.'

'But I never touched it.'

They heard a honk from the street below and the distant rattle of a tram. Effatt put a hand on the boy's shoulder, reassured him.

CHAPTER TWENTY-EIGHT

On the balcony upstairs Effatt and Quinn looked out over the rooftops, the city before them a warren of shadowy alleys beneath a shrouded moon. They had sent Kate back to Bab el Hadid to inform Madden of what had happened that afternoon. Quinn had asked her to leave out the matter of the fingerprint on the glass.

Effatt offered Quinn his packet of Camel. They lit up and stood together in silence. A searchlight battery came on, but was just as quickly extinguished. They could hear a man calling for someone and, in the distance, a group of men singing.

'Do you remember touching that glass, Joe?'

'No.'

'Are you sure? You were going through the apartment.'

'I'm certain.'

'Have you ever been there before?'

'Never.'

'Do you know Amy White?'

'I've met her at the hospital waiting to pick up Mae, that's all.'

Quinn turned away from the city and looked, through a narrow slit in the blinds, at Effatt's desk. It was as chaotic as his own. Effatt turned, too. 'I don't like this case,' he said. 'Maybe we should give it to Field Security, after all.'

'It's too late for that.'

'Why? Tell them we've found some things that concern us . . . better for them to deal with it.'

'Then Lewis will want to know why I've changed my mind.'

'He won't care.'

Quinn finished his cigarette and flicked it high into the air over the balcony. He watched it twist in the warm breeze.

'I say now is the time to bow out,' Effatt said.

'Why?'

'Yesterday afternoon it looked simple: a guy hires someone to kill his wife's lover, but now . . . too many questions. Why was Durant going to meet Macleod and that South African? It seems to me that he was involved in something, but do we want to know what it was? We've got enough on our plate, Joe.'

Quinn walked towards the balcony doors. 'I need some time to figure stuff out. I'll walk back to my office. I'll call you when I get there.'

Quinn came down the steps at the front of the station to be confronted by four soldiers, stripped to the waist, digging. They had stacked sandbags in a tight semi-circle and were creating a hole behind them sufficient to give cover to a couple of men. 'What's going on?' Quinn asked.

'Machine-gun post.'

'Here?'

'Yes.'

'Why?'

'Orders.'

The men were covered with dirt and sweat; they looked dog-tired. Quinn saw that Effatt was leaning over the balcony, watching.

He crossed to the other side of the road and walked towards the railway station. A few street urchins danced around him, but he ignored them with such steely rigour that they dropped away. This was a busy road and the cars and trucks chugged past, interspersed with gharries and the occasional tram; the air was heavy with the scent of dung and diesel. Dust caught by the *khamseen* twirled in eddies, dimly illuminated by the moon. Here and there Quinn glimpsed a cooking fire and heard the murmur of voices.

He took the butterfly necklace from his pocket and passed it from one palm to the other and back again, like a set of worry beads. Was it just the girl, or had Durant got himself mixed up in something else?

He reached the railway station. Another group of boys swarmed around him. One held up a scarab, a second a black basilisk head of Rameses the Second. '*Yalla*,' he muttered. Go away. Quinn walked through the dimly lit entrance to the concourse. Lights had been subdued in here also, so that he could only just make out the time on the great white clock. There were no trains waiting. All around, passengers stood by their luggage or sat on it. They looked for the most part like Greeks or Maltese, the kind of residents who'd have no prospect of pulling rank if it came to a crunch.

There was a long queue for the ticket office. Quinn

walked to the front, only to find that it was closed, the door bolted. He nodded at those waiting and knocked, but there was no answer. He tried again, harder this time. No-one attempted to dissuade him or offer an explanation.

He thumped still louder. 'Open up.' He heard a chair being moved, then a bolt pulled back. The entrance swung open and a short, balding European man in a grubby white and red uniform said, 'We're closed.'

'Not any more. Major Quinn, SIB.' He produced his pink identity card. 'Get me a first-class compartment set aside on the morning train to Palestine.'

'Impossible. It's fully booked.'

'I have a prisoner to move. Grade one. Make space.'

'That's still impossible. There was a near riot this morning.' The man gesticulated. He had evidently reached the stage of weariness and exasperation where he no longer felt intimidated by a pink SIB card. 'Some of these people have been waiting since last night. They'll be trying to cram the corridors.'

'What time does the train go?'

'Seven thirty.'

'Get me one first-class compartment. Set it aside or there will be no train to Jerusalem. See what kind of response you get then.'

The man's eyes narrowed in anger, but he did not dare argue.

On the top floor at Bab el Hadid, Reza sat on a desk in the centre of the atrium with his feet on a chair. He was reading a file. Beside him there was a plant, whose fronds rose above his head so that he was almost invisible.

He looked up as Quinn passed, with a lizard's unblinking stare.

The typing pool was empty, but Cohen was still at his desk, head bent over some paperwork, reading by the light of his desk lamp. Kate was leaning against a filing cabinet, flirting with Dexter. The blackout blinds had been drawn and the overhead lights extinguished.

Quinn slipped down the left-hand corridor and into his office. He closed the door, switched on his lamp, hung his jacket on the back of the chair and sat down. He began to flick through Mrs Markham's office diary, which Kate had left in the centre of his desk.

If Durant had got himself caught up in something else, then what in hell was it?

The pages recorded the endless succession of meetings. Cairo Defence Committee group, Delta Subgroup meeting, Northern Sector briefing. Every day was packed except Monday afternoon.

Quinn could see how the prospect of spending Monday afternoons in Amy White's company would be appealing. Had they checked into a room in the Continental? Had the husband found out?

He tapped the edge of the diary. The broad wouldn't talk, the husband wasn't going to give anything away, but there had to be a way in somewhere.

He turned over more pages of the diary, found an entry for a 'garden party in aid of the Army Benevolent Fund' and, two weeks later, 'Choral Evensong at the Cathedral (collection in aid of the Coptic orphanage in Heliopolis)'. He wondered if the Coptic orphanage had been a charitable cause close to Mrs Markham's heart. Three days later, amid further lists of briefings and meetings, she had written 'Mikado; tickets to be sold'.

Quinn wondered why this event had been entered in the office diary and not Durant's own. He bent closer, then reached over to the far corner of the desk and retrieved Durant's personal diary. He turned to the same page, but found no corresponding entry. For whose benefit had it been written?

Quinn sat back in the chair. Who had been selling tickets to *The Mikado*?

The conclusion came to him slowly, but with force.

He stuck his head out of the door. 'Kate?' Dexter and Cohen both turned towards him. He noticed Reza had disappeared. 'Where are Kate and Ed?' Quinn asked them.

'They were around,' Cohen said.

Quinn ran into Madden on the floor below, walking slowly up the stairs. 'I've just delivered the report to Lewis,' Madden said. 'There will be a meeting in the morning and he wanted a "working theory". I wasn't sure exactly what you wanted me to say but—'

'Don't worry about that now. Where's Kate?'

'I've just seen her down in the courtyard. Why?'

'We're going to visit Wheeler.'

'Now?'

'Yes.'

Madden fell in behind him. 'Why?'

Quinn stopped again. 'Because I ain't been smart. Durant is popular with everyone in the office, but we've accepted Wheeler's word for it that they didn't get on. He's said several times that they weren't close. And yet they had a love of music in common. Monday afternoons were kept free of meetings. Was that just for Durant? No, it was so they could *both* go to concerts at the Continental.'

'So—'

'So why was Wheeler lying about how well he knew his colleague?' Quinn said. 'That's the question.'

CHAPTER TWENTY-NINE

Wheeler's houseboat in Zamalek was a stone's throw from the bridge and no more than a hundred yards from the Kit Kat club. Kate pulled up the car beneath a palm and they clambered out.

Most of the houseboats along there had small gardens on the shore, a high hedge shielding them from the road. All except Wheeler's had a light above their entrance.

Wheeler's gate was open. Quinn slipped through it and walked down the steps to the causeway, the waters of the Nile lapping gently against its side.

The houseboat was one of the old double-storey wooden structures; its ancient timbers creaked as Quinn stepped aboard. He saw a gas light burning and ducked to look through a window. There was no sign of Wheeler. In the distance, above the Kit Kat, the spire and dome of the mosque glimmered.

Quinn opened the door and the smell of burning incense greeted him. The downstairs room was a testament to Wheeler's sophisticated tastes. It was furnished with rich red and gold carpets and cushions, brass plates and ornaments arranged along one wall beside an ornate water-pipe. The gramophone took pride of place on the dresser, with a box of records. In the far corner stood an antique Ottoman writing-desk. Wheeler's body was slumped in the chair, head back, neck exposed. His shirt had been stripped back and, in the centre of his bare chest, someone had carved a crude image of Seth, God of Chaos, and scrawled the same Arabic word: 'Liberation'.

The gas lamp hissed, a candle flickered, as if illuminating a macabre play.

Quinn broke the spell and moved forward. He put two fingers against Wheeler's neck. The body was still warm. There were shards of glass on the floor and the faint aroma of whisky and cigarette smoke. Wheeler must have knocked over his glass as he was attacked. On the wall behind the desk a framed poster adver-tised a Cairo Amateur Theatrical Society production of *The Mikado*.

'Don't touch anything,' Quinn ordered.

He looked carefully at Wheeler's face and neck, then at his hands and arms. He lifted a palm and examined the ends of his fingers. For a man, Wheeler had long nails.

'Ed. Find his telephone. Tell Effatt what's happened and get him to come here with his fingerprint guys, a photographer and a couple of detectives. Then inform Lewis, but no-one else.'

'Yes, sir.'

Madden hurried out. A few moments later they heard his soft murmur from outside.

Quinn ran his hands through Wheeler's pockets, but found nothing of substance: a few Egyptian pounds, an almost empty wallet with his identity card inside it, a handkerchief and the stub of a cinema ticket.

He turned his attention to a briefcase on the desk beside him. It was locked, so he searched for something sharp. Kate offered him a knife and he forced it. The case was old and battered, bought from a firm called Symington & Co. in the Burlington Arcade in London. The central space contained a file packed with photographs. Quinn spread them out on the desk.

They looked at them in silence. They'd all been taken in Kostandis' suite at the National Hotel.

Quinn scooped them up, flipped the file shut and handed it to Kate. 'Put this in the car.'

She did as she was asked. Quinn stepped back. He circled slowly. He could see no marks on the body, no obvious bruises or signs of a struggle. The desk was ordered, as befitted a man of Wheeler's temperament, but there was no indication that it had been hastily tidied by a third hand, as they had seen in Durant's kitchen. Quinn peeled back Wheeler's collar, looked at his neck, then took a few paces to the side and examined the angle at which he was sitting.

He glanced round the room. A window was open. He pulled it up further and looked out at the dark waters. Then he walked to a door and stepped out onto the balcony. He moved along to the section by the window, crouched down and flicked his lighter. He held it close to the deck, then ran his finger along it. It seemed to him there was ash here, but it was hard to be certain. He looked in vain for a cigarette stub.

Quinn returned to the main cabin. 'Poor guy,' Kate whispered.

'Yeah.' There was a photograph on the desk of a woman who must have been Wheeler's mother. Quinn placed it face down.

He looked through the rest of the briefcase, found

a roll of English banknotes and counted it: almost a hundred pounds, a huge amount of money. He leant towards the gas lamp and held up one of the notes to examine the print work. It was perfect, much too good to be a forgery. He looked at the others. There was no smudging and each note had a different serial number. 'Hmm,' he said. He held the first over the light again, just to be sure.

'What is it?' Kate asked.

Quinn folded the notes, slipped them into his pocket. 'Why has he got so much English money?'

Sterling pound notes were legal currency, but accepted only by the largest hotels and clubs. Most visitors to Cairo changed anything they'd brought with them into Egyptian pounds. 'Perhaps someone sent it from England,' Kate said.

'Maybe.' But it wasn't convincing. Not now that all mail had to go by sea via the Cape and therefore took for ever to arrive. Madden slipped back into the room. 'It seems strange he didn't fight more,' Kate said. 'Apart from the broken glass, everything is so orderly.'

'He must have known his attacker,' Madden said. 'How else could the man have got so close to Wheeler while he was sitting at his desk?'

'You figure he was entertaining someone?' Quinn asked.

'It seems likely.'

'There's no ashtray and only one glass, but maybe the killer threw the rest out of the window into the river.'

Quinn searched the drawers of the desk. He found bank statements and a bundle of letters. Hidden among them was a single document from the office. It was headed, 'Arms delivery to 7th Armoured

Division in area of Gerawla'. It listed in detail the contents of a convoy being sent up to the desert to resupply the 7th Armoured Division and elements of the 1st Armoured Division near Sidi Barrari.

He read through it, then handed it to Madden. 'Why would he have this here?' Madden asked, after he'd cast an eye over it.

'Check it out with the citadel. See where the convoy originated from and find out whether there was anything unusual about it, if it got through OK.'

Quinn continued his search of the desk. There was no diary or address book. He put the papers in a pile on the edge of the desk. There were no other photographs in the room, but the walls and sideboards had been adorned with care. In the alcove beside the gramophone sat a sculpture of a naked man.

Quinn examined Wheeler's records. The colonel had possessed a large selection, a mixture of classical and jazz. Quinn ducked through a low doorway and climbed the narrow spiral staircase to the floor above, the wooden struts creaking loudly. This was a smaller room, with a giant bed, the mattress covered with a white cotton bedspread. Along each side wooden blinds concealed tall windows. Quinn opened the blinds, sat on the bed and looked out over the river.

A group of street urchins leant over Zamalek Bridge, just visible in the moonlight. They were dropping something into the water below. Quinn heard them shriek with laughter. It was an elegant setting. Peaceful to the point of serene. Even the air seemed cooler than it was on the shore.

Quinn went downstairs and turned on the radio, which was tuned to the BBC in London, the measured tone of its presenter cutting through the static of the airwaves.

'In Washington, the President's closest adviser, Harry Hopkins, has said again that America's aim remains the maximum concentration of power against the Nazi threat. If necessary, Mr Hopkins said, second, third and fourth fronts will be opened. America is not training three million troops to play tiddly-winks with Germany . . .'

Quinn switched it off. 'Fact is, I figure Wheeler was scared half to death something was going to happen to him and yet he ain't suspicious of this guy.'

'It was someone he trusted,' Madden suggested. 'A friend.'

'The colonel has skin under his nails where he scrabbled at the wire. Reaching for that glass was his final act. He ain't suspicious even in the moment before it happened.'

They heard footsteps, then the boat rocked violently. Lewis came through the door, Macleod half a step behind. Reza was with them. 'Christ,' Lewis said.

For a few moments, no-one moved. Suddenly the room felt crowded. Macleod stepped forward and looked at Wheeler. He examined the wounds to his neck and chest, just as Quinn had. He checked the angle of the body, turned to the briefcase. 'Did you do this?' he asked, pointing to the broken lock.

'Yeah.'

'What was inside?'

'Pictures.'

'Of what?'

'Wheeler being fucked.'

Quinn watched the faces of the men opposite. Only Lewis appeared to show any sign of revulsion at the sprawling mess in front of him. 'Taken by whom?' Macleod asked.

'It didn't give a name.'

'Where are they?'

'In the car.'

Macleod turned to Reza and nodded to indicate he should fetch them. 'Christ,' Lewis said again. 'We'll have to tell London.' His comments were directed at Macleod, as though they were alone in the room.

The Scot's face was like granite. Lewis lit a cigarette, sucked smoke deep into his lungs. This seemed to steady him. He recovered his composure. 'So what happened?' he asked Quinn.

'Wheeler had a visitor. They had a drink, then the killer wrapped wire round his neck.'

'A man?'

'Yeah.'

'Someone he knew?'

'Seems like it.'

Reza reappeared, clutching the file in his long fingers. Macleod took it, glanced at the pictures, expressionless. He handed the file to Lewis. 'Good God,' Lewis rasped.

'Who is the wretched fellow?'

'He's a deserter. You seen him before?'

The question was directed at Macleod and Reza, who shook their heads. 'How do you know he's a deserter?' Lewis asked.

'Wheeler told me. Went by the name of Alan Jooste. You ain't ever had contact with him?'

'I've never seen him before in my life,' Macleod said.

'He was being blackmailed?' Lewis asked Quinn.

'Looks like it, but not by the killer.'

'Why do you say that?'

'The file was in the briefcase. It ain't likely the guy would leave that kind of lead behind.'

Lewis looked at Quinn. He had recovered himself now and was growing discomforted and angry. 'You know what this is going to do, don't you?'

'Do to what?'

'All of us. I took the line about this macabre image, the god of goddamned whatever, out of the original report I sent up to the chief so that you could have your case. Now look!' He grunted. 'This time there will be no choice but to put in every grisly detail. I'll also have to inform them of what we left out. You said it couldn't possibly have been an assassination. But now look—'

'It wasn't, and this ain't either.'

'So what shall I put in my report? It's a love triangle with a supremely bizarre twist?'

'Put what you want.'

'You're on very shaky ground, Major Quinn. I'd advise you to be careful what you say.'

Quinn held his tongue. Both Reza and Macleod were staring at him. Effatt and his detectives came across the causeway, but held back in the corridor. 'Perhaps you'd like to give me something I *can* report?' Lewis asked. 'I'm making the assumption you accept the two murders are connected?'

'Yeah, unless they've been made to seem that way.'

'Why would anyone do that?'

'Someone wants to kill Wheeler, knows this way we'll be confused as to the motive.'

'So what are you going to do about it?'

'We've got to find the connection. Why did Durant die first? What's the real link between him and Wheeler?'

'How long will it take?'

'We'll crack it in a week.'

'We haven't got that long.' Lewis took a pace, then stopped. 'And I want to know everything there is to know about the God of Chaos. If this isn't some Gyppo set-up, I'll eat my hat. And talk to Alastair about it. Kindly remember we're all playing for the same team.'

Lewis glanced at Wheeler a last time. His gaze lingered, then he turned away. Effatt and his detectives slipped into a corner of the room as he stalked past, but neither Macleod nor Reza appeared in any hurry to leave.

The Scot made no move to inspect anything. 'I'd like a copy of your preliminary report when it's done,' he said.

'Sure.'

'I'll have some of my boys look into this symbol. See if we can turn anything up.'

'Good.'

He moved to the door, then stopped. 'One other thing. What nationality is your wife, Major Quinn?' he asked. 'She's American?'

'What—'

'Evacuation plans, for those staying until the last minute.'

Quinn met Reza's unblinking stare, then looked back at Macleod. 'My wife is American, yes.'

'Born in the United States?'

'Born in Cairo.'

'To American parents?'

'Yes.'

Macleod nodded. 'Are there any other details of this case we should be informed of?'

'Such as?'

'No obvious suspect for Durant's murder?'

'Not one I'd want to go in a report.'

'No fingerprints found at the scene?'

Quinn hesitated. 'We're looking at a few things.'

'Nothing you want to make us aware of?'

'Not right this minute.'

Macleod walked out onto the deck and down the plank to the shore.

CHAPTER THIRTY

Effatt's eyes were red, with deep bags beneath them, but he appeared determined to try to shield his private suffering from everyone, including Quinn. 'There must be a *sufragi*,' he said. 'I'll tell them to go to the neighbours, see where he is, ask if they saw anyone come or go. Do you have any ideas?'

'Not at the moment.'

Quinn listened as Effatt instructed his fingerprint boy and photographer. The two men nodded respectfully, then began their work. Quinn watched the photographer line up a shot. The man checked they were all prepared for the flash, then triggered it.

'Anywhere in particular for prints?' Effatt asked.

'No. He's not going to find any. Try down here first, then go upstairs.'

Quinn went out onto the deck. He could just make out the distinctive shape of an egret sitting in a mimosa tree on the bank, its body silhouetted by the moon. The street urchins were still on the bridge, but as he watched, they moved in his direction, turning down towards the Kit Kat.

Quinn walked to the stern of the boat. The lights

of the Kit Kat cast a barely discernible flicker on the smooth surface of the river. Here, reeds between the boat and the shore rustled gently in the breeze. He looked up at the entrance to Wheeler's garden. A large banyan tree hung over it, creating a deep pool of shadow. He went back to the shore and climbed up to the gate. Two pots stood at either side of it, their plants well tended and watered. Indeed, the garden was immaculate. He noticed a light fitting, searched for a switch, but could not find one. He tapped the glass shade, saw there was no bulb inside. The street urchins were at the gate now. '*Baksheesh, baksheesh,*' they demanded.

'*Imshi,*' Quinn instructed. '*Yalla.*'

They didn't obey. They appeared curious, talking among themselves and pointing. Quinn tried to get a better look at the light. He put up his arm. A tall man could just reach it.

He stood there, trying to ignore the boys, then returned to the cabin. On his way, he found a light switch just inside the door and switched it on and off. It did not appear to illuminate anything else, so he assumed it must be connected to the lamp above the gate.

Effatt, Madden and Kate were waiting for him. They seemed dejected. 'OK,' he said. 'We're all tired. I have to see my wife onto a train to Palestine at seven thirty tomorrow so we'll meet at eight, go over this and split up what we need to do. Ed writes up a report, I'll deal with Lewis. Effatt?' Quinn indicated that he wished to speak to his friend outside. He took the Egyptian back across the causeway and up to the gate. He pointed at the light.

'What about it?' Effatt asked.

'Somebody took the bulb.'

'Maybe it was broken.'

'And not replaced? Take a look around. Wheeler is a particular man. I figure someone took it out and threw it in the river.'

'Why?'

'Maybe the killer didn't want anyone to get a look at him.'

Effatt looked out of the gate, then up at the light. 'Wheeler would have noticed someone removing it.'

'Why? He has a record playing, light on in the house. You can't see his desk from the bottom there. I noticed that as I came in. Let's say there are two of them. One goes ahead, talks to him, another quietly removes the bulb to make sure they can leave in the shadows.'

Effatt didn't look convinced. 'Why not just turn it off?'

'Because there isn't a switch here and they didn't know where it was.'

'It's an unnecessary precaution.'

'As it turns out, maybe. But how could they have been confident they'd kill him so clean – and quiet? What if he'd shouted, or struggled more?'

'But who could have seen them leave?'

Quinn stepped out of the gate. It was true that the entrance was not overlooked. The houses opposite were set too far back. 'Those boys are always here. Up by the bridge, down at the Kit Kat. *Baksheesh, baksheesh . . .*'

Effatt looked down towards the nightclub. The boys were indeed hanging around its entrance. 'Maybe,' he said. 'I'll get one of my men to have a talk with them.' He faced Quinn again.

'Old man, get some rest,' Quinn said.

'Rest? Impossible.'

Quinn glanced back at the houseboat. He could see Madden and Kate waiting in the doorway. 'Have you changed your mind?' he asked Effatt, quietly.

'About what?'

'The morning, saying goodbye.'

'No. Yes. Maybe. I don't know. I cannot bear to think of it.'

'The train leaves at seven thirty. I've had a first-class compartment set aside.'

'Thank you.'

Quinn moved a step closer. 'Tonight, if you need to come around . . . any time . . .'

'I understand.'

At the Military Police barracks on Bab el Hadid, there were four messages for Quinn to call home. Usually Mae only ever left one, two at most. Quinn pulled over the telephone and asked the operator to connect him. 'Hello?'

'Mae, it's me.'

'Oh, Joe . . .' She didn't sound herself.

'You all right?' he asked.

'I've been calling you.'

'I know. I'm sorry.'

'Where've you been?'

'Just working,' he said.

'Will you be home soon?'

Quinn had been about to offer a platitude. 'Is something wrong?' he asked instead.

'I don't know. I'll tell you when you're here.'

When they arrived at the apartment, a car was parked on the opposite side of the road, engine running. It moved off as Kate pulled up. They watched it go in a cloud of dust. In the short time since they'd returned from Wheeler's houseboat, the wind had got up, slicing through a velvet night and worrying away at doors and windows, unnerving in its force and persistence. Quinn pushed open his door. 'I'll make my own way to the office,' he told Kate.

'You're going back tonight?'

'Yes.'

'I'll wait for you.'

'There's no need. You should get some rest.'

'I'll wait.'

'I'll be fine.'

'I know you'll be fine, but I said I'd wait.'

Quinn ducked out against the wind, walked with head bent and eyes almost shut against the tiny grains of sand that whipped across his face, working themselves up his nostrils and into the corners of his eyes. He fumbled for the gate, walked through the tiny garden.

As he stepped into the hallway, Fraser leapt from a chair, knocking his solar topi onto the floor. 'Major Quinn!'

'Easy, Fraser.'

'Good evening, sir. I've been sitting here ever since I heard. You know, just keeping an eye . . .'

'Heard about what?'

'About the car, sir.'

'What car?'

'Oh, you haven't heard? There was a car outside. Mrs Quinn felt the men in it were . . . well, watching your apartment. There was a filthy-looking Egyptian blighter, small and wiry with marked skin like a snake.'

Quinn stopped. 'What was he doing?'

'Just standing there. Your wife went out in the car briefly and she said they followed her.'

'You speak to the guy?'

'Yes. There was a European fellow as well. I asked them what the devil they thought they were doing. They said they were on security business.'

'They show you any ID?'

'The Egyptian did. A pink card, like your own. SIB, he said. Field Security. He was a very surly fellow.'

'Thank you, Fraser.'

'What's it about, sir?'

'Nothing.'

Quinn turned the lock and pushed open his door, then shut it against a gust of wind that blasted sand into the hallway and sent it skidding into all the rooms running off it.

'Joe?'

'Yeah.' Now that he was inside, Quinn could hear the lively, upbeat sound of Benny Goodman's band.

'Joe, is that you?'

'Yeah.'

He walked slowly to the living room. Mae was seated on the rattan sofa, writing in her leatherbound diary on her lap. She closed it, placed it on the side. She wore a pretty floral dress. She had washed her hair, put on makeup. 'Is the car still there?' she asked.

'No. It's gone.'

'Did Fraser tell you about it?'

'Yeah.'

'What were they doing?'

'I don't know.'

'Who were they?'

'Security people.'

Mae looked at him. 'The Scottish guy?'

238

Quinn didn't answer.

'Is this because of what you're doing, Joe? Is it because you're still searching for the driver?'

'I don't know.'

'But this man Macleod is protecting him, isn't that your theory?'

'It's not a theory.'

'So what are they doing waiting outside our apartment?'

Quinn debated whether to tell her a little more about what had happened to Durant.

A sudden gust of wind hammered the window. They heard Rifat cough. At first, the sound was muffled, but as the fit escalated it grew louder and more wrenching. Mae grimaced. 'He must go tomorrow, Joe. I tried to take him to the zoo this afternoon, but we only got to the end of the road. Too many more days and he'll be dead.'

'I'm aware of that.'

'I hope you are. If we don't get on our way tomorrow, I'll never forgive you.'

Another violent gust of wind rattled all the windows in the apartment. Rifat coughed again. Quinn went to his door, knocked and looked in. Deena knelt on the floor beside him with a metal bowl. He was bent over it, a few bubbles of blood dribbling from the corner of his mouth. Both aunt and nephew looked up, too absorbed in their pain to do more than acknowledge his presence. Quinn withdrew. He stood with his back to Mae. Hassan was by the kitchen door.

'Will you stay tonight?' Mae asked.

'I'll be home later.'

'What happens if we can't get on the train tomorrow?'

'You will.'

'Somebody at the hospital suggested we drive to Alexandria and get a boat across to Haifa. They say there are lots of Greeks who'll make the trip for a fee.'

'That's not practical.'

'The sea air would be better for him than all the dust.'

'Alexandria is about to fall.'

Mae's eyes were fixed upon his. 'It wouldn't hurt to talk to him.'

Quinn did not answer.

'All right, Joe. I won't ask you to get involved any more, but make sure it works.'

CHAPTER THIRTY-ONE

The sandstorm had receded as swiftly as it had come upon them, tiny cyclones whipping around Quinn's feet as he trudged back to the car. Kate was asleep inside it, head resting against the window. As Quinn got in, she pushed herself upright, rubbed her eyes. 'Everything all right?'

'You should have gone. I could have driven myself to the office.'

'I'm fine.'

'You're a driver, not a slave.'

'I'm also an adult. I said I'd wait, so it's fine.'

Quinn watched the shifting patterns of sand across the windscreen. Headlights appeared in the distance, flickered towards them. The car didn't slow as it passed. 'Where to?' Kate asked.

Quinn stared dead ahead.

'Are you sure you're all right?'

'Define all right.'

'Well, I'm probably the wrong person to ask. Is it something you want to talk about?'

'No.'

'Sometimes it can lighten the burden.'

'Not this time.'

Kate tapped the steering-wheel. 'If it's any use, the one thing I learnt for sure was that, sooner or later, everyone has to let go. The only alternative is a descent into madness. I've seen it happen. I'd hate to see it happen to you.'

Quinn sat in silence. Several times he was on the point of saying something, but drew back. 'One person's grief is forgiving,' he said, 'another's is angry. There ain't nothing that can be done.'

'But either way it's a lifelong companion,' Kate said.

'That the wisdom of youth?'

'It's that of a chaplain's daughter.' She glanced at him. 'My father is a good man, for all his faults. I've seen him help a lot of people.'

'You mean you've seen God help a lot of people.'

'I mean faith.' Kate's manner was stiff, as if he had offered a personal criticism. 'There's nothing wrong with believing in something – in God, in family, in country. Where would you like to go? Back to the office?'

'No.'

'More work?'

'Sure.'

'Is that the answer?'

'There isn't an answer.'

She looked as if she wanted to contradict him, but evidently thought better of it. 'Are they leaving in the morning?'

'Who?'

'Your wife and Effatt's boy.'

'Yeah.'

'That's a good thing, isn't it?'

'Yes.'

242

She reached for the key. 'Where to, sir?'

'The Kit Kat.'

They drove in silence until they reached Zamalek Bridge. As they crossed it, they saw lights ablaze inside Wheeler's houseboat. Quinn put his hand on Kate's arm. 'Pull up here,' he said. He wondered what Effatt's men were still doing inside.

He wandered across the bridge and stood beneath the shade of a eucalyptus tree a short distance from the gate to Wheeler's garden. From here, he had a clear view over a low section of the hedge. There were four or five men inside. And they were tearing the place apart.

Upstairs, he could see Macleod and Sorrenson, another of his deputies, with several others down below. Reza stood by the gangplank, surveying the shore. Quinn was careful to keep himself out of view.

Macleod and Sorrenson heaved Wheeler's bed up against the window. The Scot had a knife in his hand and, by the light of a gas lamp, Quinn saw him carve a slit in the side of the mattress and pull out the stuffing.

'What are they doing?' Kate whispered.

Quinn turned, put a finger to his lips and pointed at Reza standing below them.

They watched in silence. Macleod and Sorrenson disappeared, as though searching the floor, then straightened again. Quinn watched the Scot look along the wall of Wheeler's bedroom. He worked across it methodically with his fingers, searching for a hidden safe or panel.

Whether he sensed movement or not, Reza shifted on his feet and took a few paces forward to the bottom of the gangplank. Quinn and Kate slipped away.

The Kit Kat was as raucous as it had been soothing the previous night, the hushed, soft tones of the Hungarian jazz singer replaced by a familiar but discordant cacophony. In the centre of the stage, the city's leading belly-dancer, Hekmat Fahmy, was shuddering through her portrayal of a woman in orgasm. The noise, the sight of her glittering costume, the glowing candles and the hazy, heavy air momentarily disoriented Quinn and Kate so that they lingered in the doorway.

Quinn's eyes were drawn to a corner table where Amy White sat on her own. There was no sign of her husband.

They took their seats at the bar and nodded at Mac, who was serving an elderly man in a fawn suit. He did not hurry. Kostandis was in his usual place. He had no companion tonight.

Kate tried to blink away fatigue. She looked at her watch.

'You want to go home, Mowbray?'

'I'm sorry, sir. I couldn't get to sleep last night for thinking.'

'I'll have a drink, find my own way back.'

'Are you sure?'

'I'm a big fella.'

'That's what I'm worried about.' She slipped off the stool, cast a glance over her shoulder at Amy White. 'Will you be all right?' she asked.

'I figure.'

'I mean, whatever's going on, you won't go back to Wheeler's houseboat tonight, will you?'

'Not tonight, no.'

'I . . .' She bit her lip. 'Just watching what they were doing at Wheeler's place, do you think they knew about Durant's death before we did, sir? That was why his apartment was in such a state?'

'Yes.'

'I see. You won't go back there tonight, though?'

'No.'

Kate tried to smile. 'I don't trust you on your own.' She appeared reluctant to move.

'You got something else, Kate?' he asked.

'No, it's just . . . Is everything all right in the office?'

'In what way?'

'I mean, I know Major Macleod has his hands full with all the protests and rumours of uprisings and all the rest of it. I'm just not sure I understand why he seems to want to be so involved in this.'

'Let's sleep on it,' Quinn said.

She turned and walked out. Mac broke off his conversation. He wiped the long wooden bar, working his way down it. 'What will you have, Mr Quinn?'

'Bourbon. Straight. On the rocks.'

Mac dropped the ice into a glass, poured the whisky. They watched Hekmat finish her performance to thunderous applause. The tables close to the stage were packed with officers who clamoured for her attention. She came down, sat on a man's knee. There were jealous cat-calls from the others. Mac leant forward, resting his elbows on the bar.

'What can you tell me about Seth, God of Chaos?'

Mac didn't blink. 'You're suddenly interested in ancient history, Mr Quinn?'

Mac never used Quinn's army rank, a hangover from the early days when Quinn had worked

245

alongside Effatt as a city cop. 'Maybe. His image was carved on the dead officer.'

'I heard you've got two.'

'There was also a word, "Liberation". Effatt says it was used by some underground resistance group before the war. Mean anything to you?'

Mac pulled open a drawer in front of him, rummaged around. He took out a thin box of matches, lobbed it across the counter at Quinn. On the front was the distinctive image of Seth, God of Chaos.

A waiter had approached the other end of the bar and was waiting to order a cocktail. Mac slid away, leaving Quinn to contemplate his glass. He looked at it, swirled the liquid and drank. Mac returned. 'I need to speak to Kostandis,' Quinn said. 'Ask him to join me at the bar. We can't talk about anything over there.'

Mac glanced at the nightclub's owner. He refilled Quinn's glass, then caught the eye of a waiter, whispered in his ear. Hekmat Fahmy had returned to the dance floor. Amy White was still on her own.

A few minutes later, after Quinn had downed another whisky and his glass had been replenished, Kostandis placed his heavy bulk on the stool beside him. He looked uncomfortable, sweaty, his neatly pressed linen suit stained at the lapels. He didn't proffer a greeting or a smile. 'What do you want?' he asked grumpily. The band was playing louder, Hekmat working towards a crescendo again. It was hard to hear.

'Who set Wheeler up?' Quinn asked.

'The man he was with.'

'You know him?'

'In a manner of speaking.'

Kostandis looked into the mirror. His own reflection was just visible through the steam, and he seemed to be contemplating it. 'Since I know deserters are your game, I figure you seduced the guy,' Quinn said. 'How long ago?'

'Six or seven months. And it was the other way round.'

'He came looking for you?'

'Well, he came in here.'

Kostandis lit a cigarette and smoked it, his bony, beaky nose appearing vast in profile in the half-light. This was not his war, his demeanour suggested. His family had been luminaries of the Cairo scene for decades, although, like most Greeks who'd chosen to make their lives here, his spiritual home was Alexandria. Kostandis still disappeared up there for weeks on end, usually in the summer. But not this year. The Germans were too close.

'Wheeler's dead,' Quinn said.

'I know.'

'You're filled with remorse?'

'Naturally.'

'Tell me what happened.'

Kostandis sighed heavily. He waved at Mac, who refilled their glasses. 'The South African came in here last night. He wanted the room.'

'How did he know about the camera?'

'None of your business,' Kostandis growled. His face had reddened.

'You had photographs taken of the two of you together?'

Kostandis did not answer.

'And he told you he was going to fuck Wheeler, wanted pictures?'

'He said an army officer would be looking for me, asking to use the suite.'

'So you knew it was a set-up?'

'Why should I have known?' Kostandis spat, sweat gathering on his brow.

'Is it the South African who scares you, Constantine, or someone else?'

'I don't like him. He's too rough, even for me. He has narrow eyes, like a wolf. But we both know he is not important.' Kostandis looked into the mirror, dragging hard on his cigarette.

'You figure he works for Macleod?'

'I'm not going to comment on that. I don't know and I don't want to, and neither should you. He said he wanted to photograph himself and this man, Wheeler. The colonel would ask to use the suite, pay for it. How was I to know what it was for? Maybe the man was too embarrassed to say he wanted pictures of himself being fucked. I don't know. Not my business.'

'How long do you think they'd known one another?'

'I've no idea.'

'What was your impression?'

'I didn't form one.'

'A week, a month?'

'Longer than that.'

'This guy works for Macleod, what does he do for him?'

'I said I'm not going to comment.'

'We know he's been running around town under Macleod's protection. Maybe there's some legitimate reason.'

'You can ask in a hundred different ways, Major, but I'm not going to give you an answer.'

'You want me to make it difficult for you, Constantine? You want me to put the pinch on?'

248

'I'm not going to tangle with Macleod and that's final.'

'If we can find the South African, we'll make it worth your while.'

'Why are you interested in him? He's small beer.'

'To you, maybe.'

They heard the distant drone of an air-raid siren. The music slowed, then stopped. The siren grew louder as it was sounded in other parts of the city. Quinn made out the pop-pop of anti-aircraft guns. He slipped from his stool, strode out of the club, Kostandis and some officers following. They gathered in the road outside, by the swaying palms, gazing up at the bright night sky. The lights of the supposedly blacked-out city stretched in front of them: the easiest of easy targets. They heard another thud, saw the flash, as the anti-aircraft guns in Ezbekieh Gardens opened up on an empty sky. A searchlight snapped on and swung wildly through the darkness.

Quinn glanced over his shoulder, saw Amy White standing by the door, head tilted towards the sky, as if she were watching fireworks. She caught his eye, held it. In the distance, they heard the rumble of an aircraft's engines, maybe two. Quinn peered into the sky, but could see nothing. A few moments later, the officer next to him pointed into the middle distance. 'There,' he told a companion.

Sure enough, two dark shapes came into view, the rumble of their engines trailing. They moved fast and came in low. Quinn waited, the crowd around him quiet. The guns in the city opened up again, the bombers dropped their load, white paper spreading across the sky and falling like big flakes of snow. The planes passed overhead, then were gone.

'It's Christmas,' she whispered.

Quinn whirled round. She was close to him, her eyes on his. She had a white silk scarf tied loosely around her neck. Her cheeks crinkled and the corners of her mouth curved in a smile. 'You want to get away from here?' she asked. 'While I'm not being watched?'

'Where to?'

'Anywhere.'

Quinn glanced over his shoulder. The others had slipped back into the nightclub. 'All right,' he said.

They did not move.

'Wait a moment, Joe.'

CHAPTER THIRTY-TWO

Quinn watched her glide back into the nightclub. He waved a cab over, issued a curt instruction to its driver. He waited. A minute passed, then two. He wondered if she had changed her mind.

She was at his side again, her white dress shimmering in the moonlight. She slipped into the cab and told the driver to take them to the Mena House at Giza.

The taxi rattled through the night, her long body pressed lightly against his. Quinn held his silence and watched the crumbling buildings grow smaller until they petered out altogether.

The driver bumped down a dirt track to the Mena House Hotel, which rose like an oasis from the desert, a tall palm swaying alongside its fortress-like tower. They clambered out, but instead of entering the hotel, Amy walked on up the dusty road towards the Great Pyramid of Cheops. It seemed still more immense in darkness.

Quinn tried to help her onto the first ledge, but she batted away his assistance and hitched her dress almost to her waist to reveal long, slim legs. The local

Bedus caught sight of them, charged over, shouting in Arabic – climbing up without a guide was forbidden – but Quinn and Amy ignored them, kept going, and soon their protests faded.

Amy was fit and Quinn struggled to keep up, his breathing ragged. 'Come on,' she said, over her shoulder. 'What are you waiting for?'

It was a long climb and they had to swing themselves bodily over each stone. They halted once or twice, but neither spoke.

And then they were at the top, standing on a large square stone platform, the apex of the Pyramid itself long since removed to be used in other buildings. They strolled to the edge, looked down at the patchwork of lights that stretched into the distance. 'My God,' she said. 'It feels like the top of the world.'

'You been here before?'

'Never. And you?'

'Only once.'

Quinn walked to the middle, looked out over the head of the Sphinx to the vast nothingness of the desert beyond. The top of the Pyramid was like a dance floor, about twelve feet square. Amy was beside him.

He did not move.

Her eyes were locked on his, the skin on her neck smooth as silk in the moonlight. A temperate breeze tugged at the strands of her hair. She went to the edge of the square and sat, facing the patchwork of lights. 'It would be a perfect place to watch a bombing run,' she said. 'Do you think they come straight overhead?'

'Cairo's never been bombed.'

'But it's only a matter of time now, isn't it? Why aren't you enforcing the blackout?'

'The pilots follow the course of the Nile so it wouldn't make much difference.'

'What were they dropping tonight? Confetti?'

Quinn went to the edge, sat beside her. 'Propaganda. Counterfeit Egyptian pound notes with a message on the back – these will be worthless in a few days' time.'

Amy stared into the darkness. She tapped her heels against the stone. 'How long do you think it took them to build it?'

'This Pyramid took twenty thousand men thirty years. They calculate that a stone must have been laid every two minutes for the whole of Cheops's life.'

'And who was Cheops?'

'They say he was a monster, who was so greedy he sold his daughter's sexual favours – a one-ton stone for every trick. That's her tomb there.'

'How do you know that?'

'My wife was a curator at the Metropolitan back home. This used to be her passion.'

Amy sat forward, placed her hands on her lap. 'Did you give her the photographs?' she asked.

'No.'

'Why not?'

'Does it matter?'

'How is the boy?'

'He's fine.'

'Are they going to Palestine?'

'Yeah.'

'When?'

'Tomorrow.'

'And you'll stay on alone?'

'I guess so.' He waited for her to explain why he'd been invited here, but she seemed content to absorb the night in silence. 'I thought you were going to Alexandria,' he said.

'My correspondent spent the day fighting with the censors. He says he won't risk his neck unless he gets to print the truth.'

'So you're staying?'

'No. He'll calm down and we'll go up to the front. If not, I'll drive up on my own. I bet if I start early enough I can make it there and back in a day.'

Quinn took the end of the silk scarf and unwound it until the bruises and red welt on her neck were revealed. She made no move to stop him. He touched the skin on one side of her throat, then the other. 'You were in love with Durant?' he asked.

'No.'

'He in love with you?'

'It's possible.'

'You had an affair?'

'Not an affair.'

'But you—'

'Once or twice.'

'Your husband find out?'

There was another long pause. 'Yes.'

Quinn wrapped the scarf carefully round her neck again. He settled it so that it concealed her bruises. 'Thank you,' she said. She held his gaze, then faced the desert. Quinn watched a car come down the road towards the Mena House Hotel. It had made no attempt to dim its headlights for the blackout. 'My husband wasn't here on the night Durant was killed. He went to Suez in the morning and didn't come back until yesterday afternoon. It couldn't have been him, if that's what you're thinking.'

'He get someone else to do it?'

'I doubt it. Who could he have got?'

'Where is he tonight?'

'I'm not certain.'

'When did you last see him?'

'This morning.'

'He met someone in the bazaar today. A deserter, name Jooste, a nasty piece of work.'

'I don't know him.'

'But your lover did.' He looked at her. 'Why did you bring me here, Mrs White?'

'Does there have to be a reason?'

'There's always a reason.'

'I wanted to tell you that it would be better if you left on the train with your wife tomorrow.'

'Why would it be better?'

'Because you'd be away from this.'

'Kostandis made a similar threat.'

'It's not a threat.'

'A warning, then.'

'My husband is a businessman. The work he's been doing involves some senior officials at the palace and in your own high command.'

'What work is he doing?'

'I don't know precisely.'

'Then how do you—'

'I hear things. I'm no fool.' Her voice had dropped an octave. 'Rommel is coming. There's money to be made, a great deal of it, and I know my husband well enough to be sure that he'll make it.'

'How is there money to be made?'

'I can't tell you that.'

'Who does it involve?'

'I don't know individual names.'

'You said senior guys in the high command.'

'It's an impression.'

'You got to give me more.'

'I'm trying to help you.'

'What about officials at the palace?'

'I can't say. I don't know.'

'Then why bring me here?'

'I've tried to explain that already.'

'You wanted to help? That's a reason?'

Her face flushed. 'It isn't enough?'

'When a woman informs a cop her husband is committing a crime, I ask myself why she's telling me this.'

'Well, maybe you should stop thinking of yourself as a cop. Looking at you, I'd say that wouldn't hurt.'

'Is this what Durant had gotten himself into?'

'You're not listening, are you? What is it, Major Quinn? You think you've got to be the last man standing? This case is your responsibility, only you can solve it? But what does it *matter*?'

'It always matters.'

'In a week's time, the swastika's going to be flying over the citadel and you'll be in Palestine or in prison.'

'Maybe so, but until—'

'Then tell me why it matters.'

'I'm a cop, it's a crime.'

'It's that simple?'

'It's always that simple.'

'Or is that just a convenient excuse? Maybe you should straighten out your own life the way you solve a crime. Or is that too difficult?'

'I didn't come to talk about my life.'

'So why did you come? To conclude a case? Is that why you're here?' She fixed him with a steady gaze. 'Can you stop thinking like a cop? I'm trying to make

256

sure you don't get squashed, but now I'm wondering why I bother.'

Before he could say anything else, she was gone. She had slipped off the stone and was already descending into the night.

They didn't talk on the ride back into town. Amy stared out of the window, lost in thought. He sat back, closed his eyes, let his head roll with the rhythm of the car.

When they reached Garden City, there were no lights on in her apartment. She glanced up at the darkened windows, turned toward him. She offered her hand. 'Good night.'

Her palm was cool to the touch. For a moment, it looked as if she would lean forward to kiss him, but instead she pushed open the door.

He tumbled out behind her and they faced each other a yard or more apart. 'Good night,' she said again.

'I'll need to talk to you in the morning. Make sure you're—'

'Good night.' She walked away.

He waited for her to glance back over her shoulder, but she kept moving until she had disappeared from view.

Quinn let himself into the apartment, slipped the keys into the silver tray and leant back against the wall, his face illuminated by thin slivers of moonlight. He heard a cough, heavily stifled, but otherwise the corridor was quiet.

Quinn walked to the boy's room, stopped outside it. He thought of the many nights he'd come home late and sneaked into Ryan's room to kiss him good night and stroke his dark hair.

He tapped his fingers on the wall, watched a car's headlights swing across the living room.

He stepped into Ryan's room. Deena was asleep on the spare bed, still fully clothed and with her back to him, her body rising and falling with each breath. Rifat was in Ryan's bed. Quinn was about to withdraw when he saw that the boy was awake. 'I'm trying not to wake her,' Rifat said. 'She is very tired.'

Quinn looked down at the metal bowl, which contained a small pool of dark liquid. 'How you feeling?' he whispered.

'I don't feel very well, sir.'

'You don't have to call me "sir".' Quinn picked up a glass. 'You want some water?' Before the boy could reply, he turned on his heel and went to the kitchen to pour a glass from a jug on the side. He put it on the floor by the bed. Rifat was still looking up at him. Quinn searched for something to say. 'Your father's looking forward to having you back already.'

'Were you with him tonight?'

'Yes.'

'I don't think he wants to see me any more.'

'That's not true.'

'He knows that I'm going to die.'

'He hopes you'll be—'

'It frightens him, doesn't it?'

Quinn moved to the cane chair in the corner and sat. This was where he used to read to Ryan. Rifat turned onto his back, placed a hand beneath his head and looked up at the ceiling. Quinn watched him, listened to the wheeze of his skeletal chest. 'There's no love like that of a parent for a child,' he said. 'When you're ill, we're frightened. But you will recover. You must.'

'Why must I?'

'Because the only alternative is darkness, for all of us.'

'I liked the stories he told about working with you.'

'He is a great man.'

'Is he your friend?'

'Yes.'

'Is it dangerous being a cop?'

'Sometimes.'

'Do you think one day I could be a cop in America? I have seen all the movies. My father says they will make my English better.'

'You can do anything you want.'

There was a long silence. 'I would like to grow up,' Rifat said.

His body was convulsed by coughs. He doubled up and blood dribbled from his mouth into the metal bowl, then fell in large globules. Quinn got up, knelt in front of him and placed an arm round his shoulders. Deena crouched beside them. 'It is all right, sir,' she whispered, as she picked up a cloth from the side and wiped the sweat and blood off Rifat's face. Her hair was dishevelled, her face full of sleep.

Quinn waited a few moments, then retreated. He watched, but Rifat did not meet his eye.

Quinn passed silently through to his own room, where Mae lay asleep with her back to him. He could hear her breathing. She still had her finger in her diary, as if she had fallen asleep while writing. Quinn removed it and placed it on the side. He resisted the temptation to glance inside.

He took off his holster, shirt and trousers and lay down on the bed beneath the mosquito net. Mae stirred, but did not wake. He wiped the sweat from

259

his forehead, then lay still, looking up at the pattern of light and shadow on the ceiling. He waited for the boy's coughing to resume.

Quinn sat bolt upright. His head spun, his face pressed against the net. 'Joe,' Mae whispered, 'not again.' She was next to him, awake, her hair tousled.

'I can see him.'

'Stop it.'

'I can see the car. It was him.'

'Joe.'

'I can see you leaning against the Ford in that dress and I can see the man's face. It was him.'

'Who?'

'The South African. The one I've been hunting.'

Mae took his head in her hands, forced him to look at her. 'Please.'

'There's nothing I could have done.'

'I know that.'

'He never tried to stop the car. I swear it.'

'Look at me. Please stop this now. You've got to sleep. This cannot go on . . . We're both tired. You've got to rest . . .' She let her hands fall to his shoulders. 'Please, tomorrow is an important day for me. Let's sleep now, all right?'

'Yeah.'

'You promise?'

'Yes.'

She pushed him gently down onto the bed, her blond hair brushing across his face as she kissed his forehead. She lay beside him, rested her cheek on his arm, placed a hand on his chest. 'Enough now, Joe.'

CHAPTER THIRTY-THREE

At Cairo's railway station, as the first rays of bright morning sun tumbled onto the concourse, many of the city's Europeans were fast losing the civility that they liked to think set them apart.

There was only one train today. Too many people wished to get onto it.

An English civil servant from the railway department stood in the centre of the platform in a sand-coloured suit and a shirt that had frayed at the collar. He fanned himself with his hat. He was harried and harassed on every side, surrounded by a thick phalanx of angry civilians each with an incontrovertible right to be on the train. Kate had informed Quinn quietly on the way to the station that the navy had evacuated Alexandria overnight. Panic was setting in.

The railway official had posted Egyptian guards in uniform at each door, even outside those of the third-class carriages. They were turning people back, disconsolate latecomers sitting on trunks and packing-cases beneath a long plume of smoke that drifted along on the still, close morning air. In the distance, tall palms and a clear blue sky were all that could be seen of the city they so desperately wanted to leave. A guard saw a couple of young Egyptian men trying to climb onto the roof of a second-class carriage and chased them away.

Rifat sat on Mae's case close to the engine, his aunt alongside him in a cloud of steam. She was holding him upright, cradling him to her chest.

Quinn waved to attract the civil servant's attention. The man looked in his direction as he tried to still the insistent arguments of the people around him. 'Three passengers for Jerusalem,' Quinn said. 'One is a medical patient. I asked for a first-class compartment to be cleared.'

The man gestured at the people around him. 'Full,' he said. 'The navy has evacuated Alexandria. Gone to Port Said, Haifa and Beirut. So now there is panic.' He clearly did not approve. 'Everyone wants to go. There's another train this evening.'

'I told one of your colleagues last night I need a compartment,' Quinn said.

The official was exasperated. 'And all these others, are they to be on this train too? It's full. *Full*. And there's nothing—'

'Major Quinn, Royal Military Police. This pair is gonna get on the train, or it ain't going.' He produced his pink warrant card. 'I've got a medical emergency. You need to clear out a compartment.'

The civilian frowned. 'What kind of emergency?' He looked down to where Rifat and Deena were sitting.

'Surgery.'

'What kind of surgery?'

'A heart complaint.' The official was still looking at Rifat. Quinn was praying the boy would not be overcome by a coughing fit.

'Is it contagious?' The official wasn't convinced.

'How can a heart complaint be contagious?'

The man grunted, then stalked towards the nearest first-class carriage.

Quinn walked back up the platform. 'Are we on, Joe?' Mae whispered, as he stooped to take hold of the case. Rifat was watching a snake-charmer entertain the waiting crowd on the far side of the platform.

'Yes.'

'I heard the family over there saying Alexandria's being evacuated today.'

'It is. The British Navy's left already.'

Quinn turned, walked back to the first-class carriage and climbed up into the corridor. The occupants of one compartment were being forced out. They had realized Quinn was responsible and glowered at him as they were shepherded away.

Quinn went back to the door and ushered Mae, Rifat and Deena forward. He took hold of the boy's arm and helped him up the steps, then along the corridor. Rifat had not coughed once on the journey from the house, but a new fit overtook him now and Quinn laid him down across the leather seats. He held the boy's hand as Deena slipped into the compartment. The official had not yet withdrawn. 'Look here, that doesn't sound like a heart complaint.'

Quinn shut the door. 'The boy's sick.'

'I know what that looks like.'

'It ain't none of your business, Mister.'

'It damned well is if you're putting an infectious passenger on my train. He's a Gyppo boy, for God's—'

'Watch your tongue.'

The official was red-faced with fury. 'Why can't you take him through by ambulance?'

263

'If you can find one, we'll do just that.'

The man grunted again and withdrew. Quinn opened the compartment door a fraction to let in some air. Rifat tried to sit up. Deena held him, but Quinn could tell the boy was straining to see if his father would come. 'Goodbye, Rifat,' he said.

'Do you think he will come, sir?'

Quinn examined the boy. 'Maybe he feels he's said goodbye. He believes he'll see you very soon.'

Rifat slumped back and stared at the ceiling.

Quinn stepped out. Mae preceded him to the end of the corridor. The engine let off a burst of steam, then shunted the train forwards, pitching her into his arms, her clean, sweet-smelling hair pressed against his face. She rested just a moment, then separated herself from him. They faced each other in silence. Mae smoothed her dress. 'You know where you're going?' Quinn asked.

'Yes.'

'You send me a telex as soon as you get in.'

'Of course.'

Quinn watched an Egyptian family trying to beat the guards and get up onto the roof. Some of the Europeans on the platform were on their feet, as if half contemplating a similar attempt. 'As soon as the surgery's done,' Mae said, 'we should be able to think about coming home.'

'Mae—'

'I've given Hassan a strict set of instructions, so everything should run smoothly. But they won't buy any food unless you tell them on a Monday morning what you want.'

'I know that.'

'You'll need to leave a list or—'

'Mae.'

264

'Look after yourself, Joe.'

Neither budged. They did not move closer together; nor did they fall further apart. Neither knew how to say goodbye. 'It won't be long,' he said.

'No, it won't be long.'

They were silent again.

Out of the window, Quinn saw Effatt running past. He was holding the hand of his younger daughter, who wore a lilac dress with a bow on the back. His other son ran behind.

Quinn thumped the window. 'Effatt!' The Egyptian stopped dead in his tracks, saw them. He swung into the corridor, his forehead shiny in the half-light. 'Here,' Mae said. 'Just here.'

They watched him slip into the compartment, witnessed Rifat's smile. Effatt sat on the bunk opposite, then fell to his knees and took the boy in his arms. Over his father's shoulder, Rifat watched Quinn and Mae. He was still smiling.

Effatt would not let his boy go. When he finally released him, his cheeks were wet with tears. He touched Rifat's face, ruffled his hair, but remained kneeling in front of him.

Quinn and Mae moved back to the end of the carriage. Quinn climbed down onto the platform. Mae had composed herself now, overjoyed at Effatt's arrival. 'It's going to be all right,' she said.

'Sure it is.'

'I feel it, Joe.' She was having to shout to be heard above the noise of the steam and the hubbub of the station concourse. 'We're doing the right thing.'

Quinn smiled back at her. He glanced up at the clock. There was only a minute until the train was due to depart. A whistle blew.

The engine let off another burst of steam and, as it cleared, Quinn saw Macleod and Reza striding purposefully towards him. Kate trailed behind them.

He watched them approach, curious. Kate had just driven himself, Mae, Rifat and Deena to the station.

Macleod was at his most dour. 'Good morning, Major Quinn,' he said. He looked up at Mae. 'I'm afraid I'm going to have to ask you both to come with us.'

Neither moved. 'What?'

'Please come with us.'

'Me?' Quinn asked.

'Both of you.'

Quinn glanced at Kate's pale face. 'My wife is on her way to Palestine,' he said.

'That may be, but I'm going to have to ask you to leave the train and come with us.'

'I don't get it.'

'The train won't leave until your wife is off it, Major.'

'Why?'

Macleod glanced about him. 'It's a matter best explained in private.'

'We can delay the train a few minutes.'

'This is going to take more than a few minutes.'

Quinn looked at him.

'Please ask your wife to step down, Major,' Macleod said.

'That's not possible. My wife has to take a sick child to Palestine for treatment.'

'All being well, she may be able to go in a few days' time.'

'A few days?' Quinn glimpsed Mae's face.

'Major Quinn, please do not make this any more difficult, unpleasant or humiliating for you and your wife than it has to be.'

'You're arresting us?'

'Yes.'

'On what grounds?'

'I'd prefer to explain in private.'

'Upon whose authority?'

Macleod pulled a sheet of paper from his pocket. 'That of Colonel Lewis, in consultation with the Defence Committee.'

Quinn examined the paper. He struggled to focus on the words in front of him.

'I would ask you once more to co-operate,' Macleod said. He had lowered his voice an octave. 'If you resist, I have permission to use force and I should tell you I shall not hesitate to do so.'

'On what grounds are we being detained?'

'Suspicion of espionage.'

267

CHAPTER THIRTY-FOUR

Mae stepped slowly down from the carriage, but as soon as her feet touched the platform Reza slipped past her and climbed the steps. 'Where's he going?' Quinn asked.

'Detective Effatt and his boy are also to be detained.'

Quinn turned and followed the Egyptian into the carriage. 'Major Quinn!' Macleod shouted.

He took hold of Reza's shoulder. The dwarf turned, looked at him with unblinking eyes.

'Major Quinn!' Macleod was in the corridor.

'Don't let him take Rifat, Joe,' Mae said.

Quinn towered over Reza, but their faces were now only inches apart. 'Get back,' Quinn instructed. Effatt and his boy were looking anxiously out of the compartment window.

Quinn picked up Reza and swung him bodily around. The Egyptian hissed and lashed out with his boot. As soon as his feet touched the ground, he landed a vicious punch in Quinn's stomach. The door of the compartment opened and Effatt stepped out. 'Joe,' he said.

Mae was shouting. Macleod pulled out his revolver

and fired it once through the ceiling. He and Quinn confronted one another. 'That's enough, Major,' Macleod said, pointing the revolver at Quinn's chest.

'You're not going to take the boy.'

'Step aside, please.'

Quinn didn't budge.

'You're being arrested on suspicion of espionage. You're not in a position to dictate terms.'

'What's it got to do with the kid?'

'Unfortunately your relationship with Detective Effatt brings him under suspicion,' said Macleod. 'How can we be sure what you are really taking to Jerusalem?'

'For God's sake, Joe,' Mae said.

Reza moved towards Rifat, but Effatt blocked the way. He scooped up his son and faced the doorway. 'It's all right, Joe,' he said.

It was hot already and, in the back of the jeep, they were crushed close together. Mae's eyes searched Quinn's for answers he could not provide. Effatt cradled his son, resting the boy's head on his shoulder while Deena held his bag close to her chest. No-one spoke.

Inside the barracks, they were ushered up the stone steps of the main building to the top floor. Quinn saw Madden watching him. Everyone in the office knew what was going on.

Sorrenson was waiting outside Macleod's suite of offices and took them down to the briefing room at the far end of the Field Security corridor. It had a tall window, through which the bright morning sun streamed, three seats and a desk. Effatt was ushered past the door. 'Where are you taking him?' Quinn asked.

'To another room,' Macleod said.

'What are you going to do with them?'

'They'll be answering the same questions.'

'The boy is sick.'

'That is of no interest to me.'

'For Christ's sake, you—'

'Be careful, Major Quinn. I assure you threats will not help your cause, or that of the boy.'

Quinn and Mae were invited to sit. Another officer appeared. 'I'm sorry, sir. My name is Captain Denislow from over at GHQ. Brigadier Collins's assistant, working with Colonel Lewis.' He smiled reassuringly. 'If I could ask your wife to accompany me I will look after her. Major Macleod would like to speak to you alone.' Denislow smiled at Mae. 'I'll rustle up a cup of tea and we've some Turkish delight, if that's any incentive.'

Quinn caught sight of Reza. 'No,' he said, standing abruptly.

'I'm afraid there's no choice, sir.' Denislow followed the direction of his gaze. 'I shall ensure she comes to no harm.'

'She stays here.'

'I shall make it my personal responsibility to ensure she comes to no harm, sir. I assure you there's no cause for concern.'

'That runt doesn't get anywhere near her.'

'Of course.'

'Take her to my office.'

'Well . . .'

'That's an order, not a request.'

Under the circumstances, Denislow could have taken offence at this, but, like Madden, he was a diplomat of the old school. He inclined his head. 'As you wish, sir.' He opened the door to usher her out.

270

She hesitated. 'What the hell is going on, Joe?'

'Give me a few minutes.'

A split second after she had disappeared from view, Macleod and Reza rounded the corner.

The Scot and Quinn faced each other across a wooden table. Reza slipped onto a stool beside his boss, took out and lit a cigarette, fixed Quinn with a hostile glare. Macleod shuffled some papers. Quinn could see his photograph on one. 'I'm afraid, Major Quinn, that as a preliminary precaution, I'm going to have to ask you to surrender your revolver.' Macleod's Scottish brogue had grown broader. He spoke with the confidence of the almost absolute power he possessed.

Quinn didn't move.

'I should remind you that you are under arrest on suspicion of espionage. And that it was requested politely.'

Quinn kept still.

'We have an armed guard outside and I will call upon his assistance if you cannot co-operate.'

Macleod's manner was so formal, it was as though someone else was listening. Quinn removed his holster and slung it onto the table. 'Do you have any further weapons?' Macleod asked.

'No.'

'Please take a seat.'

'What's going on?'

'That's what I'm hoping you'll be able to tell me.'

Quinn sat. Macleod consulted the papers before him again. 'Where were you born, Major Quinn?'

'What's this about, Macleod?'

'Would you care to have me repeat the question?'

'Who knows that you've got me here?'

271

'The commander-in-chief has been informed, as, of course, has the Cairo Defence Committee. A telex is being composed for London. We have also told the appropriate officials at the American Legation.' Macleod forced a thin smile. 'Colonel Lewis was of the view that you would insist upon such a step, as you are technically an American citizen as well as a British Army officer. We have completed it on your behalf.'

'I'm being charged?'

'Not yet.'

'I get legal representation?'

'Of course. But in the current climate I should inform you that such a request may only serve to convince our superiors of your guilt. So far, after all, you are only being questioned.'

Reza smiled – which told Quinn all he needed to know. They had planned this carefully. 'If my wife comes to any harm, you'll pay the price.'

Macleod raised his eyebrows. 'Will I?' He leant back. 'If she passes through this process, I will personally arrange to escort her and Effatt's boy all the way through to Jerusalem. If not, one or both of you will be shot for espionage. Shall we continue? Let me repeat. Where were you born?'

They heard Rifat coughing. 'The boy is sick,' Quinn said.

'I can see that.'

'If he doesn't get to Jerusalem, he stands no chance.'

Macleod and Reza both stared at him. Reza smiled. Quinn stood, shoved the table back. 'Sit down, Major Quinn.'

'You cowardly—'

'Sit down! If you continue with these outbursts, I

shall have you removed to the cells and everyone else will have to wait. We'll see how well the boy fares then.' Quinn sat. Macleod examined the papers in front of him again. 'I believe matters will become clearer if we can just proceed with the questions, or do you decline to answer? I repeat once again. Where were you born?'

'Read the file.'

'It says Belfast.'

'There's your answer.'

'What year did you go to the United States?'

'1912.'

'You were ten at the time?'

'Correct.'

'Your father was a Catholic?'

'If that's what it says.'

'An enemy of British rule in Ireland?'

'Only with a few glasses of Guinness in him.'

'Why did you emigrate to New York?'

'It's a long story.'

Macleod looked down at the file again. 'You joined the New York Police Department in 1920?'

Quinn didn't answer. This was all information culled from his enlistment papers.

'A beat cop, then a precinct detective and a long spell in Homicide?'

'You want to get to the point, Macleod?'

The Scot shut the file. 'Would you prefer us to interrogate your wife?'

Quinn glared at him.

'How does a cop from New York wind up in the British Army in Cairo?'

'You know the answer.'

'I'm aware, as we all are, of the small matter of a

273

murder – and I do not use the term lightly.' Macleod put his elbows on the desk. 'But why did you come *here*, Quinn?'

'That's none of your business.'

'As I believe you are fond of saying, everything is my business.'

'Get to the fucking point.'

'Whose idea was it to come to Cairo? Your own? Your wife's?'

'Does it matter?'

'Your wife was born here?'

'Yes.' Suddenly Quinn saw what was coming and cursed himself for not anticipating it. How the hell had they found out?

CHAPTER THIRTY-FIVE

'So, it was her idea?' Macleod asked.

'I don't recall. It was something we discussed.'

'But it was your wife who suggested it?'

'We talked about it.'

'I want to be clear about this. Did the notion of coming to Cairo originate with your wife, or was it your own idea?'

'It's a long time ago. I don't recall the details.'

Macleod paused to savour the blow. 'Why didn't you tell us that your wife's father was German, Major Quinn?'

'What does it matter?'

'In the relevant box of your transfer papers to the Military Police, you've written that he was American. See here, "nationality of wife's father: American". When I asked you last night, you said your wife had been born to American parents. But that's not true, is it?'

'It's not that simple.'

'I'll ask again—'

'Her father was a German archaeologist. He left her mother when she was six months old and they came back to New York. It didn't have any bearing on anything.'

'It was a lie. And a lie in time of war.'

'I didn't think about it.'

'It was still a lie.'

'Her mother remarried. Declan was a cop, a friend of my pa's. He adopted Mae, treated her like his own daughter. To me, he was her real father.'

'I see. So, she has had no contact with her *true* father since she was six months old?'

'Not to my knowledge.'

'Not to your knowledge?'

'He abandoned them. She's never had nothing to do with him.'

'His name,' Macleod said, 'was Gustaf Müller.'

'I'll take your word for it.'

'We opened up the register, found the correct entry. Your wife was born on the eighth of August 1910 in the King George Hospital. What was her maiden name, do you know?'

'It's in my papers.'

'Miller, you wrote. After her mother?'

Quinn did not answer.

'But according to the register of your wife's birth here in Cairo, her mother's maiden name is McIlveny.'

'She started using the name Miller when she left home.'

'Why?'

'I guess it was a gesture.'

'A piece of girlish whimsy for the father she'd never known? A romantic gesture? Is that what you're saying?'

'Call it what you like.'

'Then, why not Müller?'

276

'The Germans weren't too popular after the last war. Maybe you didn't notice in Shanghai.'

'So, your wife had ... romantic feelings for her father and his home country?'

'I didn't say that.'

'Has she ever been to Germany?'

'No.'

'You're certain?'

'Yes.'

'Has she ever expressed the view that Hitler has done much that is positive for the German people?'

'For Christ's sake!'

'Please answer the question.'

'She despises Hitler.'

'Her father never made any attempt to contact her?'

'Not as far as I know.'

'So it's possible?'

Quinn stood up, shoved back the table again.

'Sit down, Major Quinn.'

'I want to speak to someone from the Legation. Now.'

'Sit down.'

Quinn glared at his interrogator. 'How the hell did you get the high command to sign off on this?'

'I think it will be plain enough. As you will see, I've barely begun.'

'I got to you, didn't I?'

'Please sit down.'

'How long did it take to put this together? This can't be just about the Durant case. You figured I'd keep going until I caught the guy who killed my son and worked out why you were protecting him. I've had you running scared.'

'I've no idea what you're talking about.'

'Maybe the guy knows something you don't want me to get to, right? Maybe it's the deserter, Jooste. What does he do for you, Macleod?'

'Please sit down.'

'Way I figure it, there's got to be a reason why you're protecting him.'

Macleod shuffled the papers in front of him. 'Major Quinn, your obsession with your son's accident at the hands of a common deserter, while understandable, is increasingly vexatious and pointless. However, it lies outside the scope of this interview.'

The door opened and Colonel Lewis stalked in. Reza stood up and fetched him a chair from the corridor. Lewis's face was grave. 'Good morning, Joe.'

'Not so far.'

'Please sit,' Lewis said.

'Was this your idea?' Quinn asked.

'Take a seat.'

Quinn did as he was asked. Macleod opened the file in front of him. He picked up a sheet, pushed it across the table. 'Last night SOE mounted a series of raids on Axis aerodromes. They had been months in the planning. Every one was a failure. Seventy-nine soldiers are dead or missing. In each case, the Germans were waiting.' He pointed at the piece of paper. 'That note was in Captain Durant's files until his death, when you removed it.'

Quinn glanced over the document. It was one of those that had been in the safe. It began 'MOST SECRET. 28 June. Sabotage Units to mount simultaneous sticker bomb attacks against aircraft on nine Axis aerodromes. Will reach objectives by parachute and long-range desert patrol . . .'

'Why did you take this from Captain Durant's office?' Macleod asked.

'It was material relating to the case.'

'How did it relate to the investigation?'

'Durant handled a barrel load of sensitive information. I figured maybe it was an issue.'

'But why did you need to take it from the office?'

'You think you've got a case with this? You're joking, right?'

'Did you know Durant?'

'No.'

'You didn't meet him prior to his murder?'

'No.'

'You're certain of that?'

'Sure I am.'

'What about your wife?'

'What about her?'

'Did she know Durant?'

'Of course not.'

'Then how is it,' Reza interjected slowly, 'that a grey Ford V8 was seen outside his apartment building the day before his death?'

Quinn looked at the Egyptian. 'There are hundreds all over Cairo.'

'A hundred, perhaps,' Macleod said. 'Maybe twenty grey ones.' He pulled out another piece of paper. 'Our Albanian friend has given us a statement saying he saw a woman get out, her head covered with a scarf.'

Quinn read the report. 'This doesn't mean anything.'

'Then what about this?' Macleod pulled another sheet of paper from the bottom of the file and slammed it on the table. It was the fingerprint report from Durant's apartment. Quinn glanced at Reza again, who had evidently been doing a tour of the Cairo police building behind Effatt's back. 'Your fingerprint was on the glass, Major Quinn. Or am I wrong?'

'So it says.'

'Effatt's men found the fragment,' Reza said. 'Strangely, you hadn't managed to locate it.'

'The glass must have been planted. I never met Durant.'

'It was planted?' Macleod asked.

'That's what I said.'

Lewis leant forward. 'Alastair, if you wouldn't mind . . . I'd like to speak to Major Quinn alone for a few moments.'

CHAPTER THIRTY-SIX

The others filed from the room, closed the door behind them. Lewis leant forward. 'Cigarette?'

Quinn took one. They smoked in silence.

Lewis picked up a briefcase he had placed beneath the table. He took out a red folder. It was stamped MOST SECRET.

Quinn opened the folder. On the first sheet, someone had written by hand: 'To be carried by courier to Colonel Charles Lewis, Director, Military Intelligence, GHQ, MEF, Cairo. FOR HIS EYES ONLY.'

Quinn turned the page. All of the remaining sheets were translations of German radio messages. They had again been stamped 'MOST SECRET. To be kept under lock and key, never to be removed from office.'

The first read:

IDA DROMEDAR TO OTTO LUCHS. CX/MSS/933/T20.
Source: Reichssicherheitshauptamt VI, Berlin.
Date: 23 May 1942. Message from Condor. All is well.

Underneath, the translator had written:

Notes: (1) Otto Luchs is IC Panzer army. (2) Information appears to have been sent from Cairo to Berlin, processed, then transmitted to Rommel via Rome. (3) Reichssicherheitshauptamt VI is more commonly known to us as RSHA VI, or Reich Security Administration VI, the department of the Gestapo that deals with foreign intelligence operations.

Quinn looked up. 'Where did you get these?'

'That's not your concern.'

The next sheet, marked CX/MSS/886/T18, revealed Condor had discovered that the British knew the location of German Air Force HQ in the desert and would attack at any minute.

The messages dated back six weeks, but gave the impression the agent had been in place longer. Most damaging was the last transcript in the folder. Transmitted only a few days ago, it contained a detailed list of every Allied unit that would be involved in the defence of the delta. Each one was broken down, with an approximate summary of the serviceable tanks, vehicles and other heavy equipment at its disposal.

Quinn passed back the folder.

'We believe some of the information, at least, came from Durant,' Lewis said. 'Take a look here . . . Condor reports the second Indian Transport Brigade has reached Cairo, is being stationed in the citadel, re-equipped and is due back in position on the twenty-sixth of June. Only someone like Durant would have had that level of detail.' Lewis looked at him. 'Do you have any comment?'

'No.'

'Well, you'd better think of one. This is not looking good for you.'

'You've got a spy. What's it to do with—'

'At the heart of our operations. Right now, that makes Major Macleod the most powerful man in Cairo. And he believes you're Condor.'

'That's a joke and you know it.'

'He places considerable emphasis on the way in which you fought to control Durant's case.'

'Like he did.'

'The Defence Committee doesn't see it that way.'

'Then you'd better call me a lawyer.'

'Joe, I don't think you've quite got the message.'

They heard a stifled cough. 'The boy's dying,' Quinn said.

'Well, he isn't going anywhere, so he'll die here.'

'If he—'

Lewis leant forward, banged his fist on the table. 'Macleod has put together a case, which has convinced the Defence Committee that you and those around you are, in all likelihood, German spies. The fate of a wretched Gyppo boy is neither here nor there.'

Quinn stood up again, shoved back his chair.

'For God's sake, Joe, sit down!'

'You're saying I'm a spy? You really want me to take that seriously?'

'I'm saying you and your wife have very substantial questions to answer. Now, I don't know—'

'My wife's got nothing to do with it.'

'Your wife, Joe, may be the problem. Sit down. Let me tell you something. One look at these documents convinces me that Condor must be an insider, an officer like you, or me, or someone close to us, do you agree?'

283

'I've got no idea.'

'Did you suppress the information about your wife's father?'

'No.'

'But you knew she was searching for memories? Isn't that one of the reasons you came to Cairo?'

'No.'

'So she hasn't looked for him?'

'He's dead.'

'She didn't attempt to make contact with his friends?'

'Not to my knowledge.'

'So you cannot say?'

'He died a long time ago.'

'And that was it?'

'This isn't going anywhere.'

'I'm doing this as a friend, Joe, believe me. At the moment, on this side of the fence, I'm the only one you've got.'

'This ain't how I treat my friends.'

'You stubborn bastard.' Lewis leant back in his seat. 'All right. It's not a question I want to ask, but how much do you know about your wife's life here in Cairo?'

Quinn did not answer.

'Does she have a lover?'

'Of course she fucking doesn't.'

'You're sure of that? How much do you know about her work at the hospital?'

'She doesn't like to talk about it.'

'She doesn't like to talk, or you don't like to ask?' It is said, Joe, that your wife has got involved with some of these men, that she has thrown herself into her work there. Of course not all of them die. Some

284

urvive and go through a long process of recuper-
ation.'

'You got an accusation to make,' Quinn growled,
then make it.'

'Major Macleod has found a witness who is
prepared to state on oath that she believes your wife
has had an affair with one, and possibly more than
one, soldier.'

'Who?'

'I can't say.'

'It's a lie and you know it.'

'Unfortunately, at the moment, I can't afford to
"know" anything.'

'You listen to every piece of gossip?'

'You're sure that's what it is, Joe? I'm speaking as
a friend.'

Quinn tried to block the innuendo from his mind.
'Speaking of friends,' he said, 'you and Macleod go
way back.'

That didn't faze Lewis. 'Well, perhaps we do. And
maybe you're right to infer – since I believe this is
what you're driving at – that we were once close.
Closer, indeed, than I would ideally have chosen. In
retrospect, we all make compromises we shouldn't,
but this is a different place and a different time. I
needed an operator, so I hired one. I've got no illusions
about Major Macleod. But I believe your crusade has
been misplaced and now he has built a case against
you, which has convinced our superiors that you're a
dangerous man. He has gone before the committee
and presented a statement on your wife's alleged
affairs. Perfect cover, he says, for gathering intelligence
from soldiers fresh from the field.'

'You finished?'

'No, I have not! I watch you and I ask myself how much you know about what Mae might have been up to. How much are you really seeing?' Lewis turned over another sheet, pushed it across the table. 'Did you know that eight months ago she went to the head of the archaeology department at the American University to enquire about his memories of Gustaf Müller?'

Quinn looked at the statement.

'She didn't tell you about this?'

'No.'

'Does it surprise you?'

'Why should it?'

But Lewis looked at him incredulously. 'Did you know that Müller is buried in the small cemetery behind the German church in Heliopolis and that your wife goes to his grave every week without fail?'

Quinn read the sheet.

'She visits it as often as she visits the grave of your son.'

'So what?'

Lewis exhaled. 'You don't fool me, Joe. I can see the shock in your face. Your wife has a German inheritance, in which she is *clearly* interested. She appears to have an alternative life at the hospital, which you know nothing about.'

'That's a lie.'

'She's in a position to have worked out Durant's value and targeted him. Her car is seen outside his flat, a woman like her is seen going inside, a piece of glass with *your* fingerprint on it is found at the scene, which you, a detective whose competence no-one disputes, did not find. Then you fight hard for the case when I'm trying to take it off your hands.'

286

'You've no evidence of anything.' Quinn could hear the defensiveness in his voice.

'We're not dealing with *evidence*. We're dealing with espionage, in a city where every single senior officer is dancing on hot coals about Condor and his messages back to Berlin. We go on like this, we'll lose the war, and you well understand that.'

They were interrupted by raised voices in the corridor. Quinn pulled open the door. Effatt stood with Rifat in his arms. Deena was in front of them, being led by Reza. Effatt had a bruised eye and a swollen lip. Blood trickled from his nose. 'They're taking us to the camp,' Effatt said.

Quinn swung round to Lewis. 'You out of your mind?'

'Sit down, Major Quinn.'

'Take him back.'

Lewis's face had drained of colour. 'You've all got to be interned. Any further questioning can be done—'

'Interned?'

'You've brought this upon yourself, Joe.'

'He's sick.'

'Sit down.'

Quinn saw the gravity of his superior's expression. This was out of his hands. He felt the first pangs of fear. 'Please, Charles. We can settle this.' He could not recall having used Lewis's Christian name before. They stared at each other, then Lewis turned to Reza and nodded. He closed the door and Quinn returned to his seat. 'What's going to happen to Effatt?'

'Forget Effatt.'

'Reza's thugs have been—'

'It's only a temporary reprieve, Joe. I did try to warn you.'

'About what?'

'You've been so obsessed with your son's accident, you've missed what has been going on right under your nose. I want to believe in you, Joe. I'm fond of you both. But I can't have any confidence that you really know what has been going on in your wife's life. And that alarms me.'

'Why me?' Quinn said. 'You asked yourself that? You're telling me Macleod and Reza stumbled across the fact that my wife's father was German by accident?'

'What do you mean?'

'They've gone out of their way to frame me. They know I won't stop until I nail the guy who was driving that car. They've been protecting him, so you've got to ask yourself why. Why are they going to such lengths to stop me?'

'We've been over this ground.'

'But you haven't been listening.'

'I've seen no evidence to suggest there is anything untoward about the day of your son's death. As I keep telling you, we'll find the man. When we do, we'll see if you're right.'

'Did Macleod know Durant?' Quinn asked. 'They ever have any dealings?'

'Of course not.'

'You don't figure they knew each other?'

'I don't see what you're driving at.'

'Durant *knew* Macleod. There's an entry in his diary for a meeting down in the Berka the night after he died. When we staked it out, Macleod and Reza turned up, along with a South African deserter, the same guy who was photographed fucking Wheeler in that hotel.'

Lewis frowned. 'Who is he?'

288

'A hired thug, but the question is, hired for what? And what's Durant doing mixed up in it?'

'What's your explanation?'

'Give me a couple of days, I'll have one.'

'To do what?'

'We find the killer, then maybe you've got your spy. Could be you're right about the information coming from Durant. Maybe they had to shut him up real quick.'

Lewis shook his head. 'I can't do it, Joe. It's too late. I'm sorry. Macleod will persuade the committee you're too dangerous to be released.'

They heard Rifat coughing outside, then Effatt's voice as he tried to comfort him.

'Effatt's boy doesn't go today, tomorrow he's going to die for sure.'

'Damn it, Joe, I don't care about the boy!'

'But I do.'

'Then you'd be well advised to care less. For your information, Macleod and Reza are aware the boy is extremely sick and view him as a useful pressure point on you, which they're more than happy to use. The committee is in full agreement.'

Quinn stood up. He wiped the sweat from his forehead, walked to the window and looked down on Bab el Hadid. There was still a crowd outside the station entrance. He heard the blast of a police whistle, saw a couple of redcaps chasing someone through the throng. 'Please, Charles. Effatt and I . . . we've worked hard for you. You know that.'

'I don't dispute it.'

'You want Condor, you need us.'

'On what grounds?'

'Macleod won't find him. Maybe he doesn't want to.'

Lewis stared at the wall. 'I can't do it, Joe.'

'Forty-eight hours and I'll give you your killer. It's what I know how to do.'

'In the current climate, the committee and, indeed, the entire high command lean heavily on Macleod. You know they do. I'm not sure I can swing them against his advice.'

'You're his superior.'

'Without his informers and the intelligence flow that comes from them, they'd be in all sorts of trouble here. They'd feel blind.'

'But he won't find Condor. You know it as well as I do.'

There was a long silence. 'Two days, then,' he said quietly. 'I've got just about enough authority left to pull that off. But not one second longer. All of the others remain under house arrest, including your wife and the boy. Otherwise Macleod and the committee will cut my head off.'

'I need Effatt.'

'No.'

'You want the result, I need Effatt.'

Lewis sighed. 'All right, but as for the rest, including the boy, there's no negotiation. They're forbidden to leave the city under any circumstances. If they try, I'll take it as evidence that you're part of an espionage ring and have them shot.'

Quinn was left on his own for the best part of an hour. From time to time, he heard raised voices from further down the corridor. It sounded like Lewis and Macleod arguing.

By the time Denislow came back to tell him he was free to go, Mae and Deena had been brought to the atrium in the centre of the top floor. Effatt stood beside them, Rifat still in his arms. The boy was sleeping, his head resting on his father's chest. 'You going to come to the house?' Quinn asked.

'I will take him home.'

Quinn glanced over his shoulder. Neither Lewis nor Macleod had emerged from the suite of offices at the end. 'Maybe it would be better if—'

'They will watch us wherever we are.'

CHAPTER THIRTY-SEVEN

Kate Mowbray drove them back to the apartment in Zamalek through roads choked with overloaded cars and trucks that had made the journey from Alexandria. Smoke hung like morning cloud over the city's rooftops. Along Soliman Pasha, long lines of people queued in the bright sun. 'They say there's a run on the banks,' Kate said. She glanced over her shoulder at the Military Police jeep behind them.

Inside the apartment, sunlight poured through the living-room window, cascading down the corridor. Hassan and the other servants helped them in with their luggage. Effatt had been escorted home by another Military Police jeep.

Mae went through to the living room, then the terrace. She sat on a bench overlooking a garden that was, despite the inclement weather, still brilliant with zinnias and bougainvillaea and red canna lilies.

Quinn stood beneath the shade of a eucalyptus. Flies swarmed around his face. He lit a cigarette, offered one to his wife. Through the hedge, he could just make out the corner of the jeep that had followed them from Bab el Hadid. Mae stared into the middle distance. She seemed as remote as she had in the months after Ryan's death. 'What's going on, Joe?' she asked quietly.

'They've been trying to frame us.'

'Us?'

'Yes.'

'Why?'

Quinn didn't answer. He didn't need to.

Mae sighed. 'So, I'm a prisoner. Am I allowed to go out?'

'No.'

'And how long will this last?'

'I have forty-eight hours, otherwise we'll be seeing out the war in an internment camp.'

'Forty-eight hours to do what?'

'To find the killer we've been hunting.'

'And why does that matter?'

'They think he's their spy.'

'I thought we were the spies.'

'Macleod framed us.'

'Why?'

Quinn didn't answer.

'And what happens to Rifat?' Mae's mouth was tight. 'Or should I guess? What would they care about him? He's only a Gyppo boy, of course.'

'They had questions, Mae.'

'About what?'

'About you.'

'What kind?'

'They wanted to talk about a grave in Heliopolis that I didn't know anything about.'

'I don't understand.'

'You went looking for your father's friends at the university,' he said quietly. 'What else did you do?'

293

'What if I did? Is it a crime?'

'You go to his grave every week.'

'Of course I don't.'

'They've been following you.'

For the first time, her cheeks flushed. 'Well, so what if I—'

'They're looking for a spy, Mae.'

'And having a German father is a crime?'

'Is there anything else you want to tell me?'

'No.'

'How about some of the officers at the hospital?'

'What about them?'

'You been giving them more than comfort?'

Mae flushed bright red. Deep in her eyes, he saw the wound he'd inflicted. 'Did you really just say that?' she asked, her voice barely audible.

'They got a sworn affidavit says you've been screwing a couple of the men.'

'A sworn affidavit from whom?'

'Someone at the hospital. They won't give a name.'

She examined him again. The truth dawned on her. 'And you believe them,' she said.

'I didn't say that. I'm asking a question.'

'You're asking me if I've been sleeping with some of the men at the hospital?' She sat completely still, her hands upon her lap. Tears crept from the corners of her eyes. 'I figured I'd put up with everything, but I never thought to hear something like that.'

'You do more than write letters for them, Mae?'

'What do you think?'

'Did you know Durant?'

'Who is Durant?'

'The officer we found hanging from a tree. There was a fragment of glass with my fingerprint at the scene. A neighbour swears he saw a woman get out of a grey Ford the day before.'

'And you think it was me?' She was bewildered. 'After all these years, suddenly, you don't know me at all?'

They lapsed into silence. 'They're trying to frame us, did you say?' Mae asked. 'Why could that be, I wonder?'

Quinn threw away his cigarette, watched the tip brighten in a gust of wind. He waved the flies from his face.

'Could it possibly have something to do with the way you go on and on about the past? I'm not surprised they get angry with you, Joe. Even if you're right and they are protecting someone, it still *was* an accident. Nothing in the world is ever going to change that.' Quinn faced the wall. 'But, sure, it's not about that, is it?' she said. 'You think you've kept it from me all these months, but you're not so smart as you think.'

'Kept what?'

'Don't make me spell it out, Joe.'

'I've got no idea what you're talking about.'

'Then you're more stupid than I thought.' She sat up straight. 'I know what you really think. I always have.'

'About what?'

'If I'd been concentrating, it would never have happened. Isn't that what you believe, deep in your heart, Joe? Isn't that what wakes you in the dead of night?'

'Let's drop it.'

'Isn't that what you think about when you're lying next to me? Isn't that what tortures you every time you touch me?'

'Leave it, Mae—'

'If I hadn't been talking, if I hadn't let Ryan go, if I'd been showing the care a mother should—'

'I said, drop it.'

'But you *won't*. You won't ever damned well drop it. Once, maybe, I thought we'd learn to live with it, but time doesn't heal all wounds, does it, Joe? Some are just too deep. You'll go on and on, thrashing around, lashing out. You won't stop until the man is dead and we're ruined. And then what?' Mae stared at him. 'Where will we be then?'

'Maybe it'll be something. Maybe we can finally go home.'

'If it wasn't for you, we'd never have left home!' She was shouting now, her eyes bright with anger. 'Damn you, Joe. Damn you and your haunted dreams. I see the accusation in your eyes every single night, but if it wasn't for you and your stupid gun, we would never have come to this wretched place and our son would still be with us.'

Quinn stared at her. 'Don't you dare—'

'Your father has been dead more than a decade. You can't bring him back. All this good-just-sheriff stuff digs us deeper and deeper—'

'Don't bring my father into this.'

'Do you think he'd want to see you acting as judge, jury and executioner?'

'For Christ's sake—'

'Look at you now. Like a wounded bull. You're so obsessed with the purity of your sorrow that you don't even realize you're about to achieve something similar all over again.'

'What are you talking about?'

'Effatt is your best friend and he'd lay down his

life for you in a heartbeat. But you won't commit yourself to helping his son because you're frightened of what that might bring. You don't want any wound to bleed like the last, isn't that right, Joe? But all you're doing is making certain he'll suffer the same fate.'

'That's enough.'

'I can see why you would believe their nasty innuendo. Am I screwing the guys at the hospital?' She shook her head. 'What kind of sick mind can think up a line like that?' She took a step away from him. 'I have Deena's number. I'm going to get him over here and we'll go by car tonight.'

'You can't.'

'I'll drive through the night.'

'They'll arrest you before you've left the city limits.'

'Not if we're smart.'

'They'll shoot you on sight. It would be reckless and I won't stand for it.'

'Well, *won't* you?'

She stood up, walked into the sitting room and slammed the patio doors in his face so hard the glass almost shattered.

CHAPTER THIRTY-EIGHT

Kate stood beneath the shade of a palm on the far side of the street, fanning herself with a book, but when she stepped out into the sunlight sweat was running down her face.

Inside the car, she refrained from asking him what had happened back at the barracks. 'I saw a friend of mine who lives down the street,' she said. 'He claimed there was a rumour the Germans had already reached Alex.'

Quinn stared ahead.

'He said our boys were pouring back in from the blue—'

'Let's get back to the office.'

They drove in silence, but it was clear that others had heard similar rumours about Alexandria. The roads were full of jeeps and trucks coated with thick layers of dust and overloaded cars heading out of the city towards Palestine. They barely impinged on Quinn's consciousness.

As soon as they reached Bab el Hadid, he asked Kate to assemble Madden, Cohen and Dexter. 'All of them?' she asked.

'Yeah. All of them.'

Effatt was waiting in his office, leaning against Madden's desk. Quinn shut the door. Effatt's nose had been cleaned, but his lip and right eye were still swollen. 'Where is Rifat?' Quinn asked.

'At home.'

'Is he—'

'He's fine.'

'They worked you over?'

Effatt shrugged.

'Look, I'm real sorry, I—'

'Let's not go over old ground.'

Quinn glanced at his friend. 'I figure I should go on with this case alone.'

'That's not your choice to make.'

'Sure, but all the same I'd like to—'

'You know what Reza will do to Rifat if they pull us in? You know what he'll do in front of me?' Effatt's eyes burned. 'They've raped boys before and they'll do it again. I'd rather kill him myself. So there is no choice now but to eliminate them. Legally if possible, but otherwise . . .' He shook his head. 'Enough of these people now. No-one likes to be intimidated in his own country.' He took out his notebook. 'Nawab is ready if you want to talk to him. And we've found Wheeler's *sufragi*. That is always assuming we still have our case to investigate?'

'Effatt—'

The Egyptian shook his head to indicate that he did not wish to talk about his son in the office.

Quinn leant back against a bookshelf. It was hard to concentrate on the minutiae of the case. 'What did the *sufragi* have to say?'

'We're talking to him now.'

'And Nawab?'

'He hasn't told me anything. You know how he likes to have an audience.'

'Whatever you say,' Quinn said, 'I'm sorry.'

'Let's not speak any more about it.'

There was a knock on the door and Kate led in the others. Dexter and Cohen stood to either side of Madden; his height made them seem abnormally short. Cohen had closely cropped dark hair and swarthy skin, allowing him to pass easily as an Arab. Dexter had thick curly hair, which framed a chubby face.

Quinn walked to the blackboard along the far wall. He tried to concentrate. In the centre, he scrawled Durant, then Wheeler. 'Two bodies,' he said. 'Now we've got to find the connection.'

They looked at him, as if unsure that he was really going to pick up the case where he'd left off. 'I suppose we've already got the obvious one,' Madden said.

'Which is?'

'They work together.'

'No two people ever got killed just because they worked together.'

'They had access to information. They were both in highly sensitive posts. We have to agree they'd be prime targets for a German spy.'

'Sure.' Quinn drew an arrow alongside Durant's name and wrote Amy White. 'That's one way to look at it. Or we can shift the images around and get a different picture, maybe a more basic one: Durant's having an affair with Mrs White. The husband's got a history of smacking her about and a sure motive. He hires someone to kill Durant, but maybe Wheeler also has to die because he knows too much about what went on.'

Quinn stopped to consider this. If it was true and the case was resolved along these lines, would it mollify Lewis and Macleod, or more swiftly consign him to an internment camp? Lewis was hunting a spy, not a jealous husband.

'But we've got no evidence to suggest that,' Madden said. 'Would Durant really have told anyone he was having an affair, let alone Wheeler? He kept it from Mrs Markham, after all. And even if he had told Wheeler, why would they have needed to kill him as well? It seems far-fetched to me. And it doesn't explain Captain Durant's connections in the Berka.'

'No,' Quinn said. 'It doesn't. But they both had sexual temptation as their problem.'

'So maybe they were being blackmailed?' Kate suggested.

'If the deserter, Jooste, seduced Wheeler,' Effatt added, 'and Amy White seduced Durant, that makes her husband a common link. We saw him with Jooste in the bazaar.'

'True,' Quinn said. 'True.' He looked at the chalk in his hand. 'Let's say Ed is right, my basic picture is too simple and we've got to look at the connections in the Berka and the broader story, then why does our friend Durant die first?'

No-one answered.

Quinn glanced at the names on the board. 'I've got a hunch Durant was down in the Berka in some way for his friend Wheeler. I've no hard evidence for it, but the colonel told me two lies and I've been trying to figure out his motive for each. He claimed he didn't like Durant and he said he only started the affair with the South African deserter last week. But you don't pay over the odds to be fucked in front of a set of

301

hotel mirrors after a couple of casual conversations in the Kit Kat. So maybe Wheeler began to get himself into hot water months ago and chose to confide in his friend Durant. Wheeler is being blackmailed, so Durant goes down to the Berka to meet the people behind it.'

Quinn tossed the piece of chalk, caught it and placed it by the blackboard. 'Ed, you've got to turn this connection inside out. Wheeler and Durant were part of the same theatrical group. Just how close were they and how much did they see of each other? Take a look at who else was part of the same group. Talk to Wheeler's office again. Who was his secretary? What does she think? Did you get anywhere with the document we found at Wheeler's houseboat?'

'Not really. The arms consignment got through without any problems. It all arrived on time. I've checked with GHQ here and up at Ruweisat Ridge. No-one could think of anything odd about it.'

'So why has he got that document at home?'

'No-one had any explanation. Mrs Markham was baffled.'

Quinn turned to Cohen and Dexter. 'I want you guys to find this South African deserter. If he's a hired thug, let's try and find out exactly what he's been hired to do.'

'What about the God of Chaos?' Cohen asked.

'What about him?'

'I read Madden's report. That seemed a pretty intriguing connection between the two murders. Why did the killer bother to do that?'

It was a question to which Quinn had not yet found a satisfactory answer. Maybe it was, as he'd first imagined, a crude red herring, but why pull the same trick twice? That did seem odd. 'You got any ideas?' he asked Cohen.

'No. It seemed unusual, that's all.'

After the others had filed out, Quinn went through to the back of the atrium and found the reference section of their rudimentary library. He pulled down a leather-bound volume and returned to his office.

He read:

Seth, God of Chaos, Lord of the Northern Sky. Figure from Egyptian mythology. In most versions, traditionally depicted as the villain. A fork-tailed canine with a long, drooping snout, Seth was master of the Red Lands – the desert. Son of Geb and Nut – earth and sky – and brother of Osiris, Isis and Nephthys, he burst unexpectedly from his mother's womb and was always viewed as an outsider. A powerful but lonely God, he prowled the desert, howling and bellowing, stirring up sandstorms and casting an envious eye towards the fertile Black Lands, ruled by his brother Osiris and watered by the Nile.

Quinn turned the page.

In his anger and solitude, Seth conceived a plot to kill his brother. He held a banquet, persuaded Osiris to lie down in a beautiful box, before slamming it shut and pushing it into the Nile. The goddess Isis searched high and low for her beloved brother. Upon finding his corpse, she impregnated herself with his seed and gave birth to a son, Horus.

Horus grew up nurturing dreams of vengeance.

The two met on the banks of the Nile and fought themselves to a standstill in one of the symbolic battles of ancient myth. In the modern system of belief, Horus most often represents the triumph of outraged justice. The forked tail of Seth has evolved into the mark of Satan.

Quinn replaced the book on the shelf and stood in the centre of the atrium. He watched Macleod's secretary, Maude, come out of her office at the far end of the Field Security corridor, deposit an envelope in the mail tray, then go back in.

CHAPTER THIRTY-NINE

Nawab was sitting on the concrete slab with his feet up close to Wheeler's body, smoking a cigarette. He looked comfortable, as if this was how he chose to take his rest. The bloodied saw was beside him, Wheeler's chest opened from end to end, the sickly sweet smell of him just detectable over formaldehyde and disinfectant. Quinn and Effatt looked at each other. Kate stepped out into the corridor and was violently sick.

Nawab let his feet drop and reached for the clip-board. 'What do you want to know?' he asked.

'Let's dispense with the game and get on with it,' Quinn said.

'How am I supposed to know what information you require?'

'We ain't exactly at the cutting edge of medical science, Nawab.'

'Aren't we, indeed?'

Nawab spoke English with a perfect Oxford accent. He spent too long alone down here, Quinn thought, and this childish, tedious game amounted to the sum total of his human contact, unless you counted

Wheeler. And he wasn't proving much of a conversationalist right now.

'Wheeler was murdered,' Nawab said.

'We'd just about worked that out for ourselves.'

'With piano wire.'

'Please, Doctor,' Effatt said.

Nawab tugged at the ends of his moustache. He had something, but he was going to spin it out. 'Less force than last time,' he said.

'Tell me something I don't know,' Quinn muttered.

Nawab raised a pudgy fist, one finger extended. 'I hold by what I said.'

'About what?'

'About Durant.'

'Which aspect of it?'

'The power of the assault, the way the wire was worked through the trachea like that and down to the bone. The savage manner it must have been pulled to and fro. I suppose you think the two murders are connected?'

'Maybe you'd like to tell us what you think.'

'It is hard to say. Of course, on the face of it—'

'Nawab.' Quinn glanced down at Wheeler's chest. 'We got two corpses and the entire British high command on our backs.'

'See for yourself.' Nawab took down a wooden tray from the side. He turned on a light that hung over the desk and pulled it in Quinn's direction. 'Here, you'll need this.' He held out a magnifying-glass.

Quinn took it and bent over the tray. He could see nothing. Bits of something. It looked like dust. 'I don't get it.'

'You don't understand?'

'Nawab, for Christ's sake!'

306

'Look at the colour.'

'Of what? I don't see nothing.'

'Of the chips.'

Nawab was pointing at the tray, so Quinn looked again. All he could see were tiny bits of paint or maybe wood chips. 'The colour of it,' Nawab said.

'It looks brown to me.'

'It's pink. Bright pink.'

Quinn straightened again. He handed the magnifying-glass to Effatt. 'What's that supposed to mean?'

'It is nail varnish. Pink nail varnish. I scraped it from around his neck and from the collar of his jacket.'

Quinn looked at the pathologist. 'So the killer was a woman?'

'It would seem so.'

'Is it possible that these fragments could have got there any other way?'

'Not in my judgement.'

'Kate,' Quinn called. As she appeared in the doorway, he took the magnifying-glass from Effatt and handed it to her. 'I'm sorry, but you've got to steel yourself and take a look at this.'

She did as she was asked. 'What is it?'

'Tiny clippings of nail varnish.'

'Oh, I see. God ... it's hard to tell. It looks like Elizabeth Arden pink to me.'

'You can tell the type?'

She straightened, handed him back the glass. 'It's not difficult. It's all the rage. I use it, so do lots of other girls.' Quinn looked at her hands, which had no varnish on them at all.

'So the chips came off in the struggle?' Effatt asked.

Nawab raised his own fingers to demonstrate. 'The wire would probably have had wooden handles. As she applies the pressure and he struggles, the ends of her fingers rub against them, or perhaps against the wire. Wheeler has skin under his fingernails, which suggests to me he struggled hard.'

'But are you saying the two murders are not connected?' Quinn asked.

'I don't know. That's your job.'

'But as a pathologist, in your opinion, are they the work of the same killer?'

'I'm not certain.'

'Guess.'

'This is a science.'

'Let me put it a different way. Is it possible Durant was also killed by this woman?'

'I said, I hold to my initial judgement.'

'So, it's not possible?'

'I didn't say that. I've been sitting here thinking about it and I don't know the answer. It's not a simple yes or no. You said Durant was kneeling down and removing something from the refrigerator at the point at which the wire was wrapped round his neck. Upon reflection I have to concede, painful as it may be, that you *might* have been right. It would explain the angle of incision. However, I still don't believe that a woman, even a strong one, could easily inflict the damage to his neck.' Nawab shook his head. 'You must understand. This is a lot of work, pulling the wire to and fro. Through the strap muscles and—'

'All right, Nawab,' Effatt said. 'I think we get the picture.'

CHAPTER FORTY

Inside Wheeler's houseboat, the body might have gone but the pool of congealed blood remained and the place looked as if it had been ravaged by a pack of wolves. The desk had been shunted to one side, all its drawers upended and the contents scattered. The books on the shelf had been thrown to the floor, their bindings torn. A pile of gramophone records lay broken and crushed and the low ottoman had been cut with knives.

'What happened?' Effatt asked.

'Macleod's men were here last night,' Quinn explained.

'What were they doing?'

'Searching for something.'

Quinn picked through the debris. He found an Ella Fitzgerald record that had escaped destruction, put it on the gramophone and pulled the needle across. He glanced at the Nubian *sufragi* who stood by the door, next to Kate. The kid didn't look a day over sixteen, a slight figure with smooth skin and large, frightened eyes. 'Where was he?' Quinn asked Effatt.

'A friend of his works for a Greek nearby, three

boats down. The man is usually away in Alexandria. Wheeler didn't like to have him around in the evenings, so he went there.'

'He hear anything?'

'He says not.'

'What time did he last see Wheeler?'

Effatt turned and spoke to the boy in Arabic. 'Around six.'

'Was he alone?'

'Yes, sir,' the boy said.

'He often have visitors in the evening?'

Effatt translated: 'He says he doesn't know. He would always leave food out, then go to the friend's house and spend the night there. Colonel Wheeler insisted on privacy.'

Quinn thought about this. 'Any women come calling? Would he recognize them?'

'He says he has only been here two months. In that time, he did not see a single visitor.'

'Not one?'

'So he claims.'

'He ever find any evidence someone had stayed overnight?'

Effatt tried again. 'No. Definitely not.'

'What about telephone calls?'

This time, Effatt's interrogation was sharper. 'He says he rarely answered the telephone. During the day the only calls were from Wheeler instructing him on what he wished put out for supper and which uniforms were to be taken for cleaning. The colonel was most particular, he says, about everything. He did not enjoy working for him.'

'That the truth?'

The boy nodded vigorously, but all Quinn saw in

his face was fear and a deep mistrust of authority. 'All right,' he muttered.

Quinn pulled back the chair to look at the desk, shoving aside a pile of files. Kate Mowbray was watching him. 'Expensive, wouldn't you say?' he asked. He was pointing at the desk.

'It looks it.'

'In fact, you might say that of almost everything in here.'

'You still think it was two people?' Effatt said.

Quinn called back the boy, who was trying to slip out of the door. 'Ask him about the light. Was it still working when he went out?'

Effatt translated. 'Yes,' he said.

'He's sure?'

'Absolutely.'

'Who does he think removed it?'

'He doesn't know.'

'I don't understand,' Kate said. 'Why do you think it was two people all of a sudden and what has a light got to do with it?'

Quinn pointed up at the gate. 'They neutralized the lamp.'

Kate frowned. 'Why would they want to do that? If Wheeler was sitting here, he wouldn't have been able to see it anyway.'

'It had nothing to do with Wheeler. They were worried someone would witness them leave.'

'How come you think there were two of them?'

'I don't believe a woman, even a strong, fit one, would risk trying to strangle a man of Wheeler's size unless she had someone to back her up. I guess one of them came ahead to distract Wheeler while the other reached up and removed the bulb by the gate.'

'Why didn't they just turn it off?'

'Because they couldn't find the switch. It's down here, inside the front door, which suggests to me they probably hadn't been to the house before.'

They contemplated him in silence. It was interrupted by shouts from a group of boys paddling past in a crude dugout canoe. They waved. One slipped into the water and swam to the side of the boat, heaving himself onto the deck. Before he could open his mouth, Effatt stuck his head out of the window and told him to go away. The boy back-flipped into the water and swam to the boat, while the others laughed uproariously.

'My men have tried speaking to the boys from the bridge,' Effatt said. 'Maybe this lot are part of the same gang. Do you want me to try again?'

'Sure.' Quinn could see Effatt was grateful to get away from the oppressive heat and smell in this room.

He began to sift through the piles of debris. He had done this so often, but it never got any easier. In the piles of paper on the floor, he found bundles of letters from Wheeler's mother, notes from friends in England and Cairo and from others temporarily billeted in Tobruk, Mersa Matruh and Bir Hacheim. They were friendly, comradely, though one or two hinted at something beyond friendship. Quinn read one officer recollecting 'that fabulous night in Cairo' and another 'aching to get out of this hellhole and be back with you in the bright lights of that fair city . . .'

Wheeler, it seemed, was not the most cautious of men.

He found some memorandums from the payroll department and bank withdrawal slips. He went through them in detail, then pulled out the bundle of

English pound notes he'd found in the briefcase last night. He held each in turn up to the light. 'What are you doing?' Kate asked.

Quinn looked out over the Nile, his back to her. He watched the reeds sway in the breeze on the far side of the water. The air was still, the night languid. He watched a car speed along the far shore. He could just see Effatt on the bridge, talking to the boys. They were dancing around him and it didn't look like he was getting very far.

'What is it?' Kate asked.

'Just the payslips,' he said.

'Is there something in them?'

He turned, let the pound notes drop onto the desk, shunting aside some of the broken records with his foot. 'No. That's the point. From what I can see, Wheeler drew a colonel's pay. No more, no less.'

Kate waited for some further insight and, when none was forthcoming, took a white handkerchief from her pocket and wiped the sweat from her forehead. 'I'm not sure I understand.'

'Where could Wheeler have got this?' He pointed to the cash on the table.

'I don't know,' she said. 'He brought it with him?'

'No, he's been here too long. He'd have changed it.'

'Perhaps he was paid for something?'

'Maybe. But why in *English* cash? That doesn't make any sense.' Quinn handed her the money. 'Take this up to the paymaster general's office.' Under the currency regulations introduced at the outbreak of war, all sterling notes had to be changed there to prevent forgeries being put into circulation. 'See what he thinks.'

313

CHAPTER FORTY-ONE

Quinn reached forward and scooped a mixture of *hummus* and *tahina* onto a piece of flat Arab bread. He took a sip of *raki*, a colourless liquid that turned cloudy when diluted with water, then wolfed the food. He was hungry and he used his finger to push *tabbouleh* onto a crisp leaf of Cos lettuce. They were in Sofar's, a small, unpretentious restaurant in Alfi Street, just a few yards from Shepheard's.

Quinn and Effatt often met there. It was a light place, crowded and friendly, the afternoon sunshine filtered by clouds of sweet-smelling smoke. It was popular with families and rarely patronized now by officers and enlisted men, which gave it added appeal.

Effatt contemplated a table full of *mezze*. He'd barely touched a single dish. 'My sister says your wife telephoned,' he said. 'She wants Deena to bring the boy over tonight. She says they will drive to Jerusalem, or go by boat from Alexandria.' Effatt was looking at him intently. 'She asked Deena not to tell me, said she needed to get out of town.'

'You sure she said that? She had to get out of town?'

'Yes.'

'What did you tell Deena?'

'I said I'd have to think about it.' Effatt picked up a piece of bread. 'You reckon we're going to solve this case soon?'

Quinn ate again. He took his time. This was what they'd stopped off to discuss. 'I keep coming back to the same question. It takes Macleod hours and hours of work to build enough of a case against us for the Defence Committee and then last night he activates it. Why? What is it he's so determined to protect?'

Effatt shrugged.

'OK, here's another question. Why would Wheeler have a list of weapons being moved in his home? You think he could have been trying to steal them?'

'For whom?'

'Amy White told me her husband was making money. Rommel's approaching, she says, the war's over, there's money to be made. She talks about palace officials, senior figures in our military. Maybe that's where Macleod comes in.'

'How?'

'Say they're stealing weapons, giving them to your people. You think it's possible?'

A waiter yelled at the kitchen. The next-door table was occupied by a family absorbed in trying to amuse its young children.

'Of course, it's possible,' Effatt said. 'There's no doubt the city is being prepared. I hear hushed conversations, whispers in the office. The rumour is that the king and some of his officials are talking to the army, the students, trying to see if some physical assistance can be offered to Rommel as he approaches. That way, they can be seen to liberate their own city. I've heard a rumour that some of the students have been training in the Mokkatam hills. With new British weapons, they could make a lot of trouble.'

'So they start a guerrilla war?'

'It's only a rumour.'

'The king is involved?'

'Not himself. He's not so foolish. It will all be done discreetly. But perhaps his officials, those close to him, along with some officers in the army, the *imams* and students at El Azhar . . . At the right time, in the right way, they could turn the city on its head.'

'Why not get weapons from your army?'

'Because they'd be lucky if they still worked.'

'But if the palace is getting a supply of British weapons, that trade would need protection, right?'

Effatt nodded.

Quinn thought about it. 'So maybe the symbol of the God of Chaos means something, after all?'

'Yes, but what? It was used before the war. Maybe it's the banner they've chosen. If Macleod's involved, perhaps the killer scrawled it on Durant's chest as a message to Field Security to take over the case and kill it off.'

They noticed Reza and Sorrenson enter the restaurant. The pair looked for a table, then caught sight of them and came over. Sorrenson was a big man, muscular and lean, with closely cut dark hair. He was handsome, in his own way, dressed in a light khaki civilian suit, bulging on one side where his revolver hung across his chest. Reza wore a newly cut dark suit and polished shoes. He carried his stick. Quinn watched Effatt stiffen.

Sorrenson had come from the east with Macleod, the third member of that cabal, if you included Lewis.

He'd been the Scot's deputy since he'd taken up the post in Field Security at the start of the war. 'I saw you went down to Wheeler's place,' Quinn said.

'Yeah. We sneaked a peek last night.'

Sorrenson was clearly trying to appear affable and Quinn wondered why he was making this admission. 'What were you looking for?'

'Oh, you know how it is. You've seen what's going on.'

'Maybe you could tell me next time before you piss all over the evidence.'

Sorrenson smiled, refusing to be provoked. 'Of course. We're keen to work together on this one. Why don't you drop in later? We can talk about the way things are moving.'

Reza had already withdrawn and Sorrenson joined him at a table in the corner furthest from where Quinn and Effatt were sitting. They were partially obscured by a pillar and a fan screwed to the side of it. Quinn returned to his food, but he could see that Reza was still watching him.

Effatt scooped up a large dollop of *hummus* with his bread and put it into his mouth. 'I don't think I ever told you but about two months ago a Hungarian girl claimed Reza raped her.'

'Who was she?'

'Some former aristocrat fallen on hard times. She worked for the Red Cross and sang up at the Egyptian Officers Club to make money. Reza picked her up, said he wanted to question her. He took her to one of their safe-houses and raped her. I listened to what she said, then I had a call from Signor Fabrizzi at the palace.' Effatt could not keep the bitterness from his voice. 'Case closed.'

317

'So, you're saying there's a direct connection between the palace and Macleod?'

'The thought had occurred to me.'

Quinn bolted his food, then reached for an ashtray and smoked as he drank the last of his *raki*. 'You figure Macleod and Lewis are still buddies?' he asked.

'Why?'

'Lewis gives the impression he's suspicious of him.'

'And you believe that?'

'I guess I do, but I can't work out why.'

'It's a bit of a coincidence that they should end up here together, then,' Effatt said.

'You'd give someone a job out of shared history, wouldn't you?'

'Not unless I liked him,' Effatt said. He waved at a waiter for the bill. 'Not unless I liked him, my friend. I'd say they are working together, for sure.'

CHAPTER FORTY-TWO

Madden sat at his desk, typing with one eye half closed against smoke twisting up from a cigarette stuck to the corner of his mouth. He thumped hard, then cursed, leaning over the keys to inspect his mistake. His insistence on typing everything himself was a source of despair for the secretaries in the pool outside. You had to try to read the reports to see why. 'You'll never guess what,' he said.

'Try me.' Quinn took off his jacket and holster and hung them on the back of the door. Effatt had returned to his own office.

'Guess who the secretary of the Cairo Amateur Theatrical Society is.'

'Got no idea.'

'Try.'

'King Farouk? The Queen of Sheba?'

'Mrs Alicia Jane Markham, wife of the district commissioner for railways.'

Quinn faced him. 'And both Wheeler and Durant were members?'

'Correct. According to Ruth.'

'OK, that is interesting.' Quinn sat. 'Should she have mentioned it?'

'Well, I don't see why. We didn't ask her about it. You hadn't got to that line of thinking when we spoke to her.' Madden picked up a piece of paper from his desk and read through it. He scooped up a few other sheets, tied them together with string and put them in front of Quinn. 'We got pushed off course this morning so I never finished my report. But they'll want one tomorrow. I've not drawn any conclusions, but there's room at the bottom if you want to add something.'

Quinn glanced through it. Madden had attached full transcripts of their interviews with Wheeler and Mrs Markham and his conversations with Ruth and the other girls from the typing pool. 'You don't really have to write things up in this detail,' Quinn said. He could never get over the English obsession with bureaucracy.

'I know you think that, but you don't have to present the report. Lewis is all right, but you try explaining to the likes of Brigadier Collins why everything isn't in triplicate.'

Quinn signed the bottom of the report, without adding any comments, and pushed it back. 'Where is Mrs Markham?'

'Her *sufragi* says she's at the Gezira. I thought I'd wait until you got back.'

Mrs Markham sat beside the pool under a sun umbrella, her eyes shielded by a pair of thick dark glasses. She was swathed in cloth, but smelt of Nivea sun cream, which had been liberally applied to a few bare patches of skin. She was watching a group of children jumping into the choppy water from the triple diving-board.

A waiter approached, carrying a tray with a single tall, ice-chinking glass. 'I supposed you would find me,' she said. She took the glass from the waiter, and asked, by means of an outstretched hand, whether they wished to join her. Madden shook his head. 'I did not work for Colonel Wheeler,' she said. It seemed to be her way of saying she had nothing to add.

'More's the pity,' Quinn observed.

'Why do you say that?'

'You might have knocked some sense into him.'

She examined her hands. She seemed to know this was flattery, but was still susceptible to it. Quinn sat. 'I wanted to talk about the Cairo Amateur Theatrical Society,' he said.

'What about it?'

'I should have listened more closely to you in the first place.'

'About what?'

'I asked you whether Wheeler and Durant were pals. You were surprised to be asked. Yes, you said, sure. But Wheeler had given me the opposite impression. I should have asked myself why.'

'They were very close.'

'Exactly. If I'd paid more attention to you, he might still be alive.'

She didn't seem certain about this. Maybe it was a compliment too far. 'They performed together?' he asked.

'With the society? Oh, yes. Very much so.'

'In what?'

'The last production was of *HMS Pinafore*. As I recall, they were both . . . yes, they were in the chorus.'

'How long ago?'

'It was our Christmas production.'

'You have anything from that, Mrs Markham? A photograph of the cast, a programme, a list of who else took part?'

'Of course.'

Mrs Markham lived in Bulaq Dakhrur, just to the west of Cairo. Madden navigated his way through a ceaseless procession of trams, donkey carts and pedestrians before he pulled out of the last of the suburbs and slipped into the countryside beyond. Since Kate had their official car, they were in another Austin with a clutch that slipped. Madden had trouble mastering it. He was a lousy driver.

They crossed canals and passed fields of grey-green sugar cane, fringed by feathery palms and casuarina trees. A breeze rustled the branches and danced across the crops. A succession of figures could be seen dotted across the landscape, their long smocks tucked between their legs as they worked.

They reached a railway crossing and had to wait for the interminable passage of a goods train. A truck driver honked his horn. Beside them, tethered to a tree, a water-buffalo eyed them.

Mrs Markham sat uncomfortably on the edge of the front passenger seat, next to Madden. She embarked on an explanation as to why she had moved out here from an apartment in Zamalek, but it soon slipped into a prolonged complaint about the war. It was impossible to go anywhere, these days, she said, without being besieged by hordes of enlisted men from Liverpool, Manchester and Glasgow.

Something in her tone made Quinn think how often

he'd heard similar diatribes, Egypt's white masters shrinking from the reality of the countrymen they professed to adore. The colonial experience seemed to him to be all about creating an idealized version of the mother country, where poverty, ugliness and crime could be kept at a convenient distance. After a while he stopped listening, but Madden continued to provide regular polite prompts. You could say this for the English: their manners never flagged.

Bulaq Dakhrur was little more than a mud village with a small group of European houses tacked onto its outer rim. The Markhams' home was furthest from the road, over a bumpy track splattered with donkey dung and pools of liquid left by the water-buffalo. It was a tall white building, surrounded by a wide veranda, but it looked shabby and in poor repair. As they climbed out, Mrs Markham muttered about the difficulties of finding the right workmen.

She'd told Madden they'd moved here for the children, who were now at boarding-school in Cairo, and indeed there was a swing in one corner of the garden beneath a tall eucalyptus tree. Next to it was the water-tank, but there was little evidence that its contents had been used on the lawn, which consisted only of a few tufts of grass. Quinn suspected that the move from the apartment in Zamalek might not have included the district commissioner for railways. Or, at least, in name only.

'Ahmed!' she called.

The *sufragi* shuffled out. He was an old man in a filthy smock and battered sandals. 'What would you like?' she asked them. 'Tea or something stronger?'

'Tea,' Quinn said, although he'd have preferred something stronger.

She gave instructions to the servant, then led them to the side of the house. A cat was asleep in an old rocking-chair. She tipped it onto the floor and offered them a seat on a bench, which was shedding large chunks of white paint. She slipped into the house and emerged a few moments later with a box.

Mrs Markham sat in the rocking-chair and began to unload its contents onto the table. It consisted of musical scores, programmes and old photographs. 'Do you like Gilbert and Sullivan, Major?'

'Sure,' Quinn said.

She looked at Madden and smiled – she had assessed them both accurately – then sorted through the contents of the box. She made a neat pile on the floor beside her. 'Here we are.' She handed Madden the programme. 'You do know this is where all Cairo meets, don't you? I think we can honestly say that, at one point or another, we've had every nationality involved.' She flipped through the photographs. 'Of course, it's become more difficult recently to include our Italian and German friends . . .'

Quinn ran his eyes down the programme. He could see no mention of either Wheeler or Durant, or any other familiar names, although there was a generous sprinkling of senior officers. You would never have imagined there was a war on.

Madden handed him the photographs. They looked as if they'd been taken with a box Brownie, mostly on stage, during what appeared to be a dress rehearsal, since not everyone was in full costume. There was only one of the full cast. 'They weren't given starring roles, then?' Quinn asked.

'It's a team effort.'

Quinn held up the picture of the cast. He couldn't

make them out. 'Here, let me look,' she said. She produced a pair of reading-glasses and placed them on her nose. 'At the back on the left.'

Quinn took back the photograph. Sure enough, they were next to each other, grinning.

'Rupert . . . I mean, Captain Durant,' she said, 'was a new recruit. Colonel Wheeler had been in the chorus for some time and—'

'How long?'

'Oh, since . . . well, he was certainly in the Christmas production the previous year.'

'You suggested he come along?' Quinn asked. 'Captain Durant, I mean.'

She blushed. 'Yes. He seemed rather lonely. It's such fun. A terrific way to meet people from all walks of life in the city. We've even got a Bulgarian conductor. And a Greek built our set. My husband tried to get Grand Duke Boris involved one year.'

'The Russian?'

'Yes – do you know him? A charming fellow, in small doses. Well, not very charming, but he has something about him. These former royals always do, don't you think?'

'I wouldn't know.' Quinn bent closer to the photograph. 'Would you have a magnifying-glass?'

'Erm . . . yes.'

Quinn tried to make out other faces in the cast. She returned with the magnifying-glass. 'Thank you,' he said.

He put the photograph on the table and bent over it. 'What are you looking for?' she asked. 'Perhaps I can help.'

He examined Wheeler and Durant first. They were both unmistakably happy in each other's company.

No-one else seemed familiar. 'Hold on a second.' He lowered the glass. 'Isn't that . . . Fabrizzi?'

'It would be, yes.'

'What's he doing there?'

'Why shouldn't he be?' Her manner was defensive. 'I'm sure that if the authorities considered him a threat, they would have taken the appropriate action. Signor Fabrizzi is a generous supporter of the group. He has a marvellous voice. Before the war we were able to make much greater use of it. And, of course, the king is fond of Gilbert and Sullivan.'

'Fabrizzi, Wheeler and Durant were friends?'

'Well . . . yes, I believe so.'

'So they had a contact at the palace?'

But before she could answer, Quinn was on his feet.

CHAPTER FORTY-THREE

The heat had faded, but the white walls of the Abdin Palace still glowed in the subdued rays of the late-evening sun. They drove round the great square opposite its entrance, past the tawny façades of old arcades and lawns filled with scarlet and yellow canna lilies. As they approached the gate, Effatt, whom they'd picked up on their way into town, wound down his window to speak to the guards.

The men listened for a moment, then the older of the pair went to make a call in his hut. He returned, shaking his head. A long discussion ensued. Eventually the guard waved them through. 'They can't get an answer,' Effatt explained, 'but I said I had an appointment.'

Kate slipped the car into gear and moved forward. Inside the gate, an air of indolence prevailed. Two peacocks sauntered across the road; a dog was asleep in the sunshine. Kate stopped to let the peacocks pass.

Another car started up. It came down the far side quickly and spun past them, honking at the peacocks. It was a bright red Corvette, its metal bumpers gleaming.

The car was brought to an abrupt halt, the door was pushed open and there, in front of them, stood the corpulent figure of Egypt's king, descendant of the pharaohs and ruler of one of the world's oldest civilizations. He was wearing a dark suit and sunglasses. He stared at them as if they had come from Mars.

Nobody moved.

Farouk got back into his car and drove off, wheels spinning in the grit. 'What shall I do?' Kate asked.

'Go on,' Effatt said, unable to conceal his irritation at the arrogance of his monarch.

Farouk had driven through a gate in the far corner, so Kate proceeded slowly. She drew the car to a halt, and Effatt ushered them up a dark stairway to the floor above. A plump Egyptian man in a dark suit sat behind a desk in a small atrium. When Effatt asked for Signor Fabrizzi, there was another robust exchange of views, during which Quinn understood, even with his limited Arabic, that this man was Fabrizzi's secretary.

Effatt broke off, crossed the corridor and knocked on the door opposite. Fabrizzi's secretary hurried from behind the desk, spluttering disapproval, voice shrill with panic.

Effatt ignored him and opened the door. There was a dead silence, then the secretary wailed and fell back, knocking Quinn's shoulder as he hurried away.

It was a big room, with a flagstone floor and inlaid wooden panels. A giant bookcase stretched the length of one wall, the sun splashing pools of light on the desk next to the window. Fabrizzi lay in the centre of the room, his body twisted and arms outstretched, as if in a last appeal for help.

They heard heavy boots on the stairs. A guard

appeared in the doorway. 'Leave us!' Effatt bellowed. The man disappeared.

Quinn bent down, then slipped onto his knees. He looked at Fabrizzi's neck. It was cold to the touch. 'This OK?' he asked.

'Be my guest,' Effatt said.

Quinn attempted to turn Fabrizzi a little to get a better look at the wound. But the contorted nature of his position and the rigor mortis made it impossible. He had been dead eight hours at least. The piano wire was embedded in his neck. More force had been used than on Wheeler, less than on Durant.

Quinn checked the body for any other marks or signs of a struggle. There were none. He looked at the fingernails, which were cut short. Fabrizzi had been wearing a cream linen suit, half of which was now blood red. Effatt went through his pockets, but found only a silk handkerchief and a gold watch on a long chain. On a small table beside him was a tray with a silver pot of coffee and a single cup. It had not been disturbed, and the coffee had not been drunk. Quinn glanced at Kate. She was as white as a sheet. Madden stood in the shadows behind her.

Fabrizzi's secretary reappeared in the doorway. He was shaking at the sight of his master's body. Effatt beckoned him forward. 'Tell me what happened,' he said. The man began a rambling answer in Arabic, but Effatt interrupted him. 'In English,' he said, gesturing at Quinn and the others.

The secretary took a deep breath. 'I have told the guards. They have sent for the grand chamberlain but—'

'No, I said tell me what happened.'

The man blinked rapidly, frightened eyes behind

dirty round glasses. 'This morning I knocked and there was no answer . . .'

'You have been sitting across the hall all day?'

'He does not like to be interrupted, you see. I—'

'You haven't been in here *once*?'

'Sir, you do not understand. The signor—'

'Start at the beginning,' Effatt said. 'What time did you get here?'

'At seven, just as normal.'

'And Signor Fabrizzi was not here?'

'No, sir.'

'What did you do?'

'I checked with the gate. The guards always tell me if he has come in or gone out. They said he had arrived at four thirty this morning and gone straight to his room. Half an hour later he returned to the gate.'

'And went out again?'

'No, sir. He was waiting for someone.'

'Who?'

'I don't know.' The secretary wiped his forehead. He was sweating profusely. 'The signor brought them straight through. The guards told me it was a European couple.'

'What did they look like?'

'The guards did not say.'

'Were the pair in uniform?'

'I do not know.'

'And what time did they come out again?'

'They did not come out.'

'So—'

'The king has a private entrance, I thought that perhaps the signor had taken them out that way.'

'Did he usually arrange meetings at that hour?' Effatt asked.

'No ... but ... Signor Fabrizzi is ... His movements were unpredictable.'

'Why did he go to the gate?' Quinn asked.

'I do not understand.'

'Why not wait for the guards to call up to his room?'

'Er, I do not know, sir.'

'He wanted the couple to come straight through without scrutiny?'

'Yes, well ... I suppose it is possible.'

'When do you figure he ordered coffee for one?'

The secretary looked at the pot and the single cup. It was clear from his demeanour that a wise official – and perhaps a wise guard duty – learnt not to pay too much attention to Signor Fabrizzi's comings and goings.

'What's your name?' Effatt asked.

'Zulficar, sir. Ahmed.'

'Ahmed, we need help here. Who was Signor Fabrizzi meeting this morning?' Effatt had lowered his voice an octave.

'I do not know, sir.'

'Whom do you think it *might* have been?'

He shook his head.

'Do you want us to take you down to the barracks, Ahmed?'

'No, sir.'

'Then who was he waiting for at the gate?'

Ahmed shook his head miserably. Clearly he had no idea, or was dissembling well.

'Were you aware that the meeting was going to take place?'

'No, sir.'

'What was in his diary for today?'

'There was a conference with the grand chamberlain

331

and His Royal Highness at five this afternoon. I had to inform His Royal Highness that Signor Fabrizzi had not yet returned.'

Effatt walked to the window, took hold of a long curtain and pulled savagely, until it tore free. He draped it over Fabrizzi's body. Wisps of the Italian's hair poked out of the makeshift shroud. They heard voices in the stairwell, hushed and urgent. A faint breeze crept through the open window. A fan turned on top of a chest in the corner. Quinn glanced at a giant painting of the Khan Khalili that stretched the length of the far wall.

The desk appeared unnaturally clear, Quinn thought. Either Fabrizzi was a man of consummate bureaucratic orderliness, or someone had tidied up after him. In the centre was a silver case, which contained a neat pile of oval Egyptian cigarettes, each inscribed in gold lettering with the name Simon Arzt. A business card for Claridge's Restaurant-Bar (Prop. Georges Boucherot) was propped against it. Quinn noticed a matchbox in the corner of the cigarette case. The image of Seth, God of Chaos, was emblazoned on the front, like the one Mac had shown him in the Kit Kat. He held it up, turned it over.

Then he took out a handkerchief, wrapped it round his fingers and tried the central drawer on the desk. It was locked. The same was true of those lower down. He moved back towards the body. 'Is there a key?' Effatt asked Ahmed.

The secretary shook his head.

'Shall I?' Quinn asked Effatt, indicating that he could force it.

'I wouldn't advise it.'

They heard footsteps on the stairs, and a moment

332

…ater a stick-thin man in an immaculate dark suit slipped into the room. He was entirely bald, his face clean-shaven, with alert, narrow eyes. He carried a long walking-cane, topped with polished silver. Like his master, the king, and Fabrizzi, he wore dark glasses. He faced Effatt, as if Quinn was not present. '*Qu'est qu'ils font ici?*' he demanded.

This, Quinn assumed, was the grand chamberlain, Sahouf. He had barely glanced at Fabrizzi's corpse, let alone betrayed any surprise at the murder.

Effatt answered in Arabic. The conversation flitted to and fro with such velocity and ferocity that Quinn found it impossible to follow. He understood only that their presence here was the subject of the disagreement.

The argument raged, both men apparently oblivious to their spectators. Sahouf was a relatively short man with a long nose and narrow face. He had, Quinn noticed, immaculate hands.

Sahouf strode towards Fabrizzi's body. He pulled back the shroud and bent over it, then walked briskly from the room, yanking the door shut behind him. Ahmed had gone with him. 'He wants you to leave immediately,' Effatt said.

'Maybe it would be easier.'

'No. He wants a compliant local cop he can lean on, wishes it all to be hushed up, kept from the press. No autopsy, no searches, no questions. He wants the family told it was a heart attack and a note to that effect put out to the press.'

The murmur of voices was still just about audible from the stairwell, but was quickly drowned by the roar of a car's engine. They moved to the window as Farouk's red Corvette sped through the courtyard.

Quinn glared at Kate and Ed. 'What do you want us to do?' Quinn asked quietly.

Effatt watched the car until it had disappeared from view. 'I'm going to go and speak to the guards for a few minutes. While I am out, I charge . . .' He smiled thinly. 'I request that you do not touch anything in this room. However, naturally I will not know whether you have chosen to break into any of the drawers in Signor Fabrizzi's desk. The stairs will afford ample warning of any approach. But be quick. I cannot allow you to remain for long.'

He strode across the floor, out of the door and down the stairs, walking quietly, as if to demonstrate that any approach was audible. Quinn listened to the sound of his footsteps on the gravel outside. He used a letter opener to lever open the top drawer. It was empty. He tried the one below, which was similarly devoid of contents. Someone had cleared the desk. 'Why is Sahouf so nervous if he's already removed everything?'

Quinn looked around the room. Beside him was a fake Louis XVI chair of the kind you could see in Signor Potremoli's fancy downtown showroom. He glanced at the giant portrait of the Khan Khalili, then at the other paintings that adorned the walls. 'There must be a safe,' he said.

He stood up, walked across to the picture of the bazaar and lifted it from the bottom. Madden and Kate assisted him. The wall behind was smooth and clear. They looked behind the other paintings in the room but found nothing.

'A man like this has to have a safe,' Quinn said.

'Why?' Kate asked.

'A high official, sensitive documents.'

'The palace is guarded, sir,' Madden said. 'His desk is locked. I don't see—'

Quinn bent down, took the corner of a silk rug and yanked it back, revealing dusty floorboards. He ripped up the other rugs, then pulled out the furniture: first the Louis XVI chair and a *chaise-longue*, then the ornate dresser in the corner and finally the desk. He yanked back the last section of rug to reveal a wooden trapdoor. Beneath it was a safe, pointing downwards, its keyhole uppermost. 'Mowbray,' he said, 'can you do this?'

'I can try.' Kate knelt down and set to work on the lock.

It was more difficult than the other locks and it took time. When she'd done it, she stepped back to allow Quinn to see what was inside. He found a series of letters bound together with a piece of string and a wooden box.

He laid the letters upon the desk, then opened the box. It was packed with three thick stacks of English currency. Quinn took one out and flicked through it. It contained five-pound notes – maybe a thousand sterling in each bundle.

'Good God,' Madden said.

Quinn checked the serial numbers on the notes. Each was different.

He turned his attention to the letters. They were addressed to Signor Fabrizzi, Private Secretary to King Farouk, Abdin Palace, Cairo. Each envelope was dated and marked by hand. Quinn pulled out the contents. They contained sheets of paper inscribed with lines of jumbled letters. 'Encrypted,' Madden said.

Quinn folded them. 'When we get back to the office,' he said, 'take them to GHQ, see if they can make anything of them.'

They heard a car horn and a revving engine. Quinn walked to the window and looked out. Farouk was now circling in a red Mercedes. 'Hitler sent him that,' he muttered. 'You know no-one else in Cairo gets to own a red car?'

They heard footsteps on the stairs and Effatt appeared. He walked slowly towards them. He displayed no reaction to the mess or to the bundles of cash. 'What is it?' Quinn asked.

'I spoke to the guards on the gate. They saw a European man dressed in desert jacket and slacks and a woman. Both wore hats pulled low over their faces. An alert guard made a note of the car number. It was a military plate, so I got Headquarters to look through their records.'

'What did they find?'

'It cannot be so, but . . .'

'What?'

'The car was a Ford V8. According to the plate, it was your car, Joe.'

CHAPTER FORTY-FOUR

They called it a meeting, but it felt like an interrogation. Effatt and Quinn sat in two chairs in the centre of the room. Lewis was positioned behind his desk, with Macleod to his left and Sahouf, Farouk's grand chamberlain, to his right, then a young blade with slicked-back dark hair from the embassy, called Nigel Bexley, and an official from the Egyptian Interior Ministry.

Madden and Kate had been told to return to Bab El Hadid. Through the window, Quinn could see an inky ash-flecked pall of smoke melting into the night sky over old Cairo. In the courtyard below, they were still burning documents. 'Major Quinn,' Lewis said, 'the purpose of this meeting is to establish clearly in our mind the facts relating to Signor Fabrizzi's death.'

Sahouf leant forward. He tapped his cane lightly on the floor. 'Signor Fabrizzi had a heart attack. This is what his family will be told. It is what the king will be told. It is an unfortunate matter but one that need not concern you any longer.'

'He cut his own throat?' Quinn asked.

'His Excellency is aware of what you may think,'

Bexley said. He adjusted his cuffs. 'He also knows of the investigation that you are currently undertaking. But I'm afraid you're going to have to accept this restriction. Signor Fabrizzi is off limits.'

'And I would remind you, Major,' Lewis said, his manner formal, 'that I have had the greatest difficulty explaining to some of my colleagues why you are not in custody. I have said you've been granted a short time to wrap up the case upon which you are engaged. I hope you will not disappoint me.'

'You got an autopsy?' Quinn asked.

Bexley shook his head. 'Your reputation precedes you, Major, but I would venture to suggest you will do yourself no favours here. This needs to be left in peace.'

'You go along with this?' Quinn asked Lewis.

'None of us has any choice *but* to go along with it,' Bexley said.

They were silent.

'Are you expecting me to write a report?' Effat asked Sahouf.

'No. We will arrange the autopsy.'

'It will be done by the police doctor?'

'The royal surgeon will carry it out. He is adept at such matters.'

'You figure Fabrizzi was alone when he died?' Quinn asked.

'Of course.'

'So the white couple who came to meet him early that morning had already gone?'

'Correct.'

'You know who they were?'

'It is immaterial.'

'You got any idea what they talked about?'

'None whatsoever.'

'But it must have been serious, right? To give the guy a heart attack like that—'

'Major Quinn,' Lewis said, 'you are really not—'

'You know he had a bundle of cash in his safe? Maybe three thousand sterling, hard currency. You got an explanation for that?' Quinn was still looking at Bahouf.

'It is none of your business.'

'Fabrizzi usually have that kind of money?'

'This speculation is not—'

'We found the cash along with a bunch of encrypted letters. You got an idea why he was hiding them?'

'It *is* none of our business, Quinn,' Bexley said. He had tensed. 'That's the point.'

'You sure? I thought we were hunting a spy? What does Major Macleod think?'

The Scot touched the crucifix that hung round his neck. 'About what?' he said.

'You knew Fabrizzi, right? He was a contact. What do you figure he was doing with the money?'

Macleod stared at him. He did not deny that Fabrizzi had been one of his contacts.

'I would remind you, Major Quinn,' Bexley interjected, 'that we live in complex times. We need the continued support of our friends in this city and we shall do our utmost to ensure we get it.'

Quinn ignored him. 'Fabrizzi was looking to buy guns?' he asked Macleod. 'You figure that's what he was doing?'

'It's an interesting idea. What makes you say that?'

'Wheeler had a connection with Fabrizzi. We found some of the same batch of cash hidden in his houseboat. And we got reason to believe the colonel might have been interested in getting hold of a shipment of weapons.'

'For what purpose?'

'Maybe he was selling them on to the palace.'

Macleod glanced at Sahouf. 'And why would they wish to buy them?'

'I figured you'd have worked that out for yourself.'

Colour appeared in Macleod's cheeks. He shifted uncomfortably in his seat. 'Can you prove any of this?' he asked.

Quinn said nothing. He held the Scot's gaze.

'Answer the question, Joe,' Lewis said crisply. 'Can you prove it?'

'Not yet. But it would be an interesting racket, right? You funnel off weapons for hard currency. Worth killing to protect?'

'How do you suppose Colonel Wheeler was going to get his hands on a consignment of weapons?' Macleod asked.

'He was going to steal them.'

'All by himself?' Reza asked.

'He had accomplices.'

'Who?'

Sahouf tapped his cane impatiently. 'This is ladies talk. Signor Fabrizzi has had an unfortunate accident This is not your city and not your country. I forbic you to pursue the matter. Is that clear?'

Neither Quinn nor Effatt answered.

'Is that clear, Joe?' Lewis asked.

'Sure.'

Quinn and Effatt stood. 'Is there anything else you'c like to tell us, Detective Effatt,' Macleod asked, 'i relation to the death of such a high official?'

Effatt shook his head.

'Nothing that should be brought to our attention? No hint as to the identity of the European couple seen at the palace first thing this morning, no number-plate for a car?'

Effatt shrugged. Macleod turned to Quinn. Their cards were clearly on the table: now it was war.

'Very well, then.' Lewis got up. 'I think we're all in agreement. Thank you for your time, gentlemen.'

CHAPTER FORTY-FIVE

As Effatt's driver pulled out of the gates at GHQ, a black Fiat accelerated away from the dusty kerb behind him. It sat on their tail all the way to Effatt's headquarters. Neither of them mentioned it, but as soon as they were in the main building they climbed the stairs and slipped out onto the terrace. Down below, the Fiat sat motionless with its engine running. The life of the street swirled around it – lights blazing, horns blaring, shouts and yells mixed with the sound of an electric generator – but its occupants did not stir. 'Who are they?' Quinn asked.

'Reza's men.'

A door opened below. Reza himself and another, much taller, Egyptian man got out. They leant against the side of the Fiat, smoking. 'Not too subtle,' Quinn said.

'They don't need to be subtle.'

Effatt looked out over the rooftops, lights twinkling against the blackout. The sky was blazing with stars, a bright moon silvering the distant Pyramids and the desert hills beyond. Reza and his companion sheltered beneath a line of palms on the far side of the road.

'Whoever is fixing you up,' Effatt said, 'he's doing it well. Every step we take, they sink you deeper. They can find a glass with your print, get a spare set of plates for your car.'

'Macleod has spent months—'

'Are you sure it's Macleod?' Effatt asked.

'What are you saying?'

'It doesn't seem his style. It's not Reza's, anyway. What about those closer to you?'

'What do you mean?'

'You heard me.'

'Like who?'

'Maybe you should look at everyone. Ed, Kate. They've got the access and they know enough to—'

'Ed and Kate are loyal.'

'You're certain?'

'Of course I am.'

'Well, seems to me that Macleod would send Reza round and he would rake your house with gunfire. You know what he's like. We've both seen a hundred thugs like that. Maybe he has a racket, but it's *just* a racket. He's not a spy. I think you're being fitted up by someone who knows you better, maybe even someone who cares about you.'

'Why do you say that?'

'They've cut three men's throats, Joe. What's to stop them cutting yours? But they haven't laid a finger on you.'

'Not yet.'

'Someone is trying to get you to back off. This is Cairo, for God's sake. If someone wanted to get rid of you, you'd be picked off the street and put through a meat mincer or buried out in the desert.'

'You thinking of someone in particular?' Quinn

walked to the balcony. He had the uncomfortable feeling he'd guessed the direction of his friend's thoughts.

'No.'

'Go on, Effatt.'

'You think Mae could have lent your car to someone?'

Quinn stared out at the old city. 'Maybe.' Effatt came closer, draped an arm round his shoulders and they stood together, content to absorb the night in silence.

'You think someone could be blackmailing her?' Effatt asked.

'About what?'

Effatt didn't answer.

Quinn took a taxi back to his apartment and the black Fiat followed him.

As they reached the darkened bridge to Gezira and passed a lumbering number-seventeen tram, he stole a glance over his shoulder. The car was twenty-five yards behind, its driver making no pretence at discretion or concealment.

He watched the moonlight glistening on the rippling waters of the river. The Nile was speckled with white sails all the way to the horizon.

The roads in Gezira were deserted, a sign, maybe, that many Europeans had left. The taxi turned right by the church of St Joseph and glided to a halt outside the apartment. The black Fiat joined another already waiting on the far side of the street.

Quinn got out and paid the driver. He walked up the path. There was no sign of Fraser on the porch or within. The block was unnaturally still, as if all its occupants had vanished. His front door was locked. He fumbled for his key, opened it and stepped in.

He walked down the corridor, moving from light to shadow and back again. He reached the end. The blinds in the living room had been drawn and it was almost entirely consumed by darkness. His eyes searched the shadows, scrutinizing each shape.

'I'm here,' Mae said.

Quinn made her out, sitting on a chair in the corner. He moved to the centre of the room so that he was facing her. 'Did you find your killer?' she asked.

'No.'

'Does that mean we're going to be taken to an internment camp?'

Quinn moved to the window. Light from an apartment upstairs fringed the branches of a casuarina tree. He listened to the sound of the cicadas. He could just make out the shape of the two Fiats beyond the hedge. 'You try to go out?' he asked.

'You told me I was a prisoner.'

'You call anyone?'

'No.'

'You call Effatt's place?'

'I haven't called anyone.'

'You didn't speak to Deena?'

'No.'

Quinn closed the blind. Now he knew she was lying. He walked past the shelf by the window, stopped to look at a photograph of the three of them seated together on the lawns of the Gezira. It had only been taken last spring. Mae had Ryan on her lap, her arms wrapped round his tiny body. They were all grinning at the camera. 'Do you remember how it was, Joe?'

He had his back to her. 'No.' He picked up the picture. 'I see the images, but I can't get a hold on how it felt. It's like it happened in a different life, the memories all fuzzy and out of focus.'

'Sometimes in the night, when you're frightened, I see you clearly. The old you. The real you. But that's all we have left.'

Quinn glanced at the clock on the wall. It was almost eleven. He watched the second hand crawl round the dial. He thought how often he had stood there and watched that clock. 'I should have made more time for him,' he said.

Mae sighed. 'He didn't expect to have a father who was like a mother. I've told you a thousand times.'

'I've got to go out now.'

Mae didn't bother to argue.

346

CHAPTER FORTY-SIX

It took twenty minutes to walk to the other side of Gezira Island, maybe another ten to cross Zamalek Bridge to the line of houseboats on the far bank. There had only been one Fiat left outside the apartment and it followed him for about half a mile, then doubled back, as if its occupants were concerned they were being lured away by a decoy.

Quinn was hot and he moved slowly along beneath the line of palms on the quay. He heard the Hungarian singer from the Kit Kat across the water, her languorous voice carried on a faint breeze. A couple of men stood next to a red Mercedes outside the club's entrance, smoking and conversing in subdued voices.

If the nightclub was far from empty, it was still much less crowded than usual. There were tables to spare, even along the far side, next to the river. Farouk was in the corner, flanked by two girls – different ones from the previous evening – and surrounded by body-guards.

Quinn's gaze was drawn to the table closest to the piano, where Charles Lewis sat with Amy White.

Neither appeared to notice his entrance. And after a few moments, he began to imagine that they were pretending not to have done. He took his seat opposite Mac, the Egyptian's face impassive in the light of the candles all around him. 'Evening, Mr Quinn.'

'You all right, Mac?'

'Fine, sir. Just fine.'

Quinn looked down the bar. 'Been practising your German? Rumour has it you're gonna need it soon.'

Mac smiled. From beneath the counter, he produced a wooden photograph frame. Inside it was a picture of Adolf Hitler. 'Don't tell me,' Quinn said. 'A gift from Mr Kostandis.'

Mac replaced the frame. He took up a clean white cloth, began to dry glasses. 'I think you need a drink tonight.'

He poured a double, perhaps even triple shot of Scotch, slung in some ice. Quinn glanced in the mirror at Amy White and Charles Lewis, whose heads were now close together. Lewis was laughing and he swept the hair off his forehead. Quinn saw her hand drop down beside the table. He thought she had placed it on his knee.

Lewis whispered something to her and she tipped back her head and laughed with him. 'The broad got new company?' Quinn asked.

'It looks like it,' Mac said.

'You seen them together before?'

'No.'

'They been together long?'

'An hour.'

'The husband been in?'

'Not tonight.'

Quinn glanced over his shoulder again. He slipped

348

off the stool. 'When I've gone, go to the broad, whisper her husband is waiting outside.'

Quinn went through the lobby and out into the clammy warmth of the street. He lit a cigarette, then strolled along the quay, looking into the houseboats. They were all shrouded in darkness, as though abandoned. A fly landed on his cheek and he waved it away. He felt the sting of a mosquito's bite behind his ear.

'You were looking for me?' The dome of Amy White's head was ringed with light and she wore a pink silk dress, a cream scarf round her neck. Her long hair was caressed by the wind, which pulled the dress tight round her slim waist, smoothing it across the contours of her stomach. She watched the direction of his gaze.

He offered her a cigarette, lit it. 'You think I was your husband?' he asked.

'No.'

'You know it was me?'

'Of course.'

Quinn turned to walk along the quay. Amy came with him. They passed ten or twenty yards in silence. 'Where is he?' Quinn asked.

'At a meeting.'

'What kind?'

'I didn't ask.'

They had reached Wheeler's houseboat. Her smile faded. 'I figure you know this place,' he said. He reached out a hand before she could reply. 'Maybe we should take a look.' She hesitated, then accepted his offer. His heart beat a little faster. He led her down to the wooden walkway, listened to the water lapping gently against the shore.

In the living room, moonlight was reflected off the river. He watched her face. She was looking at Wheeler's desk, the debris around it and the pool of dried blood dimly visible in the shadows.

He led her on up the narrow staircase. The wooden slats creaked beneath their feet. At the top, he faced the window. A few lights from Zamalek dotted the bank on the far side of the river. He watched her scan the shore. She leant against the window-frame, slid down until she was sitting on the ledge. 'Please don't make this into another interrogation,' she said.

'Then why did you come?'

'Because I wanted to.'

Quinn sat beside her. 'Look,' he said, 'maybe I need a little help.'

'What kind?'

'When we found Durant's body, it felt like we'd got a straight motive. He has a lover, the husband's jealous.'

'My husband wasn't here.'

'So he hires someone else to do it. I figured it had to be simple, because most homicides are. But then we get another body, now a third. Turns out the men are connected, knew each other: two officers and a palace official.' Quinn touched his head. 'Now I'm trying to figure out what the connection is. What in the hell were they doing that makes someone want to kill all three of them?'

'I have no idea.'

'Your husband knew Fabrizzi. He knows the deserter we've been hunting.'

'I didn't come here to talk about this.' She stood up.

'What did you expect, ma'am?'

350

'My name is Amy.'

'So why did you come, Amy?'

'Maybe I still feel you should be spared the fate you appear hell bent on. But I don't suppose you'd accept that as a motive.'

'You say something similar to Durant?'

'You're nothing like Durant. I'm sorry I can't help you.'

Quinn moved to block the door. 'You sure about that? The other night you seemed to know all about it.'

'About what?'

'Making money. Wasn't that what you said it was about? Your husband, a bunch of palace officials and senior officers . . .'

Her face flushed. 'I told you that to give you a chance to save your neck, not so you could ask more dumb cop's questions.'

'We got information that says Fabrizzi was nailed by a white couple.'

'And suddenly you think that's us?'

'You and your husband got all the wrong connections, ma'am.'

'May I leave now?'

'Ah, come on.' He softened his voice. 'You telling me you really want to burn with him? I don't believe that. It's why you're here. It's why I'm trying to help you.'

'I can't do any more.'

'Supplying guns to the palace, is that what they've been doing? What's your husband's angle?'

'I've never said anything like that.'

'What did you say? "Rommel's coming, there's cash to be made"?'

351

She tried to move away, but he grabbed her, fingers pressing into the flesh of her upper arm. 'You're hurting me.'

'Sit down.'

'Let go.'

'Your husband killed a boyfriend, ma'am, then maybe I'd understand, but this is starting to feel like something a whole lot bigger.'

She looked into his eyes. 'I can see you very clearly. Don't forget I've spent many long hours discussing you with your wife.'

'I'm not here to talk about my wife.'

'Seems to me, right now, you're looking for a lifeboat, Major Quinn. But I'm not the right one.'

'You've been here before.'

'You think I murdered this guy? Is that what you're saying?'

'I got the images, but you can make the picture.'

She took a step closer, brushed his shoulder. 'I make the picture and it could be the last thing you ever see.'

'I'll take that chance.'

'That's the wrong choice. In two weeks, the war will have gone, moved on, and none of this will matter.'

'Make the picture. Tell me what they're doing. How are they making money?'

A burst of automatic gunfire shattered the windows, bullets whipping past their ears and ripping apart the woodwork. Quinn dived onto the floor beside the bed. He covered her with his arms.

The noise was like thunder, splinters of wood raining from air thick with dust. She clung to him, arms round his shoulders, soft hair in his eyes, nose and mouth. He could feel her fingers digging into his back and her breath on his neck.

He held her to him. She pulled him tighter, her body pressed to his.

Quinn closed his eyes. The boat rocked gently.

And then, as suddenly as the storm had begun, it was over. A single shout pierced the silent night. They heard a car accelerate away.

She did not move, eyes close to his, her dress rucked up at the waist to reveal bare legs, a trickle of blood from one ankle visible above the red strap of her shoe.

She tried to move, but he held her. 'No,' she said. She fought free, lunged for the stairs and hammered down them. The boat rocked again as she ran across the gangway and back onto the shore. He moved to the window, looked out. She slowed to a walk, smoothed her dress, as if trying to compose herself. There were more shouts now, from further down, in the direction of the Kit Kat. Quinn looked out of the other window and saw a dark Fiat driving away over the bridge towards Zamalek.

He walked out onto the balcony and glanced up at the stars twinkling above. The night could hardly have appeared more peaceful.

He lit a cigarette, inhaled deeply, then blew smoke into the warm air. He noticed his hand was shaking.

At home, Quinn tried his best to block out the moonlight in the lounge with a bunch of towels, then lay down on the couch and stared up at the ceiling. He wiped away the sweat on his forehead and top lip with his shirt sleeve. The night appeared even more suffocating when he was horizontal.

He had spent a few minutes watching his wife's sleeping figure next door and now he tried consciously to fill his mind with memories of her. It was difficult.

He thought of their life on Seventh Street and the days when Mae's stepfather used to push them towards McSorley's in a big box-cart.

The memories were real enough, but he could not relate the Mae he saw in his mind's eye to the woman who lay asleep on the bed next door.

He closed his eyes, but despite the intense fatigue his mind turned from one train of thought to the next, without letting up. He got up again and slipped out onto the terrace.

He lit a cigarette and strolled round the garden. In the corner, he heard the hiss of a hose being used to water a flowerbed. A dog from the neighbouring garden started at his approach and scuttled back through a hole in the hedge. Quinn could see Fraser's tiny light on in his room at the back of the apartment building.

He took a few paces to his left, so that he had a clear view of his own bedroom window. Mae had not drawn the curtains fully and he could just about make out the light from the hall.

He waited, watching, thinking.

After a few minutes, he strolled down the veranda and out onto the road. As he headed off on his nocturnal walk – the last resort of the incurable insomniac – he noticed that the black Fiat did not bother to follow him.

Who was it they were really keeping a watch on, he wondered, and why?

CHAPTER FORTY-SEVEN

Quinn gazed down on the crowd outside the station. That morning, in an attempt to still panic, the authorities – perhaps the district commissioner for railways – had decided to post two civil servants outside its entrance. They were dressed in crisply laundered tropical suits and had clipboards with lists of passengers they were permitted to allow through, but it was a comically hopeless task. Newspaper boys shouting, 'Bourse! Bourse!' darted between them. Others barged their way past, or distracted them in argument.

Quinn watched a Rolls-Royce pull up outside the station entrance and disgorge a rich Levantine family, travelling with grandparents and a horde of children. He wondered why they wanted to cram onto an overcrowded train. Maybe they were Jews.

It was a subject the British chose mostly not to discuss. He'd heard that the Palestinian authorities were denying Jews entry.

The roads were choked, dust hanging in the air with the acrid smell of exhaust fumes, the constant toot of horns still more vexatious as a dawn chorus. He looked up at the kites circling above. The orange hue of the morning sky was melting into the same unrelenting vivid blue.

Quinn pulled the window shut. The office was quiet. There was no sign of anyone packing or preparing to leave. Smoke could still just about be seen twisting into the sky over GHQ, but no-one had been issued with rifles or instructions for a last stand in the streets outside, as Churchill had demanded.

Kate appeared in the doorway. Her hair looked glossy and she wore bright pink lipstick. 'I went by your apartment, but the guy on the porch said you'd already gone. He said you left hours ago.'

'I should have called.'

'What have you been doing?'

'Figuring some stuff out.'

'Like what?'

Quinn closed the door and returned to his desk. 'I appreciate your loyalty, Kate. You know that, don't you?'

'Why do I suspect there's a "but" on the end of that sentence?'

'I've got no right to ask you this.'

'To ask me what?'

'I've been going over this case all night. But every way I come at it leads me back to Major Macleod.'

She waited.

'Durant, Wheeler, Fabrizzi, the South African thug we picked up in the Berka . . . Macleod has links with them all.'

'It doesn't mean he killed Durant and the others.'

'Maybe not, but he's got something to protect. The man who killed my son was working for him. I'm certain of it. I'd swear that car was turning in at the

356

gate in the moments before the impact. Why would he have been coming here?'

'I don't know.'

'A year on and they don't have a single lead. Not one. So, I have to ask myself, why are they protecting this guy? Why don't they want me to get to him? What does he know? There's some connection here to this case, I'm sure of it.'

'Sir—'

'There'll be trouble if we get caught. You know that.'

'Caught doing what?'

'I won't break into this circle unless I can get into his office and his files. The real ones, not the crap he serves up to us.'

The colour drained from Kate's face. 'But—'

'I know it's locked up at night, but we can come back here together.'

'Christ.' She glanced over her shoulder. 'Sir, I can break the locks – at least I should think I can – but they guard it. You know how paranoid they are. Someone from the uniform division comes up here all through the night.'

'Not all the time.'

'Well, isn't it every quarter of an hour, at least? When I've been working late, it seems they're up every five minutes. And sometimes they unlock the offices and check inside – I've seen them do it.'

'Kate, if you don't want to—'

'I'll do it. When?'

'It's going to have to be tonight.'

She ran a hand through her hair, sighed heavily. She glanced at the clock on the wall, then at his desk. Quinn had unloaded the cash from Fabrizzi's safe in neat piles. 'Are you planning your escape?'

'Not yet.'

'Have you counted it?'

'Yes. Three thousand eight hundred.'

She whistled. 'Gee. They always said Farouk was rich.'

'Something tells me it doesn't belong to him.'

'You think it might have been Fabrizzi's money?'

Quinn leant back against the window-frame. 'Why would a palace official need such a bundle of *English* cash? That's what I can't figure out. What did the paymaster general have to say about the notes we found at Wheeler's place? Real or forged?'

Kate looked embarrassed. 'I couldn't find him when I went up there. I meant to go back. I'm sorry.'

Quinn was loading the cash back into the satchel. 'All right. Let's go now. If it ain't about sex, it's got to be about money.'

On the road, they hit a line of vehicles pouring into the city from Alexandria, a continuous rag-tag collection of jeeps, overloaded cars and trucks. They swung in behind a Bedford, the jerboa of the Desert Rats barely visible through the dust on its side. Beyond, columns of smoke rose like flowers in search of the sun through the shimmering haze. 'Do you think it's true?' Kate asked.

'What?'

'That the Germans have reached Alex.'

'No.'

'What will we do if it is?' she asked. 'I mean, will we have to do anything with the office?'

'Like what?'

'Move documents or—'

'We've got nothing to interest them. They'd find

out there's crime in Cairo, but they'll figure that out soon enough.'

'They'll have all our personal details.'

'But we'll be gone. Moved on to a different war. Or dead in a ditch.'

Kate evidently found it impossible to accept the notion that they were just going to get into a jeep and depart, the office fans still whirring, the telephones active. And that was always supposing they weren't made to fight until the last man, or woman. 'We could leave them the number for Shepheard's,' Quinn suggested, but she didn't smile.

Kate passed through the great stone entrance to Saladin's citadel and drove up the gentle incline, then swung right beneath the tall Turkish spires of the Muhammad Ali mosque. She continued on through another gate to an inner courtyard and parked between a tennis court and the back of a white stable block.

There they watched two Egyptian gardeners watering a patch of lawn. A group of horses was led round the corner, hoofs clip-clopping along cobblestones. Quinn pushed open the door, got out.

He led Kate past the façade of a tall ochre building with battered wooden shutters and down through neatly tended flowerbeds to another courtyard. In the corner was a door marked 'Office of the Paymaster General, Currency Exchange'. Quinn knocked and went in.

The man who rose to greet him had a sandy moustache, upon which was visible the remnants of his lunch. He was a cheerful-looking fellow, belly pushed tight against his webbing belt. He had a livid face and ruddy cheeks, too long burnished by the colonial sun.

Quinn offered a hand. 'Major Quinn, chief investigator, SIB. This is my colleague, Kate Mowbray.'

'Major Jenkins.' The man stuck out a pudgy hand.

'Mind if we sit down?' Quinn said, pointing at the chairs beside them.

'Help yourself.'

He sat, Kate alongside him. They noticed packing-boxes stacked along one wall. 'There's something I'd like your help with,' Quinn said.

'Ask away. Always delighted to help the SIB.' Jenkins glanced admiringly in Kate's direction, eyes focused on the middle of her chest.

Quinn reached into his pocket and took out the bundles of sterling notes. 'I'll ask you to treat this as confidential.'

'Naturally.'

'I'd appreciate it if you could avoid discussing it with anyone.'

'Absolutely. Mum's the word.'

Quinn spread out the notes on the desk. 'Are they real?'

Jenkins busied himself examining them. He held each up to the light, then looked it over with a magnifying-glass. 'Yes,' he said. He looked pleased to demonstrate his expertise in such company. 'Yes, they appear genuine to me.'

Quinn was looking at the ledgers stored along the far wall. 'You keep a record of every transaction that comes through the office?'

'Well . . . yes.'

'Mind if I take a look?'

'Yes . . . I mean, of course.' Without asking for an explanation, Jenkins took down the books from the shelf and piled them on the desk. He handed one to

Quinn. It was a thick ledger with 'January 1942' scrawled on the front cover. 'You got one for each month?' Quinn asked.

'Yes.'

Quinn opened the accounts for January, passed another volume to Kate. Jenkins didn't move. 'Can I help?' he asked.

'No,' Quinn said. 'Thanks, but we'll be OK.' Jenkins slipped discreetly to another office.

Quinn turned to the ledger, opened it. A puff of dust rose into the air. At the top of the first page, someone had written by hand: 'Please note Bank of England standing instructions. Serial numbers of all banknotes must be recorded at time of transaction.'

Below, the details of every exchange had been neatly written out, the name of the individual inscribed alongside how much they had changed and at what rate. There were few names of officers and men – if they changed English currency, they must have done so through the black-market. Almost all entries related to businesses and most were well known in the city. Groppi's, Shepheard's, the Kit Kat club, the National Hotel and many others popped up again and again. Mostly they were exchanging relatively small sums, a few pounds here and there. Neither did Quinn recognize any of the individual names recorded in the final column. The transactions had been completed by clerical staff.

'What am I looking for, sir?'

Quinn looked up at Kate. 'Fabrizzi had a pile of English cash so we've got to work out why. He's a top Egyptian official so it don't make no sense to me. Maybe there's some pattern in the amount being changed here to tip us off as to what the hell he was doing with it or where it came from. Maybe we can prove Macleod, or Wheeler, or Durant, was being paid for something.'

Quinn kept reading. He heard a band strike up, obliterating the distant hum of the old city beneath the walls of the citadel. He forced himself to concentrate. There were no familiar names. Only about half of the book had been filled, and when he reached the end, he shut it and moved on to the next. Kate had February, so he picked up March. He flicked through the pages, trying not to skim. Numbers, numbers and more numbers.

He stopped, doubled back. The sums did appear to be getting bigger. If Groppi's, Shepheard's and all the other mainstays of expatriate life in Cairo had been changing at most three or four pounds a week in January, by March it was more regularly eight or nine.

Quinn kept on going. The totals fell again and he was just about to abandon the theory when they rose to ten pounds or more. He looked at the serial numbers. They were all different. He went back to the start of the month and began again, trying to see if there was any repetition – any indication that forgeries were in circulation. He looked at Kate, who was bent over a ledger on her lap, knees raised. 'Kate, what do you figure was the average amount being changed in a week during February?'

'The average amount?'

'By the hotels.'

She checked the pages in front of her. 'About four pounds, sometimes five. Why?'

'By the end of March it's reached ten.'

Kate pushed her glasses up her nose, raising her knees further. 'How do we know these places change all the English currency they have here, or only a proportion to keep the authorities satisfied? Maybe they take the rest to the bazaar, or wherever will give them the best rate.'

'But why would the percentage change?'

Quinn returned to the book in his hand, flicked to the end of March, then swapped the ledger for the one covering April. For the first two weeks it was a similar pattern, but towards the end of the month the sums rose again. For the last week, the average sum being changed by all the hotels and restaurants was fifteen pounds.

Up five pounds.

Quinn worked on to the end. He swapped the ledger for one covering May. Here, during the first two weeks, the average sum being changed was between twenty and twenty-two pounds, but for the last week it jumped again to just under thirty.

He took out a notebook, jotted down some figures. By the last week of June, the figure had risen to thirty-five. 'The sums go on rising. Five pounds, then up to ten. The end of April, we got fifteen. At the start of May, it's around twenty, but in the last week of the month it's up to thirty. And now we got thirty-five.'

'So what's the explanation?' Kate asked.

Quinn took the ledger for February from her and went back to the start. He wrote in his notebook the serial number of the first note to be exchanged, kept it in front of him, then ran through every other entry, trying to find a match. Forgers always repeated serial numbers. It was not cost-efficient to do it any other way.

The process took Quinn ten minutes or more, and when he'd finished, he picked the second serial number and started again. Kate appeared absorbed in her own task. When he'd finished, he looked at her. 'I figure the obvious explanation would be that someone is forging currency, putting it into circulation gradually so as not to attract attention. But none of the numbers match.'

'I don't understand,' Kate said.

'Forging banknotes ain't easy. So far as I know, only national banks can get out a few thousand notes with individual numbers. For a forger, it's way too expensive to go for that level of detail so they produce ten different numbers, maybe twenty. If there was a big influx of counterfeits, I figure we'd see numbers being repeated.'

'Then why are the sums increasing?' Kate asked.

'I don't know, but I think it started at Shepheard's.' He pushed the ledger towards her. 'See here? There's a big hike in this week, beginning the twenty-third of February. They change more than twenty pounds. The hike is not repeated in any of the other businesses and the next week it drops right back down to normal – two pounds. I'd figure the increased supply can be dated to that week.'

CHAPTER FORTY-EIGHT

At Shepheard's, Quinn dodged street-vendors and taxi-drivers and mounted the steps towards the terrace and the robed dragomen who guarded its entrance. Inside, in the relative cool of the lobby, a group of disconsolate officers in drab battledress stood before the message board, evidently waiting for buses from Air Transport Command to take them out to the aerodrome and back up to the desert. The hotel was busy, officers and expatriate civilians huddled in small groups.

Quinn surveyed the hallway, with its rich Persian rugs, granite pillars and statuettes of bronze maidens. *Sufragis* in crimson- and gold-embroidered jackets or long white *djellabas* drifted unhurriedly between tables on the terrace. Straight ahead, small groups of rich Cairene women examined the contents of Mansour's jewellery shop. In the corner, a teleprinter burbled. There might have been a run on the banks and queues at the railway station, but the atmosphere of panic had yet to pervade this bastion of colonial rule.

Quinn walked over to look at the message board where they put up the news wires. He and Kate read simultaneously. Admiral Harwood of the Royal Navy, it said, had been forced to consider the impact of heavier air-raids and the possibility that the city of Alexandria might be captured. He had therefore decided to split his fleet between Port Said, Haifa and Beirut. The evacuation had been completed without warning, but the Germans had not yet reached the city. There was no word on whether they had broken through. The battle for Egypt continued.

Quinn knew how much the high command hated journalists referring to it as the 'battle for Egypt'. It unnerved the locals, they said. But even the BBC was using the phrase.

He walked through to the garden and screwed up his eyes against the sun. The lawn was filled with small tables covered with spotless white linen tablecloths and heaped with flowers. Bougainvillaea cascaded over the wooden trellis and a single palm rose high above the building, its smooth trunk like burnished silver. The tree's giant fronds moved gracefully in the breeze, long shadows drifting across the grass.

The Swiss manager, Charles Lederer, was talking to two army officers, sweat on his brow but not a mark on his spotless white linen suit. He was a big man, hearty and jovial. In a corner beyond him was the familiar entourage that surrounded Egypt's king. Grand Duke Boris Vladimirovich was with him, but also the unmistakably lean, handsome figure of Avril White. The American was deep in conversation with the king, making his points earnestly.

Quinn slipped through the tables until he was beside the manager. 'Mr Lederer, we ain't met. I'm Joe Quinn, Special Investigation Branch, and this is my assistant, Kate Mowbray.'

Lederer betrayed no hint of surprise, as if this was an everyday occurrence. Quinn glanced at the two officers with whom he was conversing. Both were captains, with the blotched red skin that betrayed a recent spell in the intense heat of the 'blue'.

Without a word, Lederer ushered them up the steps to the lobby, and his office beyond Reception. It was a small, hot room, with a single fan and two leather seats in front of a large desk. 'Coffee or tea?' he asked, then picked up and rang a silver bell.

'Tea, please,' Kate said.

'Do you have any news?' Lederer asked.

'About what?'

'From Alex. I've been calling friends all morning, but the telephones just ring and ring.'

'No,' Quinn told him.

A waiter came and Lederer spoke to him in Arabic. Then he turned back to them. 'At any rate, what can I do for you?' He must have sensed that Quinn was not a man who liked to gossip.

Lederer had a round, wide face and an unruffled manner, as if he was used to dealing with every type of guest and complaint. He was obviously a passionate jazz fan: the walls were adorned with pictures of some of America's great musicians. From somewhere in the hotel, Quinn could hear 'Lili Marlene' being played on a gramophone. 'I'd like to see your guest register,' he said.

'Might I enquire why?'

'It's a homicide.'

Lederer raised his eyebrows, but Quinn's tone had not invited further discussion. The Swiss stood, sweat in thick beads now on his forehead. He went out to the reception desk and returned a few minutes later with a leatherbound book. A waiter arrived behind him with a tray of tea. He served them while Quinn looked at the ledger, flicking through the pages until he reached the week of 23 February.

He scanned the names.

There were none he recognized. A Sanderson from America, Christian name Gerald, travelling alone. A Polish couple, a Greek officer, what looked like a Russian prince. A great number of British army officers.

Kate had been sitting alongside him, following his eye over the pages. 'Nothing here,' she said.

'But the twenty-third was a Monday, right? So they'd have been bringing in the money from the week before that.'

Quinn went backwards. It didn't take long to find the entry he had half suspected would be present.

Mr and Mrs Avril White had checked into the hotel on 18 February. According to the registration details, they had arrived from Casablanca, via Cape Town. Quinn swung the book round. 'You remember this couple?'

'Of course.'

'That's White out in the garden now with the king's party.'

'Yes. I believe I did see him.'

'You got a copy of his bill?'

'I'm not sure—'

'I'd like to see it.'

'Yes ... of course. You understand, a hotel of this type—'

'Like I said, we got a homicide.'

'I see.' Lederer pushed himself out of his chair, took a damp towel from the tea-tray and wiped his forehead. He scanned the bookcase and pulled down a leatherbound file. He checked through it, then replaced it and took another. Eventually he placed a bill on the desk, neatly written out in a flowing hand.

Quinn looked at White's spidery signature in the bottom right-hand corner. 'Mr White paid in English currency, cash?'

'It would appear so.'

'You handled the transaction yourself?'

'No.'

'You get many guys who pay such a large bill in sterling?'

Lederer tilted his head as he tried to work out the purpose of the question. His aim was evidently to shield his client from any awkward questions. 'I cannot say it's unusual.' He studied the transaction, as if seeking evidence to support his claim. 'Newly arrived from Cape Town. Naturally—'

'Most new arrivals change their cash, right? Unless they're moving right on.' Quinn glanced through the file. Other bills were paid in Egyptian pounds, or by banker's draft, quite a number sent directly on to the GHQ accounts division. He couldn't find another that had been settled in this way. 'Why do you figure the Whites decided not to change their money?'

'I don't understand.'

'You remember whether they paid for anything in Egyptian pounds? Bar bills, tips . . .'

'I'm afraid I still don't see the purpose of the question.'

Quinn leant forward. He hadn't touched his tea. 'Cairo is being pumped with English money – two of our victims had fistfuls of it – so we got to nail where it came from, right? It starts in this week, here in your hotel.' Quinn pointed at the file. 'Only the Whites paid this way, so it has to be them. But I can't figure out why they were reluctant to change their money.'

Lederer saw that he was expected to answer. 'I . . . as I said, arriving from Cape Town . . . Mr White is a businessman, so perhaps—'

'Then he'll have known the best way to pay a bill is to change money on the black-market.'

'I'm sure Mr White would not indulge in such—'

'Any clerk in this hotel would have done it for him.' Lederer fingered the offending bill. 'I'd be grateful,' Quinn continued quietly, 'if you would go and tell Mr White that we wish to speak to him. I'm sure you will find a way of indicating that it isn't a request.'

'But he is in a meeting with the king. It would be unconscionable for me to interrupt—'

'Then I'll do it.'

Lederer scuttled out.

Kate sipped her tea. 'It's funny to think of Rommel here.'

Quinn looked at her.

'Joking aside, this is where he will come, isn't it?'

'Yeah.'

'I guess we'll all be reassigned in Jerusalem, if we make it that far. Won't we?'

'I ain't thought about it.'

There was a soft knock and Charles Lederer entered. 'The king's party has left. Mr White will see you in the garden.'

CHAPTER FORTY-NINE

White had not moved from the table deep in the pool of shade. He was fanning himself with his fedora, dressed in an immaculate white linen suit, shirt and tie.

'Mr White?' Quinn said. 'You met my assistant, Kate Mowbray.'

White nodded at Kate, dropped his hat on the table, then stood up to offer his hand to them in turn. They took seats. 'Some tea?' White asked.

'No, thank you.'

The garden was less full now. The Russian prince had moved to another table and was conversing with two Levantine women, but Quinn noticed he kept glancing in White's direction. At the top of the steps into the hotel, a member of Farouk's security detail watched them. 'My friend Charles Lederer has indicated you wish to speak to me, so . . . please.'

Quinn sensed White was on edge, although every ounce of him was strained towards giving the opposite impression. 'I have a few questions, if you don't mind. Just routine . . . matters we've got to straighten out.'

'You're still on the case, then?' White looked him dead in the eye. 'I'd heard you'd been removed from it.'

'I'm still here, Mr White. Last time I looked anyway. You arrived in Cairo in February?'

White took out a silver case. 'Cigarette?' They both declined. He lit one for himself.

'From Casablanca?' Quinn asked.

'Sure.'

'Via Cape Town?'

White smiled, displaying a row of immaculate teeth. 'I'm not aware of another route, unless one wishes to brave the battlefields of the northern desert, which may appeal to my wife but not, I'm afraid, to me.'

'She's a brave woman.'

'Foolish, some might say.'

Quinn wondered what he meant. 'You stopped off in Cape Town?'

'It would be a crime to pass such a beautiful city and not enjoy what it has to offer.'

'How long were you there?'

'Two weeks.'

'And then Durban?'

'Yes.'

'And before Cape Town, Casablanca, and before that . . . Lisbon.'

White fanned his face slowly.

'How long you in Portugal?'

'Does it matter?'

'Mrs White's father still there?'

White betrayed no surprise that Quinn knew about his wife's father. Like an experienced chess player, he was waiting to see the direction of his opponent's game.

372

'Her father has a bank account in the city?' Quinn asked.

'I haven't the slightest idea.'

'You didn't set one up for him?'

'I don't recall. I suppose I did.'

'You transfer money from New York?'

'With respect, Major, I cannot see how this has any bearing on your investigation.'

'I'm sorry.' Quinn tried to keep his tone emollient. 'I'm just trying to get things straight in my head here. You understand . . .'

'Not really.'

'I've got to figure out why you chose to travel with so much cash in sterling and where you picked it up.'

'Well, if it will help you, I got a large withdrawal from the Standard Chartered Bank in South Africa. I received the money by transfer from New York. In the current circumstances, one can never be sure if the ship one is travelling on is going to reach its destination and, if not, where it will end up. I like to be covered for all eventualities.'

'So you arrived with a suitcase full of cash?'

'If you want to put it like that.'

'You didn't change it when you got here?'

'Is that a crime?'

'No,' Quinn said. 'But, see, it's curious. Most people come to Cairo know, or are very quickly told, that they'll get a better deal if they change their currency on the black-market.'

'I'm not sure that—'

'How did Colonel Wheeler end up with some of the money?'

'What?'

For the first time, Quinn saw a chink in the armour. He acted surprised. 'I just figured you'd paid off some small debt or . . .' He left it hanging.

White did not flinch, but an eyelid was fluttering again. He did not deny knowing Wheeler. 'Please get to the point.'

Quinn glanced around the garden. Another of Farouk's goons had joined his colleague on the steps. Two middle-aged expatriate women were ushered to a table. 'Where did you meet the colonel?'

'I don't recall. The Kit Kat, probably.'

'You ever go to his houseboat?'

'No.'

'What about your wife?'

'That's a question for her.'

Quinn held White's gaze. This man, he thought, was shedding his civility with consummate ease. 'What about Signor Fabrizzi? I recall you were meeting him in the bazaar.'

'What about him?'

'He's dead. You heard that?'

'Yes.'

'He was a friend?'

'A contact.'

'You paid him a substantial amount of money.'

White could see he was being manoeuvred into another admission. 'That's none of your business.'

'What was it for?'

'It's a private matter.'

'Maybe Fabrizzi was using it to buy guns. You know about that?'

'No.'

'But you gave him the money?'

'I'm not prepared to discuss that.'

374

'How much you give him, Mr White?'

'As I've said, several times, it's a private matter.'

'You in oil? That's your business?'

'Yes.'

'You looking for government contracts?'

'I'm looking for oil, then the right to pump it. When the British stop raping Egypt, there'll be money to be made here. I'd like it to be American companies that help put the country back on its feet. Maybe, given your new loyalties, you don't agree.'

'It proving a successful venture?'

'It's too early to tell.'

'You were doing something similar in Casablanca?'

'Yes.'

'Why did you choose to move on?'

'It's under the sway of the Germans. Maybe you hadn't noticed.'

'I thought that Germany was where your family made its money.'

White smiled again. It was not a pleasant expression. 'I see my wife has been talkative.'

'The king know you were paying one of his officials here?'

'Have you talked to the palace about this?' White asked.

'Not yet.'

'Then I would advise it, before you get involved in matters well above your level.' He pushed back his chair. 'I'd love to sit here and discuss this with you all day, Major, but I'm afraid I have a business to run. If there's information you want, ask for it. I'll do all in my power to assist. If you've an accusation to make, make it. But if insinuation is your sole intent, I shall wish you good day.'

'Thanks for the advice,' Quinn said. 'I'm getting plenty of it.'

'Then perhaps you should heed it.'

White picked up his cigarette case, slipped it into his pocket. 'I can't say our conversation has been enlightening, Major, but I hope I have proved to be of some assistance.' He stalked back into the hotel.

Quinn and Kate watched him go. 'I think you upset him,' she said.

'You don't say.'

'Was it wise? I mean, he seems to have the right alibis. Maybe the money he gave Fabrizzi was just a bribe.'

'You telling me it's a coincidence he knew all three of our victims?'

They stood up and walked through the garden. By the time they reached the hotel lobby, they could hear the rhythmic chants of a street protest approaching. Small groups of soldiers and civilians were waiting for it to pass. Quinn noticed that Amy White was among them.

She was wearing a plain khaki top and trousers, a khaki bag slung over her shoulder, as though she was about to go to work or had recently returned. She was examining a camera in her hand, her hair wrapped tight at the nape of her neck. She drifted out to the street and he made as if to follow, but felt Kate's hand on his arm. 'Sir, is this wise?'

'What?'

'You know what I mean.'

'I've no idea.'

'Well . . . it's just . . . All right.' She released him.

CHAPTER FIFTY

Outside, the chants grew louder. The protest was close by, occupants of the street caught in the momentary drama of its approach. Taxi-drivers climbed from their vehicles. Hawkers carrying camel saddles, leather bags and an array of 'priceless' scarabs stopped their incessant hustling. The clientele of cafés and shops opposite spilled from the doorways. On the terrace, conversation was subdued, all faces turned to the street.

Amy glanced at the camera again, then raised it to her eye. She adjusted the bag, so that it was more comfortable. 'What did you want with my husband?' she asked, as he came close to her.

'I want to talk to you,' he said.

'We've done enough talking.'

'In private.'

She looked at him, then at Kate who stood at the top of the steps. 'About what?'

'I need to know what your husband's doing here.'

'Ask him.'

The chants were growing louder. Quinn bent closer to her. 'I know you arrived with a suitcase full of money. I want to know what he's doing with it.'

377

At that moment, the protest came into view. It was moving fast. The young students at the front carried banners, most of which bore the slogan '*Bissama Allah, fi alard Hitler*'. Others, glued to long wooden poles, depicted the British-imposed prime minister, Nahas Pasha, with a red cross through his face, and the leader of the main opposition party, Dr Ahmed Maher.

And then there was another, more sinister in appearance.

It had upon it the mythical figure of Seth, God of Chaos, ringed in black.

Quinn took two quick steps towards Amy. She had the camera to her eye. 'I need a favour,' he said. 'The placard with the image on it . . . the one of the Egyptian god, can you get a shot of it and the guy who is holding it?'

She ignored him, moved away. He could tell she had no intention of helping him.

The protest moved swiftly. Quinn kept his eye on the placard. A young student was holding it, one sweaty face in a sea of them. The chants were loud and angry, punched out to the rhythm of feet pounding in the dust. He followed, felt Kate's hand on his arm once more. 'Where are you going, sir?' Her face was bright red.

'You saw the sign?' he asked.

'Don't,' she said, 'the mood is ugly.' She had not let go of his sleeve.

Quinn shook off her hand and kept moving, past a row of taxis, parked cars and then a string of horse-drawn carts that had been forced over. Dust kicked up from the street caught in his throat and he pulled out a handkerchief and held it across his mouth. Amy was close to the protestors, camera raised, so close she looked as if she would be carried away like flotsam on an outgoing tide. She stopped, framed, fired off a shot, then moved again.

And then she slipped from view, as if sucked under.

Quinn plunged into the crowd. He found her, surrounded by shouting men. One kicked her hard in the stomach, a sweaty, dark, unshaven face bellowing with anger, the sound drowned in the greater noise of the crowd. Quinn heard glass breaking. A rock had been thrown through one of the windows at Shepheard's.

Quinn gripped Amy's shirt and bag, pulling her to her feet. The young man who'd assaulted her surged forward so Quinn dropped the bag and swung a punch, felling him with an easy blow. He swung twice more – two more bodies scrabbling in the dirt. But he was fortunate that most of the protestors had moved off and those that remained were still throwing stones at the façade of Shepheard's and hurling abuse at the British officers who were watching from the terrace. He noticed that one or two had discreetly drawn revolvers.

He heard the blast of a police whistle, and the air was filled with the heavy thud of horses' hoofs. A couple of stragglers threw a last volley of rocks, then hurried off.

Quinn glanced around, but could see no sign of Amy. He picked up her bag and followed the protestors, trying to catch sight of her. He reached the crossroads, then stopped to watch the protest disappear. As soon as it was gone, a call to prayer began nearby, as though one activity had given way naturally to the other. Quinn turned back.

When he reached the hotel, there was no sign of

Amy or her husband. Waiters and porters were sweeping up the broken glass and debris. Charles Lederer stood in the lobby, effusively reassuring guests and scolding his security guards, though it hardly seemed their fault. Quinn looked for Amy in the garden, on the terrace, even in the Moorish Hall.

Kate waited patiently. He had little choice but to leave Amy's bag at the porter's desk.

They headed for the office. As she drove, Kate took out a packet of Celtique cigarettes and lit one. She knew he hated the taste and smell so didn't bother to offer him one. He thought she only smoked them when she was irritated or angry. 'I don't know how you can smoke those things,' he said.

'They're very popular. You should broaden your taste.'

'You might as well roll a bunch of eucalyptus trees.'

Kate sent a plume of smoke billowing into the space between them. They had been temporarily halted by an altercation between a camel and a donkey – or, at least, their respective owners. A boy selling sherbets and sweetmeats rushed forward and knocked on the window. 'Is she very beautiful, sir?' Kate asked.

'Who?'

'You know who.'

The boy was still tapping at the window. 'What are you trying to say, Miss Mowbray?' Quinn wound down his window, gave the boy a few piastres, but shook his head to indicate he didn't want a sherbet. He rolled the window back up. Kate tooted to try to persuade the camel driver to move his charge aside. Quinn took out a handkerchief and wiped his brow.

'It just doesn't seem the time or place to be, you know . . .'

'You know what?'

'Right.' She was sweating profusely. 'I'm not a fool, you know.'

'You're a driver, Mowbray, so let's drive, shall we?'

She accelerated for a few seconds, then stopped. She took out the keys and threw them at him. 'Drive yourself.'

She got out. A small crowd watched the spectacle, as a muezzin droned from a minaret behind. Quinn opened his door, leant over the hot metal roof. 'Kate.' She was marching away. Another boy tugged at his shirt. 'Kate!' She wasn't listening. He got back into the car. 'Shit.' He swung into the driver's seat, turned the key and followed, pulling past the camel. He wound down the window. 'Kate . . . all right – look, stop. I apologize, damn it.'

She faced him. They had now attracted a crowd stretching thirty yards or more. 'I'm not going to work for someone who insults me,' she said. 'Especially given what you've been asking me to do.'

'All right. I didn't mean it. I apologize.'

'I'm sure a hundred other people are willing to be your driver, if that's what you want. If you look hard enough, you might even find one who breaks locks.'

'There's a war on. There aren't too many drivers.'

'That's not—'

'It's a joke!'

'It wasn't funny.'

'Sure. Please, get in.' He moved aside, made room for her. She complied. 'I need to break her to break the case, that's all,' he explained. 'I'd say she's a victim, as much as Durant and the others.'

'It's a convenient line.'

He faced her. 'Look, I apologize, right? I appreciate your loyalty, I've said that already. I wouldn't stand a chance in this without you. I've made that clear.'

'Loyalties can be easily confused, don't you think?'

'Maybe,' he said. He drove off again. 'Maybe so.' He didn't know quite what she meant, but in her current mood he didn't like to ask.

CHAPTER FIFTY-ONE

In the office, all the interpreters and secretaries in the central atrium on the top floor were packing files into large wooden crates. Ed Madden was waiting in their cubicle, seated behind his desk, fiddling with the lamp and reading a paper. He leapt to his feet, like a man who had been sitting on hot coals. 'Hello, sir.'

Quinn motioned for him to sit. 'What's going on?' he asked, gesturing at the activity outside.

'We thought it best to be prepared.'

'For what?'

'We couldn't find you, didn't know where you were.' Madden was apologetic. 'I've left this office, but once Macleod gave the order to start packing up, I thought it best to take some measures in case we're forced to move in a hurry.'

Quinn shifted behind his desk. 'You know something I don't?'

'About what, sir?'

'Rommel. Is he here yet?'

'No. But there are new orders from Lieutenant General Henderson. The centre of Cairo is out of bounds from eight tonight until seven in the morning and all officers are to carry revolvers.'

'That should make all the difference.' Quinn sat down. 'Macleod has ordered everything packed up, you say?'

'Yes, sir.'

'When?'

'A few hours ago.'

'Why?'

'As a precaution,' he said. 'The order only applies to the Field Security corridor, but I thought we'd better do something as well, just in case.'

Quinn moved to the doorway and looked out. Sure enough, there were crates all the way down the corridor leading off the far side of the atrium. 'Damn,' he muttered.

'I'm sorry, sir?'

'Nothing.'

Quinn returned to his desk. He took Wheeler's banknotes from the drawer, then those they'd found in Fabrizzi's safe. He assembled them in rows. 'Ed, you got a notebook?'

Madden reached into his pocket.

'Go downstairs and send a telex to the Bank of England. Mark it urgent, for immediate attention. Say we've found notes with the following serial numbers . . .' Quinn reeled off each in turn. 'We want to know what history they have on any or all of them. And ask if they've come across any examples of forgeries involving many *different* serial numbers. If so, we need some details. By the way, anyone seen Effatt?'

They shook their heads.

'He been in today?'

'No, sir,' Madden said.

'We get a report back from his fingerprint division about Wheeler's place?'

'It's on your desk.'

'What does it say?'

'Nothing. They found Wheeler's prints and those of the *sufragi*, but no others.'

Madden turned and left the room. Kate went with him, as if not wishing to be in Quinn's presence any longer.

Quinn reached down to open the bottom drawer of a tall mahogany filing cabinet. He flicked through until he found the folder marked 'Opposition Groups'. The reports inside had been written by the clerk of a now defunct committee, a former Oxford academic who'd been unable to hide his sympathy for those opposing British rule. He had made a point of noting that Britain had promised independence to Egypt after the last war, a pledge upon which it had yet to make good.

Quinn flicked through a file on Hasan el Banna and the Muslim Brotherhood, then another on the Free Officers Association and the Ring of Iron. It referred to the boiling anger of the Free Officers as a result of the Abdin Incident in February: 'May not have a fondness for the king, but to see him pushed around by a patronizing and arrogant foreigner like Ambassador Lampson, made to change his government by the threat of tanks at his gate ... public humiliation ... rallied opinion behind him ... final straw ... hope Rommel breaks through soon.'

There was no reference to Signor Fabrizzi or the God of Chaos anywhere in the files. A few minutes later, Madden reappeared. 'If you were an Egyptian, trying to create a movement of national rebellion,'

Quinn said, 'then you ain't going to choose the ancient god usually associated with Satan as your symbol, right?'

'Unless you wanted to frighten people.'

'It'd make more sense to choose Horus, symbol of outraged justice. Unless, of course, the movement was not instigated by an Egyptian.'

'Inspired by a foreigner, you mean?'

'Yeah.'

'You think Fabrizzi worked for Italian intelligence?' Madden asked.

'Maybe.'

'He found two good sources of information in Durant and Wheeler and was pumping them?'

'Then who killed them?'

Madden shook his head.

'You got any news about Jooste?'

'No. Cohen and Dexter have been working all their informers and contacts, but no-one seems to have heard of him.'

'Kind of odd, wouldn't you say?'

'Perhaps it is, sir, yes.'

'Are you all right, Ed?'

'I'm fine.' He looked miserable.

'Something you want to tell me?'

'No, sir . . . no.'

'Something on your mind?'

'No.'

'You applied for that transfer yet?'

'Not yet.'

'There's nothing that says you have to. You know that, right?'

Madden didn't answer. His brow was furrowed with concentration. 'Ed, I know about measuring oneself against a father's expectations. Trust me, it never leads to any good.'

'What do you mean by that?'

'You've got to lead your own life, not the one you think your father wants. It usually turns out you were mistaken anyway.'

Madden looked up at him. 'Is your father still alive?'

'No.'

'He was a policeman as well, wasn't he?'

'A patrolman.'

'How long ago did he—'

'A long time.'

'Did he—'

'He was killed as a result of an investigation I was running.'

Madden hesitated. 'I'm sorry. What happened?'

'It's a long story.'

'Most things of that nature usually are.'

The kid wanted to know he was not alone in the way he felt. 'There was a lot of corruption on the force,' Quinn said. 'I was ambitious, wanted to make a name for myself. Ever since, I've thought, maybe if I hadn't pushed so hard – tried so hard to impress him – he'd still be alive. So the lesson is, don't lead the life you think other people want, Ed. Every which way you may come to regret it.'

Quinn moved to the window and stood with his back to his deputy, looking down at the courtyard below. He lit a cigarette and watched the jeeps come and go. He tried to ignore the clock on the wall beside him, upon which time marched inexorably forwards.

'Thank you, sir,' Madden said. 'You've been good to me. I really don't deserve it.'

Something in Madden's voice – an unnatural

penitence – made Quinn turn. His deputy was staring at the floor, lost in thought.

Quinn walked back out to the atrium and watched one of Macleod's clerks loading a crate in the far corridor. He looked at his watch. How much material, he wondered, would Macleod have spirited away before nightfall?

CHAPTER FIFTY-TWO

Kate put her head round the door. 'Fifteen minutes,' she said. 'Almost like clockwork.'

Quinn went over to her. For the past hour, Kate had been sitting in a corner of the lobby, pretending to examine a file, but in reality keeping a careful watch on how often the duty guard from the uniform division came up to check on the Field Security corridor. 'He unlocked the door to Macleod's office and looked inside on the second round,' she said. 'I'll go back and wait. As soon as he turns the corner of the stairs next time, I'll come and get you. But we mustn't push it. We've got ten minutes, then we'll have to get out. I don't know how easy it's going to be to lock the door afterwards.'

She slipped out. Quinn tried to read over a report Cohen had typed for him detailing their fruitless search for the South African, Jooste, in the city's bazaars and back-streets. It was just after eleven. He wondered how Effatt was doing tonight. He'd come in earlier, but Quinn had sent him straight home again. Rifat's condition had deteriorated markedly.

Kate came in. 'All right.'

Quinn switched off his desk lamp and went out into the atrium. He could still hear the footsteps of the retreating guard on the stone landing below. Kate reached Macleod's door and dropped to her knees in front of it. She had a metal tool in her pocket and worked it carefully into the lock. She took out a small torch, switched it on and handed it to him.

The lock wouldn't turn. She lifted his hand up, so that the torch was shining through the glass panel at the top of the door. 'Damn.' She tried again. Light from the stairwell glistened off her forehead, which was damp with perspiration. Quinn wiped his own face with a handkerchief. 'Hold still,' she said.

Finally, the lock gave and they were in. Quinn swung the torch beam across the filing cabinets that stretched the length of the far wall. There was a packing-case in the corner, full of books and manuals. Quinn tried one of the cabinet drawers, but it wouldn't budge. 'They'll all be locked,' he said.

'Eight minutes left. Which one do you want me to start with?'

Quinn looked along the line. None of the cabinets was marked with anything. 'This side. Then work your way along.'

She knelt down again. It took her a minute to open the first lock and slide open the drawer. Immediately she moved on to the next, taking the torch from him.

'I need some light,' he said.

He took Macleod's lamp from the desk, placed it on the floor and turned it on. 'For God's sake,' she hissed, 'take this.' She gave him the torch and continued her work. Quinn switched off the lamp and bent over the cabinet.

The files were stored in alphabetical order: 'Abdin

Incident', 'Anglo-Egyptian Treaty', 'Azzam Bey/Territorials' . . .

He pulled out a file headed 'Hasan el Banna/Muslim Brotherhood'. It was huge, full of closely typed reports. Most were signed by Sorrenson or Reza, some by Macleod. All the agents they quoted inside the organization were referred to by number only: agent fifty-three, agent twenty-seven, and so on.

Quinn turned to the most recent report. He read swiftly, the thin beam of his torch darting from one side of the page to the other.

Rommel's approach considered profound opportunity . . . desire to welcome him into city with uprising . . . no shortage of recruits flowing in from the mosques and universities, especially El Azhar . . . important to be seen to be liberating themselves from yoke of British rule, but still no more than talk. Agent twenty-seven says Field Security perceived to be too strong and too much in control . . . Plus the impossibility of getting hold of good weaponry to tackle Britain's superior firearms and skill. No action planned or pending. All quiet on this front. No movement from Hasan el Banna. Internal exile continues. Threat neutralized.

Quinn muttered to himself. Kate broke the lock on the next cabinet. 'Seven minutes,' she said. He gathered up the file and replaced it. Sweat ran down his nose and dropped onto the floor.

He flicked through the next cabinet, pulled out a file stamped 'Free Officers'. Like the one on the Muslim Brotherhood, it consisted of typed weekly reports based on agents' testimony.

Agent eighty-nine continues to report that strength of feeling steady or even growing ... sense of outrage and national humiliation at Abdin Incident remains chief topic of conversation among the group and all like-minded officers throughout the armed forces. General view expressed daily that something ought to be done. Rommel will be welcomed. Statement to be prepared to this effect by agent eighty-nine himself. He will let us have a copy as soon as it is complete to allow for counter-measures. All officers are desirous of some form of action to assist Rommel, but no leadership is forthcoming. Talk of looking to younger officers like Sadat, but our continued close monitoring of all likely candidates hampers decision-making. Fears as to inadequacy of Egyptian men and munitions should British decide to turn their wrath on any rebellion. In summary: talk, as before, but no attempt at action. Agent eighty-nine expressed a willingness to be part of a stay-behind network in the event Rommel takes the city in return for substantial payments into neutral account in Lisbon or Switzerland. Given track record, future loyalty must be considered suspect in this regard.

This report, like the others, had been signed off b Macleod.

'Four minutes,' Kate said. She returned to the firs cabinet and locked it again, then went on down th row.

'It's all a pack of lies,' Quinn said. 'If there's rebellion in the making, they're not reportin anything.' He put away the file and continued to flick through others. There was nothing for 'God of Chaos', or 'Chaos'. One stamped 'Jews' contained a list of every Jewish family in the city. In a file on the 'Kit Kat Nightclub', Quinn saw a reference to Mac being one of his own informers. There was no mention of Kostandis, except to note that he was the club's owner. A little further back there was even a file on Alexander Kirk, the American minister to Cairo. 'A candle burns day and night in his residence', it said, 'in front of a picture of his mother . . .'

'Two minutes,' Kate said. She broke into the next cabinet. Quinn moved to it. His fingers danced across the top of the files until he saw the headings 'Mae Quinn and Joseph Quinn'. 'Got them,' he said.

Mae's file was empty – as if the papers had been recently removed. His own was as thick as a James Joyce novel.

'Sir . . .'

He knelt on the floor. It was full of statements taken from men who'd been interviewed in connection with Ryan's death, tens if not hundreds of them, interspersed with the anodyne reports Macleod and Sorrenson had typed up for circulation through GHQ. A few had comments from Lewis scrawled in the margin: 'Why aren't we getting any further on this?' and 'Major Quinn most anxious at slow progress of investigation, any chance we could speed things up to a conclusion?'

Quinn had never heard of most of the people they'd interviewed. None had been there, or had heard of the incident or of a 'Major Quinn'. Most were deserters arrested for something else. 'Sir, we've got to go.' Kate was locking the cabinet next to him.

'Hold on a minute.'

'If they catch us . . .'

He stood. 'I'll take the contents of the file.'

'No! If they find it missing, there'll be hell to pay.'

'Then I need a few minutes.'

Kate did not argue, but he could tell her eyes were fixed on the clock on the wall. She moved to the door.

Quinn scanned each page, but found nothing of any consequence; the file consisted of useless statement after useless statement. 'Time's up, sir.'

He didn't move.

'Joe! Time's up.'

'Here.' He pulled out one of the last sheets in the file. It was a report on the death of his son, stamped 'Field Security, strictly for internal circulation only'. Halfway down the page, a name had been blacked out.

'Joe!'

Quinn held up the paper, put the torch behind it and shone the light through. The first three or four references had been obscured with thick black ink, but lower down, he could make something out. The man who had been driving the car that killed his son was referred to as agent thirty-one.

'He's coming,' Kate hissed.

Quinn shoved the papers back into the file and pushed the cabinet shut. He could hear the man's footsteps. He saw the beam of his torch and dived down behind the desk. Kate had pressed herself to the wall behind the glass door.

The footsteps came closer, but the guard did not break his stride. He continued on down the corridor. Quinn waited. He was lying flat and placed his forehead against the cool parquet floor. He heard the man turn and come back. There was a gust of wind from an open window somewhere in the atrium and it nudged open the door.

The guard stopped. Quinn heard him grunt, take hold of the door handle and step in. He shone the fat beam of his torch across the wall, past the cabinets, then over the desk.

Quinn waited. He could see Kate's feet. He cursed silently.

The guard grunted again and shut the door. He fumbled for his keys, then Quinn heard the lock click. He waited until the guard's footsteps receded, then scrambled up. 'For God's sake, come on,' Kate said.

Quinn returned to the cabinet, pulled out the file and the last sheet he had been looking at. He handed it to her. 'Agent thirty-one. But it doesn't tell us anything unless we can find out who the hell these agents are.' He looked about him. There were three more filing cabinets in the row. 'Try the last one.'

It took Kate another minute or two to break the lock, but the files proved a disappointment. They were the final part of the alphabetical reference section – 'Zagazig riots' and so on. Quinn went through to the secretary's cubicle next door and found more cabinets along each wall.

'Do you think they even keep a record?' Kate asked. 'Maybe it's all in Macleod's head.'

Quinn ignored her and sat behind the Scot's desk. Both the central drawer and the cupboards to either side of it were locked. 'Try these, Kate,' he said.

'Hold on, sir. Reza is right outside the front entrance, talking to some of his men.'

'He'll be going to the uniform division. Hurry up.'

'Joe . . .'

'Come on, Kate.'

She did as she was told. These locks were easier to break. The first cupboard took less than thirty seconds, but there was nothing in it. He told her to forget the central drawer and try the other side. This had a different mechanism and took longer. She pulled open the door to reveal a filing system, which slid out on rails. Quinn inhaled sharply. There were no agent numbers. All the records were stored in files marked alphabetically. He pulled out the first folder and placed it on the desk. The top sheet had a photograph of a man in uniform: Lieutenant Aziz. By his name, Macleod had written 'agent sixty-one'. He was a member of the secret Free Officers group.

Quinn searched for agent thirty-one. His heart sank as he worked through file after file. He came to the last. Kate was by the door, looking out. 'Joe, we have to go.'

He found it. The face staring up at him had hollow cheeks and piercing eyes. It was Jooste. His real name was Alan Van der Riet, he worked as a mechanic in the garage at GHQ and the file recorded that he was agent thirty-one.

'Sir!' Kate hissed. Quinn slammed the file shut, pushed it back into the drawer. He could hear voices outside. 'Reza!' she mouthed at him.

He beckoned her through to the secretary's cubicle. A full-length blind concealed a small alcove. Quinn pushed Kate in, followed her and closed the blind. Around the side, he could just about see the doorway. Reza came through and switched on the light. He glanced about him, then walked over to the window and looked out, then examined the floor in front of the filing cabinet.

He frowned, then turned slowly and walked directly towards them.

CHAPTER FIFTY-THREE

As Quinn watched Reza's approach, he reached for his revolver, then realized he'd left it in the holster on the back of his chair.

He was about to step forward to push the Egyptian out of the way, when Reza altered course. He went instead to a cabinet on the far side of the room and rummaged through it, noisily. Quinn could no longer see him. He glanced at Kate.

Time crawled by.

Reza pushed the drawer shut, but did not move. A minute passed, maybe more. He paced towards the doorway, so that Quinn could just see his face. Reza was thinking, his cane in his hand. He tapped the end of it against the door, then moved into the room beyond.

He switched off the light, but still did not leave.

At last, he closed the door, locked it again and was gone, footsteps receding. Kate waited long enough for him to be well clear before she said, 'You bastard. That was all your fault.'

They let themselves out, Kate locked the door and they moved swiftly across the atrium to their own office. As soon as they were safely inside, she rounded on him. 'He knew we were there.'

'No.'

'Yes, he did. That was a trap. The creep had been waiting for us. He knew you'd be unable to resist. He knew we were coming.'

'Easy. There's nothing he can do to us.'

'That's a lie and you know it.'

'I've got the name. The man who killed my son is listed in the file as agent thirty-one. And agent thirty-one is your compatriot, Jooste, real name Alan Van der Riet.'

'So how do we find him?'

Quinn smiled at her. 'It's all in the file.'

The garage at GHQ was situated in a long, low wooden hut in the corner of the compound. It was sheltered by a line of palms that stood between it and the wire. Somebody had scrawled 'Transport Division' on a board and nailed it to a post.

Quinn and Kate had been sitting in the Austin, beneath a palm, for much of the night. Quinn had tried to send her home, but she wouldn't hear of it.

They had watched people arriving for work since the first rays of dawn sunlight had illuminated the horizon, but as yet there had been no sign of Alan Van der Riet. It was getting hot. 'If he's a deserter,' Kate said, 'maybe he doesn't work here any more.'

'He's not a deserter.'

'But—'

'He's been using false names and cover stories in case he gets caught. I figure he's been working here all the time, totally legit, moonlighting for Macleod and Reza when they need him.'

Kate fanned her face. Quinn looked at his watch. The guy ought to have arrived for work by now if he was coming. 'All right,' he said, 'we'll go take a look around, speak to a few people, but be careful what you say. We don't want anyone to tip him off.'

They pushed open their doors and stepped out. Inside the garage, thin beams of sunlight illuminated a row of vehicles. Vera Lynn was playing on a gramophone, barely audible above the bang and clatter of the mechanics.

Quinn walked down the centre of the concrete floor. No-one paid him much attention. A man with silver hair raised his head from a wheel and looked up, a cigarette stuck between cracked lips. 'Yeah?'

Quinn kept walking. Some of the mechanics stopped what they were doing to watch him. He reached the end. There were only a couple of men left. One was washing his hands in a basin in the corner.

Van der Riet turned, caught sight of them, then calmly resumed what he was doing. He dried his hands on the towel. 'Turn around,' Quinn ordered.

Van der Riet threw the towel in his face and lunged at Kate. He wrapped an arm round her neck, placed a revolver to her head. Instinctively Quinn drew his own, but he was too late to intervene. They watched each other for a moment, then Quinn walked forwards, forcing the South African to retreat. 'Stay where you are!' Van der Riet hissed. 'I'm not bluffing.'

Kate's eyes radiated fear. They hit a door, stumbled into the sun. Van der Riet looked around for a car, but Quinn blocked his escape route and pushed him towards the perimeter fence.

The South African passed the line of trees and

retreated until he hit the wire. Quinn took aim. 'Let her go,' he said.

Van der Riet pushed the revolver hard against Kate's temple. 'I'll kill her.'

'Then do it.'

Kate's eyes widened. 'Get back,' said Van der Riet.

'Last chance.'

'I said, get back!' He swung his revolver from Kate to Quinn.

'Go on,' Quinn said, 'shoot.'

Van der Riet stared at him.

'Go on, you piece of shit, shoot!'

'You can't touch me!'

'You killed my son. I can do what the fuck I like.'

Van der Riet tried to hold his arm steady. It had begun to shake.

Quinn fired. Blood spurted from the South African's arm and his revolver looped into the air to land in the dirt close to the wire. Kate staggered into the fence.

The South African writhed in agony. Quinn heard shouts. He straddled the man and lowered his revolver until the tip of the barrel rested on the bridge of Van der Riet's nose. The South African clutched his wounded arm, but Quinn snatched his hand away. 'If I'd wanted to hurt you, I would have done.'

'You can't touch me,' Van der Riet said again. 'You wouldn't dare.'

'Want to bet?'

'They'll find you.'

'Do I look like I care?'

'They'll take your wife.'

Quinn grunted and shoved the gun down against his mouth. 'People like you . . .' As he looked into Van der Riet's eyes the world receded, the sound around

401

him a distant hum. He saw the terror there. He began to depress the trigger. It would be worth it. He could hear those feet pounding in the dirt, see the boy's hair tugged by the wind.

'I'm sorry,' Van der Riet muttered. 'If that's what you want.'

Quinn hesitated. 'Is that all you've got to say?'

He didn't answer, so Quinn smashed his forehead with the butt of his revolver. Van der Riet screamed and tried to roll away, but Quinn held him tight. 'Is that all you've got to say?'

'It was an accident.'

'Nothing is ever *just* an accident.'

'I didn't see him. He—'

'You were drunk.'

'No!'

'You *must* have been drunk.'

'I—'

'You had time.'

'No! You saw it. The girls were talking by that car and—'

'You were staring at them?'

'He ran out into the road. One minute the street was empty, the next he was there. You saw it yourself.'

'You didn't touch the brakes.'

'I had only a split second to—'

'You *had* time.' Quinn shook his neck. 'You had time and you took my boy.'

'I didn't mean to kill anyone. Please, I beg you.'

Quinn looked down at the pathetic, imploring figure below him. This wasn't how he'd imagined it would be.

'They're going to get your wife,' Van der Riet said.

'She's the pretty blonde woman, right? They've been talking about her. Maybe they'll—'

'Why has Macleod been protecting you?'

'Macleod?'

'You heard me.'

'I – I just work here and run a few errands sometimes.'

Quinn lowered his revolver and began to force it into the South African's mouth. 'Please.' Van der Riet's voice was shrill. 'All right, I can help you.'

'You don't deserve help.'

'I've got information, I know stuff. I know what's been going on. I know where the guns are.'

'Which guns?'

'Macleod's. They're—'

'You been stealing guns for Macleod?'

Van der Riet nodded, his eyes still on the barrel of the revolver. 'Where are they?'

'I can show you. You'd never find the place yourself.'

Quinn watched him. He waited.

He took hold of the man's collar. 'You cross me, I'll kill you. Now get up.'

When they reached his apartment in Zamalek, Quinn left Kate with her revolver pointing at the South African's head and instructions to pull the trigger if he moved so much as an inch.

There was still a black Fiat parked under a banyan tree outside the front of the building, but Mae sat unharmed in the sitting room, eating an early lunch off a tray on her lap. 'What's happened?' she asked. 'You look terrible.'

Quinn leant against the edge of a table and tried

to still the pounding in his head. He took out a handkerchief and wiped his face. 'You OK?' he said.

'What harm could possibly have come to me in here? There's some food on the side.'

'I ain't hungry.'

'You look as if you haven't eaten for days.'

Quinn wanted to say something conciliatory, tell her he'd found the South African, but reticence had become a too persistent habit. What was there left to say? What was compelling enough to break the silence?

'I'm going to send someone down,' he said. 'David Cohen. He'll keep an eye on you, make sure you're all right.'

'You think I'm going to fall over and hurt myself in here?'

'He'll need to be inside.'

She stared at him a moment, then returned to eating. The only sound in the room was that of metal against china. 'Good night, Mae,' he said, but she didn't reply.

CHAPTER FIFTY-FOUR

Effatt lived in Giza, to the west of Cairo, at the end of a dusty street not far from the Pyramids. An old wooden door gave way to a tiny stone garden, which had once been the pride and joy of Effatt's wife, its rafters overhung with bougainvillaea. In the corner, a *dekka* – a low bench made of sun-dried mud and draped with coloured shawls and fustian – ran along two walls. In front of it were two brass tables, with intricately patterned iron legs.

A lizard darted across the wall.

Quinn heard a rasping cough, which grew more hoarse and wretched. He ducked in through the door to the house. The interior was cooler, the sunlight blocked out by blinds, and palm-oil lanterns of coloured glass flickered on the walls.

Rifat's brother and sister sat on a wooden bench covered with a bright orange shawl. They had cotton masks over their mouths. Quinn nodded a greeting, but they looked at him with dispassionate curiosity. He passed through to the bedroom. Effatt was holding his son, and Deena clutched a tin bowl.

The boy was consumed by another coughing fit,

his thin body racked by the convulsion. Effatt held him until it had passed, then laid him down and led Quinn to the garden. He went back into the house and returned with two glasses of mango juice, then took out a packet of Turkish cigarettes. They smoked in silence, watching a lizard bask in the sunlight on the far wall. 'I do not think he will be going,' Effatt said. 'It is too late.'

'It's not too late,' Quinn said. 'Not yet. Not for you.'

They considered this as they drank the juice. 'I cannot put him through the journey.'

His friend had aged, Quinn thought. His eyes and cheeks were puffy from lack of sleep. 'You have a boy,' Effatt said, 'you hold him in your arms. You see him cry, feed him when he is hungry, hold him when he is lonely, scold him when he is angry. You watch him grow stronger as you feel your own strength ebb. You think of what he will become, of whom he might marry, of what hopes and dreams he will cherish, but you never imagine you will see him die. That is something you never believe you will see.'

'You won't have to.'

'I have failed him. In my heart, I know it. I have failed to protect him as a father should.'

'Effatt—'

'Do not lie to me. I have seen what it has done to you. And now it is my time. I know that. How will I live through it? Do you believe in God, Joe?'

'You do. That's what matters.'

Effatt sighed. 'Who can believe in God at such a time? I'm sorry. He is calmer now, but yesterday I could not leave him.'

'I understand.'

'Now we must go. You have come for me. There is work to be done.'

'Stay here. This is where you belong.'

'Joe, I—'

'You've got to stay.'

'I will come. Deena will care for him. There is time yet.'

'Effatt—'

'I cannot sit here and wait.' His voice was crisp with tension.

'OK,' Quinn said. He waited, with a heavy heart. 'I came because I found the man who was driving that car. He's with us. You were right. Macleod and Reza have been stealing guns. He knows where they are.'

'You believe he is telling the truth?'

'He knows I wanted to kill him.'

'But they must have guessed you would find him, Joe. Maybe it's a trap. We should wait.'

'There isn't time.'

Effatt dropped the cigarette, stubbed it out and went back into the house. Quinn followed. It was deathly quiet.

He waited in the hallway. The children watched him.

Quinn took out a coin and handkerchief to perform a trick his grandfather had taught him. The boy smiled – he must have been five, maybe six – but the little girl stared at him with large round eyes.

He tried another trick, and this time the boy leant forward to see how it was done. Quinn showed him, then gave him the handkerchief and coin.

He could hear hushed voices. Through the doorway, he saw Effatt sitting on the bed, leaning towards his son, Rifat's arms round his back. The boy was sobbing.

407

Quinn forced himself to return to the courtyard, where he sat and waited. It was another fifteen minutes or more before Effatt appeared. Quinn put an arm round his friend and together they walked out into the glare of the sun.

CHAPTER FIFTY-FIVE

The South African led them to a suburb called Maadi,
just to the south of the city. It had once been a village,
created at the turn of the century by a group of
Sephardi entrepreneurs who had bought land along
the railway that linked Cairo to Helwan, but it had
long since been swallowed by the city. Now it was a
quiet, exclusive suburb, the preserve of bankers,
brokers and civil servants.

Quinn was in the back, Van der Riet jammed
between him and Madden. He leant his face against
the window and watched a traffic jam on the river
unravel. The owners of a group of primitive Nile boats,
ghiassa, were shouting at each other, running up and
down beneath their lateen sails to push other craft
away with long poles. Close to the nearest bank,
fishermen had formed their boats into a circle and
were beating the water with paddles of tightly woven
palm leaves. One or two fish caught in their trap tried
to leap free, flashes of silver in the sunlight.

The car sped past a group of egrets, sitting hunched
like vultures in a mimosa tree. Out on the river,
flamingos, pelicans and kingfishers added an

occasional splash of colour, but the light in the flat countryside was pale.

They reached Maadi, nestling against the Nile, only the rooftops of its churches, mosques and synagogues rising above the level rows of houses. Quinn gazed at the parched lawns. The properties were set comfortably in their own land, simple bungalows alternating with the kind of tall, imposing mansions you would find out in Connecticut or Long Island. They swung towards the Nile again, ran along its banks until they reached a yacht club. Van der Riet directed them up an incline, then down to the outer edge of the suburb, where the houses were less grand, surrounded by sand rather than burnished grass. Kate turned up another hill.

They pulled onto a concrete forecourt in front of a low bungalow with its blinds pulled down. To the left of the house was a dusty patch of garden, to the right a long warehouse with a tin roof. A small group of Arab men squatted on the ground behind a truck, playing a game of dice.

'This the place?' Quinn asked Van der Riet.

'Yes.'

'You been here before?'

'Yes. The weapons are stored in a warehouse in the yard.'

The game of dice had stopped. The men were avoiding their gaze. Kate took out her revolver. Quinn noticed that Ed Madden's face was sheet white. 'Easy,' he said. 'Easy.' He opened the door, stepped out. Effatt did the same. Quinn was closer. '*Assalamu aleikum!*' he said. Peace be upon you. The men did not move.

Effatt took a few paces towards them, the soles of his shoes crunching pebbles loudly against the

410

concrete. He greeted them, then fired a series of quiet, but urgent questions. One waved towards the house, another shrugged.

'Something's not right,' Effatt muttered. 'You want to go on?'

'Let's take a look.'

Effatt walked to a wide steel gate by the front of the house. Quinn pushed Van der Riet in front of him.

The gate led to a concrete yard, which ran the length of the warehouse. In its centre was a steel door, big enough to drive a truck through. It was bolted shut. Quinn looked over his shoulder. Kate and Madden were close behind.

Effatt walked to the end of the warehouse. 'Joe!' he hissed.

He was pointing at a small green door. Quinn propelled Van der Riet in front of him as Effatt depressed the door handle and stepped inside.

The interior was gloomy, but not dark. Immediately to their left, three steel steps led up to a deserted office with a tall glass window that overlooked the floor. If this had once been a factory, it was now filled from end to end with boxes covered with thick canvas sheets. Effatt moved to the closest pile, took one end of a sheet and yanked it clear.

They were faced by rows of gleaming rifles stacked between piles of wooden boxes. Effatt pulled down the next canvas sheet, then the next.

Quinn examined one of the boxes. It was nailed shut, so he searched for something with which to prise it open. He found a pair of metal pliers, wedged one end in and snapped off the lid. He rifled through the straw packing and pulled out a gleaming machine gun.

Van der Riet stood in the middle of the floor. 'You stole all of them?' Quinn asked.

'Yes.'

'Who with?'

'Reza and some of his men.'

'Wheeler tipped you off when a consignment was being moved?'

'I don't know. I did as I was asked and took the cash.'

'You were told to fuck Wheeler?'

Van der Riet didn't flinch. His confidence had returned. 'Yes.' Quinn glanced about him. He could see nothing amiss. 'What about Durant? You—'

'I never had anything to do with him. I heard what happened to him, but it was nothing to do with us.'

Quinn looked at the guns. 'Where were all these going?'

Van der Riet hesitated. 'I had to meet some student leaders from Al Azhar.'

It was evident he'd been here more than once before. Quinn walked down the centre of the room, through the bright sunlight, which poured through a metal grille. The floor was dusty and he coughed. The warehouse was maybe fifty yards long and boxes of weapons were stacked along each wall, enough to start a war. 'You figure Fabrizzi was paying for all this?' Quinn asked Effatt. 'You think that was what the money in his safe was for?'

'I guess so.'

'Jeez. It's a big operation.'

'No wonder Macleod didn't want us on his case.'

Quinn faced the South African. 'You ever meet Fabrizzi?'

'No.'

'But you knew he was paying for all this, right?'

'Like I said, I did what I was told, took the cash.'

Quinn moved towards the steel door. 'So you went out to steal 'em and Macleod sold them on. That what you're saying?'

As Van der Riet opened his mouth to answer, a single bullet passed through the centre of his forehead and the rear of his skull exploded.

Thunder broke all around them. Bullets whipped through the still air and ricocheted off the walls and ceiling. Quinn dropped flat. He saw Kate fall, then Effatt. The weight of fire dislodged a pile of rifles and sent it tumbling to the ground. He rolled behind them.

Madden cowered on the ground out in the open. Effatt and Kate lay still in the centre of the field of fire.

Effatt moved. He saw the cover, rolled in behind it. Blood poured from his leg. Quinn moved to tend the wound, but Effatt shook his head. 'Ed!' Quinn bellowed.

Madden didn't move.

Quinn crawled out, loosed off a single shot with his revolver then spun back. Kate was still lying, motionless, in the middle of the floor.

The firing stopped, but the sound rang in Quinn's ears. They heard a scraping sound, a brief cough. Dust filled the air. Madden had curled into a ball. Quinn rolled towards him, slammed into his side. He grabbed him by the collar, dragged him on all fours towards the cover.

No-one fired.

They slumped down, Madden shaking like a leaf. Quinn turned to Effatt's leg: he'd taken a slug in the calf, but no artery had been severed. Quinn took off

413

his jacket, tore at the thin cotton. Effatt shook his finger to indicate again that he was all right, but Quinn ignored him. He used a piece of cloth to clean away some of the blood, then lifted his friend's ankle a few inches. Effatt gripped his shoulder in pain.

Quinn examined the wound. The bullet had passed right through. He bound it tight.

The guns opened up again. The fire was more accurate this time, picking out their position, bullets pinging off the rifles in front, so that they had to lie flat.

It stopped. Quinn raised his own revolver, fired another shot.

'You can't win, Major.'

It was Macleod's voice. Effatt's eyes, like Quinn's, darted around, looking for a way out.

The room was silent.

'You'll hang for this, Macleod,' Quinn shouted.

'Is that so, laddie? If I were a gambling man, I'd not rate your chances. Ten men against a pair of revolvers?'

But Quinn didn't think Macleod had ten men. The gunfire, though deafening, had not felt like the work of ten weapons.

'I can see the girl moving,' Macleod said, 'and I don't see any blood on her. I'd say she's playing dead. If you surrender, I'll spare her and Effatt. And Lieutenant Madden. It's you I want.'

'We've all seen what you're doing, Macleod.'

'But who would believe them? By the time they came back, there would be nothing here.'

'And how would you explain nailing me?'

'We'd find a way. You'd be surprised what money can buy.'

414

'Whose money?'

'It doesn't matter. Money is money, Major. As a cop, you should have learnt that.'

'Even if it's from Rome or Berlin?'

'The money's not from Berlin. You'd better look closer to home. It's American money, brought to ensure the Egyptians get their country back. You think your friend Effatt is going to object to that?'

Quinn didn't offer an answer. Before he could think of one, Madden was on his feet, revolver in hand. He was running towards Macleod and his men.

CHAPTER FIFTY-SIX

There was a single shot. Quinn rolled sideways, got to his knees, then his feet. Madden was halfway down the warehouse. Ahead of him, a man was slumped forward over a pile of rifles.

Kate stirred, began to get up. Quinn ran, Effatt half a step behind him.

Madden yelled something, then fired another shot. There was a burst of gunfire, but it missed him, smacked against the wall. The room around Quinn blurred. He had their hiding-place in his sights and was careering towards it. He fired a shot and the response whistled past his ears.

And then the giant room was silent.

He stopped running. Madden stood ahead of him, leaning over a pile of rifles. Kate was there too. Quinn walked slowly up to them.

Macleod lay on his back, a single bullet hole through his temple, blood oozing from his skull onto the dark rifles beneath. Next to him, Sorrenson was slumped forward, shot through the chest. Madden examined the bodies, then put his revolver back into its holster.

Quinn heaved Macleod onto his back. He gazed

at the impassive face and distorted skull, absorbing the fact that he was dead. He kicked aside the Beretta and reached down to examine his pockets. He removed a wallet and the cross that had hung round Macleod's neck.

It didn't seem conceivable that the man had gone.

Then he turned to see Effatt splayed out on the floor. 'Effatt?' he heard himself ask.

There was no answer.

Quinn reached him. Effatt had been hit in the arm, the chest and the shoulder. He tried to speak, but blood dribbled from the corner of his mouth. 'Jesus . . .' Quinn dropped to his knees. He pulled back Effatt's shirt and tried to stifle his shock. It was a lung shot. 'Kate,' he said quietly. 'Get the car into the courtyard.'

He retrieved his jacket and began to tear up the rest of it. He took a long stretch, pushed it under Effatt's body and tightened it over the wound, then did the same again. 'Ed, we gotta turn him. Bad lung down.'

They manoeuvred him gently onto his side. 'We'll keep your good lung working,' he told Effatt. 'You'll be fine.'

Madden bent down beside Quinn and together they lifted Effatt. The Egyptian shut his eyes. 'Hold on,' Quinn urged him. 'We get you to the car, it ain't gonna hurt so much.'

They staggered out into the hazy air. Quinn heard the Austin being started as he stumbled through the courtyard. The car tore towards them. As soon as it had stopped, Quinn opened the rear door and lowered himself carefully onto the back seat, with Effatt. He and Madden manoeuvred him in the last few inches and turned him onto his side. Madden jumped into the front seat and Kate swung the car round. 'Where to, sir?' she asked.

Effatt had shut his eyes. 'Effatt!' Quinn hissed. The Egyptian looked at him. 'Keep your eyes open. We go on talking, OK? That way we'll be there before you know it.'

Kate was already driving towards the Helwan road. 'Where to, sir?' she asked again.

Quinn tried to think. Effatt's best chance was a military hospital in Cairo, but it was quite a distance. Helwan was too far away. He didn't think there would be a medical facility in Maadi. 'Go to the Scottish General,' he said.

Effatt's eyes were still open, his head rocking from side to side. They watched each other as Quinn tried to hold him steady. 'There is a lot of pain, my friend,' Effatt said.

'Ten minutes and we'll get some morphine into you.'

'Will it take the pain away?'

'Sure it will.'

'Is it a betrayal of my God to say that I do not wish to die?'

'You're not going to die. I won't allow it.'

'Do you think he was listening to our conversation earlier? Now the correct order is restored. I will not have to see Rifat die, after all.'

'Effatt—'

'Should I be frightened?'

Quinn tightened his grip on his friend's hand as they sped along the course of the Nile, the tips of the Pyramids visible beyond its far bank. Effatt's lips moved. 'I feel weak,' he said.

'Hold on.'

There was a long silence. Effatt's eyelids fluttered and closed, but Quinn shook him awake. 'You'll look after them?' Effatt murmured.

'It won't come to that.'

'But you will?'

'You don't have to ask, but it's not going to come to that. A few more minutes and you'll be in surgery.'

Effatt was breathing a little more easily. 'Will you tell him I love him, say that I'm sorry?' he said.

'You've nothing to be sorry for.'

'Perhaps if I had not been frightened I could have done more . . .'

'Effatt, cut it out.'

'I cannot bear the thought of him dying alone.' Suddenly he was gasping for air, a terrible sound. 'It breaks my heart,' he whispered.

'Open your eyes, Effatt.'

'I am tired.'

'Open your eyes.'

He did so, but it was clear the effort was becoming harder to sustain. His eyelids drooped. 'Be careful, Joe. Somebody has been watching you.'

'For Christ's sake, hold on . . .'

'I'm tired, Joe. So tired . . . Oh, it hurts.'

'Please.'

Quinn cradled him. Tears stung his eyes, and his body shook. Effatt's eyes were dulled by pain and intense fatigue. 'Goodbye, Joe. Give them my love.' His eyelids closed.

'Effatt!' Quinn whispered. 'Effatt! Please.' Tears dropped onto his friend's impassive face. 'Effatt, not long now . . . please . . .' Quinn searched for some sign of life. 'No,' he muttered. 'Please, God, not him. Effatt?'

*   *   *

419

Quinn sat alone in the morgue, facing his friend. It was the same cold, lifeless room in which he had stayed up all night beside the body of his son. Effatt had been covered with a cotton sheet, but his head was still visible. A cotton identification tag was attached to one of his toes. Quinn could not yet accept his death as an incontrovertible fact.

He realized Kate was behind him, but did not turn. 'I'm sorry to interrupt, sir.'

He did not answer her.

'It's just that it's been more than two hours. Ed and I are worried that if you don't go to see Colonel Lewis, and he finds out what happened from someone else, he may jump to the wrong conclusion.'

Quinn did not move.

'And we thought you would want to tell Effatt's family yourself.'

Quinn got slowly to his feet.

CHAPTER FIFTY-SEVEN

Lewis was in his usual chair. Brigadier Collins sat by the window in a crisply laundered uniform, his bald head shiny and red from too much sun. He was wearing reading-glasses. Next to him his secretary held a notebook open on her lap. In the far corner, Bexley, the Foreign Office official, was sitting with legs crossed, smoking.

They were all gazing at him curiously.

Lewis leant forward and placed his elbows upon the desk. 'Ed has informed us of what happened, Joe, and I'm sorry. We all are. Effatt was an outstanding policeman and a wonderful human being. In normal circumstances we'd leave you be, but as I'm sure you will appreciate we must have a full explanation.

'If I understand this correctly, Joe, you believe that the weapons you found were stolen. But I must say that we have had no reports of any consignments going missing.' Lewis looked at him. 'And any such report would surely have been brought to the attention of SIB, would it not?'

Quinn met the gaze of those piercing blue eyes. He tried to clear the fog in his mind. What had Effatt said? *It's a bit of a coincidence that Macleod and Lewis should end up here together . . .*

'Who was Macleod selling these weapons to?' Lewis asked.

'Fabrizzi.'

'What was Fabrizzi doing with them?'

'Supplying them to students and radicals.'

'Was this the first consignment, do you think?'

'I doubt it.'

'Where was Fabrizzi getting the money from?' Bexley asked. 'And was he working alone, in your estimation, or with the approval of the king?'

Quinn could not shake the image of Effatt's last imploring stare, or the sense of disquiet he had communicated as to whom they could really trust.

'Ed,' Lewis said, 'perhaps you would care to answer that.'

Madden cleared his throat. 'Yes, sir. Well, Signor Fabrizzi had a significant amount of English cash in his safe, as I think Major Quinn told you yesterday. It looks like it came from an American couple, the Whites, who arrived in Cairo three or four months ago. Avril White is in oil, so Major Quinn thinks he might have passed the money to Fabrizzi as a bribe. It is therefore possible that if Signor Fabrizzi was purchasing these weapons from Major Macleod he was acting without the knowledge or consent of the king.'

'What kind of bribe?' Collins asked.

'White has been trying to secure oil-exploration contracts for his American parent company.'

Lewis picked up a piece of paper and pushed it across the desk to Quinn. 'We got this from London overnight,' he said.

Quinn read:

IDA DROMEDAR TO OTTO LUCHS. CX/MSS/933/T21. Source: Reichssicherheitshauptamt VI, Berlin. Date: 23 May 1942. Message from Condor in Cairo. Plan for street by street defence of city. Last ditch desert line at Alamein, forces weak behind, delta wide open. Urge all speed. Arrival of New Zealand Division imminent, 8th Armoured and 44th Infantry near behind. 51st Infantry arrival end July. 2nd US Armoured scheduled Suez 5 July. 300 Sherman tanks, 100 Liberators in transit from USA, 2 Heavy Halifax squadrons from England. More follows.

Quinn looked up. 'Why are you showing me this?'

'Do you think it possible,' Collins asked, 'that Major Macleod was Condor?'

'What evidence have you got for it?'

'We're hunting a spy, Major, this isn't about evidence.'

'Everything is about evidence.'

'We're highly suspicious, Joe,' Lewis said, 'that some, or possibly all, of Condor's material, including this latest despatch, may have originated from Durant. If Major Macleod was Condor, everything begins to make sense. He was blackmailing Durant and Wheeler, sending information to Berlin and attempting to instigate a local rebellion with Fabrizzi's assistance.'

'Macleod wasn't a spy.'

'Why not?'

'Because there's a big difference between someone who's working for his country and a corrupt, money-grubbing bastard whose only interest is in lining his own pocket.'

They looked at him in silence.

'All the same,' Collins said, 'we still think that—'

'Macleod came straight from Shanghai, right?'

'So far as we know.'

'He ever go to Berlin?'

'Not to our knowledge.'

'So how come he's suddenly broadcasting straight back to Gestapo headquarters. You figure he learnt that on the boat from China?'

Collins edged forward in his seat. 'I cannot say that we find your attitude wholly helpful, Major Quinn. May I remind you that it is only thanks to the good offices of your superior here that you are not currently languishing in an internment camp. I believe Colonel Lewis had set a deadline, which passed some hours ago. If you cannot contribute to the investigation, I shall insist that you be detained immediately. It seems perfectly logical that Macleod was Condor and that he killed Durant, Wheeler and Fabrizzi. It also seems to me that, despite running this so-called investigation, you don't have any other ideas.'

'I wouldn't say that.'

The room was silent again. 'What do you mean, Joe?' Lewis asked.

'We're getting closer all the time.'

'Would you care to share your thoughts with us?'

'Well, to begin with, it's a man who sure knows *us* all real well. He is aware I keep a photograph of my son in my desk, knows the registration number of the car my wife uses and is aware a spare set of plates is kept in the garage. He can lift a glass with my print on it and drop it at a murder scene. He's able to pick up the telephone and tip off Macleod that we're about to turn up at a warehouse in Maadi.'

Quinn looked at the faces opposite. Lewis held his gaze. Ed Madden stood against the wall, head down. Kate was so close to him their hands were almost touching.

'Can you be more specific?' Lewis asked.

Quinn looked him in the eye. 'Not yet.'

open the door and walked across to the ...

CHAPTER FIFTY-EIGHT

It was dark when they reached Effatt's house, but an
oil lamp above the door created a pool of light in
which Deena led the children in a game of hopscotch.
Quinn asked Kate to kill the car's engine and switch
off the dimmed headlamps.

They watched Rifat's brother dance about. He
kicked up light puffs of dust, the others clapping and
laughing. Deena took him into her arms and swept
him off his feet.

Now it was the little girl's turn. Her bow bounced
as she skipped. She bent down to pick up her stone
and toppled over. There was more clapping, but she
wanted to go on. The boy intervened and provoked
an argument. Deena sent them both back to the start.

Quinn willed himself to move, but his eyes were
fixed upon the tableau in front of him. It was a game
he and Mae had played as kids on Seventh Street.

Now it was Deena's turn. Quinn wondered if she
would notice the car. She threw her stone and hopped
quickly to pick it up. 'What shall we do?' Kate asked.

'We'll wait.'

He rubbed dust from the window. A stray dog was

sniffing around some refuse. They could hear the sound of a generator. There was a café at the end of the street and its door swung back loudly as a couple of men emerged from it.

The little girl must have heard Rifat cough, because she tugged at Deena's sleeve and the game halted. The boy was left to play alone. He saw the dog and chased it away, laughing.

'Do you want me to do this, sir?' Kate asked.

'No.'

Quinn looked towards the entrance. He pushed open the door and walked across to the house. Inside, the garden was dark, a string of oil lanterns spilling tiny pools of light onto the palm-leaf matting that covered the floor. Effatt's house sandals were positioned close to the door, a simple cotton tunic on a peg above them.

Rifat cried out in pain. Quinn steeled himself and walked through the hall to the bedroom.

'Major Quinn,' Deena said.

They absorbed the expression on his face. Deena laid Rifat down and hurried towards the door. She did not quite block her nephew from view. 'He is not here,' Deena said.

Quinn stepped into the room. His chest felt as tight as a drum. He took a few more paces and Rifat's eyes followed him. Quinn sat on the bed. He noticed for the first time just how like his father the boy was: they had the same eyes, lips, nose and hair.

'Is Father with you?' asked Rifat.

Quinn picked up a tattered cloth camel from the bed. It had been well loved. Rifat took it from him. He held it to his chest, then tipped forward suddenly into Quinn's arms.

Rifat gripped him. Quinn felt his own fingers dig deep into the boy's ribs. Rifat's body seemed as fragile as a bird's. 'My father is dead, isn't he? The bad men killed him.'

Quinn glanced at Deena. She sank onto a bench and sat motionless.

There was a long silence.

'What did they do to him?' Rifat asked. 'Did they kill him with a gun?'

'Yes.'

'Was it because he was going to catch them?'

'Yes.'

'Were they robbers?'

Quinn hesitated. 'Yes, I guess they were.'

'He was good at catching bad men, wasn't he? Is that why they wanted to kill him?'

Quinn nodded.

'Did they want to kill you too?'

'Yes.'

Rifat looked at the wall. 'So it's lucky they didn't.'

Quinn didn't answer.

'Will I see him when I'm dead?'

'You're not going to die, Rifat. We have to get you better.'

'He said I must not die before him and now I haven't.'

The boy tried to smile. Deena put her head into her hands, and attempted to stifle her sobs.

'What do we do now, sir?' Rifat asked. 'What will we do without Father?'

'We have to take you to Jerusalem. You have to keep strong for me a little longer.'

'But if I die, I'll see him sooner, won't I?'

'He'd want you to live, though. For him.'

Rifat studied him for a moment more, then turned over to face the wall. He was very still, as if he had ceased breathing.

Quinn stood up. Deena followed him out of the room and they sat close together on a bench in the hall. 'He is at the Fifth Scottish General,' Quinn said. 'I'll be back soon to make whatever arrangements are necessary. You'll get all the help you need. Do you understand, Deena? Whatever you need . . .'

Rifat called for her and she muttered a soothing reply. She lifted her head, wiped her cheeks. She glanced at Quinn once more, then returned to her charge.

Quinn heard her soft whispers, then another lifeless silence descended on the house.

Kate pulled up outside Quinn's apartment. He noticed immediately that there was no black Fiat or military police jeep parked outside. 'Do you think they've given up on the house arrest?' Kate asked.

'No.'

'What do you think has happened to Reza? I mean, he wasn't at the warehouse anywhere, was he?'

'Stay here.'

Quinn got out and walked towards the dimmed light at the front of his apartment building. Fraser was nowhere to be seen. The door to the apartment was ajar. It was dark inside. 'Mae?' he called.

He moved along the corridor to the bedroom. The mosquito net had been hitched up, the bed not yet slept in. 'Mae?'

He reached the living room. Cohen lay sprawled in front of him, his body twisted, a pool of blood round his head. Quinn crouched down. His colleague had evidently been hit hard with something heavy: the back of his skull was a bloody pulp. Quinn straightened again. 'Mae!' he shouted.

He ran through to the kitchen. 'Hassan? Mansour!' He checked their quarters out at the back, then the yard and its entrance. There was no sign of anyone.

He went to the telephone and asked to be connected urgently to the duty desk. He had to wait a moment or two before the call was answered. 'Duty desk, Macleish speaking.'

'Macleish, it's Quinn. I need everything you've got down at my apartment in Zamalek. Cohen's dead, looks like my wife's been abducted. Get hold of Madden and tell him to bring Dexter and Nawab. Put a call out to all officers – they should look out for a blonde woman, early forties, about five eight. Possibly travelling with Reza or one of his associates.'

'Christ.'

'Find out Reza's residential address, get a patrol car round there. Search the place thoroughly, including the basement if it has one. If that doesn't turn up anything, get Keble or someone from the records division out of bed and tell them to work through every one of Reza's known assistants and associates.'

'Of course, sir.'

'I'll need every man you can find out on the streets.'

Kate was in the doorway. Quinn replaced the receiver. 'What's happened?' she asked.

'Cohen's dead.'

'But that's . . .' She frowned. 'Is your wife all right?'

'She's gone.'

'My God. Do you think . . . I mean, has Reza—'

'I don't know.'

Quinn returned to the living room. Kate followed

430

in silence. He examined Cohen's battered skull, then looked for some sign of the implement that might have been used. He tried to think clearly. Panicking wasn't going to help Mae.

The body lay in the middle of the carpet. There was no sign of a struggle. Either Cohen had known his attacker and had not suspected his motives, or the assailant had slipped through the door unnoticed. 'I'll speak to the neighbours upstairs,' Quinn told Kate. 'Try those across the street.'

The door to the terrace was ajar. Outside, a mosquito coil was burning on the floor. Quinn found an empty glass and a full ashtray. He turned over the ashtray and separated out the cigarettes to check they were all Craven A, her favourite brand. He sniffed the glass.

He walked through to the apartment's central lobby and shouted for Fraser. He checked the veranda, then knocked on the door of his room. When there was no answer, Quinn nudged it open.

Fraser lay on his back on the floor. His face had been smashed – his nose was bent, his eye and cheek hollow, his grey moustache stained with blood. Quinn bent over him. The fan was still turning, the pages of a novel flapping beside it.

CHAPTER FIFTY-NINE

Quinn returned to the lobby and climbed the stairs to the top floor. He knocked on the door of apartment three. 'Mario, Lucia, it's me, Joe.'

He heard footsteps, then hushed voices inside. A light came on and the door was pulled open by a frightened, grey-haired man. 'Joseph?'

'I'm sorry,' Quinn said. 'You seen Mae tonight?'

'Mae?' Mario Rispoli was an elderly man, a teacher of music at the American University, with a pelt of white hair. 'No.' He spoke quietly in Italian to his wife, then shook his head. 'Is everything all right?'

'You didn't see her leave?'

'Well, no . . .'

'You hear anything? Any shouts?'

'Shouts? No. We heard the car being driven away about an hour ago. I thought it was you.'

'You heard someone getting into the Ford?'

'Yes. I think so.'

'You sure it was the Ford?'

'It was from the driveway, just below.'

No-one else in the block had a car. Quinn strode through the apartment to the window, but the driveway was shielded from view by a row of trees. 'You hear anything else? Any shouts or signs of a struggle?'

'A struggle? You mean . . .' His face had drained of colour. 'No . . . no.'

'Tell me exactly what you heard.'

'The side door below was opened and a few moments later the car started. I assumed . . . Is everything all right, Joseph?' But Quinn was already heading for the door.

He ran down to the lobby, out of the side entrance and through the line of trees to the drive. The lean-to where they usually left the Ford was empty.

Quinn looked up and down the drive. If it had been Reza, why would he have taken Mae's car?

A police jeep pulled up in the street outside. Quinn met Madden and Macleish at the front and led them to his apartment. 'Nawab will be here in a minute, sir,' Madden said.

'The caretaker's out back.'

'Is he—'

'He got hit in the face with the same kind of implement.'

Madden could not tear his eyes from Cohen's smashed skull. 'What do you want us to do?' Macleish asked.

'Help Kate. She's talking to the neighbours. Go all the way down the street. The Italian couple upstairs reckon they heard someone going out in our Ford about an hour ago.'

'Your car, sir?' Ed asked. 'Why would Reza want to steal that?'

Quinn ignored the question. 'See if anyone can recall the last time they saw one of those black Fiats sitting in the road outside.'

As soon as they'd gone, Quinn began a methodical search of the apartment, starting in the living room. There was no indication that Mae had been forced out into a car and he was certain she'd not have gone without a fight.

He sat at her writing desk. The top had been cleared. This in itself was nothing unusual. He pulled open the drawer. Inside, there was a pile of letters and papers, a map and her leatherbound diary. He turned it over and untied the leather straps. He had been tempted to open it before but never had. He leafed through it. Each page was filled with Mae's neat, orderly handwriting. He turned to the last entry.

Got another letter from Ma. I have fought against the temptation to be irritated by the way in which her attempts to draw me home have been shorn of all subtlety and are no longer couched in the language of my 'best interests', but instead her own. However, as I contemplate how I shall reply, I cannot find any further reasons to stay.

Much as it breaks my heart to make this admission, to myself, or to others, the truth is that I do not believe Joe would miss me. There is not a day that goes by now when I do not replay in my mind the memories of our life together. I still cannot imagine a world beyond him and, for some reason, I am drawn to the earliest recollections of our time on Seventh Street and all the many days of laughter that made up our childhood. I am conscious that it is not just love I will lose, but my past. Perhaps that is why I have fought it so long.

Quinn turned the page.

However, I do not think I can fight any longer. The optimism we felt in the early days here, the hope that this might prove a new beginning and our enthusiasm for the city itself have wilted in the heat of this summer. Joe has another case. An important one, he says, but I have lost the ability or will to determine whether this is true or not. It is his escape route, a fact he will not acknowledge to himself, let alone me. Maybe if we had someone else to blame we could draw strength and unity from it, but Joe still runs from guilt like a man determined to hound himself to death. He pursues the man who was driving the car, but I think even he knows what a disappointment this will prove if he ever finds him. Once in a while I see flashes of the old Joe, of the humour and love, but they are mere glimpses, tiny windows on the past. Perhaps he is the man I always knew when he is with others, or some version of it. I have begun to suspect as much. I see the light in Amy White's eyes at the hospital when she talks of him, watch with amusement – and, yes, some jealousy – the admiration that shines from the face of his driver, or assistant, or whatever she is. Perhaps one of them will have him when I'm gone.

I wish I could say that I did not care.

But what does he know of my life here? What does he know of what has happened to me, of what I've become? Only friends like Marjorie prevent my loneliness being overwhelming. He accuses me of having an affair with some of the men at the hospital, but it only serves to remind me how much there is that he does not even begin to understand. I have tried everything I can think of, but I am, and will always remain, the mother of his murdered son. Guilt stands between us like a lead weight upon which all our efforts founder. Will he forgive me for the path I have chosen?

I do not know any more.

Quinn flipped back through the pages. He glanced at some of the other entries. Mae wrote about the hospital and the trauma she endured as each new soldier she had comforted slipped away. She referred to their neighbours, expressing her concern at what fate would befall the Rispolis upstairs.

As Quinn tried to bind up the diary, a few papers slipped out of the pocket in the back. There was a bill from Cirurcel and another from the small shop down the road that made reproduction furniture. There was a receipt from Amar, the tobacconist on Kasr el Nil, for the box of Havana cigars she'd bought him for his birthday.

He folded them away and stared at the wall ahead. *Will he forgive me for the path I've chosen?*

What had she meant by that? He went to the bedroom. He found Mae's drawers still packed with clothes, but the small canvas grip that was usually tucked beneath her dressing-table had disappeared. So had the photograph of Ryan she kept by the bed. He looked for her passport and handbag, but found neither.

He stood by the window, lit a cigarette and listened to the cicadas. He could just make out the faint sound of a jazz band from the direction of the river.

Will he forgive me for the path I have chosen?

*   *   *

436

Quinn found Kate in the street. 'I need the keys,' he said.

She hesitated, then gave them to him. He got into the Austin and sped through the streets. Cairo seemed emptier than usual.

It was not Marjorie Stubbs who came to the door first, but her *sufragi*. When Quinn placed his pink SIB card against the mosquito screen, the man withdrew, and a few minutes later Marjorie appeared. She was trying to tie a white dressing-gown round her waist and smooth her hair at the same time. She was a big girl with a square jaw, bleary-eyed from sleep. 'Joe?'

'Sorry to trouble you so late.'

'What is it?'

'It's about Mae.'

'Is she all right?'

'I don't know. She's gone. An officer I had guarding her is dead.'

'My God. What—'

'Maybe she's been kidnapped. But the Ford has also disappeared.'

Marjorie Stubbs was dumbfounded.

'I'm sorry, but I needed some answers. I figured you would be likely to know.'

'About what?'

Quinn was reluctant to articulate this: 'They say there have been others. Soldiers. Maybe more than one.'

'I'm sorry, I'm not sure I understand.'

'They say she's got a lover.'

'Who does?'

'There's an affidavit. Someone at the hospital told them my wife's had one of the soldiers as a lover,

437

maybe more than one. I figured you might be able to tell me who it was.'

'I've never heard anything so preposterous in my entire life. Your wife has a lover? We must be talking about a completely different woman.'

Quinn was silent.

'You cannot seriously think,' she said, 'that Mae would—'

'She's gone missing. I have to know where she is. Maybe she's in trouble.'

'Mae would no more have taken a lover than gone to the moon. I would have thought you, of all people, would understand that.'

'Have you seen her?'

'No. She's not been at the hospital the past few days. Not since the anniversary of . . . not since I last saw you. Is she all right?'

'Did she give you the impression there was something else on her mind?'

'Like what?'

'Anything.'

'Oh, Joe . . .' Marjorie sighed. 'You know . . . The boy, of course. Apart from you, it was just him, really. That was what she talked about.'

'There was nothing else?'

She shook her head. 'I don't know what you're looking for.'

'Thanks for your time,' Quinn said.

'Is she all right?' Marjorie asked. 'Where do you think . . . ?'

But Quinn had already reached his car.

He drove to Effatt's house out in Giza. Deena answered the door. 'I'm real sorry, Deena,' he said, 'I'm looking for Mae. Has she been here?'

438

'Yes.'

'She came to pick him up?'

Deena nodded. 'I thought that—'

'How long ago?'

'One, two hours.'

'She was alone?'

Deena frowned. 'No, not alone.'

'There was a man?'

'Yes. I thought . . .'

Quinn felt the blood pounding in his head. 'A white man?'

'Yes.'

'Describe him.'

She was taken aback. 'I am sorry, Major. I was not . . He stood by the door, it was not in the light. He had on a . . .' She gestured with her hand to indicate a hat.

'He was a soldier?'

'No. He was dressed . . .' Like him, she indicated.

'Tall?'

'Yes.'

'As tall as me?'

'Yes . . . I think, yes. I'm sorry, sir. I was saying goodbye. I did not—'

'He have dark hair, or light?'

'I do not know.'

It was clear she had barely registered him. 'You see the car, Deena? Was it a grey Ford?'

She shook her head. She had been in no mood to notice the make of a car.

Quinn thanked her and returned to the Austin, but did not immediately start it. He wound down the window.

He watched the tiny house, which was bathed in

439

moonlight on this cloudless night. The lamp she had switched on in the hall was not immediately extinguished. A dog barked, answered by a second. There was a light on in the café at the end of the road, and a small bird sat on the telephone wire that stretched between it and a pole.

Quinn looked at the café a moment, then slipped in the key and pressed the starter.

Back at his apartment, Kate and Madden were in the living room. Kate was fast asleep in a chair. Madden stood by the window, so absorbed in his own thoughts that he did not hear Quinn arrive. He started violently. 'Easy, Ed,' Quinn said. 'You all right?'

'Sir, Nawab has been. He took the bodies. We thought it best.'

Quinn watched Kate. 'I need you to do something for me,' he told Madden. 'Go back to the office, see if you can get a cable up to the Palestine border. Give them my wife's description and the Ford's registration number. Ask them to look out for her.'

'But I thought—'

'Just make sure they know.'

'What shall I tell them to do if they find her, sir?'

'Hold her up. I need to speak to her.' He pointed at Kate. 'You'd better take Mowbray with you.'

Both men looked at her, but neither moved. 'What happened outside Effatt's house this afternoon?' Quinn asked.

'What do you mean?' Madden was on edge.

'Either of you go into that café at the end of the street there?'

Madden frowned.

'You go in to take a leak?'

440

Now Madden flushed. 'I'm sorry. We took it in turns. There was never any risk that Van der Riet would escape.'

Quinn stared at him. 'That was a real brave charge this afternoon for a man who doesn't want to go to the front line.'

'Sir, I'm sorry about Effatt. If I'd known that—'

'I was admiring your courage.'

Madden did not say anything: he did not appear to know what his superior was driving at.

'You'd better get some rest,' Quinn said. 'Both of you.'

After they'd gone, Quinn walked through to the bathroom and splashed water on his face. According to the clock on the wall, it was a shade after three. He used the sheet from the bed to try to block out the slivers of moonlight that crept in through the shutters, but as soon as he lay down, he knew that sleep would prove impossible. He went to the hall, picked up the telephone, dialled the duty desk at Bab el Hadid and asked to speak to Macleish, who told him they'd heard nothing. There were no reported sightings of his wife anywhere in the city.

Quinn replaced the receiver. He tried to work out what time Mae would have left Cairo. He didn't think she'd make the border crossing into Palestine – assuming that was her intention – until mid-morning at the earliest.

He sat down by the telephone. Loneliness descended on him. He glanced at an old photograph of Mae on the hall table. It had been taken outside her parents' apartment building on Seventh. Quinn picked it up and gazed at her warm, affectionate smile.

It seemed to belong to a different life. It occurred to him that, despite everything that had happened this past year, he had never tried to imagine life without her.

CHAPTER SIXTY

Quinn spent the dawn hours sitting by Macleish's desk, smoking incessantly, but no information of any value came in. There was a brief flurry of interest when a blonde woman was detained by a patrol working close to the citadel, but as soon as Quinn got there and saw the battered car she'd been driving, he knew it wasn't Mae. It turned out to be a Hungarian dancer who wouldn't give her name.

When he got back to the barracks at Bab el Hadid, Quinn went up to his office on the top floor. The first thing he noticed was that the Field Security corridor once occupied by Macleod and Sorrenson had been sealed off with white tape. Dexter, who had been watching him, slipped over. 'I'm sorry, Major Quinn.'

'What's happened here?'

'Brigadier Collins's orders, sir.'

Quinn pulled down the tape and pushed open the door of Macleod's office. He walked in. 'Jesus.' The whole room had been stripped: there was not a book on the shelf, or a pen on the desk. The filing cabinets were empty. Through a half-open door, Quinn could see that the small cubicle usually occupied by

Macleod's quiet Scottish secretary, Maude, had also been cleared out. Dexter was behind him. 'When did this happen?' Quinn asked.

'They came last night.'

'Who is they?'

'Reza. About ten others. They had orders from Colonel Lewis.'

'Reza?'

'Yes. I tried to stop them, but the papers appeared to be in order. He didn't argue, just showed me the documents,' Dexter told him. 'Maude had packed up a lot of the office anyway. They shoved the rest into crates and took the whole lot away.'

'Where is Maude?'

'Reza put her in a jeep. He told her she should go home and pack and he would have the car take her on to Jerusalem.'

Quinn walked to the window, opened the glass door and stepped onto the balcony. A long line of jeeps, trucks and Austin Tillys had been assembled along the right-hand wall of the courtyard below. The workshop door was open, a mechanic rolling a tyre towards the nearest jeep. Dexter was still behind him. 'You seen Kate and Ed this morning?' Quinn asked.

'They're both in your office.' Dexter looked at his shoes. 'I never got a chance to say, sir, but I'm sorry about Effatt.'

Quinn muttered a reply. He watched a jeep speeding through the gate. He'd spent much of the night replaying in his mind the chronology of the previous day's events. They had driven Van der Riet from GHQ to here. Kate had waited in the car while he'd gone in search of Madden. Then they'd driven straight to Effatt's house.

Who would have had time to make a call? And where else but that café could it have been made from?

He crossed the atrium and walked down to the ground floor. At the bottom, he swung left and strode along the corridor past the cells and up a flight of wooden steps to the switchboard operator's room. Three women – one English and two Egyptians – sat side by side, close together, wearing bulbous earphones. They were startled by the interruption, but the incessant buzz of the switchboard commanded their attention. 'Yes, sir, of course . . . Good morning, Lieutenant Dexter . . . Yes, sir . . . Good morning, Lieutenant Henderson . . . Hot, sir, yes, it is . . . Shepheard's? Of course . . .'

The Englishwoman realized he wasn't going to go away, so took off her headphones and swung her chair to face him. She stood. 'Can I help?'

'I'm Major Quinn.'

'Of course.' She offered her hand. 'Molly Pearson.' She tried to stifle a deep cigarette cough. 'Excuse me. One so rarely gets to put a face to a name.'

The calls kept coming. 'Of course, Sergeant Baxter . . . Hello, Central . . . Good morning, Lieutenant Madden . . .'

'I'd appreciate your assistance,' Quinn said.

'Of course.'

'Who was on duty yesterday afternoon?'

'I was. Lucilla Parsons was supposed to be on the afternoon shift, but her *sufragi* called in to claim she was sick. They say she's already gone to Palestine and, if that's right, I must say that I will . . .'

Molly's voice trailed off as she saw that Quinn could not have been less interested in the politics of the telephone-operators department. 'You were here alone, ma'am?'

'No, I had Celia Gordon with me. I've told Lieutenant Mottisfont half a dozen times that we need a third person for each shift, but I'm afraid he does precious little about it.'

'Where is Miss Gordon now?'

'Mrs.' Molly Pearson smiled thinly. 'Her old man's been up in the blue for months. I should imagine she's down at the Lido, where any sensible girl would be in this heat.'

'You worked here long?'

'Too long.'

She tried to smile. Quinn thought she was the kind of woman who enjoyed the war in Cairo and wouldn't be in any hurry to leave. 'You recognize the voices of most of the people who work in this building, right?' He could see they prided themselves on it. He had guessed as much. 'You recognize my voice?'

'You're an American, Major. You're not difficult to detect.'

'And Macleod, with his broad accent?' She nodded. It was clear they knew everyone, listened to everything. 'Was it busy yesterday after lunch?'

'Oh, yes . . . pure hell. Non-stop. Normally things tail off, but ever since that wretched Rommel started his advance, it's been getting more and more bloody.'

'Major Macleod receive many calls?'

'I suppose so. It's hard to recall precise details. Of course, we've heard . . .'

Quinn smiled, tried to relax her. He could see she was wondering what he was doing there. 'It's a skill, I guess, being able to recognize someone instantly by their voice.'

'I'm not sure about that.'

'I'm surprised they haven't found a greater use for you at the coal face of the war.'

She was flattered, and he could see that she thought she could have made a greater contribution to the war effort.

'How about Lieutenant Madden?' He imitated Madden's clipped vowels. She smiled. 'You've met my deputy?'

'Once or twice.'

'He's quite a catch, I hear.'

'So they say.'

The women behind were trying to listen. 'You recall Lieutenant Madden placing a call to Major Macleod around three, maybe a shade after?' Quinn asked.

'I'm sorry, Major, I don't.'

'Maybe his voice was real quiet, could have been some kind of tip-off.'

'I couldn't say.'

Quinn took a step towards her. 'Ma'am, I know it's difficult, but if you could think real hard . . .' His voice was low, conspiratorial.

'I'm sorry, Major.'

'You don't remember thinking, How come Lieutenant Madden sounds so anxious? I can't figure out what he's talking about?'

Molly Pearson's enthusiasm for him, and for this conversation, such as it was, had evaporated. She knew she'd been played, Quinn thought, and was showing signs of resenting her susceptibility to an attractive man. She was never going to admit to listening in to the conversations of the top brass. 'Thank you, Miss Pearson,' he said. 'I should have come down here long ago.'

CHAPTER SIXTY-ONE

Quinn walked back up to the second floor, home of the uniform branch. Men were milling around now, chatting in small groups, their immaculately blancoed webbing belts betraying no hint of an army on the verge of capitulation.

The central area was tall and airy, with a balcony at the front overlooking the square. A couple of redcaps stood there, drinking coffee and smoking. On each of the walls tall metal bookcases were packed with equipment: khaki bulletproof vests, webbing belts, rain covers, machine guns, visors and riot batons.

As he passed the duty desk, Quinn stopped in front of Macleish, but the sergeant shook his head morosely. 'Still nothing, sir. I'm sorry.' Macleish was supposed to have gone off shift at dawn.

'You sent another cable to the border?'

'Yes, but still no word back. Is there anything else you want us to do?'

'Maybe there is something. We still got a contingent in Alexandria, right?' he asked.

'A small one.'

'Get hold of them. See if anyone matching my wife's

description has been sighted or checked into a hotel there. She'll almost certainly have Effatt's son with her.'

'Why would they take her to Alexandria?' Macleish asked.

Quinn shrugged. He'd not yet told Macleish that it was possible she'd left of her own free will. 'If they're trying to make a break for it, we assume they'll head for the Palestine border. If it was me, I'd go up to Alexandria and get one of those Greek speedboats to run me through to Haifa.'

'We'll give it a try.'

Quinn patted Macleish's shoulder and walked on down the corridor towards a pair of offices at the far end, occupied by Mottisfont, head of Personnel, and Keble, chief of the uniform branch. The men were polar opposites: Mottisfont small and round, with livid orange hair, a bushy moustache and a narrow face, Keble tall, slight and good-looking. Mottisfont listened to what Quinn had to say, but made no comment on his request. It took him ten minutes to find the file. When he returned, Quinn took it to the window.

LIEUTENANT EDWARD MADDEN
1st Battalion, Grenadier Guards.

Born: London, 25 July 1920.

Education: Eton College. Trinity College,
    Cambridge.

Enlisted: 10 December 1940.

Next of kin: Lord Carmichael, Glendower
House,
    Gloucestershire.

Languages: fluent in both German and Italian.

Arrived Cairo: 28 February 1941.

Assigned: GHQ Cairo, office of Military
    Intelligence.

Underneath, someone had scrawled: 'Reassigned,
Special Investigation Branch, Major Joseph Quinn, 12
April 1941'.

'Need any help, Joe?' The voice was Keble's, and
Quinn swung to face him. Keble was smoking a pipe,
one hand in the pocket of his khaki jacket. 'I don't
know if I was sorry to hear about Macleod,' he said,
'but we certainly are about Effatt.'

'Sure.'

Keble frowned. 'Are you all right, old man?'

'Yeah.'

'You don't seem quite yourself.'

'I need some help.' Quinn closed Madden's file,
dropped it on the window-ledge. 'If there was a theft
out in the field, a real significant one, of weapons,
or ammunition, it would be reported in the first
instance to the duty desk here, right? That's the
procedure.'

'Of course.'

'Even if it was stolen from one of the camps around
the city?'

'Absolutely.'

'So the desk officer has to decide whether to call
us or Field Security?'

'That's correct.'

'So he'd call Madden or Sorrenson?'

'When Lieutenant Sorrenson was alive, yes.' Keble
sucked on his pipe. He was frowning.

'You noticed a load of thefts of weapons and ammunition,' Quinn asked, 'say, over the past three or four
months?'

Keble smiled thinly. He appeared to sense a buck being passed. 'Joe, with the greatest respect, that's your remit. That's SIB territory. You're the investigator.'

'OK, but even if a desk officer passed on details of a crime straight away, he'd still log it, right?'

'We've spent half the war writing bloody incident reports.'

'Where are they stored?'

Keble gestured for Quinn to follow him.

The incident reports were held in row upon row of green box files in an airy room on the far side of the central hallway. There was no evidence that anyone had thought to begin packing or burning them. When the Germans arrived, they would find plenty of information on what the British Army had got up to in Cairo, for all the good it would do them.

Keble melted away.

The boxes were marked by month and stored in chronological order. But there were a lot of them, the inevitable result of having several hundred thousand Allied soldiers in and around Cairo.

Quinn began in the present and worked backwards through endless badly typed reports. Even though he'd worked here since the outbreak of war, more or less, he'd never imagined the volume of crimes that were logged. Most of it was petty stuff: affray, drunkenness, vandalism. Sometimes the fights were more serious.

But there were no incidents of arms being stolen.

He kept going. He became slipshod. The reports had not always been stored in precise chronological order before he started, but once he'd finished with them, they were a mess.

After an hour and a half, he'd gone back at least six months and found not a single report of the theft of arms from British bases anywhere in the delta. He walked to the window. There were more men in the courtyard, two or three jeeps with their engines running. Maybe they were preparing for another sweep of the Berka.

He noticed a series of notebooks on the bottom shelf and took one out. On the inside page, someone had written 'Duty Officer's Log'. It was full of neat entries.

It took Quinn less than half an hour to find the information he'd been searching for. An entry recorded the theft of 'substantial amounts of ammunition (at least twenty-four boxes) from 2nd Indian Transport Brigade Temporary Headquarters'.

The desk officer had referred the case to Lieutenant Edward Madden.

Quinn double-checked the relevant box file. The report of the incident had been removed.

He ran up the stairs. Dexter and most of the secretaries looked up from what they were doing and stared at him. He banged open the door of the office. Kate swung round. 'Where is he?'

'Who?'

'Madden.'

'I don't know—'

'Stay here.'

'But, sir—'

He was gone again. He stalked across the atrium, stormed through the offices opposite. Kate had ignored his instruction. 'What are you doing?'

'Go back.'

He'd reached the top of the stairs. He took hold of

the banister and jumped down them three or four at a time. Kate struggled to keep up. 'I don't understand,' she said.

But he was well ahead of her now. He went through the uniform division, checked Keble's office and the central atrium, then returned to the stairs. Kate caught up with him. 'Please stop a minute.'

Madden was standing outside by a palm. He and Quinn stared at each other. Madden began to run.

CHAPTER SIXTY-TWO

Quinn shouted, but Madden was past the guards at the gate before they had woken from their sun-drenched reverie. One knelt, raised his rifle to his shoulder. 'No!' Quinn yelled, but it was too late: he had loosed off a round.

Madden sprinted across Bab el Hadid, a tall, ungainly figure swaying through the crowd, kicking up thin wisps of sand. Quinn forced a battered Lancia saloon to a halt and followed him across the square. Madden was twenty yards in front, heading in the direction of Shepheard's. A donkey cart emerged, clip-clopped in front of him and Quinn ducked behind it, then swerved to avoid three men travelling on ancient bicycles.

Madden turned right towards the Berka. He side-stepped a herd of goats, stumbled, hit a fruit stall and fell, sending the fruit, the scales and an old man flying. He picked himself up. They were only ten yards apart now.

They flew into the Berka's crowded streets and the sights of Cairo swam past the periphery of Quinn's vision: a boy being carried on his father's shoulders, another driving goats down an alley, a group of men holding hands, scratching their beards and laughing.

They entered a narrow lane. Quinn had a clear shot. He took out his revolver, aimed for a line of washing and fired.

Madden slowed, then came to a halt. He turned round. Quinn approached, the revolver pointed at his chest. Madden looked exhausted, his face white. It was a tiny alley, not more than five feet across, and it was dark.

Quinn hesitated. Had he been led here? 'Take a walk this way,' he said. He saw Kate emerge into the alley. 'Stay there,' he instructed her. 'Keep walking,' he told Madden. 'Put your hands against that wall.'

Quinn stepped forward. 'Wide!' He kicked Madden's legs apart, removed a revolver and threw it onto the ground, then checked to make sure he had no other weapons. A group of children and an old man gathered in the gloom of a doorway. They whispered to one another, pointing at the weapon in the dust.

Madden sank to his knees. 'Get up,' Quinn ordered. He bent down, picked him up, then hit him in the flank. Madden's face was consumed by pain as he bent double. Quinn kicked him so hard in the chest that he spun back onto the ground. 'Joe!' Kate yelled.

'Stay out of this.' Quinn went after his deputy, who was curled up on the ground. 'Get up,' he commanded. Madden rocked. 'Get up!'

Madden pushed himself to his feet. He tried to bolt, but Quinn caught his jacket and swung him through a doorway, tearing the dirty curtain and smashing into a shelf of earthenware pots. Madden tried to wrestle free, but Quinn slammed him back hard.

A woman emerged from the next room, a boy caught in her skirts. Quinn took out his revolver. He placed the barrel against his deputy's chin. 'Sir,' Kate said, 'for God's sake.'

'OK, Lieutenant Madden. Now you've got to start talking.'

He could not, or would not, speak.

Quinn cocked the weapon. 'You made sure every report was passed to you. What'd you sell yourself for, Ed?'

'I—'

'You tipped him off about our trip to that warehouse?' Madden's eyes widened. 'You murdered Effatt.' Quinn pushed the revolver up so hard that Madden winced with pain. 'You told them we were coming. You knew they were waiting for us.'

'No! They told me nothing.'

'Who was it you spoke to? Macleod?'

'It was always Reza.'

'What about Lewis? They answer to him?'

'I don't know.' Quinn jerked the revolver. 'I swear it.'

'Keep talking.'

'I – I don't know what to say.'

'You took their money, Ed?'

Madden closed his eyes in shame. 'Never.'

'Then tell me why.'

'They asked me whether I wouldn't prefer to be at the front. As a Guards officer, they said, a transfer could be easily arranged.'

'That's it?'

'No.'

'What else?'

'They said they knew about . . .'

456

'About what?'

'About some of the things I did.'

'Like what?'

'Sir, I—'

'Something your father wouldn't have understood?' Quinn had lowered his voice. 'Is that what it was? A sin of the flesh he'd never accept?'

Madden hung his head.

Quinn loosened his grip. 'Van der Riet trapped you in front of those mirrors?'

He gave a barely perceptible nod. 'Sometimes Reza would come to my apartment at night. He never knocked, just let himself in and slipped into my bedroom. I would wake and he'd be there, standing by the bed.'

'What did he ask you to do?'

'I was to scoop up any reports of the theft of weapons from camps around Cairo and make sure they were destroyed.'

'Why couldn't they do it themselves?'

'They wanted to make sure you didn't hear of it.'

'What else they ask you to do?'

Madden looked at the floor. They heard the sound of whispered voices from the street outside. A stray dog put its nose in, then scampered away.

'What else?' Quinn barked.

'On that first night, after we discovered Durant's body, Reza came to my apartment. I'd double-locked the door, but I woke up suddenly and he was there, sitting in a chair by my bed, watching. He said they wanted to be informed of every development in the investigation.'

'Why?'

'I didn't ask.'

'Did you know I was going to be arrested?'

Madden nodded miserably.

'It was you who took the photograph from my desk and cut it up?'

'No, that wasn't me. I swear it.'

Quinn eased the barrel of the revolver back an inch, his eyes still on the young man's face. 'But you told them we were coming to the warehouse?'

'I had no idea they would be there. I knew what they were doing. It didn't take a Cambridge degree to work it out. I thought they'd move them.' Madden hung his head again.

'Where is my wife? What have they done to her?'

'I don't know.'

'Where have they taken her?'

'Sir, I never heard her name mentioned.'

Quinn grabbed Madden's lapels and slammed him into the wall again. 'Ever since we found Durant's body, they've been trying to make me suspect her – the sighting of her outside Durant's apartment, the fingerprint on the glass, the number-plate on the car.' Quinn brought his face close to Madden's. 'So don't tell me you don't know what they've done with her.'

'I swear, sir, her name has never been mentioned.'

'Van der Riet said they were going to "take" her. Where?'

'I don't know.'

Quinn slammed him back again. 'Where *is* she?'

'I have no idea, sir, I swear to you . . .'

Quinn eased back his revolver, then let his arm fall to his side. He glanced out at the dusty footpath, then looked back at his deputy and saw the misery in his face. 'Tell me why they wanted to know about this investigation. What was Durant's connection in the Berka?'

'I've never asked.'

'Guess.'

'I think you were right. Wheeler got into trouble and looked to his friend for help. But I don't think Reza and Macleod knew what was going on. They didn't kill Durant and the others, but they were worried our investigation might lead you to them.'

'So who did kill Durant?'

Madden stared at the floor. 'I think it was Condor. And I believe you think so, too. Someone was treating both Wheeler and Durant as sources of information. The same man was funding Fabrizzi and his incipient rebellion. That could only have been Condor. It would give him a motive for all three murders.'

'And who is Condor?'

'I don't know . . . Will I hang for this, sir?'

Quinn did not offer him an answer.

CHAPTER SIXTY-THREE

He put Madden into a cell. While he was signing him in with the officer on the corridor, Dexter rounded the corner with papers in his hand. 'I'm sorry, sir. They said you were down here. I thought you'd want to see this.'

FOR THE IMMEDIATE ATTENTION OF HEAD OF SIB, MILI-
TARY POLICE, CAIRO. In answer to query, serial
numbers match deposit in bank in Lisbon.
Account name Ernst Glauber. Possibility of sophisticated forgery. SIS believes connection Gestapo
foreign intelligence, RSHA VI. More to follow.

There was a second sheet.

FOR THE IMMEDIATE ATTENTION OF HEAD OF SIB, MILI-
TARY POLICE, CAIRO. Further to earlier response,
money in circulation with these numbers almost
certainly sophisticated forgeries by German
Foreign or Military Intelligence with assistance
of Reich Central Bank. SIS confirms similar notes
recovered during espionage operations in Britain

and Ireland. Appears to be Gestapo not Abwehr operation. Proceed with caution.

Quinn read through the telexes again. 'When did these come through?'

'Last night. Sorry, sir, it's a bit chaotic down there and I've only just been to check. Is there anything you'd like me to do?'

'Get a uniform team from Macleish and pick up the Whites. You have permission to use force if they resist, but make sure they come back alive.'

'Won't I need an Egyptian police liaison officer? They're civilians.'

'Then get one, but be quick.'

As Dexter hurried away, Quinn glanced through the window in the cell door. Madden sat on his bunk, knees to his chest, shaking.

Quinn called for the guard and told him to open the cell door. As he did so, Madden looked up, tears pouring down his cheeks. Quinn stepped in and handed his deputy the telexes. Madden read them and looked up, unsure what to make of this gesture. 'The Whites had Gestapo money,' Quinn said. 'Maybe that's your answer, or part of it. They couldn't have been acting alone. There must be someone else on the inside.'

'But—'

'Whoever it is, I don't figure it's you. So get up there and help Dexter round up the Whites. I ain't ever going to mention any of this again and I'd advise that you don't either.'

Madden sat still. He didn't know what to say. He jumped to his feet. 'Sir, I—'

'Get on with it,' Quinn growled at him, and Madden darted free.

Quinn picked up the telexes and slipped into the corridor. 'Joe!' Lewis was standing in an alcove opposite the guard's desk. He took Quinn's arm and drew him towards the window. 'What's going on, old man? You're chasing Madden now? What's he saying?' He saw the telexes in Quinn's hand, took them. 'What's this?'

'The sterling banknotes are forgeries.'

'What does that mean?'

'Looks like we found your spy. Or one of them.'

Lewis read through the telexes. He seemed to be struggling to concentrate. Quinn looked out of the window and saw Reza standing in the courtyard next to Lewis's staff car. 'Who is it?' Lewis asked.

'Avril White brought the money to Cairo.'

'Avril White? You think he's Condor?'

'Part of it. Maybe Condor is an operation, not an individual.'

'Are you sure? Avril White's a respectable businessman – an American, like you.' Lewis handed back the telexes. 'We've got teams of men sweeping the Berka for this radio, but they turn up nothing again and again. What has Madden—'

'You cleared out Macleod's office pretty quick,' Quinn said. 'Why did you need to do that?'

'If Rommel gets here and finds all his—'

'But he's not here yet.' Quinn jerked a thumb at the window. 'You got Reza working for you now?'

Lewis took a pace closer. 'Not you as well, Joe. You know, they're asking questions over the other side now – how did Alastair get a job here? Was he really operating alone? Was he selling more than just rifles? They've asked London to trace people who were out in Shanghai with us.'

'You feeling the heat?'

'I put myself out on a limb for you, Joe.'

'You know what Macleod was doing?'

'Of course I didn't. The trouble is, when they talk to people about Shanghai, it's not going to be so easy.'

'You knew what he was like.'

'But it was different then. At least, I assumed it was. Making a few compromises to get rich out there is one thing, but to betray your country? How could I have imagined he'd go that far, for God's sake?' Lewis took a pace closer. 'I've backed you to the hilt, Joe. Macleod asked for another chance and I gave him one. We all deserve that, don't we?'

Quinn didn't answer.

'It takes all sorts in a war, Joe. People like you, like him, like me. I had no idea he'd pull a stunt like that, I give you my word on it.'

Suddenly Lewis appeared terribly weary. Quinn guessed he'd been here before, or a place like it. He didn't know whether that made a difference.

Quinn went straight up to the uniform branch. As he rounded the corner, Macleish emerged from behind his desk. 'Sir, I was looking for you. I think we might have something. I got a call back from Alexandria. A woman using your wife's name made a reservation yesterday at the Cecil Hotel.'

'Where is she now?'

'They don't think she checked in, but they've sent a patrol to have a look now.'

Quinn sprinted down the stairs and out into the heat of the courtyard. Kate was standing by the car. 'I need this,' he said. 'I'll be back tomorrow.'

'Tomorrow? Where are you going?'

'Alexandria.'

'I'll come with you.'

'No. I'll go alone.'

'Sir, you're exhausted. At least let me drive.'

CHAPTER SIXTY-FOUR

Kate drove towards the Nile, then turned north onto the road to Alexandria. The sun caught each triangular white felucca sail on the river and reflected off the water, the palms on the far side pale and grey like feathers. A black ibis stood on a sandbank. A flight of white egrets skimmed overhead. On the horizon, a misty blue sky shimmered with the heat of the desert. The roads were still full, battered cars stacked with luggage, young children riding on the roofs. Most of the occupants were Egyptian.

Kate reached a roadblock manned by three soldiers. Next to it, another group was digging a long trench by the side of a canal. She wound down her window. Quinn leant across and proffered his pink SIB card. 'Good day, sir,' the sergeant said. 'Where are you going?'

'Alexandria.'

'We're advising people to turn back. Some of the local police have shed their uniforms and we've had reports that bandits have been stopping and robbing cars.'

'I'll take the chance.'

The sergeant peered suspiciously into the back of the car. There was no arguing with the pink SIB card, but he was still reluctant to allow them to pass. 'We're advising people not to travel alone, sir, only in convoy.'

'It can't wait.'

'There's a rumour going around up in the delta that we're planning to burn everything as we retreat. That's why they're all coming south. They're pretty steamed up.'

'Thanks for the warning.'

The sergeant took a pace back and Kate accelerated away. 'They seemed jumpy,' she said.

Quinn didn't answer and they continued in silence, Kate weaving through pedestrians and livestock until they were clear of the city. The desert road was obliterated in parts by sand and this caused bottlenecks with the oncoming traffic. The Austin didn't have sand tyres, so Kate drove cautiously. Once in a while, they saw a group of men pushing a car that had strayed too far from the road.

The traffic thinned, but did not cease. They passed a few abandoned vehicles, piles of old tyres and empty petrol cans stored in the lifeless scrub.

Quinn took out a handkerchief and wiped the dust from his eyes and cheeks. Kate craned forward uncomfortably, eyes close to the windscreen. Cars and jeeps flashed past. Most appeared to be travelling in convoy.

They saw the rows of Nissen huts at the airfield at Ameriya. Quinn listened to the insistent drone of aircraft above. When they were well past it, there was a huge explosion and he turned to see fire climbing into the sky. A bomber had hit something.

Quinn's neck ached. He glanced at his watch.

They'd be lucky to reach Alexandria by nightfall.

The cars coming the other way became less frequent. They overtook a convoy of military jeeps and lorries and passed through several villages that – apart from the odd cooking fire – appeared deserted. The road grew lonelier.

They saw Alexandria long before they reached it, bright shafts of light piercing the night sky, and the rumble of explosions rolling across the desert. The blasts grew more frequent with each passing mile.

The city's streets were brightly lit by the fires, but Quinn and Kate noticed that the houses were shrouded in darkness. Alexandria had been bombed for months and the inhabitants took the blackout a lot more seriously here.

The city was eerily empty. There were no cars, or outward signs of life, only the occasional blast of a siren. Kate drove past a few homes with bunting, including one that had a swastika hanging from its balcony. The salty tang of a fresh sea breeze was laced with the aroma of smoke and petrol. A lone despatch rider roared past.

They approached the Corniche. Quinn had last been here with Mae the previous summer when, like thousands of other Cairenes, they had sought the cooler climate of Egypt's coastal city.

Kate turned onto the seafront opposite the San Stefano casino; the horizon was smeared a vivid orange by fires in the quarter beyond the Western Harbour. On summer evenings, the city's inhabitants could normally be seen drinking beer in the cafés along the front, watching Romanian dancers and *gali-gali* conjurors plying their trade for a few piastres. But tonight the cafés were boarded up, the streets empty, a few signs left to sway uselessly in the breeze.

The sea was calm beyond the line of palms. One or two boats were crossing the bay, looking for mines. Kate pulled up in front of the elegant Moorish façade of the Cecil Hotel. As Quinn got out, he saw a small swastika and an Italian tricolour entwined outside a window further down the quay.

If the Germans didn't win, there were going to be folk here who'd regret the eagerness of their welcome.

The Cecil Hotel was like the *Mary Celeste*. A porter leapt forward to open the door and search for his non-existent luggage, fans turned on the ceiling and the tinkle of piano keys could be heard from the bar, but there was no sign of any guests.

The receptionist treated him as a curiosity, but not necessarily a welcome one. Clearly they had expected their next guest to be a German officer. Quinn produced his pink SIB card and placed it on the counter, but the receptionist gave no sign of the respect that once would have been its due. Your days, his expression suggested, are all but done. Quinn picked it up again. 'I'm looking for my wife. She should have checked in here last night. Name of Mae Quinn.'

The receptionist shrugged.

'Mae Quinn. Take a look.'

The man gestured towards the bar and the sound of men singing.

Quinn crossed the marble floor. The ornate bar was empty but for three men in dusty khaki jackets, hidden behind the piano by a cloud of smoke. They were still singing, loudly and out of tune; whatever musical ability they might have possessed had been obliterated by alcohol. A lone barman watched Quinn. In the corner, a window was open, the sea breeze tugging at a long cream curtain. The shutter beyond it was closed to observe the blackout regulations. Alexandria might be about to fall, but no-one wanted to be the last casualty of its war.

'Good God!' the man at the piano exclaimed. 'More guests! Come and join us.'

Quinn moved closer, but he guessed these men were journalists and had no desire to be drawn into conversation. Who else would be foolish enough to remain here? The man at the piano had a cigarette in his mouth, eyes half closed against the smoke. He did not interrupt his playing. 'Chester Morrison, *Chicago Sun*.' He raised one hand. 'These are my colleagues, David Stern from *TimeLife* and Zac Marriott from the *New York Times*.'

Quinn nodded.

Morrison stopped playing. 'What brings you here, my friend?'

'Some routine business.'

'Routine business? Ha! Nothing's routine here any more.'

Another explosion rattled the windows, but this time it was more distant. None of the men around the piano paid it any attention. Morrison returned to the keys.

Quinn went back to the reception desk. 'I'm looking for my wife, Mae Quinn,' he repeated. The man grabbed the register and spun it round. There were few entries, but Amy White's neat, rounded handwriting stood out. There was no sign of Mae.

'Mrs Quinn hasn't checked in?' he asked. 'She had a reservation for last night.'

'No, sir. She's not here.'

469

'Which room is Mrs White in?'

'Is she expecting you?'

Quinn looked at the board of keys on the far wall. Only one set was missing, for room eleven. As he walked towards the stairs, Kate appeared from the alcove that contained the house telephone and toilets. 'Where are you going?' she asked.

'Amy White's here, but not Mae. Why don't you go check the other hotels?'

'There's no sign of—'

'None.'

'What if she's armed? Mrs White, I mean. If what you were telling me earlier is true, then maybe the Whites are here to escape.'

'Why would they come up here to escape?'

'It's closer to the front line.'

'So what? They'd stand no chance of getting across.'

'But surely—'

'It now occupies only a narrow strip between the sea and the Qattara Depression around Alamein. If they tried to get over, they'd be shot by our side or their own.'

'Then how would they get out?'

Quinn frowned. 'I don't know. Get someone who knew the Western Desert and take the long route across to Libya. Steal a plane and ditch it once they were past their own lines. I've no idea.'

Quinn climbed to the airy landing on the floor above. Room eleven was at the end of a long corridor, overlooking the sea. A window was open by its entrance, smoke from distant fires drifting across the line of palms on the Corniche and the flat sea beyond.

He knocked and waited.

'Hello?' she called. 'Who's there?'

The door opened. She wore khaki trousers and a thin white linen shirt, the outline of her figure silhouetted against the light behind. 'Joe,' she said. She stepped back and ushered him in. 'I saw your wife this afternoon,' she said. 'You've missed her.'

'She was here?'

'Yes.'

'In the hotel?'

'No, on the quay.' Amy dimmed the lights, moved to the window and pushed open the shutters. The night glowed orange as a thin sliver of cloud floated across the moon. They could hear the guttural rumble of a boat's engine in the bay. 'Down there. She was getting onto a fishing-boat with the Egyptian boy. She was carrying him.'

'You sure it was her?'

'Yes.'

'You speak to her?'

'No. I was just walking along the quay.'

'Where was the boat?'

She stepped closer to the window. 'There's a hut down towards the end . . . Come, I'll show you.'

CHAPTER SIXTY-FIVE

Only the porter saw them leave the hotel. They crossed the road and strolled along beneath the palms, listening to the sea lapping against the shore. Ahead lay the little fortress of Qaitbey, so small and perfectly formed it looked as if it had been built for toy soldiers. Beyond it, they could see fires raging in the native quarter by the Western Harbour.

There was a hush. Even the sirens had faded and the boats had disappeared from the bay. The city burned in silence.

They reached the tip of the peninsula beyond the fortress and looked back towards the hotel. 'There,' she said, pointing at a wooden hut at the foot of some stone steps.

Quinn went down and looked in through the window. He could see nothing, and no boats were moored at the quay. 'She went on a boat?' he called up to her.

'Yes.'

'Alone?'

'There were two fishermen.'

'No-one else?'

She shook her head.

'You see her go out into the bay?'

'Yes.'

'She didn't come back?'

'Not that I saw.' Amy looked at him. 'I'm sorry, Joe. I'm sure she'll return.'

Quinn faced the water. There was a long silence. 'She notice you watching her?' he asked.

'I doubt it. I was walking along here and she was at the top of the steps. I thought she looked familiar. As I got closer I realized it was Mae, but she had got onto the boat by then and she didn't acknowledge me. Where do you think she was going?'

Quinn walked to the top of the steps. 'What car was she in?'

'There was no car.'

'She'd carried the boy all the way along the quay on her own?'

'I suppose so.'

He stood in front of her. 'Cigarette?' he asked.

'No, thank you. You knew she was going to leave, didn't you? I'm really sorry.'

Quinn lit his cigarette. 'I ran into your correspondent,' he said.

'Chester?'

'What do you plan to do here?'

'He wants to check in at El Daba early tomorrow, do twenty-four hours on the front line, then run back to Cairo to file. You know, the heroic last stand, doomed to failure ... What next for Cairo?'

Light from the fires glinted in her eyes and imbued her skin with a soft glow. 'You want to tell me what you're really doing here?' he asked.

473

'There are lots of things I'd like to tell you, but I don't think it's wise, do you?'

'All the money your husband brought here was forged by the Reich Central Bank.'

She turned her head towards the flames.

'Which makes one or both of you a spy,' he said.

'I'm a Jew. You think I want to assist in the annihilation of my own people?'

'You're a Jew, sure. And I been trying to figure that out. How could you be a fake, right? We checked out a Weinberg family arriving in New York in the Thirties and it's all on the level. You know about life on Seventh, so you haven't stolen an identity.'

'Why should I?'

'But something doesn't fit. I've been going over everything you've said, looking at the image, to see where the crack is. And then, on the journey up here, I get it. What was it you told me, that they'd taken your mother away and left you and your father with only one way out?' He shook his head. '*Reichssicherheitshauptamt* Six.' She looked down. 'The word chill your blood, Amy? Reich Security Administration Six – the Gestapo. They took your mother, but left the rest of you? No, that ain't real. I can see your value to them. Your father was an engineer, you went and lived in America, so your back story is perfect. You talk like a native New Yorker. You're young and beautiful.'

'I don't have to listen to this.' She began to walk away, but he gripped her shoulders. 'Now you've got to talk. Nowhere left to run.'

She shrugged free and sprinted down the quay.

He followed her back to the hotel and up into the unlit corridor. The door to her room was shut and locked. He knocked. 'Let me in,' he said. He took a step back and kicked. The door gave, slammed against the wall behind. She stood by the window, a revolver in her hand. 'Get away from me.'

He stepped into the room.

'I'll say you tried to assault me,' she said.

He watched her. 'You going to let me help you?'

'No-one can help me.' He moved further into the room. The muzzle of the revolver followed him. 'They took my mother away and we never got her back. Then they came for my father. They asked me whether I wanted to help them. Yes, I spoke English, like an American. I had a story that was true. As you say, I'm young and beautiful.' Her mouth curled in disgust. 'You want to know what it was like, Joe?'

He didn't answer.

'Down in a cell they took off my clothes and made me stand against a wall. They looked at me, smoking cigarettes and laughing. Then they asked me to lie down on the bunk and tested my suitability personally. First one, then two more together. They took their time, of course. Not bad, for a Jewess . . .'

They watched each other in silence. 'I'm sorry,' he said.

'What use is sorrow? My father is still there, waiting. When we're done here, I'll have to go back, to that cell and that wall and that bunk, and those men and their leering, laughing faces . . .'

He took a pace closer. Her eyes were misty. He reached out a hand. 'It's all right.'

'No. It's not all right. Nothing is ever going to be all right again.'

'You've got to stay here now.'

'And leave my father to his fate? Is that what you

would do, Joe Quinn? I don't think so. I don't believe that's in your noble code of detective honour, is it? This isn't some domestic dispute on Seventh, solved by turning a blind eye.'

'You figure they'll let either of you live?'

'I don't know. But it's a chance I have to take.'

Quinn sighed and closed his eyes.

'See, Joe, I understand you. I have from the first moment I saw you in that hospital. We're two drowning swimmers looking for a life-raft. Except you already had one, you just couldn't see it. And now she's gone. And even though you're trying to hide it, I can see your agony all the same.'

'White's your minder. He came with you from Berlin?'

'I don't even know his real name.'

'But there was someone here already, right? Someone on the inside, directing you both.'

'I'll say you broke into my room.'

'You seduced Durant. That was your job. But you didn't expect the guy to fall for you.'

She did not answer.

'You stole the papers while he was asleep. But that night something went wrong . . .' Quinn looked at the gun. He noticed her hand was shaking. 'You going to kill me, Amy?'

She stared at him, her face white.

'If you're going to do it,' he said, 'then be quick. I'd do the same.'

'No,' she said. 'You wouldn't.'

'You're a spy, Jew or not. You give me the gun, you'll hang.'

The light of the fires fell squarely on her face. Quinn looked from her head to her hand and back again. He waited. 'Go right ahead. I ain't got nothing to live for. You know that.'

'There's always something to live for.'

'Is that what you've found?'

'Yes.'

They stared at each other in silence. Her eyes glazed and he moved towards her.

CHAPTER SIXTY-SIX

Quinn caught her, lifted her up. He took her to the bed and laid her down gently. 'I wanted to kill you,' she whispered.

'I know.'

She touched his cheek. 'What shall I do?'

'We'll think of something.'

She gazed at him for a moment, then glanced away. He realized he could do nothing more hurtful than offer a false promise or basis for hope.

Amy took his hand and turned over so that her back was towards him. She pulled him closer and he lay on the bed beside her. They held hands, fingers locked. A series of blasts rocked the Western Harbour and the quarter beyond. Each time, the room shook and a blaze of light created new patterns on the floor, walls and ceiling. Between explosions, the city was eerily quiet and he could hear her breathing. They grasped each other, parted, then held each other again. He could feel the warmth of her palm and the thump of his own heart, but she did not turn.

Eventually Quinn got up, lit a cigarette, then closed the shutters and put up the blackout curtain. He

dragged the chair to the bed. He offered her a cigarette, but she shook her head. Silence stretched out.
'Aren't you going to sleep?' she asked.

'No.'

'But it is I who should not wish to hasten the dawn,
isn't that so? What hope can it bring for me?'

This time he did not answer.

'I'm grateful to you, Joe,' she whispered. 'I'm
happy you're here.' She lay back and stared at the
ceiling, then closed her eyes. After half an hour,
perhaps more, he heard the rhythmic sound of her
breathing. He sat absolutely still. His head sagged
as fatigue crept over him, but he jerked himself
awake. He tried to think about what she had said.
He thought of how it had begun: of Durant's body
hanging from the tree. What had gone wrong that
night at his apartment and why did Wheeler and
Fabrizzi have to die, too?

Accumulated tiredness dragged him eventually into
fitful sleep and he awoke to the dull sounds of a hotel
clattering and banging into a new day. There was a
shout. A shutter was slammed against a wall on the
floor above. Quinn could hear someone scrubbing the
corridor.

Amy slept on. He watched her peaceful face as light
crept round the edges of the blackout curtain and
stretched towards her.

The dawn let in other thoughts, too.

He went to the window again, pulled back the
curtain and looked down on the quay. There was no
sign of activity around the hut at the bottom of the
steps, or boats moored along it.

He stood, motionless, eyes fixed upon the hut.

There were no boats in the harbour. It occurred to

him that the fishermen had, of course, long since left, to protect their craft from the bombs.

Quinn let himself out quietly and walked down the corridor. Kate stood in the shadows. She stepped forward, her face consumed by an expression he could not place: confusion, perhaps, or sadness. Disappointment? Or something else? 'I knew it would happen,' she said.

He did not answer her.

'I couldn't find your wife.'

'She's gone.'

'Then I'm sorry.'

They stared at each other. Quinn didn't like witnessing her disapproval. 'I thought you were a loyal person,' she said.

'Mowbray—'

'I'll wait downstairs until you're finished,' she said. She turned and walked away.

'Kate . . .'

She didn't break her stride and Quinn cursed silently. He returned to the room at the end. Amy was still asleep, her unblemished face peaceful. He tore away the blackout curtain and turned back the shutters. She pushed herself upright. 'Are you all right?' she asked.

'We need to talk.'

'About what?'

'Where's Mae?'

She frowned, still only half awake. 'I told you, I saw—'

'Don't lie to me. The fishing fleets must have left days ago.'

She sat on the edge of the bed.

'Where is she?' Quinn asked.

She raised her knees protectively. 'I told you what I saw.'

'Amy, please. Don't lie to me.' She let her chin drop, swung her legs to the side of the bed and bent her head. 'Did you see my wife leave from the quay?'

'No. I got a call a few minutes before you arrived. I was told to keep you here as long as I could.'

'Why?'

'They didn't say.'

'You were told to seduce me?' he asked.

'Yes.'

'From the start?'

'Yes.'

'Who by?'

'All the orders come from him.'

'White?'

'No. It was him who called me, but he only does as he's told.'

'So who does it come from?'

'His code name is Condor. That's all I know.'

'How does White make contact with him?'

Amy stared at him. She turned to face the window and looked out to sea. 'Fishawy's,' she whispered, almost inaudibly. 'Each day at noon. But they don't always meet. Sometimes there is a package left, or a note . . .'

'Were you asked to tell me that?'

'Yes,' she said.

CHAPTER SIXTY-SEVEN

Quinn glanced at his watch. He stood in the heat of the sun in an alley close to Fishawy's. It was eleven forty-five. Amy was beside him.

The alley ran down the back of the café, past the kitchen. The owner of a shop selling copper pots beckoned them in and, for a moment, they took advantage of the temporary refuge. A storekeeper sat on a tiny stool, reading a copy of *El Messa*. A couple of men walked by, sandals flapping against the dirt.

The owner of the store tried to interest Quinn in his pots. A young boy measured Amy's feet for a pair of slippers. 'Good price,' he said. 'Cheap.' He was insistent.

'*Imshi*,' she said.

'*Khelim*?' he asked.

She shook her head. Quinn moved forward, but she gripped his hand, her eyes on his. 'Be careful. They will be prepared.'

Quinn edged into the alley. It was dotted with men sitting in pools of shade, reading or watching. He moved down to the kitchens. The staff stopped only for an instant as they caught sight of him, then carried on with their work. Perhaps it was his imagination, but their shouts seemed louder today. One took down a hookah, another carried a single cup of coffee on a silver tray across the narrow strip of alley to the back of the café.

The inside of Fishawy's was empty, except for an Egyptian man in a dark business suit who sat beneath the stuffed alligator, reading a newspaper. One waiter set the coffee beside him, another prepared a water-pipe, the air, as ever, filled with the sweet aroma of Me'assell tobacco and cardamom. A hawker dressed in little more than rags knelt at the man's feet, polishing his shoes.

Quinn inched forward, trying to afford himself a view of the alley at the front. He could see the wooden mirror along the far wall and a bench covered with a coloured rug. White was sitting with his back to them, head down, smoking a cigarette, a cup of coffee on the table beside him. He was dressed in a white linen suit, a fedora pulled low over his forehead. It was impossible to see his face.

Quinn waited. He glanced at his watch. It was eleven fifty-two. The aroma of tobacco from the water-pipe was stronger, charcoal lumps glowing as the businessman sucked air through water.

White hadn't moved. Two elderly men sat at a table next to him, deep in argument. The waiter brought hookahs and coffee without interrupting them. A group of schoolchildren passed, their excited voices fading quickly into the bustle of the bazaar. A couple of waiters leant against the wooden shutters, just out of the sun.

It was eleven fifty-eight. 'I see him,' Amy whispered at his shoulder. Quinn turned to look at her, but did not move. When he swung back, Kate was coming down the alley from the direction of Al Hussein Square.

She ducked into a shop front. He had told her to stay further back. He looked at his watch again. It was eleven fifty-nine.

A man playing an accordion drifted into the café. He sang to White, who waved him away. The two elderly men concluded their argument with a bout of laughter and backslapping. One almost choked on his pipe.

It was midday. White stubbed out a cigarette and took a sip of his coffee. He placed the book he'd been reading face down on the table and looked up the alley towards Al Hussein Square. A waiter shouted. An argument began in the kitchen. Quinn's eyes were fixed upon the alley opposite.

And then she slipped out of the shadows.

Mae strode forward and took her seat opposite Avril White.

CHAPTER SIXTY-EIGHT

The world all but stopped. Mae listened as White tilted his head forward and spoke, gesturing aggressively with one hand. She leant back and, for a moment, they sat in silence. Her face was impassive, her emotions impossible to read. Surely she would catch sight of him?

Or was she deliberately failing to do so?

Quinn shuffled a few inches to his left to give himself a better view of his wife and, as he did so, White stood and disappeared up the alley towards the square. Quinn could just make out his fedora passing from sun to shade and back again, as he ducked beneath long cotton smocks hanging from the shop fronts.

Mae did not move. Quinn realized she was a prisoner. She was bait.

A call to prayer erupted from the mosques nearby.

Quinn walked forward slowly. As he took a seat opposite her, she looked up at him with hollow eyes. 'It's a trap, Joe.'

'I know.'

'I'm sorry,' she said. Her eyes radiated a

vulnerability he had not seen in a long while. She looked lost. 'They made me go and pick up Rifat.'

Quinn glanced about him. 'Where are they?' he asked.

Before Mae could answer, Kate emerged from the shadows and walked towards them. She took off her cap, shook out her hair and pulled back the seat next to Mae. 'You've caused us a great deal of trouble,' she told Quinn. 'I'm sorry it has to end like this.'

He stared at her.

'I worried on the way to Alexandria that it was all over and I would finally have to kill you, but you gave me the answer, even if you didn't know it. I would like to have stayed to see Rommel take his rightful place here, but now we're left with no choice.'

'You cut all those throats yourself, Kate?'

'Not by myself, no.'

'Why did you kill them?'

'Durant was supposed to be making love to your new friend, but he caught us photographing his documents. We tried to recruit Wheeler months ago, so he knew White's true identity and Fabrizzi knew mine. They all had to go.'

'Macleod worked for you?'

'No. We gave Fabrizzi the money for his rebellion. He was supposed to do the rest. We heard from him that Wheeler was weak and could be blackmailed. But in the end Durant proved a better target.'

'The symbol of the God of Chaos was to persuade Macleod it was something to do with his racket and take over the case?'

She looked at him. 'Yes, but I've protected you, Joe. I hope you understand that. I could have killed you at any time. But now I'm glad I didn't.'

'You going to tell me why you turned traitor?'

'I'm a loyal person, Joe. It makes me sad that you never seemed to appreciate that.'

She was staring at him intently, with an expression he couldn't decipher. He glanced at Mae, who watched him steadily. 'This ain't what I call loyal,' he said.

'Then how little you know. My father's parents were killed in a concentration camp created by the country you so diligently serve. I gave you many opportunities to put your family, your friends and your life before your ego, and you failed every time.'

'So you serve the Nazis?'

She pushed her round pebble glasses up the bridge of her nose. 'There are many reasons, but I wouldn't expect you to understand them. Hitler has solutions for Africa to which we must listen. Quite soon, we'll have a government of our own and we have much to learn. But now I need a safe route out of here. The boy is in a jeep outside. I will trade him and your wife for a plane and a guarantee of safe passage.'

'A plane?'

'Yes.'

'That's impossible.'

'Well, it was your idea. As you reminded me last night, it's too risky now to try and get across the front line and I have neither the skill nor the equipment to get us across the desert to Libya. You will follow us to Ameriya, where you will use your position to requisition an aircraft.'

'That's insane.'

'If you succeed, I'll leave your wife and the boy unharmed in the jeep.'

'You'll never make it.'

'On the contrary, it's the only way. Mrs White will

have to come with us. Once we're airborne, I'll take my chances.'

'She won't go.'

'Then you'll have to persuade her.' Kate smiled thinly. 'That's a dilemma I'll let you resolve all by yourself.'

'You'll kill her anyway.'

Kate glanced over Quinn's shoulder in Amy's direction. 'We have her father. She would never abandon him.'

'You'll be shot down by your own side.'

'You'll provide us with parachutes.'

Quinn looked at her. It was only a short plane ride up to the front line. They'd have a fighting chance of making it over, then jettisoning the aircraft.

He glanced at his wife once more, tried to offer her reassurance, then walked through to the alley behind Fishawy's. 'I know what they want,' Amy said, before he could speak.

'They want a plane. If I can find one and give them safe passage to take off, they'll leave Mae and the boy.'

'They insist I must go with them?'

'Yes.'

'Because they think you won't shoot down the plane if I'm on it?'

He nodded.

They were silent.

'I'll do it,' Amy said. She was staring at him and he saw the pain deep in her eyes.

Quinn turned. Immediately, Kate shepherded Mae up the alley. She did not look back.

CHAPTER SIXTY-NINE

Outside, Quinn hailed a taxi and gesticulated at the jeep, which was already disappearing down the narrow road in front of them. Amy sat beside him.

He took in nothing of the journey, his eyes fixed on the jeep kicking up dust ahead. He kept glancing over his shoulder. Where were they? Why were they not following?

He thought he could just make out a jeep in the distance.

The taxi passed through three Military Police roadblocks and sped along the empty desert road to the barbed-wire perimeter of the airbase. They reached the barrier and pulled up before a long row of Nissen huts. Kate got out before Quinn could speak to his wife or Rifat. White had reversed the jeep away and was speeding round the back of the runway to the far side.

The door of the nearest Nissen hut was open and this was evidently the office of the base commander. There were craters outside it. Quinn entered without knocking, followed by Kate and Amy. The room was small and airless, a couple of desk fans circulating stale heat. Two secretaries banged on typewriters while the commander spoke loudly into his telephone. The wall behind him was covered with a map of the Western Desert. Next to it was a blackboard with lists of planes and sorties and the locations of all Allied airbases out in the field. Everywhere there was evidence of names, numbers and locations being hastily changed to keep up with the reality of battle.

The commander looked at them, but did not interrupt his call. He put down the receiver, but it buzzed again immediately. He ignored it. 'Good afternoon,' he said.

One of the secretaries came over to answer the call. 'Ameriya . . .'

The commander was distracted. In the end, he took the receiver. He listened for a few moments. 'That's right, sir . . . Yes, we got the plane back, but he's finished for the foreseeable future . . . Yes, seven down now . . . We can't keep up this rate much longer, the men are exhausted . . .'

The call went on, the commander sharing his frustrations with a superior. Quinn looked out of the grubby window at the airstrip and the hangar on the far side. White had parked his jeep beside a line of aircraft, widely spaced to make them more difficult to destroy from the air.

The commander terminated the call. He gazed anxiously out of the window towards the horizon, as if searching for a returning aircraft. He showed no interest in the interlopers. 'What time did they leave?' he asked his assistant.

She glanced at her watch, although clocks hung on the walls. 'Three hours ago, sir.'

490

The commander cursed beneath his breath and sat down again. Quinn took out his pink identification card and placed it on the desk. 'Look, I'm sorry to impose, I can see it's a bad time.'

'It's always a bad time.'

'I'm Major Quinn from the Special Investigation Branch.'

The commander looked at them. He had a pleasant, even handsome, face with sandy hair combed neatly across his forehead, but appeared strung out to the limit. The telephone rang again. He was about to take the call. 'I need a plane for a few hours,' Quinn said.

The officer picked up the receiver. 'Yes,' he said. 'All right – but make it quick. No . . . No, that's far too long. By this afternoon at the latest.'

He put down the telephone. 'I'm sorry, what did you say?'

'I'm going to need a plane for a few hours.'

'A plane?'

'Yes.'

He seemed confused. 'What kind of plane?'

'Whatever you've got. We've three people to transport.'

'To where?'

Quinn didn't answer. The commander sighed. 'I suppose this is another piece of damned SOE business.' He glared at them. 'You people are the absolute limit. Where are your papers, then? Or don't you bother with that any more?'

'There hasn't been time. You can get verbal authorization from Colonel Lewis if you need it.'

The commander picked up Quinn's identification card and examined it. 'Some kind of espionage caper, I suppose.'

'It's an investigation.' Quinn smiled thinly. 'Unfortunately time is short and the stakes are high.'

The man sighed. 'Who's the pilot?'

'My assistant can fly a plane,' Kate said.

'He can pilot a Gladiator? You'll just about squeeze three in, but that's all I've got.'

'Yes.'

The man seemed surprised at their acceptance. He picked up the telephone and asked to be put through to GHQ. When the call was answered, he told them to connect him with Colonel Lewis.

They waited.

'Colonel Lewis . . . Oh . . . When's he back? Not till then?' He was frowning. 'No, don't worry, I'll try later.'

He terminated the call, looked out again at the landing strip. He examined Quinn's card more closely, then pushed it back to him. 'You're in luck. Planes I have, it's the men to fly them I'm short of. But you'll have to take your chances. It's not been maintained and I can't spare anyone to do it.'

'I'll need parachutes,' Kate said.

The commander frowned. 'In the rear of the hangar. When am I going to get it back?'

'In three hours,' Kate said. 'No more.'

The phone rang again and the commander answered. He listened, immediately lost in the complications of his war.

Kate led the way to the taxi and got into the back. Quinn sat next to the driver and gestured for him to go across the tarmac to the jeep that had parked on the other side.

He was reluctant, but eventually complied. Twenty yards from the jeep, Kate banged on the man's seat to get him to stop, then clambered out. 'She comes with me,' she said, pointing at Amy. 'You stay here. I'll take the jeep down to the far end of the strip. Remain here until we've taken off.'

Amy made no move to get out. They watched Kate as she crossed towards the hangar. Mae was still seated in the back of the jeep, as immobile as a statue, her blond hair blowing in the breeze, her arm round the boy at her side. She turned towards him.

They waited.

'What will you do, Joe?' Amy asked.

He didn't answer. He looked back towards the Nissen huts and the entrance to the base. He saw a jeep pull in, then another.

'What is it? Do you have men waiting?'

'Yes.'

'Then tell them to shoot.' She gripped his arm. 'I'm sorry for the pain I've caused.' She pushed open the door.

'Wait,' he said. She hesitated, eyes searching his. Their faces were close. He could smell the sweet scent of her breath. 'Wait,' he whispered.

'Goodbye, Joe.'

She got out and walked away, without looking over her shoulder, back straight and footfall steady. She reached his wife, but no intimacies passed between them. Mae did not glance at Amy, or at him, her eyes now on the plane at the far side of the runway.

White emerged from the hangar clutching a parachute in each hand. He strode towards the plane at the furthest end of the row. A mechanic came forward to help him start it and, a second later, the engines roared into life. Quinn got out of the car. He walked close to the edge of the tarmac and watched the

Gladiator begin to taxi. He heard a loud clunk as Kate put the jeep into gear.

It careered down the runway. The plane reached the far end of the strip and turned.

The jeep reached its open door. Quinn watched Amy get down and move across. For a moment, she seemed to hesitate, but was pushed quickly inside.

Two figures remained in the jeep.

The door of the plane was shut. Its engines swelled and, almost instantly, it was propelled down the strip. Quinn saw two men with rifles crouching at the side of the Nissen hut. A third had a machine gun. Madden and Colonel Lewis stood alongside them.

Quinn watched, heart thumping. The plane was careering towards them. 'No!' he shouted at Lewis. He ran forward, waving. 'No!'

The plane was almost off the ground. Lewis raised a hand, held it aloft, then swung it down firmly. The soldiers opened fire, machine-gun bullets thumping against the fuselage. For a moment, it looked as if it would make it. Quinn saw – or imagined he did – Amy's face in the window as the plane flew past, ten feet or more off the ground and climbing. But the machine-gunner kept firing and now a plume of smoke was coming from one of the engines. The plane dipped, its engine spluttered and it dived towards the desert floor. A few seconds later flames from the explosion shot into the clear blue sky.

Through the shimmering heat, Quinn saw Mae get down from the jeep. She began to walk slowly towards him.

She stopped, hair blowing across her face.

For a long time, neither moved. Then Quinn ran. As he came closer he saw that Mae was smiling.

THE END

THE MASTER OF RAIN
by Tom Bradby

'An immensely atmospheric, gripping detective story with just
the right mixture of exoticism, violence and romance'
The Times

Shanghai. 1926. Exotic, sexually liberated and pulsing with life,
it is a place and a time where anything seems possible. For
policeman Richard Field, it represents a brave new world away
from the past he is trying to escape. His first moment of active
duty is the brutal and sadistic murder of a young White
Russian woman, Lena Orlov. The key to the investigation seems
to be Lena's neighbour, Natasha Medvedev. But can he really
trust someone for whom self-preservation is the only goal?
With the International police force riven with rivalries, it is soon
clear that Field must take his own way through the investigation.
And in a city where reality is a dangerous luxury, Field is
driven into the darkness beyond the dazzle of society to a
world where everything has its price and the truth seems
certain to be a fatal commodity . . .

'Nigh on impossible to put down . . . This intelligent thriller
brings Shanghai to life as *Gorky Park* did for Moscow'
Time Out

'Rich, dark, atmospheric, this fine novel captures time
and place perfectly. A great crime story that ends up in a
place you won't predict'
Lee Child

'The atmosphere and menace of Twenties Shanghai are brought
to vivid life as the backdrop to this gripping tale'
Daily Mail

'*The Master of Rain* is that rare thing: a truly epic crime novel,
brilliantly researched and superbly executed'
John Connolly

0 552 14746 X

CORGI BOOKS

A SELECTED LIST OF FINE WRITING
AVAILABLE FROM CORGI BOOKS

14586 6	SHADOW DANCER	Tom Bradby	£5.99
14587 4	THE SLEEP OF THE DEAD	Tom Bradby	£5.99
14746 X	THE MASTER OF RAIN	Tom Bradby	£6.99
14900 4	THE WHITE RUSSIAN	Tom Bradby	£6.99
14951 9	THE DA VINCI CODE	Dan Brown	£6.99
15169 6	DIGITAL FORTRESS	Dan Brown	£6.99
15176 9	DECEPTION POINT	Dan Brown	£6.99
77140 6	BANGKOK 8	John Burdett	£6.99
15405 9	THE MESSIAH CODE	Michael Cordy	£6.99
14604 8	CRIME ZERO	Michael Cordy	£5.99
14654 4	THE HORSE WHISPERER	Nicholas Evans	£6.99
14738 9	THE SMOKE JUMPER	Nicholas Evans	£6.99
14923 3	THE VETERAN	Frederick Forsyth	£6.99
15044 4	AVENGER	Frederick Forsyth	£6.99
14877 6	DYING TO TELL	Robert Goddard	£6.99
14878 4	DAYS WITHOUT NUMBER	Robert Goddard	£6.99
14879 2	PLAY TO THE END	Robert Goddard	£6.99
14901 2	WALLS OF SILENCE	Philip Jolowicz	£6.99
15021 5	THE ANALYST	John Katzenbach	£6.99
15106 8	THE MADMAN'S TALE	John Katzenbach	£6.99
15065 7	THE CRIME TRADE	Simon Kernick	£6.99
14970 5	THE BUSINESS OF DYING	Simon Kernick	£6.99
14971 3	THE MURDER EXCHANGE	Simon Kernick	£6.99
14585 8	MEAN SPIRIT	Will Kingdom	£5.99
15238 2	LAST LIGHT	Andy McNab	£6.99
15239 0	LIBERATION DAY	Andy McNab	£6.99
15019 3	DEEP BLACK	Andy McNab	£6.99
15173 4	THE UNKNOWN SOLDIER	Gerald Seymour	£6.99
15043 6	TRAITOR'S KISS	Gerald Seymour	£6.99
14816 4	THE UNTOUCHABLE	Gerald Seymour	£6.99
10565 1	TRINITY	Leon Uris	£7.99